A Woman, in Bed

A Woman, in Bed

— by Anne Finger —

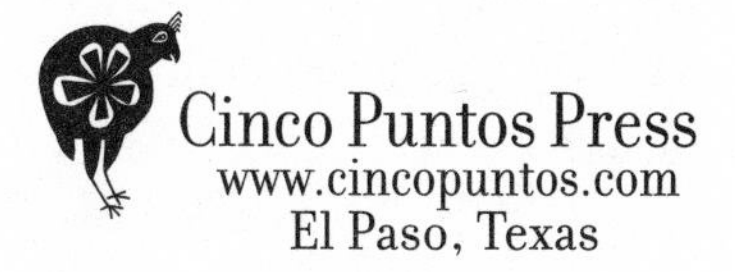

Cinco Puntos Press
www.cincopuntos.com
El Paso, Texas

 For further information, write Cinco Puntos Press, 701 Texas Avenue, El Paso, TX 79901; or call 1-915-838-1625.

Printed in the U.S.

FIRST EDITION
10 9 8 7 6 5 4 3 2 1

Library of Congress Cataloging-in-Publication Data

Names: Finger, Anne, author.
Title: A woman, in bed / Anne Finger.
Description: First edition. | El Paso, Texas : Cinco Puntos Press, 2018.
Identifiers: LCCN 2017033096 | ISBN 978-1-941026-74-8 (softcover) | ISBN 978-1-941026-75-5 (ebook)
Subjects: LCSH: Women—Sexual behavior—Fiction. | Self-realization in women—Fiction. | Married women—Fiction. | Adultery—Fiction. | BISAC: FICTION / Historical. | FICTION / Literary. | FICTION / Contemporary Women. | SOCIAL SCIENCE / People with Disabilities. | GSAFD: Love stories.
Classification: LCC PS3556.I4677 W66 2018 | DDC 813/.54--dc23
LC record available at https://lccn.loc.gov/2017033096

Many thanks to Sheila Black for her thorough reading
and to Michael Northen for sending Anne Finger our way.
Pioneers, all of you.

The cover painting, "Empty Bed," is by Helen Masacz.
Used by kind permission of the artist.
Book and cover design by El Paso's own Anne M. Giangiulio.

For Judy Greene

Hunger

Simone Clermont stood in the larder of her mother's house, the door ajar a crack to let light in. Marcel had sucked her dry and he was now sleeping, dazed on the laudanum of her breast milk. She overheard her mother and Cecile, the kitchen girl, making supper for the boarders, pots clanging, the grumble and murmur of their voices, the chop-chop of knife against cutting board. In the dim light, she could make out the bags of flour and sugar, the jars of preserves—apple, raspberry, quince. The tub of butter. Supper was three hours away, and she was starving. She would have been perfectly within her rights to march into the kitchen, make straight for the icebox, help herself to the remains of last night's beef stew or the leftover trifle. Her mother might cluck and fuss, though she was in Simone's debt. But like a naughty child, she had sneaked into the larder. She wanted to leap up and pull the ham down from its ceiling hook, gnaw hunks free with her incisors: eat and eat and eat until billows of flesh hung from her. Nature, that old hag, wanted to have her way with Simone. She was like the goose being fattened up for Christmas dinner, who came waddling across the yard, honking with delight as gruel was slopped into its trough, past the tree stump that served as a chopping block with its faded sepia stains of blood that had pulsed from the necks of chickens, ducks, this goose's progenitors. What was in store for Simone? She had as little sense as that wambling goose, only a premonition that nature was up to no good.

If she were to eat the entire jar of raspberry jam she was holding in her hand, she wouldn't be satisfied. She shoved it back on the shelf. Stalking out of the pantry, she called, "I'm going out for a walk."

Her mother appeared in the kitchen doorway, knife in hand, the blade glistening with the membranes of the rabbit they would dine on that evening, calling out to Simone's retreating back, "Oh, don't take the child out in this wind."

Simone turned on her heel. "I'm not taking Marcel. He's asleep."

"And if he wakes up?"

"He wakes up. You can pick him up. Or let him cry."

Her mother regarded her daughter's broad rump with satisfaction. Simone was no longer a slim-hipped wraith floating through life. Her thickened hips were ballast, weighing her down, steadying her passage.

Wind

Her mother blamed her daughter's restlessness on the scirocco, the hot wind that began in the heart of Africa, swept across the Sahara and the Mediterranean, bending the heads of the royal palms along the Boulevard du Littoral in Cap d'Antibes so they resembled a line of giraffes with necks curved downwards to munch on low leaves.

Simone had to shove hard against the wind to open the door. A determined foe, the wind caught her skirts of pale blue, threatening to lift them up over her head. Simone, grabbing her skirt, let go of the door, which slammed with a resounding crack, echoing throughout the house.

Later, there will be a row:

—Just because you got up on the wrong side of the bed, you needn't slam the door and give us all headaches.

—I didn't slam it. Why must you always think the worst of me?

The cat, lurking at the corner of the house, startled by the sound, leapt. The cat was in love with Simone, with her smell of breast milk and yeast, with her disregard for the gifts of sparrows and field mice left for her on the stone doorstep every morning. The cat was not a pet, it had simply taken up residence in the barn. A good mouser, as its belly gave evidence.

Simone's frock was not just out of fashion but ungainly. Sick of the maternity chemise in which she'd lumbered through the last months of pregnancy, the months since Marcel's birth, but unable to fit into her regular clothes, she'd rummaged through the closet of her old bedroom, and pulled out this dress, which had belonged to her dead sister Elise, moving the buttons over on the sleeves, hitching up the excess fabric with its belt. The sleeves flopped about her arms like deflated balloons, the skirts worked their way free of the sash, threatening to trip her up, so her locomotion was almost Chaplinesque: she took a few steps, then hitched the skirt up on the left side, a few more steps, then gave a yank to the right. It was so hot she had dispensed with undergarments, save for the fortified nursing brassiere.

Marcel, cast out of the nirvana of sleep by the door's bang, mewled twice and then drew in a deep breath, preparing to let loose with a wail.

Simone, pausing at the back door, scanned the road for the bicycle of the postman, M. duPont. He was a kilometer distant, pausing at the crest of a hill, ready to savor the moment when gravity would reverse its effects, no longer a force to be struggled against but one which would send him gliding down.

He will have a letter for me, Simone told herself. She had finally, after laboring over many drafts, told her husband, Luc, how the birth of their son had shaken the foundations of her being. She could not bring herself to write, *My cunt throbs when Marcel nurses, while my mind is filled with unwholesome fantasies. I have come close to stimulating myself for relief while nursing. I am becoming a monster. You must come to me. Or let me come back to you, even if there are fevers in Turkey that put our child's life at risk.* Instead, she had written: "I fear for my emotional balance. I cannot tell you how desperately I long for you, need to be with you."

Rabbit

Jacques Melville—along with his companion Albert—was trudging along the cobblestone streets of Juan-les-Pins, both men with heads bent down against the wind, their trousers flapping against the rails of their bones, Albert describing the charms of his boyhood summers *chez Vidal*. They did not look at the recently erected cenotaph listing the names of the Great War dead, those whose bones lay jumbled with the remains of friend and foe in the mass graves of Verdun and Ypres.

"Just promise me," Jacques raised his head, "that we won't sing troubadour ballads in the parlor after dinner."

"Afraid so, old chap," the last two words in English.

Marcel wailed. M. duPont leaned back as he coasted downhill and allowed the wind to dry his sweaty brow and neck. Marcel's cry roused Simone from her reverie. She lifted her skirt in her hand, pretending—to no one save herself—not to have heard her son's wail, and walked down the path. Jacques shrugged his rucksack more firmly onto his back, a soldier headed into battle.

Jacques had been gadding about France with his university chum Albert for nearly a month. The two of them were bound for the penultimate stop on their journey. They were sick of living out of their rucksacks, of drinking weak coffee served by frugal landladies, of the musty scent from their socks, never quite clean after having been washed in cold water sinks of hostels, of their aching feet. Jacques, for his part, was also sick of Albert. (Albert will never grow tired of Jacques. Forty years later he will still be dining out on tales of this ramble: *Ah, let me tell you a story about living off the fat of the land. It was years ago, decades, I was traveling with my friend Jacques—Jacques Melville*—and here he will pause to let that name sink in—*and we came upon a lemon tree, unfortunately surrounded by a stone wall some three meters high…*) Albert, aware that Jacques—never lighthearted—was becoming more and more phlegmatic, kept attempting to josh him out of his mood, although as Albert grew more antic, Jacques became more taciturn. Albert was whistling snatches from tunes—*It's a Long Way to Tipperary, The Internationale*—holding up his hand to show the fur of sand adhering to his sweaty palm, saying, "Just think, yesterday these grains of sand might have been under the heel of a Bedouin's camel in the Sahara." He rabbited on about the effects of the scirocco on the psyche: "Those teetering on the brink of insanity"—illustrating by pretending to walk a tightrope, spreading his arms, then staggering—"may fall over the edge, while for those like you and me," Albert continued, "it merely heats up the brain a bit, as a glass of absinthe might, bringing a pleasurable touch of insanity—"

"Those like myself, at any rate." Jacques winked. "After dinner, I shall plead a headache, and excuse myself from the forced after-supper gaiety."

"You're such an old stick."

"I can't help it," Jacques said, smiling for the first time since they disembarked from the train. "I was born this way. Most infants wail at birth. My mother says I stared at her as if to say, 'Why have you brought me here?'"

The hot wind had whipped up Albert's already curly hair, making it look like spun sugar. When they started on this journey, Albert had a cap in his possession, but it had long since disappeared. He resembled a whirling dervish, but instead of being surrounded by vast skirts, he was surrounded by the ghosts of lost objects: undershorts left to dry on the railings of balconies in pensiones and forgotten there, books left behind on the seats of second-class compartments of railway cars, combs, socks.

M. Dupont, rolling down the hill, his mail bag slung across his chest, saw the tiny figure of Simone starting down the path, and thought: What a devoted wife! M. Dupont didn't trumpet about his opinions regarding Simone's faithfulness, as he later kept to himself the fact that she was receiving, in addition to the twice-weekly letters in her husband's ornate hand, other letters, also written in a masculine hand, with the name J. Melville in the upper corner and a Paris return address. M. Dupont hoarded his secrets with a sense that he had a pile of riches locked within him. A secret told is one no more, and he did not want to squander his treasure. His being so tight-lipped caused consternation amongst his fellow townspeople: not only were we born on this land where the sea seeds our lands with salt as the Romans did the fields of Carthage; not only are we thus dependent on the whims of holiday-makers who may decide, after we have built them hotels with sea views, turned our family homes into lodging houses, set up restaurants and cafés in which they can dine on bouillabaisse and *tourte des chasseurs—Oh, yes, madame, it's very authentic—as a matter of fact, from an old family recipe;* who may then decide our town has become a tourist trap and decamp en masse to some other locale to begin the whole process anew; not only are we cursed with the hot winds sweeping in from Africa in the summer, and the cold and fierce mistral in the winter, but we have a postman who shrugs and juts out his lower lip when one tries to wheedle the slightest bit of information out of him—such is our lot in life!

M. Dupont, having reached Simone, and working the pedals of his bicycle so it remained in place, reached into his bag and held the letter aloft.

Simone lifted it to her nose, inhaling the scent of her husband's Upman cigars, then tucked it into the sash of her dress, and strode off towards the promontory, to the grove of cypresses bent by the wind.

Marcel's arms and legs cycled furiously, while downstairs his grandmother, in response to Cecile's question, "Should I go fetch the baby?" said, "No, no! Crying gives his lungs exercise."

In the front garden of a deconsecrated monastery turned asylum for the local cripples, idiots, and ancients without relations, toward which the postman DuPont was cycling—carrying the bill from the local miller—a woman furrowed her brow, squinting at the work dangling from her knitting needles, invisible to all save her, redid an errant stitch, and set back to her work. Seated next to her, his face turned towards the sun, a blind boy, his left hand hugging his right shoulder, his right hand clasping his left, rocked back and forth. On his way there, the postman Dupont passed another knitter, Mme. Gratoit, one who did not knit garments of air but of wool, who rocked back and forth—although in a chair designed for that purpose, her foot on the cradle of her newest babe, her seventh, all alive and quite healthy, five boys and two girls—with the pride of a gardner with a green thumb.

Jacques

Jacques Melville was a few years too old to be traipsing about France, carrying a knapsack and wearing clothes in need of the attention of a laundress' starch and irons. By way of contrast, the man who was to become Simone's husband, while he had shown up at the Vidal door on foot, had done so because his touring sedan had developed engine troubles, which necessitated him finding a night's lodging. He'd not only worn a cream-colored linen suit, crisp despite the sodden heat of the day, but he had also presented his card to Mme. Vidal, ivory paper engraved with black: Luc Henri Clermont, *ingenieur en chef de la linee Athens-Istanbul, Compagnie Internationale des Wagons-Lits et des Grands Express Européens,* and did not flinch when Mme. Vidal quoted him a price five francs above her usual charge. (Albert will manage to get a price five francs below the usual by looking imploringly at Mme. Vidal, citing the ties of affection that bound them and that both he and Jacques were students.)

Jacques' behavior was made even more unusual by the fact that he had a wife and infant son back in Paris. By all rights, he should have progressed to the stage of life where for the holidays one rents a place at the seaside—described as a villa, which proves to be a ramshackle cottage, and where one spends the month battling the sand which finds its way into the chinks between the clapboards of the exterior walls, and from there to the flesh of the half-eaten peach left in the larder, the gaps between one's toes, the cleft in one's posterior—and traipsing about in a half-stupor from the sun.

His wife, Sala, knew that such a holiday would not be much of one for the females in the family (Sala's widowed mother lived with them), what with the ubiquitous sand, the preparing of meals in a kitchen with dented pans and a temperamental gas ring, not to mention the dealings with the local greengrocers, butchers, and fishmongers who saw it as their duty, almost religious in nature, to get the longer end of the stick in their dealings with the summer people. Better for Jacques to head off on his own, burning off some of his wanderlust while Sala stayed in Paris. This arrangement was quintessentially modern—a marriage in which the distaff partner pursued her own ambitions and brought in her own income—but also evocative of ancient tribal societies, where women tended garden and child, while men ventured out in bands, returning home with the kill. If the marriage appeared to outside eyes to be rather unconventional, it was still to Jacques' taste altogether too conventional.

Albert thought it was his friend's preternatural seriousness which had led him to make his odd marriage to Sala, a marriage in which there was not only little evidence of passion, but one in which the two partners seemed yoked by sullen resentfulness, more typical in marriages of decades-long duration. The two even seemed to bear an uncanny resemblance to one another—so much so that they were occasionally mistaken for brother and sister. The features which on Jacques' masculine visage—the leonine brow, the deep-set eyes, dark and brooding—rendered him handsome had the opposite effect on his wife. Her square forehead suggested the prow of a Chinese junk, while her thick dark eyebrows, which met just above the bridge of her nose, gave her face a feral cast. He used tweezers to pull out the errant hairs of his brow, although he was careful not to take his pruning so far he seemed a dandy. Sala disdained such interference—for one thing, she hardly had time to lollygag about plucking at hairs.

Prior to her daughter's marriage, Sala's mother had not kept a watchful eye on her daughter's chastity. Both mother and daughter were advocates of free love. Mme. Prusak had raised her daughter to be forceful and independent—*Don't let anything stand in your way! You've got to fight for what you want!* Alas for all involved, Sala brought this attitude to her most intimate relations. Jacques' response to his spouse's attacks was to grow more diffident, which only increased his wife's fury. Their marriage was well on the way to becoming one in which one partner is long-suffering and the other a harridan. The reason spoken aloud for Mme. Prusak moving in with them was that she would run the household while they each pursued their vocations, but in fact her primary purpose was to function, not as a drudge but as a duenna, one who prevented the untoward intimacies of full-bore rows.

As the name suggests, Sala's family was of Russian extraction, her parents political exiles who had narrowly escaped the hangman's noose, fleeing their homeland with the clothes on their back and a single valise containing a bar of soap, a razor, and items of underclothing, Russian translations of *The Iliad, The Odyssey,* and *The Communist Manifesto.*

Like any good babushka, Mme. Prusak sang lullabies to her grandson, but the songs were ones she had learned in clandestine meetings, so that later, when Frédéric would hear marchers moving through the streets of Paris singing *Arise ye prisoners of starvation, arise ye wretched of the earth*...he would be filled with a desire to sleep.

Husband

When Simone reached the grove of cypresses, their branches sculpted by the sea winds into long green strands, she seated herself on a flat boulder and pulled the letter from her waistband.

"Thank you for your most recent letter. I wish I could report better news on this front. The delayed railway ties have at last arrived, but are of such inferior quality that a good half of them are unusable. The summer heat is already ferocious—well over 40 degrees many days and has been accompanied by a plague of red chiggers. The natives spend more time scratching themselves than working. I do not mean to burden you with concerns which more properly belong to the masculine realm, but only to underscore that it is quite impossible for me to either come to France or for you to return to Turkey. You must draw of your reserves of inner strength, both for your own well-being and for that of our child."

She was too shocked to cry.

Her hands formed into fists—Luc would no doubt have chuckled had he seen them—fists as helpless as those of Marcel. In one of these fists was the letter, crumpled into a ball. Until now, she had kept every letter he had written her, tied up with a pale blue ribbon in a packet.

She described Luc as *mon mari*, but if she knew English that language's equivalent would strike her as far more apt, with its allied meaning of one who manages a farm: the verb *to husband*, to govern thriftily and well.

Luc did not love her, she saw that clearly. He loved the idea of her, the image of her in her pale gown, gliding down the stairs, her blonde hair upswept atop her head, with a few errant tendrils tumbling down. He loved her laughter, her charm. He loved the words "my wife," he liked to escort those words to gatherings, to introduce them to his colleagues and connections. He liked to slip the hand of those words through the crook of his elbow and give them an affectionate pat. (The fault was not entirely on Luc's side: she had fallen in love not so much with Luc as with his adoration of her.)

The wind made the hairs on her arms stand up on end, while beads of sweat gathered in her pores.

A quarter of an hour later, Marcel had indeed worn himself out with crying and fallen back asleep. M. Dupont had delivered the miller's bill to the institution, and Albert had just said to Mme. Vidal, who had chided him for arriving unannounced, "Oh, but I wrote you! I'm sure I did."

"No matter." Even with the financial assistance given her by her son-in-law, she was not in any position to turn away guests. Moreover, not having seen him since the start of the war, she had assumed him dead. She supposed it about all young men unless she knew otherwise.

Easier to jumble all those bones into the mass grave of her imagination than to wonder about each one: Did he survive? Is he staring at the wall in some veterans home in the countryside? Here was one resurrected.

His arrival did mean that she would have to turn her bedroom over to the two young men, sleep in the sitting room.

"Oh, there's Elise!" Albert cried, recognizing her sky blue frock.

"No. Elise, she..."

"Oh," Albert said, putting his hand on Mme. Vidal's shoulder.

"Three years ago...the Spanish," using the local name for influenza. Mme. Vidal withdrew herself from Albert's touch, fearing loss of her composure. "That's Simone."

In the autumn of 1918, it seemed that death, that old glutton, had finally had his fill, pushed his chair back from the table, patted his rotund belly, lit a cigar, said, "I couldn't possibly eat one more thing." But then he caught a smell wafting in from the kitchen. Light and clear, the perfect thing after the meal he'd just devoured, those lads tasting of mud, quite on the gamey side. He cleansed his palate with ruddy-cheeked farm boys too young for the army, their fresh-faced sisters, old women smelling of apple blossom bath powder, barefoot imps with gap-toothed smiles from the slums of Manchester and Berlin and Bombay. How quickly they went down, clean as a fruit sorbet.

Elise came home from a hike one afternoon, her cheeks in high color, sat down, put her hand to her breast, and spoke her last full sentence, "I'm rather flushed."

Simone had been the one her mother had fretted over: not only too thin, but given to bouts of melancholy and novel-reading. Consumption seemed inevitable. A cough caused her mother to banish her to the sleeping porch so that the winds could carry the tubercle bacilli away. Simone's good health did not prove her mother wrong: quite the contrary, it was evidence that Mme. Vidal's methods had been successful.

Mme. Vidal swiped her hands against each other, shaking off the dust of the past. "Yes, yes, and Simone is now married woman." As if on cue, Marcel began to wail. "And I am now a grandmama. Walk up to meet her, Cecile can see to your things."

Wind

"Albert!" Simone cried, "Albert! Albert!" She raced down the path towards him, sending pebbles skittering, crunching cypress needles beneath her feet. As she ran, she allowed the wind to carry off her husband's letter.

Albert was surprised at her pell-mell race towards him. It wasn't something he could imagine the Simone he knew before doing—motherhood had released a hoyden she'd kept well hidden.

He quickened his pace, his footsore companion trudging behind.

She threw her arms around his neck. He wrapped his arms around her, lifting her off the ground, swinging her around: an embrace a brother might give his kid sister. He pressed himself against her, making her breasts, swollen with milk, ache.

Simone slipped her arm into Albert's and, her head against his shoulder, they walked towards Jacques, who leaned against a boulder to await them.

When they were a couple of yards from him, a gust of wind caught her skirts, sending them up around her, as if she were drowning in that expanse of blue. Jacques glimpsed the dark triangle of her pubic hair, her legs.

"Oh," she cried, tamping her skirts down with her hands. It seemed they might become a parachute, the wind billowing them into sails and lifting her into the air, buffeting her away. She'd drift over her mother's house, calling down, "*Le vent*! The wind! Goodbye, Mama! Goodbye, Marcel!" Who knew where she might end up? The scirocco might die down as suddenly as it had sprung up, and she'd be sent on an earth-bound plummet. Or she might waft down, landing in Aix or Lyon, a wind fallen gift from the heavens.

It was only Albert, tethering her to earth, who kept her from rising.

Jacques had smoothed down his hair that morning with a cream and the resulting stiffness of his locks caused two tufts to rise on either side of his temples. This, combined with the shape of his face—an inverted triangle ending in a tapered chin—gave him a slightly diabolical mien. The irises of his eyes were so dark they were nearly indistinguishable from his pupils.

"Allow me to present my dear friend, Jacques Melville. Simone Vidal—"

"Clermont."

"Ah, yes, she has broken my heart by marrying."

Unlike Luc, who had clicked his heels—although of French stock, he had been raised in Alsace—and bent to kiss her proffered hand, Jacques extended his own hand in return. By this gesture, he showed himself as a modern man who had thrown off prewar fustiness.

It all happened in a fraction of a second:

His hand, in the empty air, a few centimeters from hers, waited. He allowed it to rest there, thereby forcing her to lean forward, to be the one who grasped hold of his hand. He returned almost no pressure. His hand was so soft that it reminded her of touching her husband's genitals when he was unaroused. There was an air of ironic detachment in his manner, as if he were an anthropologist who had spent so long in the field he now viewed the customs of his own tribe as curiosities. Simone relaxed her hand. Just when it seemed it might slide away from Jacques', he squeezed it, hard enough that the shadow of a wince passed across her face, while a wry half-smile crossed his.

And then it was over. The smooth waters of the everyday closed above them.

Linking arms with both of them, Simone chattered about the other guests—an Alsatian bird watcher who made bird calls at the table; a British major, a summer visitor of many years standing, who had become quite forward with Simone of late: "I suppose he's heard married French women are known to take lovers and wants to put himself first in line. Oh, it's quite sickening."

"Ah, Simone, your gallants are here, to defend your honor!" Albert stepped backwards and made a mocking bow. "Aren't we, old man?"

"Certainly," Jacques said drily.

"You'll have to indulge my friend. He's a genius."

"You flatter me," Jacques said, not bantering, but flat out. He was not about to make his intellectual prowess a joking mater.

When Simone returned with Jacques and Albert, Cecile greeted her with, "Your mother's got a headache, she's lying down upstairs."

Her mother, who'd risen when she heard their footsteps coming up the path, appeared in the doorway as Simone reached the top of the stairs. "Just because you got up on the wrong side of the bed, you needn't slam the door and give us all headaches."

Hobble

Simone changed for dinner out of that ridiculous dress of Elise's—*really, what had she been thinking*?—and into a silk hobble skirt the dressmaker in Constantinople had run up, copying a Poiret design from a fashion magazine—although she'd grown too stout to fasten the hooks and eyes. She tried to get into her pre-pregnancy corset, but even with all her tugging and pulling, it wouldn't fasten.

Elise's corset had to be around here somewhere. At twelve, Simone had watched her elder sister grappling with the hated contraption, with its sweat-yellowed laces and the tears in the satin where her fat had fought against it, rubbing the red marks it left on her flesh when she freed herself from it.

After her death, some of the townspeople had advised burning her bedding, her clothes, while others had expressed horror at the notion

—Oh, no, the smoke will carry it into the air, it will be everywhere.

—Better to bury her things.

—Ah, and have it get into the soil itself, we'll never be free of it.

When she opened the top drawer of Elise's bureau, the smell of her sister rushed out at her, and she slammed it shut.

She covered the gaping waistband with a tunic.

They gathered in the parlor before dinner and then went in, the gentlemen escorting the ladies. Albert was the one who took her arm. Jacques squired two giggling daughters from Lyon. It was a small enough thing, Albert being the one to take her into dinner. And yet—if only she could have slipped her hand through Jacques' arm. Tears welled in her eyes—her innate moodiness no doubt exacerbated by the weather, her maternity. She swallowed hard, determined to keep her emotions in check.

Fifteen people were seated at a table meant, at most, for twelve. Throughout the dinner a chorus of *pardons* and *excusez-mois* was murmured as elbows butted against one another. Mme. Vidal frequently rang the bell which summoned Cecile and whispered to her to clear away whatever she could.

Present that night at table was, in addition to the families from Rouen and Lyon, the retired British major who had spent his summer holidays *chez Vidal* for over a decade—with an interruption, of course, for the Great War. He greeted each newcomer with the sentence, *"Je parle tres bien le francais,"* although he seemed to feel that correct pronunciation and intonation were affectations. Also, the female birdwatcher from Alsace, who carried on a monologue, "...at first I thought it was a peregrine falcon, but when it took wing I realized it lacked the requisite white throat. And then..." quite oblivious to the fact that no one paid her the slightest mind.

Mme. Vidal had been forced to take in lodgers when her husband, a commercial traveler for the wines of the Château Cabrières, had died unexpectedly. At first, she had trouble attracting customers—there was ample competition for paying guests, especially in the off-season, and it seemed that she might have to throw herself on the mercy of her peasant family. The laws of familial obligations would have required that they be taken in, but Mme. Vidal and her two daughters would have been expected to share a single bed in a room under the eaves, the girls to slop the hogs and feed the chickens, winnow the hay—*the one who doesn't work, doesn't eat*—their skin turning brown, their hands growing calloused and their prospects for marriage, save to some country bumpkin, dim. Elise, with her child-bearing hips and strong shoulders, would have been the more favored in that department.

But then Mme. Vidal let it get about that at her lodging there was a charming daughter, Simone. (The elder daughter, Elise, a good-hearted, flat-footed sort, was not mentioned.) Granted, Simone was no great beauty, but then again she had none of the haughtiness of those who saw themselves as a reincarnation of Venus. Comely and flirtatious, she was just the thing for the salesmen and railway inspectors and army officers on leave, far from home. And not just for them—when the summer holiday makers descended, Simone formed passionate friendships with the daughters, with long walks on the windswept strand, and the exchange of pressed flowers and sentimental poems, so that the next season, when the besotted daughters declared that they simply must return to the Vidals, their indulgent papas gave in, overruling the wives' protestations that this year they had hoped to go to the mountains.

Simone's life had not been all flirtation and romance. She eviscerated and plucked chickens after Elise had chopped off their heads. Afterwards she'd find pin feathers stuck to her face, flecks of chicken blood. At dinner, she and her sister each took a wing, their mother the back, leaving the breasts and thighs for the boarders. There were linens to be changed, pots to be scoured, greengrocers and fishmongers to be haggled with. Dishes to be washed, passageways to be swept. At the end of the evening, a lodger was sure to appear in the just-cleaned kitchen and say, "I do get a bit peckish at bedtime and was wondering if I might poke about in the icebox."

After the war, her mother read aloud to Simone the statistics about the dearth of marriageable men, thrusting under her daughter's nose the bar graph in the newspaper: the topmost line representing the number of able-bodied men of marriageable age, and the line underneath—five times as long—the number of women. Simone was to understand that she was one of the infinitesimal black dots which made up the lower line, each point a single, love-starved woman.

"There simply aren't enough men left. They say for a while at least, we'll become like primitives and one man will have many wives. I suppose the church will have to go through some folderol and allow it. …"

Her mother turned the most casual of conversations into a dirge—a one-woman Greek chorus—staring into the middle distance, gazing at a future in which crow's feet would appear at the corners of Simone's eyes, her winsome laugh grow brittle, and the dewy virgin would become the desiccated spinster, until at long last Simone's hymen would be broken, not with a thrust from her lawfully wedded husband's member but in her grave by the relentless mouths of worms and voles, maggots and slugs hatching in her womb.

Like a prince in a fairy tale, Luc Henri Clermont had appeared in his cream-colored linen suit, clicking his heels and doffing his hat.

When Simone, great with child, was sent from the miasmas of Turkey to lie-in safely at home, Mme. Vidal understood the balance between the two of them had shifted, given that she was now assisted financially by her son-in-law. Simone, a matron, could hardly be expected to bewitch as she once had. Still, she might have made a bit of an effort to rouse herself from her sullenness, so when the woman from Rouen asked, "How much longer will this wind last?" Simone, instead of merely staring out the window at the clouds scudding across the sky, could have said, "Oh, after these winds have been through, the sky is so clear—I would swear when you stand on the bluff you can see the coast of Africa!" or "If it's windy tomorrow we'll put on a play! It will be such fun!" Mme. Vidal shot her daughter glances: *Come now, no one enjoys a grouchy hostess. And do quit picking at your food.*

Simone was even hungrier than she had been earlier, but while struggling to hook the waistband of her skirt she'd made a promise to herself to get her figure back. She was a keeper of vows, especially ones made to the god of vanity.

Colonel Addams beat the edge of his spoon against his wine glass, and in the startled silence that followed, declared: "*Je porte un toast à Mme. Vidal, une femme estimable, et à cette excellente maison*!"

Jacques whispered to Albert, "What are we drinking to?" Albert shrugged, clinked his glass against Jacques', and downed a good slug of wine. The Alsatian birdwatcher resumed her monologue: "…the sound of the ortolan is rather like this," and made a series of chirps and clicks. "Yes, you're right," she continued, as if someone had responded, "it isn't particularly melodious, almost insect-like, in fact—" while the mother from Lyon issued a series of *sotto voce* reprimands to her children, and the retired British major asked Jacques, in his idiosyncratic French, where he was from. Simone, in order to prevent the possibility of Jacques saying—as another guest once had—*What language is he speaking*? exclaimed, "Yes, do tell us where you are from!"

"Nîmes." The headache which Jacques had planned to plead had now arrived.

"Hoo-hoo-hoo-hoo-hoo. Do you hear the difference? It's subtle," the Alsatian birdwatcher said. "Let me repeat…"

Albert, embarrassed by his friend's monosyllabic response, added: "My friend lives in Paris. And before that, Madagascar."

"Ah," the mother from Rouen asked, "what were you doing in Palestine?"

"Palestine?"

"I believe, dear," her husband corrected, "that you are thinking of Damascus. Madagascar is—some place else."

"An island," Albert put in, "off the coast of Africa."

Jacques eyed the curve of Simone's breasts, smaller than they had been this afternoon. *She must be breastfeeding.* His wife, Sala, a doctor, had of course gone with bottle-feeding. He imagined the mouth of her infant sucking at her breast and, feeling himself become aroused, inched his chair closer to the table.

Blue

In Istanbul, the Prussian blue that formed the backdrop of Luc's blueprints of the trestle bridges that would span the canyons and crevasses, the tunnels that would bore through mountains, stained his fingers, despite his scrub brush. (He cared for his body as he did for his polished wood and brass engineering tools, which he buffed with a chamois cloth before returning to their leather cases.) He would touch her with his tinted hands, leaving a stroke of blue on the edge of her jaw, a smudge circling her breast like a faint tattoo. A deep blue, almost a bruise, where he had thrust his fingers inside of her, worked the heel of his palm back and forth. She would forego her customary bath, wanting to keep the traces of his lovemaking on her skin.

One day, Luc had come home and seen a pile of Turkish books higgledy-piggledy on the floor next to her chair on the verandah. His wife told him she had engaged a young poet of their mutual acquaintance to tutor her in the Turkish language.

At dinner that night he said: "*Ni devus lerni Esperanton. Ĝi estas malŝparado de tempo por lerni turkan.*" Simone laughed.

His dignity wounded, he brought his linen napkin to his mouth, wiped his mustache and lips.

"I'm sorry. What did you say?"

"I spoke in Esperanto." He stopped himself from saying *my dear*. "The universal language. We should learn it, speak it to our children when that time comes. It is a waste of time to learn Turkish."

"The letters are so beautiful. My favorite are *kaf* and *çim*." She stroked the shape of the letters in the air.

He knew at that moment his wife would not be faithful to him. It was not the tutor he feared being cuckolded by—the man's tastes did not tend in that direction—but by a gerund.

Despite knowing that truth, he plowed on: the Turks themselves were abandoning the Arabic alphabet, changing to the Roman, part of shedding their Ottoman past, becoming modern, just as they intended to scrub the language clean of words that had been borrowed from Arabia and Persia. (Beware the gifts foreigners leave at your gate, even if these are only Arabic words for *pus* and *wisdom*, the Farsi words for *enemy* and *footloose*.)

The poet told her there was no word for *être* and *avoir*, "to be" and "to have" in Turkish. "How do you say, 'I am…', 'I have…'? she asked. "Ah," he said, "we do not say such things as crudely, that is, as directly, as you Europeans—I mean, you Western Europeans—do." She wanted to dive into this language, to swim in its waters thick with silt, in that sea of the past and shame and languor, to allow a tiny bit of the foul water to seep into her mouth.

Jacques

The company—save for the birdwatcher who retired early, since she left the house before dawn, carrying bread, a hunk of cheese wrapped up in a cloth, a thermos of blackstrap molasses and hot water, and Mme. Vidal, who napped with Marcel in Simone's room—adjourned to the parlor after dinner, sorting itself onto the various settees and armchairs.

"I'm afraid," Jacques said to Simone, "I must take my leave—"

The look that passed over her face, in the seconds before she regained her composure, was one of desolation.

Seeing it, Jacques added, "—despite your charming company…I've a terrible headache."

"Ah, yes, yes, no doubt from the scirocco."

The lady from Rouen offered aspirin, which Jacques declined, saying he needed to just lie down and give his eyes a rest.

Simone drove off her sense of abandonment by becoming gay to the point of freneticism. She sang, only slightly off-key, an arabesque she'd learned in Turkey, which brought a round of applause from the assembled guests. Simone cranked up the victrola and Caruso sang an aria from Pagliacci. "A miracle!" the father from Lyon declared. "It's as if he were right here in the room with us!" although when Caruso reached the phrase *una smorfia il singhiozzo*, his voice began to deepen and slow, and Simone rushed to turn the crank again.

The daughter from Rouen, sensing that her mother had taken a dislike to Simone, shifted from her position on the couch next to her parents to a footstool next to Simone, from which position she could gaze upwards as she said, "Tell us all about Constantinople."

Simone wove the words *scimitar, pasha, fez, Blue Mosque, harem, Nubians, odalisque, minaret, casbah, opulent* into her conversation, the words with which Luc had seduced her. "And do you know the title the Ottoman sultan took for himself?…Let me see if I can remember it all," and she held up her left index finger: "The Emperor of Emperors, Sole Arbiter of the World's Destiny, Refuge of Sovereigns, Distributor of Crowns to the Kings of the Earth, Master of Europe, Asia and Africa—"

"Not of Europe!" the major grumbled.

"—High King of the Two Seas, the Shadow of God on Earth."

In the midst of her list, Jacques had reappeared with a book in his hand. "The light up there was really quite impossible for reading—if you don't mind, I'll just—" and he indicated a nook, as far as possible from the assembled company, into which he cocooned himself, even going so far as to turn the chair in it away, so that his back was presented to the other guests.

"The sick man of Europe," the major coughed. "Turkey, that is." He mumbled a bit: the words "Gallipoli" and "butchers" rising out of the rumbling brook of his muttering.

Simone, although not known for strong opinions, ventured one now: "It seems to me both sides can be said to be guilty of—well, butchery."

The major answered her with a glare.

Hereafter, he will be neither avuncular nor sly towards her: he will treat her as if she does not exist. To hear the British Army criticized by a flighty girl, one who had been living amidst the enemy, allowed herself to be seduced by them…

The major rose. He inclined his head and said, "If you will excuse me, please," and marched out of the parlor, ramrod back, head high.

He will finish out his stay *chez Vidal* but in the future will holiday in Brighton. He'd put up with a lot for the sake of the sunshine—their gussied-up food, for a start, sauces covering the meat which for all one knew was rancid. Good, straightforward English cooking, that's what he'll dine on in the future. Blood sausage, spotted dick, winkles. And none of those syrupy liqueurs they'd plied him with after dinner; a good pint of British bitter. Years later, after the Fall of France, he'll know: *I was right about those frogs all along*.

"Oh, dear." Simone rose to go after him, but Albert gestured to her to stay.

To break the awkward silence, Albert said, "Ah, but perhaps it's true that this was the war to end all wars. Shall we raise a glass to peace? In our time and for all time!" But the toast to peace did nothing to lift the gloom that had descended on the room. To speak of peace reminded them of the war.

Albert clapped his hands together. "I have it, on very good information—from the lady herself—" he gestured towards Simone.

"Ah, Albert, you mustn't repeat things we ladies have—"

"—that our lovely hostess not only went to a costume party—"

"Oh, Albert, no," she said.

Hearing the grace note of shame in Simone's voice, Jacques perked up, made a quarter turn towards the group.

"Yes, not only did she go dressed as a Turkish janissary—"

"Oh, we're back to the Turks again, are we?"

"But her husband, the absent and no doubt estimable Chief Engineer Clermont"—Albert raised his glass—" accompanied her, also in costume—and she has a photograph of the two of them. Go fetch it for us, Simone."

"Maybe one of the others would like to entertain us for a while," Simone said. "Perhaps a song or the recitation of a poem?"

Albert and the mother from Rouen responded at the same time, Albert saying, "Oh, don't try and wiggle out of it. Go and fetch the picture," while she said, "I'm not much of a one for poetry," and then, in a lower voice, "Waste of time if you ask me."

"If you don't go and get the picture, I shall start declaiming poetry. Which will greatly annoy at least one of your guests," Albert winked.

Simone returned with the studio portrait which showed her with ballooning trousers and a flowing coat, a glued-on mustache, a scimitar, felt boots and turban, while Luc wore an embroidered red caftan. A veil covered the lower half of his face, revealing kohl-rimmed eyes.

"Who is the Turkish lady with you?" the Lyonnaise woman asked.

"That is my husband. In costume. For the party."

"Do they all dress like that?"

"More and more you see women in modern dress. Especially in the cities…he wore a veil to hide his mustache." Simone twirled both her index fingers before her face to indicate that her husband's mustache was no mean thing.

"They treat their women badly, don't they? The Arabs."

She sensed Jacques was looking at her and turned her head. And sure enough, he was giving her a look she couldn't quite decipher. Was he saying: What a ridiculously old-fashioned dandy this husband of yours must be—with his waxed and curled mustache? Did his look also convey: Yes, and you are beginning to admit the truth to yourself, that you have wed a vain and ridiculous man. But perhaps she was reading too much into it. Maybe it wasn't a look of scorn, but one of complicity. It might be that he only meant a smirking acknowledgement of their mutual superiority to those who didn't know a Turk from an Arab.

"Ah," Albert cried, "Ladies, gentlemen, your attention, please! A momentous event has occurred! Jacques Melville has set down his book. I am not certain, but I think he is about to grace us with his presence."

"May I?" Jacques asked, taking the photograph.

Albert leaned over his friend's shoulder. "Doesn't our Simone make a handsome man?"

"I prefer her as a woman," he said, giving her a look of such frank sexual regard that she blushed.

Raptor

One by one, two by two, the guests said their goodnights, and drifted off to bed, until only Jacques, Albert, and Simone were left in the parlor. Mme. Vidal, who had been upstairs dozing in the rocking chair with her grandson in her arms, tiptoed down the stairs and warned her daughter against staying up too late. "You need your sleep…" she said, glancing at the couch: *And remember, I'm sleeping on the settee tonight.*

Simone nodded back, gave a tight smile: *Oh, just sleep in my bed until I get there. I'm not about to give up the chance I have for some real company for your sake*!

Simone filched a bottle of homemade *mirto* from the pantry. "From the berries of the myrtle bush. It will give us vivid dreams."

"Are you Circe, a knower of herbs and potions?"

"This"—Albert draped an arm around his pal's shoulder—"is why we keep him around. He lifts up the tone of the gathering with his classical allusions—"

"I need to excuse myself for a minute." Simone's breasts were milk-filled and aching.

Albert yawned, "We should be heading off to bed—"

"Oh, no! I mean, not on my account. I am just so glad to have some—but, of course, if you are tired…"

A little after midnight one of the other guests came down and asked, as a special favor to the elderly, if the young people could please be a little more quiet. After that, they whispered, which made them laugh. They held their hands over their mouths, which only made them laugh harder.

A full moon shone through the window.

As she refilled their glasses, Simone's hand brushed against Jacques.

"You're warm."

"I have a slight fever—it's nothing. Probably from…" she glanced downwards, uncertain if she should say the word "nursing," wavered back and forth, will it make her seem bovine, slovenly? Not to say it would be prudish, yes, she determined to finish her sentence, to say the word, and blurted it out rather too harshly: "nursing."

"Ah, the sacrifices the race of noble mothers makes—" Albert said.

Because she wanted to drive off the notion of her being exalted by maternity, she said, "I quite enjoy a slight fever..."

Jacques' eyes fixed on her, like those of a raptor on its prey.

She'd been about to say "A fever is like wine, too much leaves you thick and dull, but the right amount..." but now to say that would make her foolish.

His eyes accused her of being a woman who needed stimulation, whether from wine or fever or the admiration of men.

The next gesture he made took her aback, laying his flat palm upon her forehead, leaving it there. Under the influence of drink—Jacques was on his third glass of *mirto*—some men reveal a hidden streak of cruelty. Jacques revealed a well-concealed vein of tenderness.

Flush

He was flushed, in all the myriad senses of that word: warm, lavish, abundant. He held forth. She and Albert basked in his talk: "In Madagascar, it was said that everyone had a spirit animal. I was quite convinced mine was the aye-aye. Have you heard of the aye-aye? No? It has enormous eyes and five fingers. A species of lemur. Difficult to actually catch sight of, it hides in the forest and plays tricks on us humans. But when I confided my belief to one of the village elders, he shook his head very solemnly from side to side and said, '*Angonoka.*'" Jacques imitated the old man's hunched shoulders, his penetrating glare, the gravely certainty with which he spoke.

"*Angon—*," Simone repeated.

"*Angonoka.*"

"*Angonoka.*"

"There. We'll have you speaking Malagasy in no time. The Europeans call it the ploughshares tortoise," Jacques laughed. "One of the ugliest animals you have ever seen—a strange protuberance of its shell under its head—most pronounced in the male of the species, resembling a plough. If my spirit animal couldn't have been the aye-aye, couldn't it have been the native bats with a face like a fox? No, alas, within me is a lumbering tortoise. Its mating is triggered by fighting with male rivals. The two of them go at it, locking their ploughs together, stumbling back and forth. Have you ever seen a boxing match?"

"No," Simone said. "Bullfights, I have seen bullfights."

"Sometimes one of the fighters knocks the other out quite decisively. But sometimes the match goes on and on, two men, punch drunk, leaning into each other, almost as if they were engaging in a strange dance, every now and again one or the other landing a blow. Resembling one of those longstanding marriages where the couple are joined together by hatred and custom, staggering around together. That is how the ploughshare tortoises fight—the male of the species."

"And the female of the species?" Simone asked.

Jacques gave a shrug.

Albert yawned. "We should be getting to bed," although none of the three made a move to rise.

Another half an hour passed, Albert yawned again. "We should be getting to bed. We must be up early, our hike to the lighthouse."

"Sleep in tomorrow," Simone coaxed. "You can see the lighthouse some other day."

"No, alas," Albert said. "There's only tomorrow. On Thursday, we leave for Carcassonne."

"You are leaving?"

"You see," Albert said to Jacques, "she adores us, she's devastated that we are going!" Simone had begun to cry.

"Didn't Albert tell you? We are on a pilgrimage."

"It's just that it's so dull here. I'm so lonely. I'll be left alone with that dreadful colonel and those squabbling families."

Albert offered her his handkerchief. "This corner is clean."

"I'm sorry, I'm sorry. You must think I'm—weeping like this." She pushed her fingers against the underside of her eye sockets and forced a rueful laugh. She shook her head, like a dog shaking off water: "A pilgrimage? What kind of a pilgrimage?"

"Perhaps we could come back." Albert cocked a questioning eyebrow at Jacques.

"Perhaps." Jacques sounded doubtful.

"Oh, no, no. It's your holiday. I don't want to—. The doctor says I should wait until Marcel is at least six months to take him to Istanbul. There are fevers there. And Luc— my husband—can't come here, because of his duties. For a while—I'm sorry, I shouldn't be airing my thoughts—it seemed that he was going to be able to come for a visit. I was looking forward…but then some calamity arose—something to do with a shipment of railroad ties, if you can imagine. Oh, I'm so sick of myself! I sit around and brood all day. Like a hen. I cluck and fuss. Tell me about your pilgrimage. What kind of a pilgrimage would the two of you be going on?"

Albert dropped to his knees, took a few steps on them, his hands pressed together in prayer. "I didn't tell you, I had a religious conversion, I'm going to become a Carthusian monk."

"Oh, Albert, you couldn't keep silent for an hour, never mind a lifetime." Simone ruffled Albert's wild hair.

"I like that. Perhaps I'll become a dog instead. Your faithful companion," and from his knees he went onto all fours, hung his tongue out, wagged his rear.

"We are going to Carcassonne to meet a poet, Joë Bousquet. A literary pilgrimage. I have been corresponding with him—he has quite a striking voice. He was wounded in the war, paralyzed, and is now unable to leave his family home."

"Come with us." Albert had gone from all fours to sitting on the floor, with his legs drawn up in front of him.

"You forget I am a married woman. I can hardly go traipsing off across the countryside with the two of you."

"Tell your mother that we've become monks. We'll make a great show of our piety tomorrow."

"And then there's my child."

"Oh, he's so small. I'll just tuck him under my arm—"

"And what would my husband say?"

"I won't tell. Jacques, will you tell?"

"Your husband should have known better than to leave you alone."

"Jacques, Jacques, put that harsh schoolmaster self away. Have some more *mirto*."

Jacques raised his hand, like a cop stopping traffic. "I have had enough. And you have had more than enough. To bed, with all of us."

At the top of the stairs, they bid whispered goodnights. Jacques lingered in the hallway, watching as Simone entered her bedroom.

Having shut the door behind her, she wept. Was she crying because Jacques and Albert were leaving tomorrow, abandoning her? Because she was ashamed of having revealed to them the depth of her loneliness? Was she weeping because she had already fallen in love with Jacques?

She pressed her fingers against her eye sockets. She would be fine, fine without the two of them. After they had gone, she would spend time with the daughter of the family from Rouen—what was the girl's name? Martine? Yes, Martine. As for her rather untoward behavior in the parlor tonight—they'd all had a bit too much to drink, in the morning no one will remember her having cried, and if they do—why it will all be covered in a hazy, alcoholic wash. As for those looks that friend of Albert was giving her—the way he had stared at her with such disdain when she talked about her husband's mustache, and his—leer, really, there was no other word for it, *I prefer her as a woman*.

She heard a bedspring creak. "You're drunk!"

"Mother!" Simone had quite forgot her mother had given up her own room to Albert and Jaques, had been asleep up here waiting for the parlor to be vacated.

"Yes, your mother." She rose in her rumpled white nightgown, wrapping a throw around her shoulders, stumbling across the room towards the door. Before she closed the door she hurled over her shoulder, "I heard you crying!"

Sate

Simone changed into her nightclothes, shook Marcel awake, offered him her nipple, hoping to fill him up so he didn't wake her later. The tug of his mouth on her breast made her cunt throb, sexual hunger as sharp as hunger in the belly.

She heard a soft rap at her door, her name whispered.

"Just a moment," she called out, rising, laying the sleeping Marcel down in his cradle.

When she saw Jacques at the open door, she thought he was going to ask her some practical question—*Where are the extra pillows kept*? *Do you have matches*?—but instead he reached out his hand and touched her face.

For six months, she had been living in a world of softness: the midwife's hands, rubbed with lanolin; Marcel's sweet flesh. The roughness of his hand shocked, excited her.

"I want to make love to you."

She did not open the door wider to admit him; nor did she slam it in his face.

He said nothing more, only stared at her.

"I believe it's usual, in this situation, to begin by paying the lady in question a compliment. To tell her that she is charming, beautiful."

"You don't need me to tell you that. You know it already."

"So I am vain?"

Again that direct stare. She was so aware of the pulse of blood in her sex she thought he might be able to sense it too.

She could do this and it would sate the yearning within her. With the feeling of leaping into a cold lake, she opened the door. "Just tonight."

"Just tonight." He shut the door behind him, pulled off her nightgown, cupped her pubic mound in the palm of his hand, thrusting his fingers into her.

She cried out, more in shock than pleasure.

"You were wet already."

She did not dare tell him she became aroused by nursing. He might run from her as if she were a primordial female, sucking men into her maw.

She thought that now he was going to trace his tongue along the whorls of her ear, bestow a line of kisses along the inside of her forearm, inner elbow to wrist, stroke the nape of her neck, but he did none of these things. He locked her in an embrace and their two bodies shuffled, awkward as a walrus on land, towards the bed. "Careful. My son's cradle." But when they tumbled onto the bed, the ropes supporting the mattress rasped against the holes they were threaded through.

"The floor," he said.

Her breasts began to jet milk. "Oh," she cried, clapping her hands over her nipples, trying to stop them from spouting.

He moved her hand away with his mouth, tasted her milk with the tip of his tongue, then guzzled at her breast like Marcel.

Never having before made love with anyone besides her husband, she had thought the sensations, the smells, the raw physical feeling of Luc's flesh moving in and out of her flesh encompassed the totality of the world of passion.

Everything about Jacques was different—the shape of his cock, the way he thrust in and out of her, the smell of him, his air of slight disdain—not so much for her as for the act itself, as if a part of him were split off, looking down from high above at these two strange, wild creatures, caught up in their rutting.

After he climaxed, he did not immediately withdraw from her, as her husband had always done, instead collapsing upon her. His breath came hard and ragged in her ear. With Luc, everything had been so much more—contained. Upon ejaculating, Luc had always risen and gone to the washstand and rubbed his genitals down with a washcloth and a soap reserved for this purpose. He had instructed his innocent bride that she was to do the same, and they had each returned to the marital bed smelling of jism and sweat, tallow and coal tar. She had assumed this was a universal human ritual upon completion of coitus—as ubiquitous as cleaning oneself after defecating. Vaguely aware of the connection between disease and sex, she feared those fluids their bodies had given off might fester and putrefy as they wallowed in them. But Jacques must know, this sophisticated man, this man whose easy gaze showed he was at home in the world of sensuality, how such routines were managed.

Her body ached from the weight of him, anchoring her, and she squirmed beneath him.

He drew himself free of her, they clambered up onto the bed, he pulled her close to him, she lay with her head on his chest, listening to the steady beat of his heart. She and Luc had never lain like this. After Luc performed his ablutions it was her turn, and by the time she returned to the bed, he would be fast asleep, snoring softly, sex functioning not so much as a soporific but more as an anesthetic.

She drifted off to sleep, woke. Was it because Jacques, half-asleep, was caressing her, or was she the one who, half-asleep, had started to caress Jacques? They made love again, gently this time, drifted off to sleep. And then—how could it be?—the sky was growing light. Jacques gave her a kiss on the forehead, a kiss of benediction. He put on his underclothes, folded the rest of his clothing into a neat packet, set his shoes upside down on top of it, and started to tiptoe out of the room.

Rock

He stopped by Marcel's cradle, crouched down, rocked it.

"I have a son, too."

Simone hoped the room was still dark enough that he couldn't see the look of shock on her face. It hadn't occurred to her that he might have a wife, and more than a wife, a child. What was he doing roaming about with Albert? Or he might not be married, the child could be the product of a liaison, he'd left some girl from the lower orders shoved off in a garret somewhere. Of course, she herself had a husband and a child, but he had known that before their encounter began.

"He's a year or so older than your baby. It's strange: a growing child destroys each earlier version of himself. I miss the helpless infant, gone forever."

Jacques brushed his index finger against Marcel's palm and instinctively Marcel's hand clasped it. It was his finger that had been inside of her, that smelled of her. What he was doing seemed sinful, almost incestuous, and yet two months ago the whole of Marcel had been inside of her, moving through her.

"May I pick him up?"

"All right. Just—"

"Oh, I won't wake him. Don't worry." He rocked the cradle, and swayed his body back and forth in time with it, so when he lifted Marcel his movement was smooth and unbroken. He lay him on his left shoulder. "Yes, I remember this weight." He inhaled deeply. "And this smell. At this stage they still smell of their mothers."

She was not naive, she wasn't, not the sort of woman who expected life to be like romantic novels—but nonetheless, there was something so—almost brutal—in the way he said *At this stage they still smell like their mothers*, as if Marcel were interchangeable with all other infants—and she were interchangeable with all other mothers.

"This one more than mine. My wife is a doctor, so she didn't breastfeed. The smell of a nursed baby is purer."

She took a deep breath and asked, "What's your son's name?" trying to sound off-hand, but her voice was tight with tension.

"Frédéric."

He laid Marcel back in his cradle, rocked it a few times, whispered, "There, there," kissed Simone and departed.

Lighthouse

It seemed to her that she did not sleep again, although that was not, strictly speaking, true: throughout the early hours of the morning she dove down into sleep and then darted just as quickly awake, moving in and out of sleep like a barn swallow swooping across the evening sky.

She did finally fall into a real sleep, because she distinctly awoke, her room filled with mid-morning light—and Marcel's cradle empty.

She washed and dressed as quickly as possible—given the lodgers in the house, it was quite unthinkable for her to come down in her dressing gown. Cecile, doing the last of the breakfast dishes, wiped a lock of hair back from her damp forehead, leaving a ribbon of grey suds on her brow.

"Sleep well?" her mother asked.

When that failed to produce a response from Simone, her mother said, "I trust our work here in the kitchen didn't disturb you."

Simone lifted Marcel from her mother's arms. He squawked slightly at the change, and her mother shot her a look, *Your own son prefers me to you.*

"Shall I get you some coffee?" Cecile asked.

"Oh, she can get it for herself."

"Thank you, Cecile."

With her small hands, it was difficult for Simone to manage the morning bowl of coffee with a single hand while she held Marcel so he could nurse. She finally clenched the rim between her thumb and forefinger, despite her mother's disapproving glare.

"What does the day look like?" Simone asked.

"Bright and sunny, as you can see for yourself."

"No, I only meant—the others, the birdwatcher, of course I know—have they gone down to the sea, or—"

"To the seaside. The major and the two families."

"And?"

"Yes?" her mother said.

"Albert and his friend?"

"Jacques. I know you haven't forgotten his name is Jacques."

Cecile walked past, lugging a pail of dishwater out to splash over the kitchen garden, the water sloshing from side to side, the heavy thump of her footsteps, the door slamming shut behind her.

"Did they go to the beach, too?"

"Curiosity killed the cat," her mother answered.

"Satisfaction brought it back."

"We have quite enough satisfied cats about the place as is. Out in the barn, and now, it seems, in the house, too."

During the remaining course of the morning, Simone managed to piece together the answers her mother had refused to give her. Albert and Jacques had risen early—the mother from Rouen had heard them whispering with the birdwatcher—her bedroom being directly above the kitchen, sound does travel—not to mention the kitchen smells! The poor woman from Rouen had never gotten back to sleep.

At lunch, the table was set for thirteen. Mme. Vidal mentioned it before anyone else could. "Of course, I'm sure no one here is so silly as to be superstitious. And who knows, we may only be twelve, sometimes our birdwatching friend's rambles allow her to return, sometimes not. She's left quite strict instructions that we are to start without her—"

"Have the young gentlemen taken their leave?" the major asked.

"No, they've only gone off for a day hike," Mme. Vidal said.

"To the lighthouse," Simone added, pleased to be in the possession of some intelligence.

"To a lighthouse?" the mother from Rouen said. "It seems a strange destination."

"You can climb to the top—I believe there are six hundred stairs—and it's a magnificent view."

"Six hundred stairs!" The mother from Rouen did not approve.

The major, to head off the threatening unpleasantness among the ladies, began a discourse on lighthouses in his execrable French. The great lighthouse at Alexandria, one of the Seven Wonders of the Ancient World, actually on the island of Pharos in the Alexandrian harbor, and it was from this word that the French word *phare* as well as the Spanish and Italian words *faro* had been derived. The lady from Rouen offered her opinion that Alexandria was in Palestine, and those at the table who knew better declined to correct her. Her husband's cousin had known a man who was a lighthouse keeper and was a very strange sort indeed. Just when it seemed the conversation might flag, the Alsatian birdwatcher returned, darting to her seat at the table, saying, "Oh, I'm so glad you didn't wait for me. I would have felt terrible had you waited. Just some soup, please, and then I'll catch up with the—but I heard you were talking about lighthouses! Once at a lighthouse in the La Coruna in Spain, right among the rocks, I saw a black stork." She clasped her hands to her bosom, leaned her head forward and looked about the table at each and every one: "Yes! A black stork. Now, as I'm sure you all know, the black stork is migratory, indeed—" While she spoke, she set her soup spoon down, and a perplexed Cecile stood in the doorway, uncertain of whether to serve the casserole or not. "It travels enormous distances, across Europe to northern India—"

Simone thought she might well go mad.

After lunch, Simone nursed Marcel. She slept (or tried to), went into the parlor and played a few hands of *beloute*, arranged and rearranged a bouquet of flowers, perched on a stool in the kitchen and polished the silver, nursed Marcel again, walked along the strand.

The table was again set for thirteen.

Mme. Vidal's satisfaction was evident as she spoke. "Our rugged young men have plans to dine al fresco this evening—at some fisherman's shack. Apparently the charms of my table can't compete with those of perching on a boulder, eating fried fish off a cracked plate."

"Ah, Madame," said the father from Lyon, "any one who would shun your estimable table—"

"Hear, hear," the major put in, in English.

"Perhaps they miss the trenches," the father from Rouen said, and then guffawed, although no one else found humor in his remark.

The suppertime topics seem to have been set: discourtesies and slights delivered to hostesses, rude guests, fair weather friends. The conversation hopscotched around the table, each story followed by laughter or tut-tuts of disapproval and sympathy, and then by the next speaker telling a tale featuring even more loutish behavior.

Jacques and Albert returned, calling *âllo* from the passageway, refusing to enter the dining room—they were filthy and smelled of fried fish. They would wash and then retire: they had an early train to catch,

"Farewell, to one and all," Albert called. "I kiss the hands of all the ladies from afar, and warmly clasp the gentlemen's hands." Jacques nodded his head in agreement. Poor Cecile—before she'd even had a chance to clear the supper things—was swabbing their mucky footprints.

Maybe

Simone lay awake all night. Despite the promise she'd extracted from Jacques—*just for tonight*—she hoped to hear his footsteps padding down the hallway, stopping outside her door.

At dawn, she heard the creaking hinges of a door being opened—slowly, slowly, so as not to awake the rest of the house—and the sound of bare feet creeping down the stairs. She raced after them.

"We were trying to be so quiet," Albert whispered.

"I was—awake with the baby. Yes, yes, awake with the baby!"

Jacques squared his rucksack upon his shoulders, shifted his weight from one leg to the other. "The train."

"I'll walk to the gate with you."

Albert raised an eyebrow. Although covered ankle to chin, wrist to wrist, she was nonetheless in her nightclothes. "Oh, no one will see me," she said, and looped one of her arms through each of theirs.

At the gate, she said, "Maybe..." allowing her voice to trail off.

It was Albert who responded: "Yes, perhaps we'll be able to stop back, after our visit to Carcassonne."

"Oh," Simone said. "Oh. But it would be quite out of your way."

"Yes," Jacques agreed, glancing at his watch. "We mustn't make promises," Jacques stopped himself from completing his sentence: *we can't possibly keep.*

"No," Albert said, kissing her hand with a flourish. "We are poets, and poets don't make promises, they have dreams. Right, old man?"

"Right," Jacques said, and then they were gone, leaving Simone standing at the gate.

Iron

A week later, she was so filled with his absence that she rose in the middle of the night and took the winter quilt down from the upper shelf of the wardrobe. She lay it on top of her, spreading her legs and wrapping them around it, but that didn't satisfy her yearning for the weight of him. So she piled her pillows on top of the quilt, but the pale replication of the sensation only made her yearn for him all the more.

No wonder he doesn't come back to me, she thought. Who would want a woman who pretends that a pile of bed linens is her lover?

She replayed the sensations of that night—his rough hand on her cheek, the thrust of his fingers inside her, the way he smelled at the beginning of their lovemaking, of bay rum and wine and onions. And how, as he sweated away on top of her, those smells gave way to something mustier and thicker, his own smell, as distinct as the whorls of his fingerprints. The way he said, "Simone, Simone." His heartbeat.

At her father's funeral, there had been prayer cards showing Mary's heart, crowned and adorned with a chaplet of roses, hovering above her breast. It looked nothing like the hearts of pigs and goats and sheep set out for sale in the market, lumpy and dripping. Simone had thought of Mary keeping the gifts of gold and frankincense and myrrh, pondering them in her heart. Mary must have had a doorway in her chest which she opened to take out her heart, and then reached into the gap for the stored gifts of the magi, which she removed to ponder—the French word is *repassant*, also used for the task of ironing—a physical action, rubbing the flasks and reliquaries, as her mother worked a dishtowel over an already dry glass or as Simone found her hand between her legs, rubbing the place for which she had no name.

Back

"He isn't coming back," Simone's mother said.

"I don't know what you are talking about."

"You know very well who I am talking about. Albert's friend. You can sit there gazing down the road forever."

"I'm not *gazing down the road*. I've got to look somewhere." She turned her head and stared at the grove of olive trees on the hillside.

"You used to moon after your father in just the same way." Her mother snapped the tablecloth as she shook the crumbs into the yard.

In the distance, the occasional dark splotch resolved itself into a wandering cow or M. duPont on his bicycle, bringing nothing more than a letter from Luc, or disappeared before it could be made out.

And then, one day, M. duPont waved, thumb and forefinger extended, to indicate he had two letters.

She opened the one from Albert before the one from Luc, skimmed through the letter greedily: *Carcassonne was a marvel, we truly felt as if we weren't in this century, or even the last...We had our dreams of returning to you, and if our purses and our circumstances had permitted we would have, but alas when we left Carcassonne we were penniless.* Her eyes raced through the letter, searching again for the letter "J." *Joë refuses to have electric lights, he says the electricity jangles his damaged nerves...*And then, at the end of the letter, in the very last paragraph, there it was again, the letter "J," the curved triangle with the fish hook hanging from it, and the letter that followed was not a single "e," the letters that followed were not "oë," the letters that followed were "acques," the word was "Jacques," and the sentence as a whole read, "Jacques seems to have taken quite a shine to you, and requests permission to write to you."

She didn't care who saw her running up the path, racing up the stairs—not her mother or the lodgers who might later say *My, it seemed as if the hounds of hell were after you* and then lift an eyebrow, waiting for an explanation. Not Cecile, who would ensure that this tidbit of information got passed all over town: *I don't know what was going on, I just know that when M. DuPont came back, she was down at the end of the road, waiting for him with a letter, hailing him as if he were a taxicab.* Simone didn't even care that the letter she had written to Albert was so hastily scrawled her pen tore the paper, and her words were a quick jumble, telegraphic: *Glad to hear that you are well. The baby and I are both fine. Tell Jacques that yes, he may write to me. I hope you will write to me, too. I will write you a longer letter soon.* And then, because the letter seemed altogether too abrupt: *The baby tires me out and I want to make the next post. I embrace you tenderly, Simone.*

A month elapsed before the letter from Jacques arrived. *Thank you for giving me permission to write to you. I hesitated only because I did not want to cause any difficulty between you and your relations—whether by blood or marriage. It has taken me so long to pen this missive that I fear by now you may have returned to Istanbul. I have been much involved in affairs here at home in Paris—the completion of a manuscript about my sojourn in Madagascar, for which my publisher is quite eager, and, also, if I can speak quite frankly, in difficulties in my household, which, alas, is not a happy one. My wife is pregnant again.*

Simone read the letter over and over again: there was no reference to their—to what had transpired between the two of them—but then, again, Simone was quite uncertain how one would refer to—sexual congress—she had no other words save those. She felt a bit like a child trying to follow a discussion at the family dinner table, knowing that the arched eyebrows, the forced coughs, the allusive words were codes she could not decipher. Was this letter endeavoring to create greater intimacy between the two of them? Or was it merely an attempt to, as the saying went, "let her down easy"? She wrote back to him, having gone through numerous drafts, trying to match her tone to his. In one version she wrote, *I am sorry to hear that your home life is difficult,* but then thought that sounded too remote. In another draft, written late at night, she made explicit reference to their lovemaking, but when she read it over in the morning she was so ashamed she ripped the paper into tiny squares. In the end, her letter contained reports of the local weather and listings of her son's latest doings, with a scrawled P.S. *I am somewhat cowed, writing to a literary man like you, I fear I don't express myself at all well, I do miss you,* and underlined the word "do."

Flush

Over the course of the next months, letters traveled back and forth between Simone and Jacques. Simone remained in her mother's home, since Luc had determined that the political situation in Turkey was so precarious she ought not to return. He continued to promise to visit her, but circumstances arose, one after the other, preventing this from occurring. If the letters between Simone and Jacques never grew any more intimate, neither did they grow any less so. Simone lived, as she had during her twelfth year, the year after her father's death, in a world removed from the physical.

The word "purgatory" had eluded the net of definition. She had leafed through a copy of *The Divine Comedy* illustrated by Gustav Doré and seen the souls in Purgatory, depicted in shades of gray—lead and slate—abject figures, draped in robes that resembled both burial shrouds and the habits of Mohammedan women, bearing boulders as they moved along a rock-strewn path that wended its way above stark cliffs and fog-shrouded crags. She tried to paste her father's face into the hollows of those cloaks. The ordinary world—the smell of the ocean, her mother's whistling as she washed the dishes, her sister Elise's guffaws—was at best an irritant. The world made sense only when it gestured to what lay beyond: the air in the church, thick with incense, the crucifix on the wall above her bed.

Now the path to the gate was the path down which Jacques had walked. The chair in the parlor was the chair in which he had sat. Even her own son was the infant he had lifted into his arms.

A thick letter from Luc arrived by special post containing a ticket for a steamship departing four days hence. Cecile and her mother packed Simone's trunks with the same roll-up-your- sleeves, get-on-with-it fervor they applied to spring cleaning. They could not wait to rid the house of the squalling child, Simone's moodiness. As for Simone, she wanted to be freed from her mother's house, but she dreaded seeing

Luc again, could not imagine receiving his caresses. She thought of pheasants being flushed from fields by hounds, taking wing to escape, easy shots against the sky above.

A week later she was in Istanbul. Luc seemed hardly to notice her diffidence, or if he did put it down to the whims of female nature: skittish, like a horse in a new barn. Give the gal a chance to get settled, and all would be fine. He was fascinated by the child, showing not only the expected paternal pride, but curiosity about the child's mental and physical processes, his rudimentary acquisition of language—"Do you see, he knows his name. Marcel, Marcel," and the child looked in his direction—"and when I put the block behind my back—Where did it go? Where did it go?" This interest was not to be confused with indulgence: he was upset that Simone had not yet begun toilet training, making her aware of the latest scientific studies which proved, quite incontrovertibly, that the foundations of a disciplined and well-ordered life were laid down by the regular excretory habits established in infancy.

The first night they were together, Luc thought it best not to press himself on her: no doubt she was tired from the journey and required some time to readjust to his presence. He did want to let her know that his—he formed the word reluctantly, even in his own mind—his love for her had not waned, and so when they lay down next to another in bed that night, he clasped her hands tenderly, and covered them with a series of minute kisses. She shocked him by becoming quite forward, initiating the marital act. At its conclusion, as in the past, he rose and washed himself, and then she did the same, even squatting down a bit—the washbasin was behind a screen—and twisting the flannel around her finger, shoving it inside her, doing her best to remove every trace of him.

When she was having sex with Luc, she imagined Jacques' presence—not that Jacques was moving in and out of her, but that he was watching them couple with a look of amused contempt.

She spent her days reading novels and staring at the blue sea and blue sky. The servants washed and rewashed the floor (they were horrified that their master and mistress wore shoes indoors) and occasionally brought her child to her.

One day, standing at the balustrade staring at the horizon, she felt a sharp queasiness and realized she was pregnant. She would be sent back to France for her parturition.

For the first time since her return to Istanbul, she smiled a smile that was not forced.

Jacques

Lumbering, flat-footed, great with child, Simone returned to Juan-les-Pins.

A letter from Jacques, penned many months before, waited for her. (She had written before she left telling him she was returning to Istanbul, that their correspondence must, at least for a while, cease.)

She sat down at the table in her room, without even removing her coat, and wrote to him. She wrote of the blue of the sea and sky in Istanbul and her disgust at her husband's body. And that, once again, another creature was within her.

The trunks unpacked, silk underthings, thin skirts, waiting for the time when her body would be her own again.

She spread her legs in front of her bedroom mirror to see her sex, swollen with the hormonal wash of pregnancy.

A girl: Odette. Weaned at six weeks. She couldn't stand the needy, tugging mouth at her breast. She did not want her breasts to once again become an obscene fountain when she was with Jacques.

She would be with Jacques again, she would.

And then, on August 1st of 1923, Simone received a letter from him, telling her he was coming south—that he would, as soon as he heard back from her with her assent to his visit, send a telegram to her mother, booking a room for a few days. From Juan-les-Pins, he would once again go to see Joë.

Her letter in response would have been delivered into the hands of M. Dupont, who would have slipped it into his satchel to jostle against the other letters therein. It could have found itself trapped between the pages of a magazine or dropped behind a desk by the slovenly postmistress in town. If those things failed to happen, it would have been put in a sack and carried from Juan-les-Pins to Aix to Paris. But the train could derail, the mail car cracking open like an egg, white letters slithering down a hillside. It was much safer to send a telegram, her words transubstantiated into dots and dashes, a series of pulses racing along black wires, arriving in Paris within minutes.

She passed the blank across the counter with the words, "Yes, come, Simone."

In a separate, larger envelope, Jacques had sent a chapbook of Joë's poems. Simone ran her hands over the rough, deep blue cover: she touched the words *spine, marrow, blood, scarf, circle, delirium* as if she were a blind woman reading Braille.

"I had a telegram from your paramour," her mother said.

"My paramour?"

"You know very well who I mean. He'll be here in three days. I hope he doesn't expect me to knock five francs off the price like I did for Albert."

Jacques found it more than a bit embarrassing: Simone's flushing and fluttering at the supper table, the way she kept suppressing the smile creeping over the corners of her mouth, gazing at him and then quickly averting her eyes. In response to Mme. Vidal's questions—*And how is Albert? Why hasn't he joined you on this trip? And what have you been up to?*—he offered, *Fine. He's busy in Paris. Finishing my manuscript.* To make up for his curtness, Simone blathered about Marcel's latest doings, the weather, and then, as if aware she sounded foolish, offered a scrambled disquisition on what she had read in the papers over the last few days, in response to which Mme. Vidal whispered, "Simone!"

⚜

That night, he heard the soft pad of bare feet heading down the hallway, pausing outside his room, the barely perceptible rap of her knuckles against his door. He did not immediately rise from his bed, where he was stretched out naked in the summer heat, reading the latest version of a hastily-printed surrealist journal.

Simone, standing on the other side of the door, her heart dithering in her chest, seeing the faint light from under the doorway—*surely, he must have heard me knock, if I knock any more loudly I may wake Mother or Cecile*. She heard the creak of the bedsprings as his weight shifted.

She bit her lip, rapped again, glanced to the left and the right: no door was opening, no one was peering into the hallway.

"Knock, knock, knock. Knock, knock, knock." He stood in the doorway, keeping her from entering.

Her eyes filled with tears.

"Come, come." He stepped back from the door, shut the door behind her, opened his arms to her.

"Ah, you poor girl," he said as she was riding him. "You poor starved child." And later, "What a fool this husband of yours is. To leave you so bereft."

In the morning she stank of him and, not daring go down to breakfast before she washed, she called out to Cecile when she heard her passing in the hallway, asking her to bring her some hot water.

A few minutes later, her mother was outside Simone's closed door, calling in, "Come down for breakfast and then have your wash. Poor Cecile is worn out already and it isn't yet eight o'clock." And when Simone did not deign to respond, "Did you hear me?"

Simone opened the door a crack, her body tucked behind it, and hissed, "I'm indisposed."

"Indisposed? But you can't have started your flow again already."

"Mother! You sound like a peasant, discussing this sort of thing—and in the hallway! Whatever will the guests think."

"Well, I only…" Simone's mother said, to the door that had been closed in her face.

Mme. Vidal's sour mood settled over the breakfast table, despite the fact that she smiled as she passed the butter and the jam—*This is from the apricot tree you can see right out that window*—and inquired politely over the guests' plans for the day, averring that the morning mist—a much better word than fog—would soon lift, making this the perfect day for a hike in the hills, and yes, also, a perfect day for the beach.

"Has our Parisian intellectual headed out already?" one of the guests asked.

"No sign of him yet this morning," Cecile put in, although Mme. Vidal had spoken to her several times about not jumping into the conversation. She was, after all, to remember her place. Not only that, but it didn't do to grumble about one guest in front of the others—they were sure to start wondering what was said when their backs were turned.

Simone, having handed Marcel off to Cecile, appeared at the breakfast table as the last dawdling guests were helping themselves to just a bit more coffee and the morning's first cigarette.

"You needn't wolf down your food, dear."

Simone wanted to depart the table before the last guest did, so that her mother couldn't take advantage of the two of them being alone to tell her she looked peaked, to ask pointedly if she had gotten enough sleep.

A floorboard creaked overhead, and Simone looked upwards, which Mme. Vidal did not fail to notice.

"M. Melville's still abed. He must be worn out—from his travels."

"I'm going for a walk," Simone announced, standing up abruptly.

"Do you think the fog is burning off?" the last lodger at the table asked, dabbing the ends of his greying mustache with his napkin. Simone feared he was working himself up to saying, "I don't mean to be forward, but do you think we might walk together—perhaps your mother and your son might join us?"

She bolted from the table before he had a chance to do so, stopping in the kitchen to give Marcel in his high chair a quick kiss. Marcel lifted his arms to her, pleaded, "With you, Mama. With you!"

She shut the door on his sobs. After all, it was for the best, she didn't want to spoil him. She hoped that Jacques, having heard she'd gone down to the strand, would set out after her.

At the gate, she realized she had forgotten her hat, but she didn't want to go back for it and risk getting waylaid by her mother. As she walked down to the shore, the wind caught in the tendrils of her hair. She could imagine her mother's reprimands: *The sun and wind will parch your hair. Your skin will turn red like a boiled lobster*. Some anti-fairy tale, golden tresses spun into straw, the princess's mottled skin making her a toad.

The morning fog was settling in, not burning off. The cove was dotted with a few bathers, a small knot undertaking calisthenics in unison. Great cormorants were perched on boulders, drying their wings or rocking on the choppy waters offshore, waiting for their prey.

The wind drove grains of sand and salt into the crevice between her teeth and gums, the whorls of her ears. As in the year after her father's death, when she had set penances for herself, offering them up to speed her father's path through Purgatory—jagged pebbles in her shoes, kneeling on the cold stone floor of the church at early Mass each morning—these physical irritations were sources of pleasure as well as pain, making her body give up its secrets.

That same year, in fifth form, she'd had her first male teacher, M. Duprée, the science master. He'd brought his microscope to school, sealing grains of sand on a slide. Peering down the brass shaft, she saw miniature shells, wave-tumbled glass, fossilized sea sponges, broken claws from infinitesimal relatives of the crab and lobster, evidence of another, unseen world. The sea she so loved, for all its majesty, was also an open sewer, a grave to numberless beings.

Her father was in the ground, worms and grubs turning him into earth. She wondered if she dared ask Mr. Duprée if they might examine dirt, too. *Media vita in morte sumus*. "In the midst of life, we are in death" did not refer to a state of the soul, but to the body, earthy and gross.

Seal

There Jacques was. Coming towards her. Yes, it was him. She stopped dead in her tracks, her heart all a-flutter. The clichés of cheap romance novels were proving themselves real, although her bodily sensations weren't solely cardiac. Other, less poetic systems were coming in to play, the outer manifestation of which was a pleasant dampness between her legs. The sea stank, fetid and amniotic.

He looked around before embracing her. "I hope I didn't make your mother suspicious."

"She can be as suspicious as she likes. My husband—well, he sends her a cheque every month. If she cooks my goose, she cooks her own. I suppose that isn't a particularly elegant way of putting it—"

He was smiling fondly at her, and she saw that he was taken by her simplicity, that those letters she had written him, in which she had endeavored to offer him a well-turned phrase, an original observation, had enchanted him when she was most straightforward.

They bent their heads together, each forming a wind break for the other, as they followed the crude path down to the strand. They stopped at a tidal pool and watched a sea anemone, with its hundred of tentacles waving in the water, both phallic and fragile. When Marcel had been inside of her, his penis must have looked like those translucent fronds, only later filling with tissue and blood. A minnow darted by and the tentacles, as skillful as the fingers of a blind man, pulled it into the stout center of the organism.

What were these translucent bits of protoplasm floating past? Tadpoles, polliwogs, a just-born guppy or jellyfish?

They came to an outcropping of rock forming a half-cave. Without any preliminaries, Jacques took a blanket from his rucksack, spread it on the sand, seated himself, and unbuttoned his flies. He yanked up her skirt, pulled off her drawers, tucking them in the rucksack so they wouldn't blow away, lowered her roughly onto him, facing away.

The world beyond them disappeared. Even her breasts, their limbs, their mouths, their smells were inconsequential. There was only his sex, her sex, the bare and frank conjunction of their movement. The God she'd worshipped all her life, the God of good and evil, of sin and virtue, was killed as they made love, murdered by his ancient mothers and fathers. The stout gods and goddesses of the barbarians reigned again, squatting around campfires, gnawing on the gristle of roasted bone, picking their teeth, farting—gods who did not know the meaning of the word shame.

And then the world came back.

The wind.

The fog.

The two of them.

The plash and funk of the ocean.

A sound, something between a honk and a bark, slowly distinguished itself from the rumble of the ocean, the cries of the gulls, the flap of the wind against their clothing.

"We aren't the only lovers on the beach today," Jacques whispered. Steadying herself with one hand against his hip, she turned.

A few feet beyond them, two monk seals were coupling lackadaisically on the strand. Their bodies, so graceful in water, were slug-like on land. The cow moaned as the bull flopped on top of her.

"Slowly, slowly," Jacques' whispered, as she pulled herself off of him. She sat on his lap, his arms wrapped around her, sheltering her. She whispered, "They can't smell us?"

He shrugged, mouthed the words, "The wind—the wrong direction—"

The seals both bellowed, roars of pleasure, cries of pain echoing off the rocks and waves.

Train

It was quite acceptable for a married woman to put her hand into the crook of the elbow of a man who was not her husband, who was a guest of the family, as the two of them walked through the streets of Juan-les-Pins, as this constituted an act of everyday masculine protection to the frail sex of which Simone was a member, although none of her family friends and acquaintances, passing them and offering a smile, a nod, a tip of the hat, could have known the pleasure it gave her to have her thin fingers wrapped around his arm, could have known she was thinking: I never before knew my hand, my very hand itself, could experience joy.

It was also quite within the realm of that which was proper for a young woman of a good bourgeois family to stand on the railway platform with said lodger, even though it might be observed that the smile upon her face revealed she was quite smitten. It was not quite acceptable, but still these things happen, it's not *comme il faut*, but nonetheless, a shrug, a wink, for Simone to have her fling with Jacques. After all, women were weak, easily tempted, and men had desires that were like the engine of that train now entering the station.

But to step onto the train with this man with the brooding eyes and furrowed brow, to travel with him to Carcassonne to visit the poet Joë Bousquet, was to cast herself outside the bounds of decency.

Simone, right foot on the step, left on the platform, hesitated for a fraction of a second, not filled with second thoughts, but rather with the desire to prolong this moment, her break with the past.

She drew a deep breath, grabbed hold of the bar, and hoisted herself onto the train.

Chez Vidal, Odette was wailing: "Mama, Mama, Mama, Mama, Mama," holding out her arms. "Mama, Mama, Mama, Mama, Mama."

They were lucky enough to find a compartment alone.

"Did I ever tell you," Simone said, leaning her head against Jacques' shoulder, "that the first man I ever loved was wounded in the war?"

Did I ever tell you...she said, as if she had told him many, many things about her life. The fact is, they have said very little to one another, and most of that in the presence of others: Albert, the guests crowded together in the parlor after dinner. The words they have spoken to one another when alone have mostly been monosyllables: *yes, there, oh, hold me, oh, yes, my God, oh, oh; oh yes, yes, right there, oh.*

He knew she had had a stout sister named Elise who had died of Spanish influenza leaving behind a dress of cornflower blue; a husband named Luc who had an ornate and ridiculous mustache and had gone to a costume party as a concubine; a father who had died some years before—his portrait hung in the lodging-house parlor. Quite frankly, he did not want to know the year of this husband's birth, his place of origin nor particulars about Simone's mother's social background, any facts that might enable him to create a smooth narrative of her life.

"I like the way things are between us now. When I feel I know everything essential about you and nothing superfluous."

She fell silent and when he realized, belatedly, that his words had wounded her, he said, "Go on," and stroked her hand affectionately.

"My father died when I was twelve years old. For a while I became very devout. I'd set penances for myself—walk with my head bent down, looking for jagged pebbles to put in my shoes. I went to Mass every day—the old crones, and me. They kept urging me to kneel on a *prie-dieu* but I liked—wanted—the sensation of the flagstone against my knees. And then there was the war—I became devoted to France—"

"Rather than to God?"

"I wasn't devoted to God so much as to my father's salvation. My mother'd say, 'You'd better pray for him. He needs every single one of your prayers.' But then, when France was invaded, it was so—concrete. I kept a map, with colored pins—black for Germany, red for France. At school, we were allowed to knit. For the soldiers at the front, as long as we used wooden needles and not steel ones. The clack of steel ones drowned out the teacher. One day, my teacher, Mme. LeDuc—I idolized her—held up my socks and said, 'These are socks for deformed feet.' "

"I suppose that was the end of her as your idol."

"Oh no. After that I loved her even more."

When vexed by her pupils' vast, collective stupidity, Mme. LeDuc slapped implements against her open palm—a ruler, the rod kept propped in the classroom corner. Sometimes she used these to rap knuckles, the tender spot where the shoulder and neck meet. Simone never felt the bite of the rod or the ruler, although she often imagined she did.

"Don't weep when you are being reprimanded," Mme. LeDuc said to her. "It's like allowing a dog to see your fear. It's true, I'm harder on you than I am on the other girls. You're not hopeless."

A trace of contempt is like a hint of bitterness in the mouth: the flesh of a veal roast can be insipid, unless dusted with tart hyssop.

Stump

"And then, Robert, who lived down the lane from us, returned from the front minus a leg. I brought him bunches of wildflowers and—even though food was so scarce then—turnips and beets and parsnips. I knitted one of my odd scarves for him. He must have already been falling in love with me then because he exclaimed over it so. He still wasn't completely recovered: there was a suppurating wound on his flesh. After a while, it began to seem that—we were intended for one another."

(Her mother had sighed and said, "Better a one-legged husband than no husband at all.")

She looked Jacques fully in the face. "I was quite frightened of him. Physically. Not frightened that he might be aggressive with me—untoward, nothing like that. Frightened of the smell of him. His wound it—it stank—it was the smell of his masculinity too. The musty wet wool. As if the smell of the trenches could never be washed completely away from him. I was— Am I telling you too much?"

"No." He saw that some day, if their liaison continued, he might grow bored by her prattle, but for now he was charmed by it.

"At the same time that I would be obsessed by the German advance, I would be haunted by the—thought of Robert's absent leg. How could I think so much about something that wasn't there?" She had heard that Jews bury an amputated limb. Was it true, therefore, that non-Jews do not bury their hacked-off body parts? In that case, where had Robert's missing leg gone? Had it been tossed in a garbage tip? Incinerated? Had the amputated limbs been collected, tucked in the spaces between the shrouded bodies of the dead stacked like firewood in mass graves?

"It seemed to me—I feel so foolish saying this now—that when I could be kind to Robert, when I could hold his hand and tamp down that feeling of revulsion, then our side would be victorious in battle."

Jacques took her hands in his. "When I lived in Madagascar, I really came to know the Malagasy people—I learned their language—I'm one of the few Europeans who's fluent in it—"

This was the third time he had told her about his ability to speak the language of Madagascar. From that fact, she didn't draw the conclusion that he was both vain and fragile, needing to trumpet his abilities. Instead she suspected he had so little regard for her that he forgot the conversations he had with her as soon as they were finished.

"Our colonial subjects are said to be primitive, superstitious, but it often seemed to me that they had a way of comprehending the world which we call irrational, but which might be better called non-rational. A Malagasy might believe that the hacked-off limb was walking about on its own, seeking to be reunited with its former body, that it haunted your mind because it saw you as a pathway to Robert's flesh."

Simone did not know how to respond to this, and, the silence making her uncomfortable, went on:

"One day—the back gate was unlatched, and he had his pants' leg rolled up, his wooden leg on the ground next to him, his stump stretched out on the bench. The end of it was covered with raw flesh, and a few dark hairs, long and spindly. They made me think of the hairs on the chin of the Vietnamese greengrocer."

"Just giving the fellow some air," Robert had said, sounding fond of his errant, missing leg, as if it were an impish kid brother who was always getting himself in trouble, who had been sent out to buy some bread in the morning and returned after dark, empty-handed, penniless, abashed, full of promises to always be good in the future.

"Are you—worried about what your reaction will be to Joë?"

"I'm afraid—I suppose, I'm afraid that he will sense my—my fear."

"He will. But he won't try to hide his reaction to—what you are choosing to call fear. Which probably also contains within it repulsion, pity. As well as fascination. He will rather force you to—well, you'll see…I must warn you. He's not a man who wastes time, who has truck with small talk."

"When you first met him," she ventured, "were you put off by —"

"I was wounded at the front," Jacques said. "A lucky wound, it got me out of the trenches but did no lasting damage. But I spent several months in a hospital. One gets used to a lot. In fact, one returns to ordinary life and finds one can't help but stare at these strange creatures without missing limbs, with unbandaged eyes, ambling along the sidewalk without the slightest hesitation or halt."

Egyptians

He dozed for a while, and when he awoke, he said: "Do you know that I'm Egyptian?"

"I thought you were from Nîmes."

"I was born in Nîmes. The town was settled originally by the Roman legions that had taken Egypt from Antony and Cleopatra. When we go there, we will walk through the ancient part of the town, see the city's coat of arms, which shows a crocodile leashed to a palm tree, representing the founders' capture of Egypt."

When we go there, when we go there.

"Caesar Augustus…" Jacques said, and then interrupted himself while he lit a cigarette. She reached up and took it from between his lips, took a drag, returned it to him.

"Caesar Augustus, no fool he, knew that having overthrown one great empire, those legions might take it into their heads to overthrow another—to wit, his own. But of course he did not want it said that he didn't treat his loyal soldiers well—so he granted them tracts of land, but in the far-off south of Gaul. These demobilized soldiers of Augustus brought with them a colony of Egyptian slaves, whose descendants intermarried with the local population, with the sons and daughters of the Romans. The researches of Friar Mendel have let us know that ancestry does not mix smoothly, a pureed soup, but rather in discrete clumps. Even now, nearly two millennia later, a child will sometimes be born with half-almond eyes and olive skin. I was such a child. I warn you—I have an ancient nature, cold and pitiless—exacting."

"I've been warned." She smiled. (Years later, he would say, "I told you, very early on, about my Egyptian nature. You mustn't wail: you knew what you were getting into.")

The train dropped them off in mid-afternoon. A few porters and taxi-drivers managed to rouse themselves to implore their business. Jacques shook them off, and they set out, their hands clasped, walking along the narrow streets, the flat planes of ancient houses and churches looming above them. The houses were shuttered, the occasional muffled cry of a cooped-up child issuing forth from behind the stone walls. Their footsteps sounded against the cobblestones: the echoes of their footsteps. The heavy mid-day meal had been eaten. The pots and pans and plates and saucers had been washed and were now set on racks to dry in the still afternoon air. Tubs of mucky water festered, waiting to be dumped in the back garden, while the inhabitants of these houses drowsed on divans and daybeds.

As their elongated shadows walked ahead of them, she rocketed out of time, saw this walled city as a ruin, when humanity itself would have ceased to exist, when these stone walls, these cobblestoned streets, might be observed by the eye of a rook, perched atop the wreckage of one of the turrets above them.

Joë

The servant who opened the door, inclined her head and said, "Mme. Melville, Monsieur." Simone fought to keep a grin from her face.

"Did you tell them we were married?" Simone whispered, as they were climbing the uneven flight of stairs towards Joë's redoubt.

Jacques shrugged: "People make assumptions."

"Wouldn't it be more practical for him to have a room on the ground floor?" She regretted the words as soon as they were out of her mouth: *practical, I sound like a peasant, not like the lover of an intellectual.*

The smell of beeswax candles, the scent given off by the polished mahogany of his bedstead, the bookcases, the musty odor of antique Oriental carpets—later, Joë would tell her that the most threadbare of them had been brought back from the Seventh Crusade by an ancestor, but she wouldn't know whether he was telling the truth or one of his delightful stories. His room seemed less a sickroom than a grotto within a church. (Simone had always been drawn to those alcoves tucked away within the majesty of cathedrals, half-hidden places safe from the masculine pomp and business of the popes and archbishops, where it was possible to imagine Mary squatting and straining to expel the holy infant in a shed which smelt of cow farts and damp hay.) Joë sat upon his bed as if it were a throne, thick blinds drawn against the afternoon light. A single kerosene lamp on the bed table illuminated the magnificent dome of his forehead. The shape of his head surprised her: she'd made a picture of him in which he was elongated, a gaunt Donatello.

"Ah, Simone! You must come to me, yes, closer, closer, I can't come to you—closer, closer, yes, there's only a single chair, let Jacques have that, you come sit right here on the bed, it's all right, I won't hurt you. I don't bite. That is," he giggled, "unless you want to be bitten.

"Closer, closer. I want you next to me. The female body gives off a heat the male body never does. Let me smell you. Yes, yes. Jacques told me all about you. Oh, and you are just as beautiful as he said. Did he tell you all about me, too?"

"He told me you were a quite talented poet."

"Ah, no, I am shattered. 'Quite talented'? Bah! Look, there's my heart, it's lying there in shards on the floor. In the military hospital, the chief surgeon gave me two cyanide capsules, he said, 'We've done all we can, if life ever becomes unbearable for you…' They're in the drawer, fetch them for me, would you? I thought I could endure anything—pain, paralysis, isolation—but faint praise, that I can't abide. Go, go, the top drawer, right over there—"

"She doesn't know you are teasing her," Jacques said.

Joë fluttered his long-fingered right hand above his heart, a gesture that might have been cribbed from the repertoire of an actress in a melodramatic film, and declared, "I am not joking."

"Come, come, Joë, the poor girl is on the verge of tears."

"Perhaps suicide isn't the right course of action here. I think instead that I ought to challenge you to a duel. Yes, at dawn, in the grove just past the duck pond. 'Quite talented!' Did he tell you, Simone, my love, that my father's head man has rigged up the most wonderful contraption for me, a combination bicycle and bath chair. I turn the pedals with my hands?" He began to mime the motions he made while propelling his device, counting, as if measuring off paces, "One-two-three—what's the customary number of paces one takes before drawing one's weapon? Is it five or ten? Simone, you'll be my second, won't you?"

"I don't—I really don't see what—"

"Joë, I warned you, she really is an innocent, a child, she's not used to the monstrous egos of poets. And anyhow," Jacques said, holding up his two hands as if surrendering, "I didn't describe you as a 'quite talented poet.' She just doesn't understand the subtle gradations."

"I'm not a child," Simone protested. "I have two children. I have traveled to Istanbul. Twice. I have overseen a villa with a considerable staff. I hardly think it is fair to talk about me in this manner."

"Ah, Simone, Simone, you must forgive me. I'm simply terrible. I create these little dramas—here, let me put my head in your lap"—and Joë leaned forward, grasping hold of his legs and shoving them to the side—"yes, there we go, now stroke my head as if I were your puppy, your bad little dog. You forgive me everything, don't you? I rather treat this little room as my kingdom, or perhaps my laboratory—"

"Jacques told me, he said that I must know, that you didn't have any truck with small talk, no how-was-your-journey and I-hope-the-weather-will-be-fine-during-your-visit. That, well, you didn't know how much time you had left, so you lived your life, conducted your relations, with great urgency. But I expected you to be—well—"

"Saintly?"

"I thought illness—your condition—would have—I suppose this sounds naive—ennobled you. That suffering would have—"

"Ah, suffering," Joë said. "For a while, it is interesting. And then, like everything else, it becomes boring."

Jacques, meanwhile, was leaning back in his chair, with the air of a critic watching a drama staged for his benefit.

Needle

Joë gave a solemn nod in Jacques' direction. Jacques stood and washed his hands in the sink in an open anteroom.

Simone heard the sound of a cabinet being opened, a faint clatter of metal and glass.

"On account of my condition, I am granted surcease from pain..." Joë said. "As a student...before the war...I sought out that substance Homer refers to as nepenthe, frequenting back alleys and the docks. I was forced to strike some dark bargains to obtain it...But I won't shock you by telling you all that. When I was wounded, my body was on fire and at the same time, I was so cold—the ambulance ride, each bump and jolt an agony—and finally, a nurse with the face of an angel saying, *this will help with the pain,* and in that moment, my whole life became utterly clear to me: I was destined to have this wound. Indeed, this wound existed before I did, and I was born to embody it.

"I'm like a man besotted with love, who bores everyone with endless babbling about his beloved...I love my wound—not a simple love, mind you, its mixed with hatred and resentment," he gave a wave of his hand, "as all real love is."

Jacques set about preparing an injection from a rubber-stoppered glass vial. Then, tying a tourniquet around his friend's arm, he slapped his flesh until a vein stood out, blue-black beneath the pale flesh.

"In English, they use the word 'painkiller.'" And here he made his right hand into the shape of a gun. "I rather like to imagine an American cowboy"—those last two words in English, the word *cowboy* repeated for the sheer pleasure of saying it. "He strides through the dusty town, spies the pain—a black blob, slithering about on the ground between the saloon and the horse rail, takes aim and fires. But in truth, this drug doesn't actually remove the pain, it's scarcely dead, only one is now able to observe it from above."

Jacques administered the injection and Simone, feeling faint, looked away. So this is what the room of a poet looks like, she thought, taking in the rows of books surrounding Joë's bed, the magazines printed on cheap newsprint scattered on the floor. The cover of one showed a photograph of a woman wearing a horned Viking helmet with her tongue sticking out, the cover of another proclaiming DOWN WITH ART! She wondered if later on she would be able to get up the nerve to ask Jacques, "What does it mean? Why is the woman wearing a Viking helmet and why is she sticking out her tongue?" and "Am I hopelessly old-fashioned because I believe in art?"

"Ahh," Joë said, as the needle entered him. "I would be a poor host indeed if I traveled to a distant shore and left my friends behind, waving to me from the dock."

Jacques drew another dose into the syringe.

"Oh, half of that. Half," cried Joë, "she's slight and this is her first time." Then, cocking his head to one side, "It is your first time, isn't it?"

"Yes," Simone murmured. "I'm a bit—what will it be like?"

"Ah," Joë said, "we are going to a place where words cannot follow."

"I am going to—demur."

"Very well," Jacques said, filling the syringe, and wrapping the tourniquet around his own arm, using his teeth to tighten it.

Joë worked his lips and tongue. "Ah, the taste of bitterness in my mouth! It lets me know that my beloved morphine is entering every pore and orifice of my body. What is it that the Bible says? 'In bitterness we find the sweet?'"

"What book of the Bible is that from?" Jacques asked.

"The Gospel According to Joë."

"Bitterness," Joë said, and then fell silent. A few minutes later, he said, "Our minds are acutely tuned to bitterness because poisons are bitter. The brain awakens in its presence. Chefs will tell you…"

"Chefs will tell you what?" Simone finally ventured.

"Hmmm?" Joë asked. "What did you say?" and lapsed into silence. After a while, a long while, he said, "Has he told you yet that he is Egyptian? Your Jacques?"

"Yes."

"And that his spirit is a tortoise. He's told you that, am I right?"

"Yes, he's told me that."

Simone wondered if she was one in a line of women who had been brought by Jacques to kneel before the altar of this demigod.

"When I," Jacques' voice was deep, "when I, I was, in Madagascar…"

"Ah," Joë sighed, "I love these stories that begin *When I was in Madagascar…*"

The thought crossed Simone's mind: Was it possible that the two of them were—she did not know the word to use—had a liaison of an intimate nature? When Joë had said that prior to the war, to his injury, he had obtained this drug on the docks and been forced to strike some 'dark bargains,' had he been referring to—she could only imagine the cover of a cheap novel she had seen displayed at a book kiosk, a sailor slouching with his hip jutted out, a sultry gaze at the viewer from beneath half-hooded eyes. In this world where all the rules were different, might friends also have—an unnatural connection? How could it be—after all, Jacques was married and Joë a paralytic. Perhaps this flirtation was, like the threatened duel, a playlet he put on to make his life in this shut-up cell more diverting.

There were so many questions she wanted to ask: How did he experience his inanimate legs? Did they seem to him to be familiar objects, like the shoes we wear daily, almost part of our corpus, but objects nonetheless? Or did he feel towards them a kind of grieving anger—the way once-beautiful aging women regard their faces, now mottled and creased by time? And as for the other business of the lower body—the passing out of waste, arousal—how were those things managed?

At length Joë said: "'To enter the kingdom of heaven, one must become as a little child.' Now that's really from the Bible. Our Lord and Savior," and here Joë gave another one of his giggles, "said it."

"Now, why did you say that?" Simone asked.

"Because I felt like saying it," Joë said.

"No, but how did it relate to—the previous conversation?"

"It didn't, my darling, it didn't. I merely said it—because I said it."

"I've changed my mind," she said, rolling up her sleeve.

Jacques roused himself from the chair, trudged to the anteroom, opened the medicine cabinet, prepared a dose for her. She watched as the needle entered her arm, saw the flesh clinging to it as Jacques withdrew the syringe. "Press your finger, there, so you don't get a bruise." His speech was slow, as if his tongue and lips had thickened.

She turned her face up towards Jacques, hoping he would kiss her, stroke her hair.

Joë, alert to drama even in this state, said, "Simone, you must understand this morphine is a god. And like the Old Testament Yahweh, this god is a jealous god. When we are before his altar, he demands that all other gods—Priapus, especially, his rival in joy—must be banished."

After a minute, Jacques said: "I had just bent down to tie the lace of my boot—" and Joë said the words along with him.

"We have had this conversation many times, your friend Jacques and I. Sometimes many times in one evening. Jacques speaks to me of his wound. Under the influence, one's tongue can be loosed. Loosed or unloosed?" He stuck out his tongue like a naughty child, and then took it between his thumb and forefinger. "What a strange appendage—the tongue," he mumbled, before letting go of it.

One's tongue unloosed? Simone wished that it were possible to insert the now-empty hypodermic back into her arm, draw out the drug—at the same time realizing that such a notion was evidence that it was already beginning to have an effect on her. What words of love for Jacques might pour unstinted from her?

"Free tongue…" Joë was saying, and said it again, and then for a third time.

Jacques turned to Simone, took her hand. "He told you we were going some place where words could not go. But they're like a dog, a dog that doesn't want to get left behind, words trot after you, looking up at you: *Take me with you*! And then begin to howl and whine."

"Your Jacques and I take this drug, and our words cease to be original, we chant a Gregorian chant, over and over he says, 'I had just bent down to fix the lace of my boot.' That is why his wound was a minor wound, a blessing, it got him out of the trenches and…" Joë's voice trailed off, then: "What were we talking about?"

"War wounds," Simone said.

"Ah, yes..." A smile flitted across his face.

The gravity in the room increased. Perhaps they were on a distant planet or in an underwater realm. Great force was required to move their limbs. Time slowed down to a crawl. Lifting one's head—my head, thought Simone, this head I am lifting is mine, it belongs to me, it is me, but at the same time it is a head and I can regard it as a concrete object in the world—it was all quite clear and terribly confusing at the same time, and when she got to the end of a thought so much time had elapsed it was impossible for her to remember where the train of thought had begun.

She heard herself say the word, "Saturn."

"Ah, this girl of yours is a poet. She's just spoken the perfect poem, a single word: 'Saturn.' It's exquisite. Simone, you must never debase your oeuvre by declaiming another word. Rimbaud knew when to stop: otherwise, he would have been one of those poets who showed great promise as a young man…In fact, I think it would be best if you ceased speaking altogether—fell into mystical silence, like Nietzsche."

The shelves of books. The drawings thumbtacked to the wall. The honey-colored light from the kerosene lamps. Gravity. Her ankle. The bell on the bedside table. An incongruous lamp with a fluted linen shade, embroidered with forget-me-nots—her mother would have exclaimed over it. An even more out-of-place vase, porcelain nymphs and satyrs, Pan's flute becoming the opening to hold the flowers—although the vase was empty.

"When," Jacques said. "When," he said again, "when I was in Madagascar. In the cities—well, the cities are cities, but in the countryside...perhaps you are back in time, or perhaps this modernity of ours is but a...I just had a very profound thought. But now I've lost it."

Decades later, Simone too will be granted this balm as a medically sanctioned release from pain. The faithful Marie-Claire will dispense it, having become not only maid and dogsbody, but also nurse.

The sight of the little glass vials of morphine lined up on the shelf will give Simone a feeling of security.

One of the poets will come to visit and deride her drug, saying "Simone, morphine as compared to opium—well, it's like the difference between sugar and sugar cane, the insipid essence as opposed to the complexities of nature, the interpretation of the dream as opposed to the dream itself.

"Picasso used to say to me: 'Opium's smell is the least stupid smell in the world. It's like the stink of a circus or a sea port.'"

Although he will feel the object of his affection far superior to hers, Marie-Claire will nonetheless notice a few vials missing after his departure. In the future, she will take the precaution of hiding them prior to his calls. And then the poet's visits will cease. Once men had been drawn to Simone by a glimpse of her finely turned ankle. Once men had been drawn to her by her willing ways. Once men had been drawn to her out of a desire for connection with or revenge upon her husband. Then men were drawn to her by a desire to make off with her morphine.

Slam

She had no memory of that first evening with Joë ending, of making her way with Jacques to their room, only knew that the next morning she was down in the depths of the ocean, trapped by the water's enormous weight as a series of sharp raps was being delivered to their bedroom door. She rose up up up up up but still did not get to the surface. Her brain was waterlogged. She wanted to take it in both her hands and wring it out.

And now sunlight was pouring through the windows, the woman who had been knock-knock-knocking on the door had entered the room, flung open the drapes, and Jacques was moaning, "Oh, for the love of God. Let us sleep."

"The young master said I was to get you up. It's long since gone noon."

"Jesus," he moaned. "Some coffee, at least bring us some coffee."

"There's no need to be rude." The woman slammed the door as she departed, returning a quarter of an hour later with a tray with a pot of coffee, bread, and cheese, still muttering, "…decent Christians…the young master said…run off my feet," keeping up her chant as she went out again, again allowing the door to slam behind her.

In the meantime, Jacques had redrawn the drapes, although a shaft of afternoon light, pouring through a gap, illuminated motes of dust filling the air.

Simone had fallen asleep in her clothes. She was shocked by how musty they smelt, how the waistband, digging into her flesh, had left a red and itchy mark, her stockings rumpled. Overnight, she had become a slattern. She'd have a wash—although she dreaded ringing for the sullen girl, asking her for hot water and a clothes brush.

Jacques downed the coffee as a Russian downs a shot of vodka. Simone stirred warmed milk and sugar into hers, sipped from the porcelain cup. He was naked. His clothes lay in a heap on the floor.

"I can't believe I slept in my clothes. And this is my only outfit."

"Ah, dear Simone, I fear I have debauched you."

He did not speak with the playfulness of the night before. His concern was shadowed by guilt.

She saw that his remorse was causing him pain. Although she did not want to make him suffer, she knew it would be futile to lie to him.

When her parents had left the peasantry behind, they had bid farewell to filth. In the hamlets and thorps surrounding Juan-les-Pins, Simone had passels of aunts and cousins and second-cousins-once-removed who tromped out to their barns and pastures through muck and mire with steps that resembled a military march. In the cold of winter, they herded their animals inside so they might share in the heat from the pigs and sheep who smelt of shit, cheese, and menstrual blood. They had permanent black lines not just under their fingernails but encircling their cuticles—and, as for their toenails, they had come to resemble the hooves of their animals. With hot water and soaps, lavender oil and nail brushes and pomades, Simone's parents had fought back against the ancestral filth threatening to ooze out from their pores, to invade the safe house they had erected for themselves with its bleached linen curtains and well-scrubbed floor—a tide of slop that would sweep them back into the world from which they had so recently escaped.

"I feel—unclean," she admitted. "Physically and—I suppose I would sound foolish if I said 'spiritually.'"

"Ah, Simone, you are so—unjaded. It's what I love about you."

The word "love" had been spoken. The word "love" floated up towards the ceiling. She would have liked to grab hold of it, but knew it would be like grasping a soap bubble: touch would make it dissolve.

"No, you don't sound foolish." He moved to embrace her, and she hung back, afraid he would be disgusted by her smell.

"Jewish women have a ritual bath that they undertake after their monthly cycle—"

"The mikvah," he said.

It didn't surprise her that he knew about it, even knew the Hebrew name: what didn't he know?

"I wish there were such a place I could go, immerse myself in purifying water."

"The mikvah," Jacques said, as he leaned back on the bed, then pulled her towards him, "must be filled with rainwater. And before a woman enters it, she must be completely clean—"

"Are you Jewish as well as Egyptian?"

"No." He paused, then rushed into the breach of his silence. "My wife is Jewish. Not observant, but—she likes to tell me about the—strange customs from which she escaped. There, there, you mustn't pout every time I say the words 'my wife.'"

"I'm not pouting, I—"

"You look as if you're about to burst into tears."

"I'm sorry! I can govern what I say but not the expressions that cross my face!"

"Let's not row. I have a wife, you have a husband. It may be awkward when—these things, these connections, people, come up in conversation, but—it would undoubtedly be even more difficult for us to communicate if we avoided all mention of them. My wife"—he said the phrase deliberately— "my wife is a very modern woman. A doctor. She likes to tell me about the superstitious rituals of her grandmothers and aunts in the Russian Pale: the sabbath goy who was employed to light the oven and switch on the lights, since they were prohibited from doing so—the Passover ritual of cleansing the house of leavened bread— the rules about menstruation and coupling. She expects me to share her disdain for them, to dismiss them as primitive…I must have some more coffee." She watched as he walked naked across the room, pouring himself another cup of coffee and downing it in a single gulp.

"Has she ever come here?"

"What is that to you?"

"I-I was merely curious."

He allowed nearly a minute to pass before he spoke:

"No. If Sala were to come here, she would start scheming for

Joë's improvement. She'd want to get him to some medical clinic in Paris where wounded veterans are trained in a useful occupation: accountancy, perhaps. She'd lecture him on the dangers of morphine and confiscate his medication. Donate it to some clinic that served the worthy poor of Paris. She'd roll up her sleeves and get to work on him." He took Simone's hand and gave it an affectionate squeeze, which he felt served as sufficient apology for his earlier sharpness.

A rap on the French doors that opened onto the garden: Simone cried out.

Jacques peeked out from behind the drapes, covering the lower half of his naked body. Joë was seated in his wheeled device, with a gold-headed cane which he rattled against the wavy glass.

Joë was saying something, but they could not make it out, and he motioned for Jacques to open the doors.

"My coy maiden," he said to Jacques.

"No maidens here." Jacques still covering himself with the curtain.

"Ah, but coy. Fling open the drapes, and look into the garden. You will see that we are in Eden. What need have we for shame?"

But surely in Eden everything had been new: each flower in perfect bloom, the pomegranate trees and the apple, the persimmon and the fig, all bountiful and fresh, while in this garden, as old as the walls that enclosed it, the trees were ancient and gnarled.

"We'll be dressed and join you soon."

"Bah! I want to see my two creations pure, unsullied by clothing—"

"We're hardly your creations."

"Don't engage in theological disputes! Just do as I command. Oh, please. At least let me see the lovely Simone, bare and pure. Simone, if I were a painter, a sculptor, you would pose for me, wouldn't you? Really, it's no different, my art is my words, but I still need the form of a beautiful woman before me."

She looked to Jacques: he jutted out his lower lip, shrugged his shoulders, and she removed her clothes, glad to be free of their stink and heaviness, dropping them onto the floor, then stood at the window, naked. She surprised herself by not crooking one arm over her breast, another over her genitals.

Joë stared at her, and then shifted his gaze to Jacques.

"Oh, you must show yourself, too," Joë demanded. Jacques stepped forth from behind the curtain, and the two of them stood there, hands clasped, side by side.

"Ah, she's a beautiful girl, your Simone." He sliced his finger through the air. "Draw the curtain, get dressed, and come and join me."

For the remainder of this visit, things among the three of them were rather prim. If Joë had need of morphine, he indulged in it alone, and in quantities sufficient only to take the edge off his pain. His flirtations with Simone were of the sort that flatter a young woman without suggesting that anything untoward might occur.

Train

Jacques and Simone went to the station together. Jacques' train was scheduled to leave before hers. On the platform, his stern masculine index finger chucked her under the chin, "Come now, come now, it's not so bad as all that, we'll see each other again."

"When?" She regretted the word before it was out of her mouth, but it had issued forth from her body like a rude, unstoppable noise.

"Ah, Simone!" Jacques said, making a quarter turn away from her. She had no doubt that he said, "Ah, Sala!" in just this same tone of voice. I'm like Odette, she thought, with her arms stretched out, her plaintive "Mama, Mama." Nonetheless, tears spilled out of her eyes and down her cheeks. She bent her head down, wiping her face with four flat fingers.

"Wait a minute." He walked away, peering at the fine print of the schedule hung on the wall. He laid a hand on her shoulder, "Let me see if I can change my ticket. There's another train, in an hour." He spoke with the station agent, passed some extra francs through the opening at the bottom of the grille—she knew how carefully he shepherded every sou—sent a telegram, no doubt to Sala, and took her arm, propelling her to a café. "This way, you will leave before me, and it's always easier to be the one who leaves than the one who gets left behind."

He was a trifle put out: he had planned on working on the manuscript in his valise during his hours on the train. (*She rubbed lard into her hair before plaiting it. Her name was Bomfomtabellilaba, her name was Lalao, her name was Marie, her name was Anisoa...When I arrived at school I realized I should have given myself more than a perfunctory wash: her smell of pig-fat still clung to me.*) Of course, he would still have the same number of hours on the train, but by ten in the evening his powers were spent. (In his thirties, he already had the unshakable patterns of a man well into middle-age: I must have black coffee first thing in the morning. I cannot do any real work—work that engages my intellect, that is—unless I have had a solid seven hours of sleep. Aubergines make my liver too heavy, I never eat them. After ten in the evening, I'm good for nothing but idle conversation, detective novels, or sex.)

Jacques had yet to publish his first book—the war, the excursion to Madagascar, the malarial lethargy with which he had returned home, the trials of his marriage to Sala had all served to thwart his literary output. Since he was no longer a young man, he could no longer produce a young man's text, no rough diamond with brilliance despite its flaws. (His book, which situated itself on the frontier between several genres—it was a memoir, a traveler's diary, a grammar of the Malagasy language, an anthropological exploration of the poetic jousts which the Madagascar natives practiced, a philosophical critique of the notion of originality—would be published some two years hence to respectful but hardly glowing reviews.) There would also be the necessity of lying to Sala—his telegram had said, "Unavoidably delayed. Back this evening." In all likelihood there would be a scene, accusations, denials. Nonetheless, he had been moved enough by the girl's plight that he had undertaken this action.

Sighs

As soon as the waiter set their drinks before them, Simone said, "I should tell you. I have written to my husband." She had in fact not yet been able to get up the courage to do so. She was lying to Jacques not so much to force his hand as to force her own.

He sighed. (How well she would come to know these sighs of his over the course of their lives together.) "Yes?" he said, already dreading the answer to his question.

"Yes."

"And?"

"And?"

"And what did you say to your husband?"

"I told him everything."

"Everything?"

"That I was here in Carcassonne, with you. That I was in love with you. That we had—consummated that love. That I had injected morphine..."

"Simone." He dropped his head, supported it with his hands, as if it were too heavy to be held up by the mere muscles of his neck. "Simone, you oughtn't to undertake these dramatic gestures. And certainly not without consulting me first."

She had thought he would be proud of her, as he had been proud when she stood naked before Joë.

"What business is it of yours, how I choose to carry out my relations with my husband?" These words were false; she was trying to conjure another Simone out of the air. They both knew full well that there was nothing in her that was not his business.

"It is not unusual for such letters, written in angry passion, to get shown to solicitors, used as evidence. I do not know much about this husband of yours. But he is a solid member of the middle-classes, who views his wife as his property—a very special sort of property, but nonetheless his property—and he will not take it lightly, you being stolen from him."

"I am not a thing. I can't be stolen."

Already, she was plotting her next lie: she would, after the passage of a week or two, tell him that Luc seemed never to have received the letter, that it must have gone astray. But then it would float through the air, threatening to land. Better to tell him she had forgotten, in her haste, to affix the proper postage, and it had been returned to her. Yes, but she would have to give it a few days, a week.

"It's true, you're not a thing. It might be better for you if you were. You are a living, breathing entity, you can't simply be stuck on a shelf, you need a dwelling place, you need food and drink, you need to clothe yourself, you need to provide for your children—although your children may well be taken away from you, after what you have revealed."

"I thought…I thought…"

"No. You didn't think. Or rather, you had one thought, but you didn't follow it through to its logical conclusion: *if I take this action, there will be this corresponding reaction*. Did you think that by this rash move you were going to put me under some obligation to you?"

"It seems you hate Sala for her excess of practicality…"

"And you thought I would love you for an excess of impracticality? Anyhow, I don't hate Sala. I don't know what I ever said that would make you think I hated her."

"You speak of her so disdainfully."

He jutted out his lower lip, inclined his head slightly to the right side. "Disdainfully? I think I see her rather clearly, as one sees anyone with whom one has such a long and daily acquaintance. I chafe at the yoke of marriage, it's true—Ah, you needn't pull that face, as if you have been seduced and abandoned. You were as eager for this connection as I was. More eager, I think."

Three days later, after several glasses of wine, looking out at a crescent moon in the deep blue sky, she did indeed pick up a pen and write, "Dear Luc, I must tell you I have taken a lover…"

Sala

In the years that followed, Simone and Jacques would have many rows over his marriage to Sala, and the lugubrious pace of his extrication from it. (As later he would have quarrels with Dominique over Simone.)

Simone, her eyes welling with tears, pleaded, "Why did you marry her?"

Jacques responded with a shrug of his shoulders.

"I didn't mean that as a rhetorical question. I really want to know: why on earth did you marry her?"

He gave yet another shrug of his shoulders.

"That is not an answer!" Simone screamed.

"It is an answer. Perhaps not a satisfactory one, but nonetheless it is an answer. The only one I have. You know full well I am dispassionate by nature. I feel about myself the way that I feel about rhubarb: I can take it or leave it. I recognize—"

"Oh, please! Not another one of your speeches!"

"You ask me for an explanation, and then when I attempt to give you one, you—"

"Oh, yes, I've heard it all before! It's your Egyptian blood! It's your phlegmatic character! It's—!"

In fact, Jacques knew quite well why he had married Sala.

When Sala was seventeen she and her widowed mother had moved into an attic room in the boarding house run by Jacques' mother. His mother had more or less fallen into the occupation of landlady, offering a room first to a relative—after all, it was little enough extra work, and the added money certainly helped their straitened circumstances—then to a friend of a friend. Once she was making dinner for five, it was scarcely any more work to make dinner for six. And once she was making dinner for six, the adding of a seventh was of little consequence.

His mother had become the family's financial mainstay because her husband had a stutter so severe it prevented him from assuming the university position which should rightfully have been his. His father's debility did not fill Jacques with shame. Indeed, his father seemed like a delicate flower, ill-suited to the crassness of everyday life. Jacques acted as his father's deputy, accompanying him to the tobacconist and the stationer, saying, *My father would like…*almost as if his father was a royal who did not deign to speak to commoners.

(Was it his father's impediment which led to him being drawn to the broken: the stuffed bear with a cracked eye, the beggars in the Court of Miracles at Nîmes, displaying their stumps and sores?)

Simone would know Jacques for more than two decades before she learnt that his mother, like hers, had taken in boarders.

Egg

Jacques' mother was aided in her haphazard profession by her flair for raising chickens. When hens grew broody, clucking and pecking when Mme. Melville went to collect the eggs and gave off plaintive cries, avian Rachels weeping for their children, she would swat at them with her apron, quite unmoved. She could spot the onset of a henhouse pox and nip it in the bud, knew the signs of and sure cure for worms in their gizzards. As a result of her knack with hens, she developed a secondary gift for cooking eggs in a great variety of forms: omelettes, eggs poached in red wine, eggs with tripe, a dish she called *croque madame*—a *croque monsieur* topped with a fried egg—although the lodgers sometimes grumbled, "Call it what you like, it's eggs again."

Sala pointed out to those who muttered, "Eggs again!" that many in this hard world could only dream of such bounty. Why, when her parents had been in exile in Siberia, they had spent a week in the dead of winter with nothing to eat but bread and salt and stewed prunes. Sala knew a better world was in birth. It made no sense to call the 1905 revolution in Russia a failure—after all, one hardly expected a child to be born after a single contraction of the maternal uterus.

Many more such pangs would be felt by the great body of history before it was delivered of its plump and long-awaited offspring: the Revolution. These metaphors about parturition came easily to her, as she was training to be a medical doctor. Those in the Party knew full well that the majority of sympathetic physicians—along with professors and engineers—would, when faced with the rigors of post-revolutionary life, abandon their erstwhile allies. There would be a great need for those like Sala, well-trained, at the ready, and without illusions.

Sixteen-year-old Jacques gazed longingly at this woman. With her simian brow, the material ghost of our animal ancestors made visible, and her declarations about the imminent earthly paradise, she seemed to reconcile in her person the quandary of how we can both be descended from the apes and aspiring to the angels. He thought of himself as a boy, unappealing and timorous. But like the ugly duckling of Hans Christian Andersen's tale he had turned, as his childhood came to an end, into a being both handsome and graceful. Little imagining that one such as Sala would take any notice of him, he did not hide his infatuation with her. He was shocked when one day, encountering him on the back stairs, instead of moving out of his way—she was on the step above him—she planted herself firmly in his path and refused to let him pass, saying, "I think you have something I want."

"W-w-what's that?" Hearing himself stutter, he feared he might be developing his father's affliction, and blushed vividly.

Sala, who had misjudged his shyness as chilly sophistication, now misread his discomfort as disdain.

"This," she said, planting her hands on his shoulders, and giving him a kiss, not of the tender, almost breezy caress of lips one imagines as one's first experience of a kiss, but a full bore attack, her tongue slipping into his surprised mouth, where it wriggled about with his own, rather like two Sumo wrestlers grappling. He moaned with both shock and pleasure, and she thrust her hips against his, with each jut of her pelvis thinking, "There, that will teach him not to trifle with a free woman like myself…There…I'll teach that stuck-up princeling a lesson." It would be difficult to say which of the two was more startled by what next ensued: a gush of fluid covered the front of Jacques' trousers, and the words "I love you" blurted from his mouth.

But despite his declaration on the stairs, this initial encounter did not immediately blossom into a love affair. Jacques had been amazed to discover that he aroused desire. Like the youth who has only been served wine at the dinner table in tiny quantities doled out by the paternal hand, but who discovers in taverns that spirits can intoxicate as well as soothe, he found himself quite drunk on his own erotic power. He flirted shamelessly with Sala's comrades, and made a fool out of a shopgirl employed at the local tobacconist. What he needed was someone older, a brother, if he had had one, or an uncle, halfway between his father's generation and his own, to guide him.

It was practical Sala who took on this role. Her first task was to remove the caul of mystery in which bourgeois society had cloaked sexual matters. She showed him the pages in her medical textbooks which contained anatomical drawings of male and female copulatory apparatuses, both internal and external, labeled with their Latinate names. He learned that the functioning of the reproductive parts was a matter of hydraulics, hormonal and sanguinary. She warmed to the topic at hand, lending him copies of Krafft-Ebbing's encyclopedic tome on the varieties of sexual perversion and Darwin's *The Origin of Species*, explaining to him that it was a strange quirk of natural selection that our sexual desires and pleasures had evolved as they had. It was perfectly possible to imagine, under slightly different circumstances, that the acts of coitus necessary for the perpetuation of the race might have operated out of pure necessity and with as little enjoyment as defecation and micturition. What a happy fluke for humanity was pleasure—the desire and longing which preceded it were perhaps not such happy accidents. Having inculcated that lesson in him, she moved on to the next, instructing him in the ethical manner in which male-female relations should be carried out. The tobacconist's girl, for instance, might find herself ruined through her dalliance with him; he should take care not to abuse his social inferiors.

Later, after they were married and marital relations had grown stale, when Jacques suggested they sample some of the practices described by Krafft-Ebbing, Sala was quite willing to go along for the sake of marital harmony—as long as they could be indulged in hygienically. If a critique were to be offered of her approach to the carnal side of marriage, it might be that she was a trifle too athletic about the whole matter, and seemed to regard it as a salubrious necessity, rather like cleaning one's teeth and taking a brisk Sunday walk, the duties one owed the body so that it would be well-regulated and do as the mind commanded.

Her hearty approach toward Jacques belied the fact that she loved him. But she was determined to be the master of her emotions, rather than have them master her. She was jealous, often crying herself to sleep in pain over his flirtations with other women. At the same time, she was proud of keeping these difficulties to herself. The sensation was not dissimilar to the one she experienced in gross anatomy, face-to-face with a cadaver. The reek of formaldehyde made her queasy, the rubberiness of dead flesh chilled her, the sight of the corpse's mottled flesh and wrinkled skin filled her with a sense of dread. Let one of the young men faint—she was certainly not going to do so and give them the excuse of her being a frail female to boot her out. Like gross anatomy, Jacques was a tough subject she was determined to master.

Their relationship continued in this manner for several years: between Jacques' affairs with various young women he would return to Sala as a ship returns to its home port.

War

The Great War had, of course, ruptured his life. Jacques enlisted in the officer corps. He learned close-order drill, the attention which had to be paid to one's uniform—clipping the errant thread that dangled from a buttonhole, polishing his boots—actually, his manservant did it for him—until they shone. And then the front lines, where he lived in what was more or less an open sewer.

Jacques spent only a few weeks in the trenches before being wounded in the leg, that injury of little long-run consequence save for the fact that it kept him in a military hospital and thereafter invalided, safe from greater harm. The pain from the wound had been terrible, but it had earned him shots of morphine. When he awoke in the field hospital twenty-odd kilometers from the front lines, he was a child again: the murmuring of the nurses melded into song, and the veils covering their hair made them seraphic. The smells of blood, camphor, and phenol reached him, as did the cries of men in pain—but on account of the morphine these did not arouse their customary associations. He babbled, as did the others around him.

When he had recovered sufficiently to be moved, he was sent to a glove factory remade into a rehabilitation hospital. The men who had lost limbs, noses, portions of jaws, the men whose lungs had been seared by mustard gas regarded Jacques with a mix of envy and contempt: he who would be left with nothing more than a scar, a preternaturally smooth and hairless expanse of skin. Having seen a living man blown to bits—up until the moment he had witnessed it, this turn of phrase had seemed just that, he could not have imagined that a man's intestines could fly through the air in one direction, while his left leg hurled off in another—Jacques could no longer pretend to himself that he was still preparing for his life to begin. A sympathetic orderly brought him hastily-printed books, and he read poems which had been written at the front by poets now dead, the manuscript having been dispatched to the publisher by a grieving sister or fiancée. If he had died, he supposed it would have been Sala who would have sent a sheaf of his writings to a literary journal, with a note that read in part, "I wonder if you might look over these poems, which were returned to me along with the rest of his personal effects..." But as he had survived, he was not eligible for posthumous publication. The poems he himself mailed off were returned to him with brief notes expressing both admiration and regret, the latter outweighing the former.

He sank into a funk as the morphine was titrated down. He could bear the pain: he missed gazing at the world from a skewed perspective.

Shortly after he was discharged from the hospital, he saw a notice in the newspaper: the department of overseas affairs was seeking teachers for a variety of positions, including ones in Equatorial Guinea, Indochina, and Madagascar. It seemed a sign from the heavens.

Pantoum

The second full night he and Simone spent together at Joë's house in Carcassonne, making love, sleeping, waking to talk, to make love again, Simone said, "Joë said"—tracing her finger through the tangle of dark hairs on his chest—"you were writing a book?" She was so fearful of making a gaffe, of earning Jacques' contempt that she formed the next sentence in her mind and repeated it several times, daring herself to say it, as one gathers up one's courage to jump into a frigid lake: "What's it about?" How stupid that question, now that it is out of her.

(Later, Jacques will write: "Master of the word you speak / Slave of the word you have spoken.")

Jacques will say, "*Kupu-kupu terbang melintang / Terbang di laut di hujung karang,*" and kiss her on the forehead.

"Oh, now I understand. Now it's all perfectly clear to me."

"Well, it's a bit complicated—I'm writing about the time I spent in Madagascar, although not of the 'colonial officer telling charming stories about the natives' genre. Mostly, I suppose, it's about *hainteny*, which is a form of oral poetry in Madagascar. The Merina people of Madagascar are probably of Malayan origin, and there are some similarities between the *hainteny* and the pantoum."

Simone will be silent.

"You must forgive me. I can be a terrible pedant. Here I am in bed with a beautiful woman, discussing literary forms."

"Oh, no, no. I'm interested. I'm fascinated by—in everything you have to say. It's just—I didn't get much of an education from the nuns. And then, when I was in Istanbul, I was trying to learn—for instance, to learn Turkish, and I did a little bit—but then—the pregnancy came, Marcel—and I was sent back here. I suppose it's all a bit—scattershot—my education, my lack thereof. It's so hard: having no one to guide me."

"Well," he will say, fondly, a bit pleased at delivering a lecture in bed—Sala would never have allowed such a thing—*I have patients to see in the morning, I need my sleep*!—"the basic form of a pantoum is that, after the first stanza, the first line of the next stanza repeats the second line of the previous stanza, and the third line repeats the fourth line."

She could understand it better if she had a piece of paper and a pencil or if she could count on her fingers.

"It all sounds a bit ponderous when you put it that way, like double-entry bookkeeping. Are you familiar with Baudelaire's—"

"Oh, Baudelaire! I've heard of him!"

Jacques will cough, "—with his *Harmonie du soir*?" And he'll recite:

> "Now is the time when trembling on its stem
> Each flower fades away like incense;
> Sounds and scents turn in the evening air;
> A melancholy waltz, a soft and giddy dizziness!
>
> "Each flower fades away like incense;
> The violin thrills like a tortured heart;
> A melancholy waltz, a soft and giddy dizziness!
> The sky is sad and beautiful like some great resting-place."

He will see she'll be about to go into a rhapsody of delight over the poem, and want to warn her off—he won't yet be ready to show her the full force of his disdain: "Myself, I'm not an acolyte of the cult of Baudelaire. I can do without the 'melancholy waltzes' and the 'tortured hearts.' I ally myself more with the Futurists: the factory gutter, the ditches filled with muddy water. But that is neither here nor there, is it, my darling?" He won't really be that close to the Futurists, he'll make that statement more as a way of shocking her.

"The notion of originality is a queer, even frightening thing to the Merina people. They repeat the proverbs as they have been handed down, because to do otherwise would be to dishonor the ancestors, who gave them this wisdom. And yet, when the proverbs are repeated, in juxtaposition to one another, they take on a certain character from what surrounds them: not just the other words, but the circumstances. And despite it all, I want to be original in this book I'm writing. Even though I've tried to shed my white skin, I'm a European."

Madagascar

On his second full day in Antananarivo, the capital, a Sunday, he had been invited to an afternoon gathering at the headmaster's house, on a bluff overlooking the city. He had scarcely been outside his lodgings, having spent the previous day unpacking, drinking purified water that nonetheless tasted of limestone, writing letters home to Sala, his parents, friends, letting them know he had made the journey from the port to the capital safely; and sleeping, his body acclimatizing itself to the heat, the attenuated mountain air. He had written to Sala: "We sailed from Zanzibar. A monkey raced, screeching, around the upper deck…The journey from the port to the capital took nine days. We were carried on palanquins by native bearers. I detest this system of exploitation, and yet find myself with no alternative but to take part in it. We passed the Dutchmen's Graveyard. So many Dutch colonists were killed by native fevers that the Netherlands gave up their attempt to take this island. King Radàma said his two most powerful generals were Hàzo and Tàzo, Forest and Fever, and any army overcoming the one would be slain by the other."

As he left his hostel, a man pulling a *pousse pousse* ran alongside of him, imploring his business, a man so thin his legs seemed those of a child's stick figure. Jacques' initial explanation and polite refusals grew less and less courteous in the face of the rickshaw puller's insistence, but Jacques could not bear to be a fat European lugged about by an undernourished native. He had never before thought of himself as stout, but compared to these locals he was.

"Sir, sir, very cheap, sir, very cheap."

Surely, though, the man needed his business. To refuse it might be to condemn him to a night of hunger. Perhaps he should just give the rickshaw-man the coins he would have charged—but no, it would do no good to make him an object of charity. The rickshaw puller seemed to assume that Jacques' insistence on walking was a bargaining tactic, that if he lowered his price enough, Jacques would climb in.

Of course, Jacques had known he was white, but his whiteness had seemed to be a thing which existed on the surface. As he labored up the hill—despite his muscled calves, he had a much more difficult time of it than the scrawny natives around him—he saw that his whiteness was in his sinews, in the way he had of holding his belly, in the way he, a wearer of shoes, walked. The taste of his tongue in his mouth was the taste of a European tongue. Every glass of wine he had drunk, every meal he had eaten, all the books he had read, the physical training he had undergone in boot camp: all of these had left traces in him. He could live like a native for another two decades and still not purge his past.

He recognized—he was becoming quite winded by the climb—that his mental processes were becoming less and less acute, as they did before he drifted off to sleep. Still sober enough to realize he was growing light-headed, he looked around for the rickshaw puller. Yes, he saw now that it would make sense to avail himself of the man's services. But the man had given up.

He arrived at the headmaster's house, pale and shaky.

"You couldn't find a *pousse pousse*?" his hostess cried.

Jacques was aware not just of the sheen of perspiration covering his face, but also that sweat was darkening the underarms of his jacket. "The idea of it, it doesn't sit well with me."

The headmaster's wife laid a quasi-maternal hand on his shoulder. "You'll have to shed some of the rather naive beliefs you've brought with you from home…This heat, the thin air, our European constitutions simply aren't adapted to them…Oh, if we had known, we would have sent our driver."

Feeling like a bit of an invalid (yes, it was true, he had a tinge of heat stroke), he allowed himself to be led to an ornate wicker armchair on the verandah, to have a cold drink, a mix of citron liqueur and seltzer water and chipped ice—how on earth did they manage to get ice here?— pressed into his hand. A servant was called to fan him; Jacques protested, "Really, I'll be fine, I just needed to sit down—"

"No, no, I won't hear of it. Our generator is on the blink, so we haven't electricity, otherwise the ceiling fans would be…it's the least we can do. If you refuse, you'll make me feel a poor hostess indeed."

Slightly ridiculous, all of this—the pasha on his throne, the palm frond fan wafting through the air above him, the women flocking around him, a harem of off-white butterflies, the afternoon heat making the perfumes and dusting powders they wore more intense—a cloying mix of the scents of so many different women, attar of roses and apple blossom, sandalwood—recalling, in a minor key, the clashing smells of rotting flesh, antiseptics, phenol and camphor in the military hospital, as their pale linens called to mind the white-garbed nurses.

"He needs a lighter suit."

"My husband has a wonderful tailor in Paris," a woman who had perched herself on the arm of his chair murmured. "His man here can take your measurements." Was Jacques imagining a hint of lasciviousness in the way she said, *take your measurements*? Surely she wouldn't be so forward, he must be still a touch addled from the heat. Wouldn't it be more practical to have the tailoring done by a local? He was certain that if he were to say that, he would be met by a chorus of fond derision, humored out of this delusion the way an inebriate is simultaneously coddled and bullied.

The woman who had seated herself on the arm of his chair fished an ice cube from her glass, ran it across her forehead, and then, tilting her head back, over her neck and collarbone.

"Margot!" another woman reprimanded, indicating with a jerk of her chin Margot's bodice, in danger of growing translucent from the melting ice. "Don't you know—my husband can explain it to you quite scientifically—homeostasis and all of that—rubbing yourself down with ice only makes you hotter in the long run."

"Oh, I don't care about the long run! I'm unbearably hot right now."

Again, he wondered if he were imagining double meanings.

Margot asked: "And what is it that's brought you to us, all the way from Paris?"

He was surprised that she knew he had come from Paris. Before the afternoon was over, he would understand how bored these members of the European community were, the thrill that had coursed through the outpost upon news of his arrival. He wouldn't have been surprised to learn that they had gathered not just the simple facts of his name, place of origin, date of birth, educational background—but that they'd even managed to get wind of the report of the medical examiner who had certified his fitness for this posting: a 24-year-old male of medium height (1 meter 78) and build (72 kgs) with no apparent deformities or anomalies. Good family history, one tubercular uncle on the mother's side. His arrival had galvanized these women, kindling hope in them. (A foolish hope, for they'd had these fantasies many times before, and just as often been disappointed.) He had let them down already by the mere fact of him. But rather than admit to their despair, they were attempting to drive it away with drinks and flirtation and banter.

Jacques answered her question forthrightly: "A desire for—adventure, I suppose."

"Oh, surely there's more to it than that?" Her eye fixed on him, determined to unearth a secret. "An unhappy love affair? A scandal?"

"Sorry to disappoint," Jacques said, although that wasn't true: in fact, he was conceiving such an animosity towards these exiles, he was pleased to dash this woman's hopes.

(His detachment drew her in, as it would with so many women over the course of his life.)

"I'm famished."

"Where is M. Lefort?"

"I think we should just go ahead and sit down without him."

"Be as ill-mannered as he is?"

"Who's M. Lefort?" Jacques asked.

"The science master."

"A bit of an odd duck."

"Get's caught up in his—oh, I don't know, books and little experiments or whatever, and loses track of the time."

"We should go ahead without him."

"No, no, I simply can't," the headmaster's wife said.

They waited. And waited some more.

Is there anything more depressing than a Sunday afternoon? Yes, a Sunday afternoon in a colonial outpost. The hangover from the previous night's over-indulgence showed no signs of abating. The enforced indolence of the Sabbath brought about a raw confrontation with what lay on the other side of the weekdays' hectic rush. One yearned to be returned to what one yesterday yearned to be released from. One had only the sure knowledge that it was the inevitable lot of our pathetic species to be discontent. There was no word for this feeling save "homesickness," and that word, like everything else, was wanting.

"Ah, Melville," the headmaster said, venturing into the female territory of the verandah. "I heard you'd arrived, a bit out of sorts. When the ladies are done with you, come and join us in the study."

"I'll come now," he said, not even going through the expected ritual protests at being forced to leave behind the charming assemblage.

When he was just out of earshot, one of the women he had abandoned said: "A bit rude, if you ask me."

"Ah, there's more to him than meets the eye," another woman murmured: if he had no secrets, she was not above creating some for him. (She would be one of those who later would spread the rumor that Jacques had a fatal disease—after all, the postmaster had told her that Melville received weekly letters from a Dr. S. Plutach—perhaps that was the surname, this doctor wrote with the scrawl notorious for his profession—at the Hôpital Necker in Paris.)

Smoke

The louvers of the windows in the study were set aslant. Shafts of light divided the cigar smoke into bands as it curled up towards the ceiling where it gathered in a murky cloud. The icy drink the women had pressed into his hand was taken from him, replaced by a neat whisky.

"I keep telling the girls that those chilled drinks only make one hotter in the long run—"

"Yes, yes, you've explained this to us before. The body's response to cold, etc." The headmaster did little to hide his tetchiness.

"Ah, but M. Melville hasn't heard this before, and it's knowledge that will prove useful."

"Our guest has only just arrived. Let him relax a bit before we offer our 'Things the Newcomer Needs to Know' lecture." With this the headmaster put his hand on Jacques' shoulder, adding, in a meant-to-be-overheard voice, "Some of your new colleagues over here I'd like you to meet," and then, in a confidential whisper, "Didn't want you to get stuck with that tiresome fellow…Perhaps I'm being harsh, we tend to know one another's faults and foibles all too well."

The circle the headmaster led him to opened all too eagerly to let him in. "Got bivouacked all right, I hope." "Digs okay for you?" Jacques took note of their tendency to use slang which was slightly out-of-date—words and expressions that had been current in the year they had left France—and moreover to pronounce those words distinctly, with inverted commas around them.

"I remember my bachelor days, that single room *chez* Mme. Maurice. Fifteen years ago—where does the time go? Had a little spirit lamp, so I could brew my own coffee—an excellent landlady, Mme.

Maurice, but a bit of a penny-pincher, and I've always been most particular about my—"

"He won't stay there long. When he's got a semester or two under his belt, I'll write to the Ministry, saying if we want to keep hold of this excellent man, we'd better increase his housing allowance."

"Yes, and a man doesn't stay a bachelor forever."

"Our headmaster, by the way, has some very charming daughters."

"Ah, come now, lads," the headmaster said, "we mustn't make poor Melville feel he's being married off in his very first week."

"Save it for the second week, shall we?"

Jacques discerned the pecking order of this place, as rigid a hierarchy as had existed amongst the hens in his mother's backyard coop, albeit one enforced by verbal rather than physical jabs.

"Lefort! At last!" A rumpled man in his thirties, with a dark splotch on his suit jacket, arrived, bumbling apologies.

Jacques did not like to think of himself as a snob, but when he sat down to dinner he could not help noting that while the table was set with crystal and fine china, the cutlery gave itself away as being plate on account of its heft.

In Jacques' boyhood home, there had been mismatched genuine silver, handed down by the ancestors who were from the petty nobility—his parents no more hid their existence than they did the other progenitors who had been shopkeepers. The door of his family home was open to anyone—even Jews and *pieds noirs*—with the sole proviso that after they left, a comment would be made, almost ritual in nature, fond and derisive at the same time, about the visitor's tendency to remark on the price of objects or his distinctive accent.

The Oriental carpets on the floor of the headmaster's house revealed themselves as parvenus by their garish colors, not muted as they should have been by decades of being walked upon, and the common rooms of the house seemed to have been cobbled together by someone who had studied photographs of drawing rooms in the homes of the prestigious. Back in France, with their mediocre exam results from provincial universities, the masters at this school would have been village school teachers, living in rented rooms, taking their meals in mean cafés where the landlord, taking pity on them for their worn suits and grateful for the effort they made with the town's youths, would have poured them a glass of the house wine, *gratis*. The headmaster would have had at most a single servant, a woman who did the work of both laundress and cook, a char who came in once a week to do the heavy cleaning, while here the headmaster and his wife lorded over a whole staff.

A dish called *coq au vin* was served, made with guinea fowl rather than chicken, followed by a *beouf en daube*, made with meat from the zebu: he wished for something frankly foreign, rather than these dishes which, purporting to be French, only awoke his longing for home. Did the kitchen staff really add vanilla and chilies to these dishes or was it only that these odors, wafting through the air, found their way into everything?

(Later, he would learn the flesh of Malagasy women tasted of cloves and *pili-pili*.)

A woman's stockinged foot, slipped free from her shoe, caressed his ankle. He deliberately dropped his napkin, bent to retrieve it, and set her foot back on the floor. When he sat back up, he saw the headmaster's wife shooting him a glare: he had made an enemy.

Like the belle of the ball, he found his dance card filled up. His vague mention of a hot springs turned into a fixed invitation. "Yes, we must go there. How would next Saturday afternoon be for you?" "Come now, you mustn't keep him all to yourself..."

Jacques felt as if he had found himself on stage, in a drama entitled "The Dinner Party" or "The Colonial Outpost," put on by an amateur provincial theater company with more enthusiasm than talent. This was only intensified when, after dinner, he took a leather bound volume down from a shelf which held Diderot, Molière, La Fontaine, Balzac—and discovered its pages uncut. A cursory examination showed nearly all the books were in that same condition.

The next day he wrote to Sala: *In the center of Antananarivo, one could swear one was in Paris—a newer, cleaner Paris as it must have looked before the grit of centuries settled on it—save for the smell of spices—anise and pink pepper and nutmeg, and of course vanilla, which underlies everything, that and the palm trees and the torpid heat.* He did not tell her of his terrible homesickness or that he couldn't shake the sense that these buildings were false fronts, that he would someday duck behind them and see they were made of plaster-covered chicken wire, propped up by shafts of lumber.

Fever

On his third week in the country, he ventured into the native market, wandering past the sellers of second-hand knives and tools, clusters of peppercorn, bundles of dried vanilla beans, past heaps of beans, mounds of rice, fruits he did not know the names of, the air growing more fetid the further into the maze of the market he traveled. A woman dozed in a rush-backed wooden chair, half-asleep, with a pipe hanging from the corner of her mouth. Every now and again, she roused herself to wave a palm frond at the bluebottles descending on the hunks of meat set out for sale in front of her. Later, he would learn the names of the things offered in the marketplace: the fruit of the baobab tree, of the cardamom plant, beans of tamarind about to burst open their pods, the stinking durian fruit, its spiked hide like a medieval mace, basket after basket of chili peppers, red ones resembling Chinese lanterns, green ones the fingers of a fat man, others with a curve that suggested the place where a woman's back gave way to her buttocks. He began to feel dizzy—the noonday sun, the smells, the press of bodies, hands reaching for him, voices calling to him, the only word he could understand the imperative: Buy! Buy! That he did not know the names of these fruits increased his sense of lightheadedness. He had a glimmer of what Adam must have felt before naming day in Eden, the mania of the physical world not yet forced into the strait jacket of language. He would leave—yes, leave—

but each way he turned seemed to lead him deeper into the market. Overcome with dizziness, he attempted to keep himself from falling by steadying his arm against a shaft of bamboo which held a canopy aloft over one of the stalls—but the bamboo pole itself was merely stuck into a basket filled with beans and it swayed, sending the raffia shelter it was holding up lurching, threatening to plummet into the goods below. The keeper of the stall screeched at him, as did several other sellers, someone else grabbed his arm, began to curse back at the women who were yelling at him.

"I—" Jacques said. "I— I—" He smiled and nodded, pressed his hands together in benediction, hoping these gestures translated across the cultural divide, and strode quickly away from both his benefactors and those who called down imprecations on his head, still reeling.

Later, when everyone was so sure that it had been the food he ate in the market which had sickened him, he inwardly disagreed, for he had felt the vertigo which to him had seemed the primary symptom of his illness before he had eaten. Indeed, it seemed that the illness had entered his body through the air—hadn't the gas attacks on the front lines let us know that air can be fatal?

It was all so strange, the odors. *There, take a deep breath, don't let them see your confusion. Find a place to sit down, have something cool to drink.* He saw a food stall, separated from the open stalls by hanging mats which nonetheless allowed one to see inside, with reed mats also covering the ground, natives hunkered upon them, drinking and eating, the low murmur of laughter and conversation.

He entered, bringing with him a pall of silence. White men never came here.

How long did he sit there, in the painful silence? Five minutes, ten minutes, twenty? He was learning that the time of the Europeans—measured steadily out in seconds, minutes, hours, tracked precisely from the place they decreed the prime meridian—had little meaning here. As one body, his fellow diners seemed to have decided that since Jacques was not going to be driven away by their coldness and they did not dare physically force him to leave, they would simply act as if he did not exist. Their conversation once again swirled around him while he drank what he would later learn was *ranonapango,* made from water added to the crusty rice at the bottom of the pan, and then ate a stew of greens and tough meat and chili peppers. He paused before spooning the food into his mouth, remembering what he had been told about avoiding the food the Malagasy ate, that European stomachs were unable to tolerate it. Someone had even drawn a parallel with dogs, which devour foods that would sicken us. What crude racialism!—my God, we're all from the same species.

His stomach began to cramp when he was only a few yards from the market place. The pains became more and more ferocious until he was forced to dash into an alley, lower his pants and squat down. He looked up to see children laughing and pointing at him, one making a great show of holding his nose and fluttering his hand to drive away the stench. That was his last clear memory. He was home—that is, home in the hostel in which he had been billeted—how had he gotten there? The whitewashed walls spun around him. Where was his mother? Had she, too, come down with this fever? Perhaps he had become his own mother, these pains were those of labor. But something had gone wrong, there was no baby, just these stools of dark water. Men appeared, standing in the doorway.

—*Chin up, old man.*

—*You were young and strong to start with. That's a point in your favor.*

A little while hence, it might be said to another newcomer, "Ask Melville. He was like you when he first arrived here, filled with all that nonsense: *underneath-it-all,-they're-just-like-us*. Tell him, Jacques…"

More and more cramping: his body was still trying to give birth. A needle went into his arm. A native woman cooled the air above him with a fan. In the corner of the room, a priest was chanting in Latin. "Tell him to go away," Jacques implored the woman. "I'm not a believer."

He had never been one of those who made a show of his scorn for religion. In his family one was baptized in the church and buried there. His father liked to declare that for Lent he was giving up krill or lark's tongue or Tahitian limes. Now his anti-clericalism no longer seemed jocular: it was imperative that the priest depart.

The woman answered him in Malagasy, her voice rising at the end of each sentence, as if she were asking him a question.

Tuum ex toto, talis esto morbundum, Domine, corde tuo, et ex tota anima tua, et ex tota mente, the priest chanted, scrambling the words of the sacrament. Jacques grabbed the arm of the woman, imploring her to speak to the priest, urge him to say the Mass properly, lest the devil be conjured up.

While Jacques was speaking, the priest ceased to do so, but once Jacques fell silent, he began his chanting again.

Occasionally, he was conscious enough to feel shame when the Malagasy woman cleaned him, daubing him with a damp cloth—the skin of his ass, his scrotum had been burned raw by the acidic stools roiling from him. His penis would stiffen as her hands brushed against it or lifted it out of the way, but these erections were like those of an infant, before desire had an object, devoid of masculine assertion. She would laugh tenderly and say something in her native tongue. One night his fever was burning so bright, it seemed he could understand her, a sickroom Pentecost: *In the midst of all this, our little soldier still stands at attention*...or, perhaps, *You see, life goes on, you're not done for yet*...The pain made him weep like a baby. She held his hand, and whispered a song to him in the language of the angels.

M. Lefort, sitting by his bedside with his hat in his hands, stared intently at Jacques.

Sometimes he was conscious enough to hear in the distance the call to prayer from the minarets of the mosques. *Allahu Akbar. Ash-hadu alla ilaha illallah.*

The words he had written to Sala hovered in the air about him: "We were carried on palanquins past the Dutchmen's Graveyard: so many Dutch colonists were killed by native fevers that the Netherlands gave up their attempt to take this island." They formed themselves into a long line and circled about him. He knew he had to catch his finger through one of the letters, snag it like a hook in the mouth of a fish and then he would be able to reel in the remainder of the sentence, gather those words in his arms, clutch them against his chest: if he were able to accomplish this, he would live.

His desire for life astonished him.

The priest came back. An anti-baptism was being carried out, Jacques' nether regions rather than his head were being daubed, not with holy water but with the foul liquid that poured out of him—excrement, not Christian blood, was the sacred fluid of this religion.

The Malagasy woman continued to sing to him and clean up after him. The ghost-white faces loomed in the doorway, the priest—who was also sometimes a one-legged beggar he had seen on the street in Nîmes in his boyhood—spoke his garbled Latin. Jacques shouted at the priest to be silent, at the beggar that he had no money to give him, and, as he shouted, realized that all the words—the panhandler's appeal, the priest's chant—had been coming from his mouth.

In the distance, the call to prayer from the minarets of the mosque. *Allahu Akbar. Ash-hadu alla ilaha illallah.*

Ghost

During this time when Jacques was in the grip of dysentery, Simone was a schoolgirl. In the heat of the summer, her thighs stuck to the wooden seat in her classroom, the sweat soaked through her garments so that when she walked home along the Chemin Raymond a damp ghost of her legs was visible on the back of her deep blue skirts.

Later, when she will be lying in bed in the dark next to Jacques he will say to her, "In Madagascar, I saw a crocodile for the first time. It was sunning itself on the bank of a river, so still that I would have stepped on it had it not been for the native who was with me, who grabbed my arm, called out. It opened a single eye, fixed it on me, not just with the implacable gaze of a member of a species who inhabited the earth long before our pitiful tribe even existed, who knows that it will endure long after our species has become extinct, but with that of a creature which had an atavistic knowledge of me."

She will treasure the words that baffle her, repeating them over and over to herself, as if burnishing a piece of silver. *Atavistic. Implacable.* She would never look them up in a dictionary, not wanting to know their meanings.

Those stories of his that began, *Once, in Madagascar…When I was in Madagascar…The Hova people of Madagascar…*He never said those words when there was light in the room, whether daylight or artificial. He only spoke those words in the dark, when the two of them were in bed, in that drowsy state he sometimes fell into after they had made love, when it almost seemed as if he were a crocodile on the bank of a river.

Lilt

One day, he hollered at the priest—who now spoke Latin with the lilt of a Malagasy—and his shout did not make the priest disappear. *Sanctam unctionem…suam piissimam.* The man's hand was touching his eyes, his ears. He was being given the last rites. It was quite impossible, he could not die. For one thing, it was the middle of the afternoon, sunlight glared through the cracks in the curtains. Death should happen at night, lit by flickering candles. He must stop the priest before he touched his genitals as he asked the Lord to forgive Jacques' carnal sins. He began to flail about, trying to get away from the priest's hands.

But he did not die. Flummoxing the doctor's predictions, his fever broke, and he traveled back down into the world of the healthy, as one descends a mountain after a climb, exhausted, filled with the aftermath of exhilaration, going down because one must go down, both longing for and despising the snug cottage below with its glowing windows.

On the day when at last he had a normal bowel movement, producing a turd that was firm and well-shaped, he stared at it in the porcelain bowl with a sense of childish pride.

A shaving mirror was brought. A grizzled man stared back at him—one of his relatives perhaps, a younger brother of his father, a black sheep whose existence had heretofore been hidden from him. It seemed comical that when Jacques moved his jaw, the man in the mirror moved his. When he lifted his hand to touch the wiry sprouts of his beard, his doppelgänger did the same. Jacques' sunken cheeks and hollow eye sockets resembled those in portraits of religious ascetics who had starved themselves for the love of God. Indeed, he found the only words he could use to recount the course of his illness were religious ones: calvary, redemption, rebirth, suffering. Muddled up with all that was a sense that he had been cleansed from within, that his body had purged itself of his whiteness, that while on the outside he still had the skin and the manners of a Caucasian, he had been freed of his color.

A colleague caught him at the mirror, clapped him on the back. "You'll be plump again in no time! You'll be back to your old self!"

Midadaka

But he did not want to become again the man he had been before his illness. From his manservant, from the women in the market, from a dictionary created by a missionary society, he learned the local language. He copied the words in long lists in his notebook, Malagasy in one column, French in the next. *Midadaka* means to babble. Several words—*akondro, boroboaka, fintsa, katakata, kida*—are translated as banana. *Fananimpitoloha* is a mythical seven-headed beast.

In Malagasy, the verb came before the object, the object before the subject so that if he were to say, "I want a banana," the desire would come first, followed by the thing desired, with the one who did the desiring the last in line.

The written word was not enough. He swapped lessons in French for ones in Malagasy with young men of mixed heritage. These men looked around Jacques' room, studying the things laid out on his bureau—cufflinks, hairbrushes, mustache trimmer, razor, aftershave—

as if they were anthropologists making notes. He was unable to persuade these men to invite him to their homes, they put him off with excuses about how noisy it was, how there was simply no private place, and he saw not just shame but fear in their excuses. He asked them about the *hainteny*, which he had read about in the descriptions of the island published by British missionaries, but they replied that it was sinful. "Why?" Jacques asked. "It is not Christian." "Why not?" "I cannot explain it to you, sir," they said, blushing and stammering.

Those men who had written the early accounts of Madagascar had been like hunters who went into remote valleys where the animals had had no human contact and so had not learned to fear them. But surely, outside the city, there were villages untouched by civilization.

He learned the exact spot on the ridge behind his upper teeth to place his tongue when he was pronouncing certain consonants, the new way in which he must purse his lips for these vowels. He knew his mouth in a way he had never before known it.

Malagasy had taken words from the missionaries, swiped words from pirates, from escaped slaves, from the Arabs, from the Dutch, from the French. The conquerers came to devour, but they were themselves, bit by bit, devoured. Malagasy words always ended in a vowel, and the lilt and intonation of its speakers made it seem close to song, words blending into the ones that had come before and those that followed. Jacques wondered if his father, who hadn't stuttered when he sang, would have been freed of his terrible burden if he had been a speaker of Malagasy rather than French.

In his rented room in Antananarivo, at ten on a Sunday night—his students' papers to be corrected and next day's lesson plans looming on the back of his desk, a sense of obligation niggling at the edge of his field of vision—he wrote, in the fountain pen with the gold nib given to him by his father: *This island floats off the coast of Africa, but not of it. Here there are no elephants, no lions, no rhinoceroses, no tigers, no apes. (Although, at the hot springs at the center of the island, when excavations were being carried out for a new bath, they did find the fossilized remains of a hippopotamus.)*

Madagascar might have sailed here from some other region, might someday take it into its head to bid farewell to Africa, and glide off to the Barbary Coast or the Bay of Bengal.

Geologists say that this island was once part of Africa, and some cataclysm broke it free. A chain of large islands once joined it to Asia, and its people hopscotched across those islands, now sunk beneath the sea.

In the parts of the city shown on his map with shaded lines to show that the cartographers had simply given up faced with these nameless curving alleys and footpaths, he found a brothel that served the local population; although he was met with suspicion, the madame—a quadroon—was not about to turn away a customer. Among the women offered to him was one so obese three ordinary women could have fit inside of her. Folds of flesh billowed around her, and he had fought down both laughter and disgust. Walking upstairs with the woman he had chosen, he had looked back to see a man with his arm around the fat woman's waist, tiny against her enormous flesh.

He chose the same woman several times in a row, asking her the fifth time he was with her if she would take him to her village.

"I do not have a village."

"Where are you from?"

"Here, I have always been here."

"And your people?"

"Here, they have always been here."

Later, he could not remember her name: had it been Faniry or Rina or Miora or Fatima? He tried another woman. Unlike the other women in the brothel, this new one seemed preoccupied, not just her face but her body itself—the slump of her shoulders, the way she held her belly—shadowed with worry. While he was making love to her, it seemed she was both there in the room with him and elsewhere. He saw, as if gazing into a psychic mirror, how his reserve could exercise an almost hypnotic hold over others.

She had learned that gloves should match and shoes should match, and so she wore identical brooches, one above the left breast and one above the right. She had learned certain gestures from European women. She cocked her head to the side and gave him a coy smile, but the gesture was a bit off, so one could tell it did not come naturally to her: One could also speak a nonverbal language with an accent. The grammar of the mother tongue could sometimes be discerned by the mistakes made in speaking a foreign language. He was aware that he was thinking too much, that his intellect sometimes got in his way—just as a quite tall man, who enjoys towering over other men, who sees the advantages that it gives him, and not just in the obvious ways, on the playing field for instance, but in the everyday course of life, nonetheless resents having to constantly keep on guard against bumping his head, the discomforts he experiences sitting in chairs made for ordinary men.

He sang to her—he was a bit drunk, he wouldn't have been able to sing otherwise—*sur le pont d'Avignon, l'on y danse, l'on y danse*. She was charmed by him, or perhaps pretending to be charmed by him.

He held out his arms in the waltz position, and she wrapped her hands around his neck and ground her loins against him.

He was beginning to find her more tiresome than charming, but his irritation proved to be the magic switch, and he grew hard and was able to do what he had come here to do, to get his money's worth.

On the shelf in the corner her treasured objects sat, including a slip of paper she had saved from a machine that gave one's weight and fortune: *You will soon have a chance to make a profitable transaction.* On the reverse, her lucky numbers: 9, 32, 21, 27, and 10.

Her name was Bomfomtabellilaba.

Afterward he asked her: "Will you take me to your village?"

"My village? I do not have a village."

He kissed her hand and called her "Bomfom."

"My name is Bomfomtabellilaba. My name is not Bomfom."

He thought she was teasing, and said again, "Bomfom."

"No! Bomfomtabellilaba!" Then, frightened that her anger might drive away a paying customer, she smiled, as if she could erase what had just passed: "Bomfomtabellilaba."

Her anger intrigued him. When he returned the following week, he again chose her.

After they made love, he asked her, "Bomfomtabellilaba," (he had been practicing saying her name all week, so it would flow easily off his tongue) "Why did you get angry when I called you Bomfom?"

"That is not the name I was given."

"Yes?"

"So it is wrong not to say it as it is meant to be said."

"Because?" he said, but she would not—or maybe could not—answer him.

Pantoum

He was full of questions, this one. He wanted to know how long she had been in the city. He wanted to know what life in her village had been like. He wanted to know why she had left the village. He wanted her to teach him words in Malagasy. She held out her open palm: "That will cost you extra." She had been intending to be flirtatious, but he reached for his billfold, pressed notes into her hand.

"Enough?"

He studied her and she studied him. She studied his studying of her. He kept asking about the village, about proverbs, about *hainteny.* "Tell me about *fady*."

"I do not know the words in French."

He smiled at this, because she knew almost no French.

She hated those smiles of his, had had enough of being laughed at.

"Tell me in Malagasy."

"I do not know what to say."

"Why did you leave your village?" he asked her. He asked her this question every time he saw her.

"I left my village to come to the city."

"But why?"

"I walked."

"But why did you leave your village?"

She answered him by nuzzling his neck or playing with his penis, not wanting to tell him that she was the daughter of a drunkard, set to enter into the sort of marriage daughters of drunkards enter into: a third wife, or a fourth, a woman who would pound manioc and carry water from the well while the first wife lay on her mat and plaited her daughter's hair or sat in the shade and stared at the horizon. She didn't want him to know that to pay off her father's debts she had stood in the flooded paddies and planted rice seedlings, minnows nibbling at her feet, her back aching, the flesh of her feet so spongy she could scrape it off with her fingernail. She didn't want to tell him that when she had walked away from her village, she had asked people sitting by the road, "How do I get to the city?" and they had pointed in many different directions, often back the way she had come. White people thought they had invented everything: they even thought they had invented cruelty.

"I wish I had shoes," she whispered in his ear. "I wish you would buy me a pair of shoes, and I would tell the other girls he loves me, loves me so much he has bought me a pair of shoes."

Mules

He came to Bomfomtabellilaba with his school satchel. She giggled when they were alone, and she said: "I will tell the other girls, my white boyfriend is so clever, he reads books while he makes love to me." She grabbed his glasses, putting them on, pretending to read a book and thrusting her hips.

Inside the school bag was not a book that her clever European boyfriend would read while he made love to her, but a pair of shoes, mules he had bought at the second-hand shop, because had he gone to the shoemaker word would have gotten all through the French community, and he didn't wish to make any further difficulties for himself. Anyhow, he told himself, she would be perfectly happy with a hand-me-down pair of shoes.

"You love me," she said. "You have bought me a pair of shoes."

He thrust out his lower lip and shrugged his shoulders. "I have bought you a pair of shoes."

The proprietor of the second-hand shop had polished them. Only someone who was familiar with shoes would realize they were run down at the heels.

"Ah, they're too big for your feet. I suppose I thought better too large than too small."

She rose to her feet, wobbled, took odd steps, almost clown-like, raising the front of her foot out of the way before setting her heel down. "I am a French lady," she said, giggled, took another step, tripped over her own feet, and fell laughing to the floor.

He sat down next to her on the floor, although he was a European and everyone knew their gods forbade them to sit on the floor. Still laughing, she took the mules off, rubbed her feet, and then put the shoes on her hands, and her hands walked a few steps like a French lady. Later, a priest will tell her that the path *Jesosy Kristy* commanded his followers to walk was a difficult one, and she will think: *Oh yes, I know how difficult Europeans make walking.*

Outside

Mme. Maurice rapped on his door. "There is a young woman, outside, wanting you." He understood from the word "outside," that she was a native woman who would not be admitted into the house.

Bomfomtabellilaba said, "I'm sorry for coming here."

He took her arm, made a half-bow to Mme. Maurice, standing sentry in the doorway, murmured, "It won't happen again," and steered Bomfomtabellilaba down the stairs.

"How did you know where I live?" he asked.

She stared at him for a moment and then said, "My father has died. I must go back to my village, I must hire a cart and I have no money."

"I will go with you."

"No."

"Very well." He turned on his heel.

"All right."

It was fortunate, he thought, that his had happened during his school holidays. She led him into the native quarter, to rent the cart and horse to take them to her village. She said to the man—apparently he was connected to her in some way, Jacques had not begun to penetrate the complications of consanguinity here—"He speaks Malagasy," and Bomfomtabellilaba and the carter withdrew some distance from him to carry out the arrangements. Jacques sensed that she was not negotiating a lower price on his behalf but figuring out how much they could get away with charging him, what her share would be.

They smelled the village before they saw it, a scent yeasty and sweet, and then the smell of dung and animal blood.

He thought he might be treated here as he had been when he entered the food stall so many months ago: as if he were a block of wood, but the locals came over to greet the two of them—everyone was quite drunk—to look him over, touch his skin, his hair, ask her questions about him. This was what it must have been like to be one of those Indians carried home in Columbus' ships, to be exhibited before the Spanish court.

Sugar-cane beer was being pressed upon him, he did not at all care for the taste of it, there was an undercurrent of anise. Still, he drank.

An ox was being dragged into the center of the village. The wattled flesh at its neck shook, and it bellowed. A youth distributed spears. A discussion ensued over whether Jacques should be given one. Although he had come here out of a desire to be a part of village life, still, he hoped he would be exempted from this rite, but in the end, he, too, was handed a spear.

After all, he was an eater of flesh, loved a rare and bloody steak. Among the civilized, this killing happened in an abattoir, men in galoshes, wearing rubber aprons, with well-sharpened knives, hidden away behind high walls. He dipped his cup in the vat of beer, downed it, refilled it, guzzled that next one down, too. Where had Bomfomtabellilaba gotten herself to?

The first of the spears pierced the flank of the ox. The animal was not going to be killed efficiently, no sledgehammer to its head, no quick slice of its throat. It was part of the ritual that it know it was dying—it too, like those who were killing it, must experience the horror of death.

The epithet with which Homer had described Hera, "ox-eyed," ran through his head. A second spear was thrust into her gut.

The drink sickened Jacques, and he, like a few others, wandered off to the edge of the clearing and vomited. A dog ventured over, tentatively at first, and then when it was not driven off, eagerly, and began to lick up the puddle of sick. Some had stumbled on their way there or back and lay where they had fallen. The vomiting sobered him up, although he couldn't, properly speaking, be said to be sober, but he was no longer immersed in drunkenness, he floated on top of it as a man in a rowboat rocks upon the waters of a lake. He was cold, despite the tropic heat.

This is what I want, Jacques thought. I want to be shocked and sickened and disgusted: I want to be shaken to my core. I fear it and I want it. I want it more than anything else on earth—more than riches, more than to be loved, more than to have adventures, more than to achieve literary fame, more than to have adulation of my peers.

He stumbled over to the vat filled with *betsa,* dipping his cup in and draining it immediately, repeating the action again and again.

When he awoke, he tried to judge the hour by the position of the stars, but his brain was still too fuddled by drink.

The smell of the ox roasting. It had been hacked apart, the pieces were being turned on spits over various fires scattered throughout the center of the village. A few meters away, the ox's head, its eyes gone dull, its mouth fixed in a grin, perhaps a grimace, looked down from a staff on the feast being made of its flesh. He reminded himself that only a hundred odd years ago human heads had been carried on pikes through the streets of Paris.

He overheard some men talking, their words ritualized, on the verge of argument, but never spilling over into actual rage. Yes, this must be the *hainteny*. He staggered over to their group, wishing he had not let himself get so inebriated.

Later, he would write:

Once, they say, there were birds the size of elephants on this island. The natives say this, and the investigations of the Europeans bear them out: skeletons have been found of a bird three meters tall, and fossilized eggs with a circumference of over one meter.

Once, they say, a race of pale, tiny people, the Vazimba, lived on this island. Some of the natives say they still dwell in the forests and are the ancestors of kings. The Europeans have found no evidence of this, and so do not believe it.

The natives say that the lemurs are our ancestors. Perhaps Darwin would find some truth in this.

A few weeks later, he saw the woman, Bomfomtabellilaba, in the street, arguing with a man who wore the *galabeya* and the tightly-crocheted cap of a Muslim, but who was so drunk the rank odor of *betsa* reached Jacques when he was more than a meter away. She signaled to Jacques with her eyes that he should not give any sign of recognizing her. He was aware of his jealousy as one is conscious of a troublesome but minor affliction—a paper cut, a hangnail.

"Who was that man?" he asked her later.

"What man?"

He did not respond, did not say, "You know very well of whom I am speaking," simply allowed her pretense to hang in the air.

"He is no one. He is not important."

"A relative?"

She used the word *havana* to describe him, a word which may mean a relation by blood or alliance—or a friend, or a lover. It can even be used to describe one's co-wife in a polygamous marriage. Translation, once it got past the simple substitution of one concrete noun for another, always became complicated, filled with byways and underground passages from which one might emerge in a completely unexpected place.

"Is he your husband?"

"He is not my husband. I think you should be happy. I think you should drink a glass of *betsa* and laugh and be happy."

Habit

He had found his way in. On breaks and holidays, he returned to Bomfomtabellilaba's village, occasionally with her, more often not, bringing gifts—bangles and knives and carved wooden boxes the Indian traders sold. He pretended to drink, sipping the *betsa* or rum he was given as a maiden aunt sips her Sunday afternoon glass of sherry, jotting notes in his memo pad.

I am like the jar that has no desire but the water.

I am like the water that has no desire but the jar.

In the village, things simply were. Not just the mid-day heat, but the air of lassitude, belonging to no one in particular. The men bending over their game of *fanorona* on a rickety wooden table with lines chalked across it. The laughing women plaiting one another's hair. The sleeping children in a pile, nestled with the pigs and dogs.

A rooster crowed in the distance.

In his off hours, he got out of the habit of wearing shoes.

He got out of the habit of speaking French.

He got out of the habit of using a knife and fork.

He got out of the habit of sitting in chairs.

He got out of the habit of having sex in the missionary position.

He got out of the habit of holding his belly like a European.

He got out of the habit of thinking in sentences with verbs.

He got out of the habit of wearing trousers.

The feel of his genitals swinging back and forth between his legs beneath his *lamba.*

The Muslim call to prayer. A lungful of air bellowing through a conch shell, echoing against the hills, carrying farther than muezzin's voice could have. At first, he had taken it to be an injured animal bellowing. It reminded him of the shofar he had heard from the synagogue in Nîmes.

The clink of bangles on the wrists of the Indian traders' children.

A bamboo arrow, blown from air-guns fashioned from a palm leaf, felling a kingfisher or a bulbul.

Destiny is a chameleon at the top of a tree: a child simply whistles and it changes color.

A shrike sounding a cry of alarm.

He hunkered on the sand, eating the meat of a turtle that had been boiled in seawater.

Long ago, not so long ago, dhows carrying slaves on their way to the sugar plantations of Mauritius had sailed past.

Mango trees.

Baobab trees.

In the shallows of the river, crocodiles, lazy in the sun, slithered over one another.

Terraced hillsides, each tiny field a different shade of green, a patchwork quilt.

In the center of the village he slept, not sleep in a solid firm block as Europeans did, alone in their beds, or at most with one other, a state firmly and decisively separated from wakefulness. In the center of the village he slept, on a woven rush mat, a woman's belly for a pillow. He had a slight malarial fever. Impossible to live as he did and not contract it. Teas and potions kept it in check. A dog licked his hand, tasting the salt of his sweat and the remains of roast pig, tentatively at first, then, when he was not shooed away, with full laps of his tongue.

He did not exactly dream, but he did not exactly think or remember, either. When he had been a boy in Nîmes—before his family had at last come into a small inheritance from a distant relative, sufficient, barely so, to enable them to leave behind the apartment within his paternal grandparents' home and move to Paris—when snow fell at night, it sometimes seemed that the flakes landing at his bedroom window were made of words. At first it was possible to decipher some of them before they melted on the glass—*mouchoir, bouleverser, rocher, faucon*—or disappeared beneath the weight of other words—*biberon, théâtral, entente, gris-vert, radiesthésie*—the heavens shaking out vast dictionaries, the jumbled words tumbling down faster and faster, blotting one another out, drifts burying the house. At such moments, Jacques had toyed with the idea of joining an order of silent monks. He imagined himself walking along still corridors, past the cells where his brothers knelt in dumb prayer, the footfalls of his mendicant's sandals echoing against the rough walls, the few words the recurring ones of the Mass, the Ave, the Pater Noster, polished smooth by repetition. Ah, but he would have had to give up the pleasures of the flesh, and, anyhow, he was not a believer. Perhaps he would ship out on a tramp steamer, talk to his fellow crew members in language so stripped down it was semaphoric.

A rooster crowed in the distance.

Bomfomtabellilaba's stomach, digesting the feast they had eaten, the potent drink, rumbled, and he smiled.

The dog having licked clean Jacques' left hand, sniffed his way around to Jacques' right hand and began on that.

Raptor

Later, the men sparred and joked with one another, repeating proverbs:

The cicada's voice is heard above the fields, but its body can be held in one hand.

One who dances without drums is laughed at.

The dead ox doesn't protect himself from flies.

He jotted down what they said in his notebook, watching them so intently that he earned the nickname "the hawk."

With the fountain pen that had belonged to his father, he wrote:

Since the Revolution, it has been the duty of sons to kill their fathers, but here in Madagascar a system of thought prevails which outsiders crudely refer to as "ancestor worship." This is a different world, where man is part of a natural order, foreordained long before he was born. Life is harmonious, the Malagasy say; and people are a great mat—that is, we are woven together with one another.

It was a paragraph he would return to again and again: he never felt that he got it right.

Jacques did not forget that there was a woman named Sala in Paris, to whom he wrote weekly letters. He complained to her about the stupidity of his fellow colonials: "I cannot tell you how the inanity of these conversations makes me long to talk with you." It was as close as he got to a profession of love for her.

Jacques washed his face with strong soap and shaved. He put on socks and shoes and trousers. He walked into his classroom and rolled down one of the maps which hung, like furled shades, at the front of the room.

"*Repetez, s'il vous plait.*" Pointing with the long wooden dowel, touching the body of France as the priest had touched him, he intoned: "*Nord-Pas de Calais, Picardie, Haute-Normandie,*" while his students droned after him. He lectured on the use of the literary simple past subjunctive, distinguishing it from the imperfect subjunctive. He pretended to still believe what he had once known with utter certainty, that beneath the cloaks of dark flesh of our overseas brethren dwelt the pure souls of French citizens.

He went, when absolutely necessary, to the soirées and Sunday afternoons put on by the fellow members of his community.

He sat on the verandah of Mme. Maurice's house and watched the women walk past with bundles atop their heads, tracking the sway of their hips and shoulders, the intricate dance they did within their bodies, beneath their still heads.

She rubbed lard into her hair before plaiting it. Her name was Bomfomtabellilaba, her name was Lalao, her name was Marie, her name was Anisoa. Through the doorway, I could see a baobab tree with children and pigs and dogs drowsing in a pile beneath it. Women walked past, balancing jugs of water or goods for the marketplace on their heads. When I arrived at school I realized I should have given myself more than a perfunctory wash: her smell of pig-fat still clung to me.

1968

Nearly half a century later, in May of 1968, his writings about Madagascar will be denounced in one of those hundreds of hastily-printed leftist newspapers which are being hawked on every street corner: the nameless women with their smell of pig fat, the children lazing with the dogs and sows. He is the voice of a colonialism which feeds not only on the labor of the oppressed but on their very souls. Although, of course, the word "soul" won't be used, as that would be evidence of feudalistic, reactionary thinking.

A few days prior to the publication of this broadside, a turning point will have occurred in his health. He will be taken to the hospital. Being hospitalized, with all its indignities—he asks for a bedpan, to which the nurse responds, "Tinkle or BM?"—means that at least he can see his Dominique.

She will read the article aloud to him, knowing he will be both amused and flattered by this condemnation: at least he is still worth damning. In language that sounds as if it has been poorly translated from the Albanian, he is called an imperialist lackey, a neocolonialist, reactionary stooge, a running dog.

He will say, "I wish this old dog could still run," but Dominique's visit has already quite worn him out, he can't get enough breath behind his words, and he sees, from her abstracted smile, that she hasn't understood what he said, but doesn't want to force him to repeat it.

He will gesture to her to come close to him and rasp into her ear: "It makes one long for Robespierre, who only slaughtered his fellow Frenchmen and not the French language."

He will sleep, and wake to the chants from the marchers, washing up like the waves of sound a theater audience makes before the curtain rises, the demonstrators ignoring the signs: "Quiet. Hospital."

"What are they saying?"

She will stand at the window, listen. "I can't make it out."

"It's a good thing I am dying. I've outlived this world. It no longer makes the slightest bit of sense to me."

Dominique will have to leave—even in the midst of all this tumult visiting hours are strictly observed—and alone in his room, as he wavers in and out of consciousness, Bomfomtabellilaba will be sitting on one side of his bed, Lefort on the other (a rationalist would, of course, say these were specters cast up by the actions of morphine on his brain), Bomfomtabellilaba polishing the pair of second-hand mules he had bought her so many years ago, Lefort sitting silently, as he had sat next to Jacques' bedside when he was in the grip of dysentery, as the two of them had sometimes sat in Lefort's room.

Fever

On Bomfomtabellilaba's dark skin, the bruises showed purple with green edges. One of her braids had been yanked out, leaving a square of raw flesh.

"Why did he do such a thing?"

"He has whiteness in him."

"I am white," Jacques said.

"You are white. He is mixed up. He makes a war against himself. You have a home you can go back to."

"This is my home, now."

"No. This is not your home."

"It's all beside the point. What's the sense of even talking about these things: the whiteness in him, his being mixed. The fact is, he shouldn't treat you this way, it can't be allowed, it's criminal."

"If I go to the Frenchmen, they will laugh at me. They will say I am a bad woman. They will say, 'The bruises are fading and hair grows back. It's not as if he took gold from you.'"

Jacques steepled his fingers. "I suppose you are right." Then: "Are there not some others, in your community, who could intervene? Friends of his?"

"He has no friends. His own brother told me, 'Bomfomtabellilaba, you must get away from him.' He'll listen to you. He'll be frightened of you. You are a *vazaha*. I'll tell him to come and meet me in a place, and you can wait outside. When he comes outside, you will tell him 'You cannot treat Bomfomtabellilaba the way you have been treating her, you cannot strike her across the face when she has done nothing wrong, you cannot pull out her hair by the roots.'"

Jacques drank beer at a table outside the bar. The man entered the house across the street—it occurred to him that he did not know the man's name, he would have to address him as, *You there*! or *My good man*, which would be awkward, demeaning. He wondered that he had never asked that most basic question: What is the name of this man who is neither your husband nor your relative? It was even more curious in light of the fact that she had been so insistent on his using her full name.

The first time he heard the man's name would be out of the mouth of the police officer: Ahmed Jacobs, that is to say, the deceased.

Jacques thought it fortunate that the man did not look unkempt: his galabeya was freshly washed and ironed, his topi set dead center atop his head. Jacques thought: it was the drunken man who did these things to Bomfomtabellilaba. I will speak to the sober man, this sober man and I will come to an easy understanding. At the end of our conversation we will shake hands. Still, he wished he knew the man's name. His hands were sweating rather more than he would have liked.

The first beer having failed to quench his thirst, he ordered a second, and, a half hour later—he couldn't very well occupy the table with an empty glass in front of him—a third.

During the questioning with the policemen, these glasses of beer—had it been three or four? Or possibly even five? At first he had been quite sure, three glasses of beer. But wasn't it true that he wasn't used to drinking beer? Yes, he preferred wine. So it was not wrong to say that he was unaccustomed to beer, especially to the native home-brewed beer which was not of uniform potency. Was it at all possible that he might have had more than three beers, might in fact have been inebriated when the incident in question took place?

"Listen," Jacques replied, "a man takes responsibility for his actions. He doesn't make excuses about having drunk too much beer, and above all, he doesn't speak euphemistically. He doesn't say 'incident' when the word wanted is 'murder.'"

"I—we, we appreciate the fact that you aren't trying to downplay what happened and your role in it. In the interests of speaking accurately, I would remind you that the word 'murder' has a very precise legal definition. Let us use the word 'death.'"

"All right, the word 'death,' then. Not 'incident.'"

The interrogation was not proceeding in the manner in which Jacques would have expected it to: the accused, that is to say, he himself, Jacques, was being spoken to in a manner that was almost deferential. He briefly considered the possibility that this was a ploy, but rejected it. Even now, in his state of shock—he kept seeing the grey jelly that had seeped out of the dead man's ear—he knew that a man of his position—that is to say, a white man, an educated man—was very unlikely to be charged with murder or even manslaughter.

"I shan't downplay this, either: The man's own brother said he had always known he would come to a bad end."

"Now did you hear this directly or—"

"She told me this."

"You are referring to the woman who goes by the name of Bomfomta-ta..."

"Bomfomtabellilaba. Yes."

"What were your feelings toward this woman?" The other policeman, not the lieutenant, asked this question. Even in the state he was in, Jacques took in the covert look of reprimand that passed from the lieutenant to his underling: this question had been blurted out too soon. Clearly, the second man was in over his head. Perhaps there was another man, a Malagasy, who usually acted as the lieutenant's second, but given the sensitivity of this matter, it wouldn't do for a native to be playing that role. We are all brothers under the skin, but nonetheless.

"I was fond of her."

The lieutenant spoke quickly, seizing the reins of the interview.

"It was a carnal relationship, was it not?"

"Yes."

"Do you love her?"

"The word 'love' is not really one which is in my personal vocabulary, that is, the words which I use to describe myself, my emotions."

"Nonetheless, if you could be said to love a woman—"

"But I have just told you, the word 'love' is not in my vocabulary."

The man—who Jacques did not yet know as Ahmed Jacobs, who was not yet the deceased—came out of the bar across the street. Jacques drained his glass of beer and walked towards him. The man was older than he had assumed: his temples were greying and the flesh of his face sagged slightly. Perhaps he was Bomfomtabellilaba's father, or her uncle.

"I know who you are," the other man shouted.

"Yes." Jacques allowed the slightest of smiles to play about his face: it would go better if he brought an air of bemused detachment to all of this. Jacques had not even finished thinking this thought when the man struck him with his left hand, a blow so hard it left a mark on Jacques' face which, by the time he was released from the jail the next morning, had darkened into a bruise, showing up against his pale flesh a brighter purple than the bruise across Bomfomtabellilaba's face, which had been the start of this whole matter. The man was shouting at Jacques, he was drunk, the yeasty stink of beer surrounded him. Jacques teetered, lolling forward and back. He had never before been struck, not even by his father. The man loomed over him, shouting in his face.

And then it happened. The air rushing out of Jacques in a tremendous "hunh," a caesura of time itself, his head was pivoting on the axis of his neck, he could hear the sound of the bones of his cervical spine wrenching against one another, and then, oddly, not the sensation of falling but of the ground rushing up to him.

Jacques stared up at the drunken man, shocked by the sudden intimacy between them. This man—whose name he did not know—saw Jacques in his rawest state. It was more searing even than the knowledge one gains through the act of copulation: the dazed closeness, the sense of having been knocked out of the world of the ordinary. Jacques could never have imagined he would feel tender towards the man who had struck him. There was something womanish in him, something he couldn't have imagined before, some thrill in submission.

At the same time, he was aware that he had to get back up on his feet, that was what a man did when he had been knocked over, he didn't lie there dazed on the ground. His usual clear-headedness had been smashed out of him, along with his wind. It would, of course, return to him. A few hours later he would be so collected that, when the police officers who were interrogating him held a confab in the hallway out of his hearing, one would say to the other, "I've never had to deal with such a cool customer, it really throws me off my game."

The man was looking down at him with a look that mingled expectation and contempt.

When Jacques had been in basic training there were certain conscripts who saw brawling as one of their duties when on leave—in addition to getting drunk and coupling with a whore. He knew of more than one friendship that had begun by one man slugging the other—an efficient way to get the business of male rivalry out of the way. It might be that way between the two of them. Although, it would be necessary for Jacques to comport himself like a man, to return the blow: to do otherwise would not be sporting.

As Jacques lumbered to his feet, the man whose name he did not yet know assumed a fighting stance, fists in front of him, bent legs, weight dancing from side to side. Because the man was drunk, the effect was comical. A crowd had gathered, and it was more embarrassment than anything else that made the nervous grin creep across Jacques' face as he, too, assumed a fighting stance, although he felt like a child playing at being a grownup.

The man shouted at him: "You are thinking this is funny?"

"Now, see here, my good man, I don't…" and the man was rushing at him, head bent down.

It was glorious, Jacques felt as if he had been given an injection of the opposite of morphine (yes, he would say later, of course, it was adrenaline). When the colonial police asked, "Was it your intention to cause the man bodily harm?"

"Yes."

This will be neither the first nor the last time that Jacques' scrupulousness about language will cause difficulties.

"It was your intention to cause the man bodily harm? Permanent bodily harm?"

"No, not permanent bodily harm. I only intended to knock him over. I should let you know," Jacques will say, holding up the index finger of his right hand as if he were in the classroom, "I have no practical experience in matters of this nature—gauging the force of a blow, as I had never before been in a physical altercation."

A glance will pass between the two officers—they would have been less surprised if he had told them he remained a virgin. Still, this will be a point in his favor.

The nervous smile that had been playing around the corners of Jacques' lips now burst into a grin of pride: the man had crumpled down—there had been a grunt, and then a low crack—and it was now the other man's turn to lie dazed in the dirt of the road. Jacques glanced at the crowd gathered around him, expecting to find smiles of complicity and encouragement, but only saw wariness.

The man rose, not to his feet, only to a sitting position.

He leaned over and vomited, and what came out of him was altogether too dark and smelled of iron as well as bile.

He cradled his head in his right hand. His breathing was labored and noisy, rasping in-out, as if a long-unused pair of bellows was being pressed in to service. In-out, in-out.

And then silence. His body slumped forward.

In the offices of the colonial police, Jacques asked more than once, "You are quite certain the man is dead?" and his difficulty in comprehending this was yet another point in his favor.

He loosened his tie, and asked the interrogating officers if the overhead fan might be turned on, a glass of water brought to him. The junior officer laid the inside of his wrist on Jacques' forehead, the gesture almost maternal, and said, "You're running quite a fever." The senior officer indicated that this fact should be noted in the record.

"It's nothing," Jacques said. "I run them from time to time."

"Malaria?" the superior asked.

"A touch."

"Have you seen a physician?"

"No." Jacques ran the glass of water across his forehead. "My native friends have given me some herbs which I find quite efficacious...Surely, this isn't relevant to the subject at hand."

In the end, it was all totaled up: the character of the deceased, Jacques' malarial fever, the native beer, his passion for the woman with the unpronounceable name, his alienation from the European community, the fact that there had been little malice involved, and that the man, after all, had struck his head on a rock: and the matter—the police officers insisted on using such words, "matter," "incident," "the unfortunate event"—was resolved by having Jacques sent home.

Bomfomtabellilaba waited for him outside of the police station.

She spat in his face as he was led past.

The wad of spit slithered down his cheek.

The native policeman to whom Jacques was handcuffed wiped the saliva from his face with the tail of his own shirt, having no handkerchief.

Dysentery had ushered him out of his whiteness. Malaria led him back into it. At his mother's house—how queer it felt to be lying in his boyhood bed—the malaria, which had been held at bay by the local remedies, ricocheted him in and out of fever. One day he was lying on his bed, bathed in sweat, and saw that the pattern of the wallpaper had formed itself into words, written in the alphabet of a language he had never before encountered—neither Greek nor Cyrillic nor Arabic—and which he was nonetheless able to decode. The writing on the wall offered prophecies: *You will recover. You will breath more easily. Your fever will depart.* The nature of this language was such that one could not speak as an individual nor to an individual. The writing could perhaps be more accurately translated as: *We will recover. We will breath more easily. Our fever will depart.* Or as: *The whole world will recover. The whole world will breath more easily. The whole world's fever will depart.*

When the disease had him in its grasp, it seemed quite possible that he was both lying on the soft bed in Paris and, at the same time, on the mat on the floor in his home on the edge of the native quarter in Antananarivo. It seemed quite logical that he was both himself, Jacques Melville, a man of European extraction who had been born in Nîmes, France. And that he was also Jacob Ahmed, a man of mixed parentage, who had been born on an unknown date in Madagascar, and whose spirit, following his death on June 17, 1919, had taken up residence in an out of the way corner of said Jacques Melville's body—perhaps in his spleen or his vermiform appendix.

At other times, Jacques was sure there was an alternate reality where, when he slugged Ahmed Jacobs, the punch landed just a centimeter to the left, and, although reeling from the punch, Ahmed Jacobs either did not fall, or fell so that his head did not strike the rock. Ahmed Jacobs had pulled Jacques to the ground, and the two of them had grappled there, almost like lovers, until they, both drunk, almost laughing, came to a stuporous agreement to call it a draw.

The next day, the fever, done with him, he would be flung back into the world, sober, cold. He would know that he was in Paris. A single soul resided in his body. A few days later, he would find himself in the throes of fever again—European logic now seemed hopelessly naive to him.

It was Sala who took matters in hand, saw that he was visited by an expert in tropical medicine, Sala who tracked his fevers, and procured the latest medicines for him. Gradually, her potions and ministrations restored him to health: the world became singular, orderly. She took it for granted he wanted to be well—how could it be otherwise?—just as she assumed that the two of them would marry. She said, "Do you think your mother will let us take the wardrobe with us to our new place?" and "I think a honeymoon would be an extravagance. Later, when I've finished my residency and you've defended your thesis, we could go on a trip to Italy. Or would you rather the Dalmatian Coast?"

Patience

Patience: the English name for the card game the Americans and French call solitaire.

A game for invalids; for lonely women on rainy afternoons; for mothers of febrile infants who, like their offspring, got half an hour of sleep the night before: this last category the one into which Simone fell.

Although the words "game" and "play" suggest lightheartedness, this was more like the despondent self-grooming of a caged monkey.

Simone slipped the queen atop the king, the knave atop the queen.

She studied the eye of the jack in profile, ran her finger along his cascading locks.

She yawned, stretched, rose, padded into the kitchen of the cold water flat in Paris to which she had decamped with the children, regarded the morning's dishes piled in the sink, filled the kettle with water to heat so she could wash them, lit the stove, and sat down at the oil-cloth covered table and smoked a cigarette. The kitchen, windowless, at the back of the flat, had a sour smell—if her mother had been here, she would have emptied out the cupboards and scrubbed them down, her rag-wrapped finger jutting into greasy corners, her elbow moving back and forth like a piston. If she had been in Istanbul, her servants would have chased not dust but the possibility of dust.

The kettle shrieked. Simone switched off the flame, stared into the mucky water in which the dishes soaked, decided she needed some air.

She looked in at Odette, who after her wild night was sleeping soundly, Marcel playing with his blocks in the corner. Simone slipped out of the flat.

That's just it, you didn't think at all, did you?

On receipt of her letter Luc had set aside his pressing obligations and returned to France, at times imagining himself forgiving his wife, at other times casting her off. She opened the door of her mother's house and met his gaze, not with guilt, not with abjection, not even with defiance, but with cold steadiness: he was helpless. He did allow her to keep the children—he felt repelled by them, creatures half her substance. Still, he did not want to be accused of being unjust, and provided an allowance, meagre but sufficient for their care.

Prior to Luc's arrival, Simone had received a letter, not from Jacques, but from Joë.

Jacques has written to me of the events that transpired after your departure from my home. I know you'll understand that there's nothing dishonorable in the two of us speaking about you. We have the honor of poets, for whom honesty is supreme. You mustn't let his nonchalance frighten you. He loves you, although his pride may prevent him from saying so.

On the strength of Joë's letter, and with the financial wherewithal provided by Luc, Simone packed a trunk, tucked her children against her, and boarded a train for Paris.

She was unprepared for the business of finding a flat—even checking into the accommodations near the train station baffled her. When the clerk behind the desk asked her, "For how many nights?" she blushed and said, "I don't know. Does that present, is that a—difficulty?"

"No, madame." The clerk smirked.

She rented the first flat she was shown—she wanted to get away from that clerk—and sent a *petit bleu* to Jacques' office via the pneumatic post telling him she was now living in Paris and giving her address. Within the hour, she was listening for the sound of his footsteps on the stairs.

He did not come, not within the hour, not within the day, not within the week. Not within the fortnight.

For the first day she had been relatively calm—although quite unable to eat. She drank coffee in the morning and wine in the afternoon and evening. She concocted stories as she gazed out the window of her flat: Sala had found the letter and had attempted suicide, swallowed one of those poisons for which there was no antidote (she was, after all, a doctor), was now lying on her deathbed. Of course Jacques must stay beside her. The *bleu* had been delivered to the wrong address. Jacques had been called away on business.

By the third day when there was no response from him she was frantic. She paid a neighbor to sit with the children and, pulling her map of Paris from her handbag, got directions from the concierge. She blushed and stammered as she outlined the route in pencil—she had never before taken the Metro, she was forced to confess—how did one—that is, go about it?

"Ah, the sweet young lasses from the countryside," he said, and laid a lubricious hand on her shoulder.

She had planned to present herself to Jacques, but then, standing opposite the building which held the office of the publisher by whom he was employed, she lost her nerve. She was like the actress in the wings, sick with stage fright, but with this difference: the actress knows she will step on stage and her anxiety will vanish. She will say her lines and her fellow actors will say theirs. Who knew what might happen if she climbed those stairs and knocked on the door? A smile might break forth across Jacques' gloomy countenance, or he might be shocked to see her, might take her elbow and propel her out of his office, down the stairs, grasping her arm so firmly he would leave a series of faint bruises.

She took refuge in a café across the street, nursing a coffee, staring out the window, her gaze fixed on the office door. The third time the proprietor asked, "Will Madame require anything else?" adding, "I have some *tarte tartin* fresh from the oven," she took the hint.

The smell—caramel, warm apples—was intoxicating. For the past three days she had eaten nothing save a bit of biscuit from Marcel's plate. Just as she took a bite, she saw Jacques emerge from the opposite doorway, was seized by a fear that he would see her and shifted her chair so suddenly that it scraped against the floor, turning her back to the window. She spat the lump of food into her napkin.

Her neighbor was fuming at the door of her apartment, Odette wailing in the background. "You said just a few errands."

"I'm sorry, I'm sorry, I— I—"

"Well, those few francs you gave me hardly cover the trouble you've put me to, my own children will be home soon…and by now the greengrocer is probably out of…" Simone fiddled with her purse, pressed one note and then another into the woman's outstretched hand—really, the amount she gave was quite generous—but the woman only sighed and rolled her eyes before stalking off.

"The lady slapped me," Marcel said.

"I'm sure you deserved it." Then: "Where? Show me...Ah, you haven't even got a bruise. Don't be a crybaby."

She sent another *bleu* to Jacques, trying to convince herself that the other one must have gone astray.

After four days, a letter arrived from him, sent by regular post:

I have received both of your communications. You must understand that I have a multitude of obligations—not just to my family—you will recall that a second son has been born—but to my colleagues and to the publisher who has contracted for my book. While I don't deny my—and here, a blot on the paper showed that his pen had paused—*desire for you, my fondness, even my need, I must also say that I suspect you are once again forcing my hand—or attempting to do so—by taking rash action. Perhaps I am wrong about this, perhaps you moved to Paris for reasons that have nothing to do with me. I will make every attempt to call on you soon. I cannot, however, give any definite time frame.* He closed, *With tenderness,* and his initial.

Two opposing armies battled in her head for the next days. One side hurled the words, *you must understand that I have a multitude of obligations, I cannot give any definite time frame, my family, force my hand* at the other side of her mind, which held up, against the bombardment *my fondness, my desire, my need, with tenderness*—puny shields indeed.

Her hunger did not abate. She held onto it as an Alpinist on a sheer rock face clings to his rope. How odd that taking in nothing solid, her body continued to pass waste. Each day she regarded her measly deposit in the toilet and thought, Surely, this is the last of it; tomorrow I shall produce nothing, and be clean at last.

That self she had been at twelve, in the glorious and harrowing period after her father's death, had been reborn: the girl who mortified her flesh, and prided herself on that mortification, then, repenting of the sin of pride, punished herself further.

And then one night, a rainy night, at last, at last, the knock on the door came. It was nine o'clock, the children were sound asleep, she had always known he would come! There he was at the doorway, lounging, his hip thrust to the left, almost feminine, wearing a beret, chewing on a toothpick, so beautiful she did not want to rush into his arms, because then she would no longer have his image before her. But she was rushing into his arms, she was laughing, saying, "I knew you would come, I knew you would," taking in his odor of wet wool and tobacco, his masculine smell, laughing, crying.

"Come now, come, come," he said, slapping her backside, like a man breaking a horse. "There, there, good girl, yes." He calmed her by holding her so tightly she could not move.

"I love you. I love you." She knew it was the wrong thing to say, but she could not stop herself.

"Let's not be foolish," he said, his voice filled with fondness. Then: "Offer me a glass of wine. I'm a bit winded from that climb."

"Yes, of course." She turned away from him, her eyes filling with tears, moving into the kitchen.

He settled himself on the couch and glanced around the spare flat, taking in the sticks of furniture, the worn floorboards, the carpet tacked to the floor. It pleased him she had come to this out of love for him.

Since she shared the only bedroom with the children, they made love on the settee: her neck would be stiff the next day from the awkward angle at which it had been pressed. "Ah," he said at one point, as his ankles banged against the sofa's arm, "we shall have to get you into better lodgings," and it seemed he had pledged himself to her.

Afterward, he pulled his wool coat over her. It was then she noticed Marcel regarding her with wary eyes from the doorway.

"Ah, Marcel," Jacques said. "My little man."

"Go back to bed," Simone ordered.

"I'm scared."

"Go back to bed!"

Marcel whimpered and retreated.

She leaned over and reached for her clothing from the floor.

"Where are you going?"

"To lock his door."

"Leave it be."

"Ah, no," Simone said.

"In Madagascar," Jacques said, "the children are exposed to the sexual act in the most natural way. I was shocked at first, but now our European habits seem unnatural to me."

They made love again, dozed, and then, after bestowing kisses on her forehead, her cheeks, the backs of her hands, he said: "I must get home or there will be a terrible row. And I simply haven't the stomach for it. But I will be back. Sooner, this time. I promise. No tears, please."

She stood in the doorway, and listened to the sound of his feet retreating down the stairs, listened to the front door close, went and stood at the window and peered from behind the curtain, watching him until he disappeared into the night.

Jacques did not come again the next night, nor the night after that, but on the third night he did. Again, at nine o'clock, unannounced. She had been determined to return his hauteur with her own, but found she was quite unable to keep herself from smiling.

"Ah," he said, stroking her hair after their lovemaking, "you are like an intoxicating drug, partaking of you only increases my desire."

She was lying with her head on his chest, he could feel her smile against his skin. Yes, he had her right where he wanted her. His attitude towards women wasn't one of which he was particularly proud, but nonetheless, there it was. He could as little wish it away as he could wish himself ten centimeters taller or fair-haired.

He developed the pattern of coming to see her two, three or even four times during the week. Once, when he was called out of town unexpectedly, he left a note telling her that with the concierge.

Pope

Jacques had begun to realize that he was not going to make his mark as a writer. He certainly could not bear to be one of those men who plugged away, receiving lukewarm reviews and dwindling audiences. Instead, he began to plot his course as the future pope of French literature—as certain Italian monsignors, at about his age, start to plan their trajectory into a plum bishopric from which they hope to jostle their way to the rank of cardinal and from there to scale the very peak of the mountain. Jacques busied himself with learning secrets, doing favors, getting others in his debt, making himself a confidante. He smothered ruffled feathers, and ruffled smooth ones. On some occasions he more or less excommunicated writers, writing scathing reviews—*I cast thee into the outer darkness*—at other times, he seized hold of someone and elevated him into the literary firmament.

Kneel

As a girl, Simone had been given lessons on the mandolin so that she might sing, in her voice made only more charming by being slightly off-key, troubadour ballads featuring weeping lovers kneeling next to bedsides and biers.

Simone was the one who ended up kneeling on the kitchen floor in her Paris flat, cleaning it with gray water and a brush. She hunched over the scrub board in the utility sink as she scoured Marcel's shirts, Odette's diapers, knuckles reddening, hands reeking of laundry soap and bleach.

All those years she was hungry. (She made sure the children never were.) At first Jacques liked the way the extra flesh disappeared from her bones, so she didn't look like a solid *maman*, but later she got to be too much of a waif.

"My God," Jacques said, looking down at her after they'd made love one day. "You're a skeleton. I feel like a necrophiliac."

She said nothing.

"Your children are plump enough."

"I don't want them to suffer for the decisions I've made."

"Ah, you and your suffering. I might as well stay with Sala, if I'm to be endlessly reproached—"

"Whatever I say troubles you. Perhaps I should just take a vow of silence, like the sisters of the discalced Carmelites..."

"You would still be able to give me those looks of yours..."

"Go, then. Go! If I am such a source of torment and trial to you."

Decades later, Simone will mistake Odette for Elise.

"I'm your daughter, not your sister."

"Oh, no, I don't have a daughter!"

That's perfect, Odette will think: you never really knew I was there.

Never hungry, true enough. But chicken only once a month, sad vegetables the greengrocer gave Simone out of pity. Sometimes, after an evening out, she'd produce filched puff pastries filled with scrambled quail eggs, crushed petit fours, wrapped up in odd bits of paper from her purse. Then it would be back to hard ends of cheese and lentil soup and the very occasional visit from a once-hungry painter who, having just sold a painting to a rich American, raced up the stairs with flowers and charcuterie and chocolate.

Jacques took her to gatherings, introducing her simply as "Simone Clermont." She would arrive so hungry that her stomach cramped and her head ached, and would endeavor to eat delicately, as if with disinterest. Glistening red and black bubbles of caviar were spread out on a groaning board alongside whimsically shaped canapés which might have been miniatures of the hats the women were wearing that season, a sprig of rosemary substituting for a feather. The artists wore workingmen's berets, striped fisherman's shirts they'd picked up at second-hand stores, still stinking of the sea, and hailed the tuxedoed waiters, "Over here, Comrade."

The Dadaists chanted their poems in cafés and at parties: "A squirrel had come to press its white belly against my heart...Musicians, smash your instruments…The white wine of remembrance ricochets off the walls…"

Simone and Jacques met some friends at a café. They were all going to the home of an American heiress—who introduced herself to everyone as simply "Sally," as if she had no surname—whose fortune had been made in a chain of markets—no, "supermarkets"— the word said in English with an attempt at an American accent. *What a word*! They said it over and over again, sprawled around the café table: "Supermarket," "Supermarket," the chain named of all things, Piggly Wiggly, although one wasn't to say the words Piggly Wiggly to the heiress, who was sensitive not so much about her origins—she proudly told the story of her grandmother's twelve children in a shack in an Appalachian hollow—as about the origins of her cash. After a few drinks *chez Sally* they couldn't resist, and someone mouthed, when their hostess's back was turned, "Piggly Wiggly," eliciting giggles which grew more uncontrollable the more they were suppressed.

A new group declared: "Smash the word!" and the cover of their manifesto—printed in black and red on cheap newsprint—showed a fist plunging into a mountain of type, the letters careening off. These bastard sons of old-hat Dada broke language from the prison house of meaning, allowing sounds to wander free.

Fever

Sometimes she longed to be ill. She longed for fever to rocket her out of the everyday, to lie in bed, to have glasses of cold water with slices of lemon brought to her, for a cold compress to be laid on her hot forehead, for the way that pain makes us know our bodies anew, as a lover's caress does.

When she did fall ill, she wanted nothing more than for her torment to end. She called upon the God in whom she no longer believed to take it from her. And who was there to lay a soothing hand upon her? To offer a bucket for her to retch in, to bear away this disgusting product without complaint?

No one.

Not Odette, not Marcel, certainly not Jacques. She knew how to seduce those of her own sex, but not how to befriend them.

And yet, when illness departed, she felt pride in what she had endured: *The thermometer read 39.5. I was so dizzy I found myself clinging to the bed, so as not to fall. I lost two kilos in as many days.*

On the odd afternoon Simone would go to the neighborhood café, where, over a long-nursed glass of wine, she'd look at the illustrated papers, hanging on wooden sticks alongside the more proper newspapers. The women of France were to look like Tartar princesses, in a profusion of tassels, sleeves that would drag in one's soup—much black, red, and gold. The silk dresses she had bought when first wed to Luc, distinctly fashionable then, were distinctly unfashionable now. She sat in the café, longing to see Jacques—*would he come by that evening?*—and longing for a gold-embroidered jacket with kimono sleeves.

Thud

The clock in a nearby church bonged out the hour in a single dull thud. "Ah, it's one already," Jacques groaned. "I've missed the last Metro."

He pressed his hands against his knees to sit upright, sighed, the air of a man about to mount the gallows.

"How—is it—a long walk?"

"A kilometer and a half perhaps. It's more the inevitable row."

In the half light, he saw her smile. "My Simone," he cupped her cheek in his hand, "you are so lacking in duplicity. In answer to that question that you don't dare ask—yes, she is aware of you. She doesn't know your name, but she is quite aware of the fact that I—that my attention is wandering, and not flitting about, as it sometimes has in the past, but has fixed itself quite firmly on an object."

Has fixed itself quite firmly on an object.

Later, Simone would become the wife, the one who made scenes, hurled accusations, who sniffed his clothing for the scent of other women. The one about whom he complained. The one his mistresses spoke of with an air of pity. *Poor woman. I know she suffers, and that I bear some guilt for her suffering.*

"Have you a cigarette?" Then: "I will leave as soon as I finish smoking this." Simone focused on the glowing tip.

"And yet, she, despite knowing that, she…"

"She is quite certain she knows what is best for me. That if I were to break our marital vow—although she wouldn't use that word, it reeks of religiosity, she'd say 'commitment' to her, to our children—I'd later come to regret it."

Sniff

One evening Jacques arrived, long past his usual hour—nearly eleven. In fact, Simone had given up on him, shed her clothing and was dozing in the bedroom, coming awake when she heard his key in the lock. His visits were random, she never knew when to expect him. (Actually, it might be more honest to say that she always expected him, was frequently disappointed.)

She pulled her wrapper around her—it had been part of her trousseau. The ivory satin had grown dingy, the blue sash worn. Jacques was glassy-eyed, attempting unsuccessfully to suppress the sort of grin a schoolboy exhibits when he has pulled one over on the teacher. Perhaps wanting to keep her from seeing this sly grin, he pulled her close and whispered, "I've woken you," stroking her hair.

"It's all right, I was merely…" Beneath his usual smell of tobacco and red wine—at the moment more pronounced—she smelled perfume.

"Where have you been?" She had tried to make the question sound light-hearted, but hadn't quite pulled it off. "I only meant—it's so late."

"At a café. One thing led to another, the conversation went on and on—you know how it is."

She drew in a quick, short breath.

He broke off the embrace. "Ah, don't sniff me! You are becoming like Sala."

It was a refrain that would be sung throughout their long engagement, their subsequent marriage. —*You are becoming like Sala.* —*Don't be like Sala.* —*You remind me of Sala.* It was the most skillful of his sallies, causing Simone to flush and incline her head downwards, as she did now, muttering: "I wasn't sniffing you. I merely—"

"'I merely,'" Jacques mocked. After a moment had passed and her eyes were brimming with tears, he softened his tone, chucked her under the chin. "You mustn't act like a schoolgirl, a reader of cheap romances. Come now, you aren't in the provinces anymore, you aren't a peasant—"

"I was never a peasant!"

"I didn't say you were. In fact, I said just the opposite. I said, 'You aren't a peasant.' And I was about to add—you are, well, at any rate, you are becoming a sophisticated Parisienne."

Truly, if Simone had been a sophisticated Parisienne she would have seized the reins of the conversation—which Jacques had so skillfully taken from her—and pointed out that he had changed the subject from his faults to hers.

Later, when they summered at La Vigie, a fortress on an island near Marseilles, Claudine, the mistress of the ragtag menage, would say to her, "Ah, men!" Then: "And you've got a particularly wily one."

"What's sauce for the goose is sauce for the gander," she told herself. It was a phrase she could imagine her own mother uttering, with her arms folded solidly across her chest. And so, a few weeks after the night when she'd been accused of trying to ferret out his sins with her nose, she made sure that he observed her flirting quite openly with one of his colleagues at a gathering. She had imagined that Jacques would respond to this first with jealous rage, then with the realization of her errors of his own ways, and, filled with contrition, would swear off his own adventures. (Jacques had been right when he said that many of her notions about affairs of the heart had been formed by the novels she'd borrowed as a girl from the lending library in Juan-les-Pins.) Her playing the coquette did not, however, bring him to heel.

Just the opposite. When they were alone in her flat, he said, "Guillaume was quite taken with you." She shrugged and made a moue.

He said nothing more for a few minutes. But when he was returning from the lavatory, he came up behind her in the kitchen, wrapping his arms around her, locking his hands on her breasts. "Would you like Guillaume to grab you like this?" His erection pressed into her backside.

"Ah, Jacques, no!"

"Imagine these aren't my hands, imagine they're his hands."

"Stop it!" Her indignation was real.

"Don't be a prude It's just a harmless bit of fun."

She came to understand that Jacques needed what he called his flirtations—which often were, indeed, just that—nothing more than winks, charming phrases, eyes meeting across a crowded room, whispered enticements—and which sometimes were far more than that. She also came to understand that what would threaten her and Jacques' bond would not be these dalliances, which Jacques took as his due—after all, faithfulness was a quality one expected in a dog, not a man—but her keeping him on, as it were, a short leash. It was Sala's very fidelity that had driven him away.

Her infidelities were proof of her faithfulness to him.

Stuff

Despite the precautions they took, she found herself pregnant.

The abortionist was a physician, also a (not very good) poet. Her abortion was paid for by a few words of written praise from Jacques, although the bargain was not stated quite that baldly. She was given a mild sedative. The nurse clapped her hand over Simone's mouth so that no one in the adjoining office could hear her screams.

"Come, come, Madame. You've given birth to two children. This is nothing in comparison." Simone writhed. The doctor flung the curette down on the table in exasperation. Bits of blood and tissue flew away from it, dotting his glasses, his cheek. The nurse, still keeping one hand over her mouth, leaned forward and dabbed at his face with a cloth. *Was this the stuff meant to be their child*? She sobbed.

"Another injection of veronal," the doctor said.

Afterwards, the nurse shouted through the fog to her, "Do you have a friend I can telephone? A friend who can come and fetch you?"

Simone staggered into the toilet. The thick pad that had been placed between her legs was soaked with deep red blood.

There was no place in that tiny office for her to rest. The exam room, where the operation had been performed, was needed for other patients. In the waiting room itself, she would be an alarming presence. She was shuttled, for a while, into the doctor's office, where she curled up on the floor, beneath his diplomas written in Latin on stiff parchment; knees to chest, arms wrapped around knees.

Something had to be done.

Through the fog of pain, she heard the words, "...I really do not mean to insist, but it is quite necessary that I speak with him...I believe if you let him know I am on the telephone, he will take the call..."

It was March, the 13th. Jacques must have walked hatless from his office, a couple of kilometers away, for when he arrived his cheeks were ruddy and his hair disheveled. He seemed put out: at being interrupted in the course of his day. At the smell she was giving off. He went outside to hail a taxi. Then he on one side, the nurse on the other, propelling her out of the office. Jacques stuffed an envelope filled with tablets into the pocket of his overcoat.

Later, it occurred to her that the doctor had never performed this particular operation before, had not imagined the aftermath.

In the taxi, she huddled against Jacques. He draped a reluctant arm around her shoulder.

"What time is it?"

He moved his arm to look at his watch—half past two—and did not return it.

She moaned. "The children."

Madame was feeling poorly, Jacques told the concierge. No, no, nothing serious. Stomach flu. But perhaps she'd be kind enough to meet the children at school.

"My children got themselves home from school," she grumbled. Simone had never seen evidence of offspring. She suspected these children—who had never been rude, shouted in the hallways, or needed to be met at the close of the school day—were fictive, trundled out to stand in contrast to her own children, ragamuffin son and daughter of a flighty mother, a mother who was known to spend the evenings reading or rambling around the city when other women were scouring pots or offering prayers to their patron saints.

"It would be a great kindness," Jacques said, giving her one of his most charming smiles. He could flirt with any woman—a flat-footed concierge in her sixties, while the woman who'd just aborted his child clung to his arm.

It wasn't the usual clatter of footsteps on the stairs, the medley of laughter and stories and pleas for warm milk and bread with butter and sugar, but tiptoes, exaggerated whispers. Their mama, their eternal, unchangeable mama was ill. It was as if the marble figure of Charlemagne in front of Notre Dame, after all these centuries of sitting astride his steed, his back ramrod straight, his scepter in his hand, had gotten down off his horse and was found bent over, his crown tucked under his arm, his features drawn in pain.

Walking

In the afternoons, while the children napped, and on evenings when she was sure Jacques would not come, Simone left the flat and walked.

On these walks of hers, passing men would look her over quite frankly. At times, women would, too. Sometimes the women were carefree gamins, charming in cast-offs. Others wore their hats at an angle, their faces in semi-shadow. A woman on the Metro smiled coyly and leaned close to her. Simone smelled garlic and yeast on her breath, saw the faint black mustache above her lip.

On these walks, she never saw Gertrude Stein lumbering down the rue du Fleuris, although on more than one occasion she did see her companion, the ferret-like Miss Toklas, coming back from the market with an aubergine or a bouquet of dandelion greens. The Americans had come. The French franc had been weighed on the scale and found wanting. The word had gone out: you can live in Paris for a song. *Over there. Over there...The Yanks are coming*. Phalanxes of Americans jostled Parisians on the pavement. Some were poets, some were not. They spoke of faraway places: Baltimore, Milwaukee, Santa Monica. "Back home, in Wichita. Wichita, Kansas..."

Simone rather liked them.

Later, after another war, another visitation of Americans will descend. The GIs will want ice water, will want to fuck the French mademoiselles, will guzzle fine wine and sing, *Oh, they don't wear pants / in the Southern part of France / and the dance they do / it is called the hootchy-koo.* When they finish a meal they will pick their teeth with little bits of wood.

She stopped before the Morris column on the corner to gaze at the posters pasted there: A concert of Erik Satie's Pictures at an Exhibition would be held...Pernod...Michelin tires...Drink Dineset...Buy a lottery ticket...Dubonnet...SNCF...Exhibit of Braque's latest paintings at... LaForest foie gras...

It was 1924. Lenin was dead. Russia would now be ruled by a troika. She had the image of a government on the move, three men in a sledge wearing felted boots, wrapped in great coats, swathed in mufflers, fur hats with ear flaps, pulled by three horses, rushing through Moscow and Leningrad, outracing the snarling wolves of counter-revolution, flinging out decrees, manifestos, pronouncements, barreling across the Russian steppes, on to Siberia, to the Asiatic republics, where stunned peasants herding their flocks of yaks would see the cloud of dust raised on the horizon, and watch the sleigh as it raced on, the wind of history breathing down its neck.

Posters for the eighth Olympiad, to be held in Paris, showed ranks of muscled men, like statues of Greek gods. The thighs of these men were swathed in drapery and palm fronds and their bodies showed none of the troublesome business of moles and body hair. Their arms were raised high in identical open-palmed gestures, which did not yet make Simone think of the *Hitlergruss*.

Slippers

Jacques was hired to write pornography for an anonymous private collector—its central character always a man with a well-trimmed mustache. Actually, Simone did the bulk of the writing, after the two of them had dreamed up the scenarios—"Two women with one man. One of them a Negress." "A bordello?" "We did a bordello last time. I think this time, something different. A port city, Genoa or Marseille. It's foggy. A somewhat seedy section of town—" "Our friend with the well-trimmed mustache goes to an antique store there." "A very erudite shop owner, a bit of a character—" "Perhaps even a grotesque. A hunchback or some such thing—" "But don't," Jacques added, "go on for too long about the antique store. Last time apparently our—employer—found the whole business took a bit long to get started—"

Simone shared Jacques' contempt for this man so wealthy he not only paid others to cook his food, clean up after him, set out his clothing, but even to fantasize for him—and yet she was thrilled at being able to help Jacques in this way.

Jacques found her an apartment with two bedrooms in a quite fantastical building in the rue Campagne-Premiere which had been cobbled together from building materials from the Turkish pavilion at the 1900 Exhibition Universelle, a building filled with painters and sculptors, their mistresses and models, aspiring mistresses and models, and a few members from the bohemian wing of the Communist Party. The leftover tile work, blocks, and arches—and a spare minaret—one also stood on the roof of the building—were stored in the basement. The builder had given little thought to petty matters like ventilation and insulation. When her next door neighbors had sex, she and Jacques could overhear every moan and gasp. He would sometimes hold an imaginary baton in his hand, pretending to conduct their tryst as if it were a symphony.

Although the children had a bedroom, she woke most mornings to find Odette curled in bed next to her, Marcel lying across the bottom of the bed, wrapped in his quilt.

An Algerian man slept on a cot in the basement and endlessly patched the house back together. He seemed to be able to speak only two words of French, *oui* and *non*.

Jacques began, on rare occasions, to spend the night. "This floor is so cold in the morning!" If she had been another sort of woman, she would have saved carefully from her housekeeping money, a few centimes here, a franc there, and when she'd accumulated enough, bought him a pair of sheepskin slippers. Having just received her monthly check from Luc, she went to a shop on the St. Germain des Pres, the sort of place where the shopkeeper smiled at you as if you were a long-lost friend. The proprietor showed her the care with which the tiny stitching had been done; told her that not only were they handmade by his wife, but the sheep were raised by his cousin.

He guided her hand inside.

His hand remained wrapped around hers.

She understood she was being propositioned, that she would be paid in a pair of lambskin slippers.

She overheard a chair creak. His wife, no doubt, in the back room, stitching slippers, her hands soft from the lanolin in the wool, her fingertips calloused from the endless pushing of the needle.

She thought of the lambs, parted from their mothers, slaughtered.

She straightened her back, showing a chilly outrage at the proposition, which she had, for a few moments, considered.

"How much?" she asked. He quoted her a price that was roughly half of what she had to live on for the month.

She bought the slippers, and also a shaving kit for Jacques. She stopped herself from buying him a pair of pajamas.

In order to pay the rent, she wrote to her mother, telling her the children had been ill, she hadn't said anything because she hadn't wanted to worry her, they were better now but the doctor was threatening about his bill. She couldn't ask Luc, she was afraid he'd upbraid her for her lack of care of them, might even try to wrest custody away from her.

In the morning, when Jacques spent the night, he would rise and slip his feet into those beautiful slippers, stepping over the sleeping Odette, curled up outside the locked bedroom door, and pad over to the kitchen table. The sound of him setting his briefcase on it. Of its latch opening. A shuffle of papers.

Sometimes, she would rise and tiptoe in her bare feet across the floor, lay her head in his lap like a faithful dog, and allow him to stroke her hair with his left hand while his right hand raced across the page.

Koroi

They traveled once to Greece. The Cycladic idols, row after row of ancient female funerary figures, with their blank faces and their arms hugging their chests, keeping themselves warm against the coldness of eternity, were shunted off in dark rooms at the back of the museum. They moved her more than the gods and goddesses of the Classical period with their muscled perfection.

Parachute

Jacques teased Marcel, "If you're this grouchy as a boy of seven, what will you be like when you're an old man?" and tried to tousle his hair, but Marcel ducked away from him.

How had Marcel gotten to be seven already?

Marcel dropped his toy parachutist from the roof, leaning out over the blocks of plaster Moorish filigree and then raced down the stairs, attempting to catch the toy before it wafted to earth.

That evening, a member of the demimondaine accosted Jacques on the stairs. *—That kid of yours makes a frightful racket, three o'clock this afternoon, woke me up. —Excuse me, he's not my son*. Jacques made a formal half-bow and withdrew. He'd have made a good general: he well understood the notion of strategic non-engagement.

Jacques' personality was sometimes described as *alambiqué*, a word derived from a process of distilling wine into brandy, involving multiple and precise heatings and coolings. (The word came from the Greek, via the Arabs, and thus carried within it a memory of the time when Europe was the barbarian periphery, in danger of being civilized by those pulsing upwards from Grenada, Sardinia, Provence, the Balkans, while Jacques' Gallic forbearers, living in mud huts, wearing stinky furs, grunted around their campfires.) The word is impossible to translate adequately into English, although the words "over-subtle" and "cunning" come closest. It is not a compliment.

Galoshes

Jacques came from his father's funeral, smelling of rain and damp earth and Sala's perfume. (The scent of Sala's perfume was new—she wasn't the perfume-wearing type: she told Jacques she had been given a bottle of *Vers le Jour* by the family of a grateful patient but he rather suspected she'd bought it in an attempt not so much to entice him as to mark him as her property.) He came through the door and put his arms around

Simone, but it wasn't really an embrace, he was propping his body up against hers. A few times before, when he'd had too much to drink, he'd treated her as an inebriate might a lamp post.

"You can't imagine how I longed for you there at the cemetery. How I hated Sala for not being you."

She envied Sala for the things she had of Jacques: his galoshes, caked with mud on a rainy day, which she must clean with some improvised implement—perhaps using the point of a pencil to remove the hardened muck that had stuck in the whorled soles. She envied her the socks and underwear and shirts worn next to his skin. She wanted to grumble as she picked up the clothing he had so casually discarded on the floor of the bedroom. She wanted to open the laundry hamper and be hit by his smell coming up from it. Simone wanted to be exasperated with him, to be sick of him, to be sullen towards him. She envied Sala the hatreds, petty and not-so-petty, of a long marriage.

She longed for a child with him. The condom disturbed her not only in the way it was not quite him going into her, but also because it was emblematic of his not loving her totally, wildly, completely, with full abandon: he was not willing to give up everything for her. Sometimes she could persuade him not to use a rubber but to pull out of her before he came—his flesh against her flesh, nothing between them, and then the gush of warm fluid, dribbling down her belly.

Fortress

In the spring of 1929, Jacques told her some friends of his were planning to spend July and August in an old fort on an island off Marseille—La Vigie the fortress was called. It had been used in medieval times as a lookout for approaching marauders. Sala's commitments at the hospital—summer was the worst time for infectious disease among the Parisian poor—meant that she would stay in town.

"I'm afraid the place is pretty rough and tumble," Jacques said.

"Are you asking me to join you?"

"If you like."

"And the children?"

"They'll be happy—the woods and the fresh air. The place is owned by—have you heard of him?—a poet named Claude Maine."

Simone always dreaded such questions.

"He's scarcely known. And justly so. Like Agamemnon, he has a sobriquet—not 'leader of men,' but 'the very bad and very sickly poet.' He has some respiratory complaint—not TB, don't worry—that his analyst—a Jungian—has convinced him will be cured by—ah, I don't know, dreaming, and then writing endless wretched poetry about his dreams. There's some family money—I think on his wife's side—she's there also, although each has a lover—but not to worry, it's all quite amiable. We'll be dining *en famille,* and there's adequate help—the idea is for it to be more or less an artist and writer's retreat."

She would not just make love with Jacques every night, but sleep next to him, night after night, waking with him. She would live in the bohemian paradise she had dreamed of: with a married couple who lived side by side, each with their own lover.

An open-roofed car met them at the train station, mud caking its wheels and splattering its fenders. "Simone, I've heard your praises sung, not just by Jacques but by Joë, but you see, even the greatest poet of our age doesn't do you justice—"

"This is Claude," Jacques interjected.

"May I?" Claude asked, leaning forward to kiss her hand. He kissed Odette's hand as well.

"Where are we going?" Marcel whined, after fifteen minutes on the road.

"To a fort," Jacques said. "It has slits in the walls from which bowmen shot their arrows."

"Will I have a crossbow and arrow?" Marcel asked, but no one answered him.

After a little while, Marcel declared: "I'm going to upchuck." Claude pulled the car over.

"Better now?" his mother asked.

"I don't like it here."

"You don't like it anywhere," Jacques said. "Get back in and stop bellyaching."

"This," Claude declared, as they rounded a hairpin turn, "is the most difficult—especially after the rains, which alas we had last night. Ah, no, no," he cried, as the back of the car fishtailed.

"Are we going to die?" Marcel asked.

Jacques said, "Some day."

The men—Marcel included—got out to push, while Simone, who had never before driven, steered them free, to cries of "Brava! Brava!"

The next morning, at the long trestle table where they shared their meals, Claude was saying, "…and then the bicycle sprouted wings…"

His lawfully-wedded wife, named, as it happened, Claudine, passed a crock of jam towards Simone. "We have a wonderful stock—if you don't care for raspberry, there's peach and also a sour orange marmalade. All homemade."

"Ah, so you are an artist in the kitchen, too."

"Me? Heavens, no! It's Hélène." Hélène was Claude's lover.

Claude interrupted the recounting of his dream to say, "If you should see Claudine at work in the kitchen, I would advise a most immediate evacuation. If she doesn't set the curtains on fire—"

"It was just that once!"

"Then she's likely to sever an appendage—if not a limb." Claude continued, "Yes, wings on the bicycle. Excuse me." He turned away and delivered a hacking cough into his hand. "And I realized, even while I was sleeping, that the bicycle, of course, represented the modern, the technological, while the wings, were the spirit. Nonetheless, although it was quite useless, I pedaled frantically…"

"Hélène will give you a few days to settle in, and then she'll set you to work like a field hand, give you a bucket and shove you out the door to gather berries. She may even give you a ladder and send you up in the orchard, after peaches and plums," Claudine said.

"But then the bicycle began to plummet from the sky, it was really quite terrifying..."

"Really?" Marcel asked.

"It was a dream, darling."

"I dream."

"And what did you dream about last night?" Claude asked.

"A duck."

"Yes, and...?"

Marcel hid his face in his mother's skirts.

"I shan't mind going out to pick fruit. I quite like the outdoors. Oh, goodness." Simone was wiping her cheeks with the backs of her hands. "I don't know why I am crying. I think it's that—oh, please, don't let Jacques know—my tears bother him no end."

"There, dear," Claudine said, reaching into the pocket of her smock and drawing out a stoppered bottle containing a murky yellow liquid.

"...having crashed into the sea—you'll notice, of course, the parallels with Icarus, although unlike Icarus I didn't perish—most excellent stuff," he jutted his chin towards the bottle, which Claudine had unstoppered and was adding to Simone's coffee.

"A lemon liqueur. Cures all ills known to man—and woman."

"Really, I don't know why I was—why I am—crying." Then: "It's a bit of an odd taste."

Claudine took the cup from Simone's hand, had a sip. "You're right." She dumped the doctored coffee in the sink, poured Simone a shot of the liqueur in a glass, a fresh cup of coffee, as well as producing a used handkerchief with which to dry her eyes from another of her kangaroo pockets.

"The lot of a mistress is never an easy one."

"Oh, I don't think of myself as —"

"No, of course not." Claudine laid a motherly hand on Simone's shoulder. "One never does."

"It's just—I live in these ridiculous lodgings, and because of the children I never—well, not never, but I do feel—it will be such a relief—"

"…and found myself in a most fantastical underwater paradise…"

"…to do something. To be handed an empty bucket, and fill it up with blackberries or plums or—"

Rabbit

Just then the redoubtable Hélène entered the kitchen, holding a rabbit by its hind legs. Simone could not help but notice that Hélène bore an uncanny resemblance to Claudine.

"Bunny," Odette said.

"Ah, the snares of the fair Hélène!" Claude declaimed, distracted momentarily from the recounting of his dream, and the two of them shared an ardent kiss, Hélène then continuing through the kitchen to the back garden, where she slit the rabbit's throat, and hung it, high enough to be out of reach of the dogs, who lapped at the fat globs of blood as they landed on the ground.

Jacques entered, eyes half-closed, gave Simone a husbandly peck—a kiss in front of everyone. Simone delighted in being able to set his coffee in front of him, to fuss about—what kind of jam did he prefer? Did he need anything else?

Hélène announced that she was going to give Simone and the children a tour of the grounds. Jacques declared he would observe nature from his favored position, seating in a chaise on the back verandah, looking up occasionally from his book.

Off they trooped, Hélène with a machete in hand. "The paths are pretty well-established, but every now and again nature takes her revenge and we have to bushwhack our way through." Brush also had to be cleared: it could feed the late summer fires.

At dinner that night, one of the painters—Simone had not quite got them all straightened out yet—called as she came down to dinner holding the hand of each child, "Ah, here come our noble savages! Kissed by the sun—" It was true, freckles were appearing on the bridge of Simone's nose.

"And bitten by the gnat," Simone said, showing a series of red bumps on her arm. Yet the country air was restoring not just her, but the children.

A few nights later, lying curled against Jacques after they had made love, she dared to say to him, "I've never been happier." She hoped he might say the same to her, but knew it was a foolish hope.

She had not thought to bring the sort of rough clothes she would need—she had rather imagined this place would be "rustic" in the fashion of Juan-les-Pins—so Claude lent her a pair of his old trousers, which she held up with a length of twine. She wore them every morning when she set out to do battle against nature, wooden clogs on her feet, her hair tied up beneath a kerchief, a rake or hoe slung over her shoulder like a carabiniere's rifle. *En passant par la Lorraine / Avec mes sabots, mes sabots*, she sang, and then clacked her clogs together (the clacking of heels did not yet make them think of the Germans).

Once, when she did this, she tumbled, went from being an upstanding woman to a puddle of flesh on the ground.

"Do you have a tendency to fall, to lose your footing?" a doctor would later ask.

"Oh, no. No," Simone will answer. She always felt, in the presence of doctors, as if she were defending herself from their accusations.

After all, we all fall from time to time, and perhaps Simone had tripped over a root or stumbled on the uneven ground. She hoisted herself back to her feet, called a cheery *I'm fine, I'm fine* to those who were rushing towards her, and picked up her song where she had left it off, *Rencontrai trois capitaines, avec mes sabots…*

The morning after her fall, there had been a blue-black bruise spreading across her thigh. Simone had felt a queer sort of pride in it.

Leaving the breakfast table where Claude had been reciting his dreams, Jacques muttered, "…the very bad and very sickly poet."

"Oh, hush. Some day he'll hear you."

Jacques jutted out his lower lip: "Perhaps he'll get angry and take back his trousers," and gave a wink.

Odette and Marcel trooped off each day with the snotty-nosed and ragged offspring of the cooks and handymen and laundresses and maids-of-all-work needed to keep the menage running smoothly, building palaces and forts in the woods, throwing stones at crows. The fortress had a number of unused rooms and when Simone couldn't find the children anywhere else, she would swing open an ancient wooden door, to be hit by a smell of mossy damp and the sound of children's whispers.

"What are you up to in here?"

"Playing," Odette would respond, in an eerie voice.

Nape

Simone and Claudine were sprawled on the sofa, Claudine's arms wrapped around Simone from behind.

"A man doesn't like to feel hemmed in."

"I'm hardly hemming him in!"

"No, my love."

Claudine shifted a bit so she could rummage about in her capacious pockets for a hankie for Simone's tears. "But he doesn't want to feel that way, no matter what the facts of the matter are."

Odette entered the room, stared for a moment at her mother, and then declared: "*Maman* is crying." She strode to the couch and clambered up on it, leaning against her mother as her mother leaned against Claudine, the three of them forming a female trinity.

Claudine's soothing caresses moved slowly from Simone's shoulders to her neck. She toyed with the down-like strands that grew from her hairline, and then began to offer a series of sweet kisses to the nape of her neck.

Odette, lying against her mother, sucked her thumb, a habit she had long since given up.

65, rue Cochin

Back in Paris, she learned Jacques' home address—she wished she had not done so, she hadn't been able to stop herself from delving into his briefcase when he was in the toilet, opening his pocket diary, where on the flyleaf was written: Jacques Melville, 65, rue Cochin, 6e, Paris. Once she knew it, she knew she could not possibly forget it. 65, rue Cochin. 65, rue Cochin. At times, during her evening perambulations after the children had fallen asleep, she would find herself outside the building in which Jacques and Sala lived. Standing across the street, she stared at the squares of light formed by the windows, wondering which ones were theirs.

One evening, she stood there for so long that a woman opened the window and shouted, "Go away, you whore!" Perhaps it was Sala. Simone wanted to scurry off, but she would not give the woman the satisfaction, whether she was Jacques' lawfully wedded wife or merely a freelance protectress of the moral order who assumed Simone was a streetwalker trolling for a customer. She willed herself to stay rooted to the spot, to stare resolutely at the window. Sala might be crying out: *—She's down there in the street right now! Staring up at the window! —Oh, don't be ridiculous! —I'm being ridiculous? Go and have a look!*

She was terrified that Jacques would say, "Now Sala claims she sees you standing outside our building at night," and the look on her face would betray her.

Although she was terrified of being discovered, still, Simone would find herself impelled to 65, rue Cochin…65, rue Cochin…65, rue Cochin as if she had no more will than an iron filing and the building itself was an enormous magnet.

Summer

The first summer at LaVigie was followed by a second. They slept on a sleeping porch they'd rigged on an old parapet. The sunlight would wake her, while Jacques—who had stayed up late, playing mah jong and drinking the local aperitifs with the other men, filling the air with the smoke from their cigars and pipes, their endless talk—moaned a little as she rose from the bed and pulled the bedclothes up over his head to block the light.

Claude would hear her singing as she set off with her hoe over her shoulder, lean out his window and call, "Good morning, my beautiful Simone, my lark who announces the dawn," and blow her a kiss.

"*Avec mes sabots, mes sabots*," she'd sing out, and click the heels of her wooden clogs together.

"Claude," Jacques said, encountering him in the passageways, "I don't mind you flirting with my Simone, just do so a little more quietly."

End

The second time she rid herself of Jacques' child, she did not go back to the doctor who fancied himself a poet, but went instead to a middle-aged woman who brought children into the world both at their time and before their time. She took a rubberized tablecloth, red and white gingham checks, the kind used in cheap restaurants where the *vin rouge ordinaire* had a whiff of diesel and flicked it over the kitchen table.

"Do you have children, Madame?"

"I—" a lump in her throat. Simone swallowed hard. Once Marcel and Odette had been the size this stranger inside of her now was.

The woman—Simone never knew her name, was not even given an alias by which to address her—did not lay a soothing hand on Simone's shoulder. Instead, she sighed deeply: No, not a weeper!

Simone—the tears were already running down her cheeks—held up two fingers.

"Any other pregnancies?" Simone raised her index finger in the air.

"Did it end on its own?" Simone shook her head.

As the woman wiped the cloth down with bleach, she said, "Five myself. There would have been—oh, twelve, thirteen—if nature had had her way." A cigarette dangled from her lips. "Take off your underclothes—your girdle and panties…just hitch up your skirt, there's no need to remove anything more…climb up on the table…It'll all be over in a minute. Open your legs."

The woman put her fingers inside Simone, a quick cramp of pain was followed by a second, longer cramp. "There, we're done." She brushed her hands together like a woman who has just finished rolling out a pie crust.

"Done?"

"Sit up slowly." She was already busy, gathering up her equipment, carrying it to the sink—the same sink, over which, in an hour or two, she would doubtless prepare dinner for her family.

"That's all?"

"In a couple of hours, you'll start to cramp. Then everything will pass out of you…If you start to run a fever—over 39 degrees—get yourself to a doctor, or if need be a hospital. Be sure and tell them you passed something small and white. You saw a tiny hand or a foot. That it fell into the toilet, and you were so distraught you flushed it away."

As predicted, the cramping started that evening. Someone who was meant to be doesn't give up its hold on life easily.

Simone imagined she had given birth to one of those children, although never to both of them. Their son would have been named Stephan, in memory of Jacques's dear friend, killed in the war. Alone in the flat, her children at school, she picked up her imaginary baby, and walked him up and down, jiggling him in her arms to soothe him.

Simone had two very real children, who would have liked something more in the afternoon than a bit of that morning's baguette, already going stale, thinly spread with butter and sprinkled with sugar. When they went to their friends' houses after school, they told her, they were given pastries from the Café de la Paix, the mothers set them out on gold-rimmed platters in their fluted paper cups.

Left

Jacques sat in the hospital corridor with his elbows propped on his knees and his head in his hands. He did not love his wife, but this—he would not wish such a thing on another human being.

A passing nun laid a hand on his shoulder and murmured his name. His first thought was that she had come to give him some news, and he half hoped it would be the worst news, because then things would be over. But instead she said:

"I will pray for your wife."

"Thank you," he said, partly because he felt gratitude, but mostly because this seemed the most efficient way to end this encounter. She stood there for another few seconds: perhaps waiting for him to say, "God bless you," but he had no intention of adding hypocrisy to his list of failings.

The year was 1933. He won't visit a hospital again for nearly two decades when an old friend will be dying in Belgium. He'll be struck by how the smell of these places has changed—no longer the charnel house odor of rotting flesh—and will thank God for penicillin.

He longed for Simone, yearned for her physical presence as he never before had.

At last, a doctor emerged, shook his hand, clapped one hand on his shoulder. Phrases swam up from the sea of words, "narcotics are controlling the pain…we've been forced to amputate her left leg… ongoing danger of infection…internal injuries which may reveal themselves in the coming days…You should go home, get some sleep, the next few days will be grueling enough without… "

"Thank you, doctor," he said, this time quite genuinely, and picked up his briefcase from the floor. He didn't head for the hospital's front door but for the call box in the corner of the waiting room.

The phone in Simone's flat rang and rang and rang as she struggled up from a deep sleep, rang and rang as she pulled on her robe, rang and rang as she stumbled to the living room.

Marcel and Odette were awakened too. Marcel stood in the doorway, watching his mother with the air of a detective taking notes.

"I'm at the hospital, there's been an accident." In response to Simone's cry—he should have thought out what he was going to say more carefully— "Not me. Sala."

"Is she. . .?"

"I need you. Come." He gave her the name of the hospital.

"Hold on, let me make sure I have enough for the taxi fare—"

"Just come. I'll meet you in front." He rang off without saying goodbye.

She turned to Marcel. "A friend is ill. Go back to bed. I'll be here when you wake up in the morning."

She ran to the taxi rank and roused a driver there.

Jacques was waiting at the front door of the hospital, paid the fare, held her, leaned into her, such dead weight she thought she might topple over.

"There's a hotel." He gestured across the street.

The desk clerk, hair askew, fetid sleep breath, lumbered towards them from a cot in the back office. Jacques did not pick up the iron key shoved across the counter towards them.

She would always remember the weight of it in her hand.

The lift—they had been given a room on the fifth floor—descended solemnly towards them. Once inside, the safety gate proved persnickety, and the sleepy man shuffled over to them, explaining—as if it should have been perfectly obvious—that one needed to shove the door—*no, no, not so hard*!—and hold your finger on the button at the same time. *No, no, you must keep the button continually depressed*!

As soon as they were in the room Jacques unbuttoned his flies, used his hand to make himself erect, flung her onto the bed, pushed into her. Simone thought of those passages from the Old Testament, ancient Hebrews rending their clothes, smearing their faces with ashes, beating their breasts and wailing in mourning. She comforted him like a mother, smoothing his hair, covering his face with kisses, while he rutted and groaned, and at last collapsed on top of her.

He began to sob.

Was she happy that Sala was dead? No, not happy. Relieved was the word that came closest, although that was not exactly right either: there was a hole in the language.

It might even be that Sala's death, instead of freeing them, would cast a pall over their future. She remembered the time at the Carcassonne train station when she had casually referred to his hatred of Sala, and he had given her the look a sadistic schoolmaster gives his dullest pupil and said, "I don't hate Sala. I don't know what I ever said that would make you think I hated her." The guilt he had always felt towards Sala, no longer shadowed by its twin of resentment, might rise to the surface: he might even come to feel that Simone had ruined a marriage which despite its difficulties had been solid, companionable.

Although the room was not cold, and she had remained nearly fully clothed during their coupling, she began to tremble with fear.

He lifted himself up onto his elbows and stroked her hair.

"Ah," he said, "ah, you poor girl. You know nothing of what is going on."

"She's dead."

"No, no."

"No?"

"No."

"Ah, the way you were—"

"What did I tell you?" He pulled himself out of her, stood up, tucked himself back together, smoothed his clothing, sat down on the bed.

"Only that there had been an accident."

"She was crossing the road. It was raining. The lorry's brakes—she was thrown quite a distance. They've amputated her leg. There's always the danger of infection, and perhaps internal injuries."

"Which one?"

"Her left. Why does that matter?"

She held him while he sobbed wordlessly against her, while he sobbed and sobbed and sobbed.

He slept; she did not. She could smell the histories of the others who had passed through these rooms: the sausage, sweat and beer stink of a Swiss commercial traveler; a spinster's odor of sawdust and clay; other couples who'd made love on this mattress, all that remained of their passion a faint odor of musk.

At last she broke the embrace: dawn was coming, she had to get back to her children. She was halfway down the hall when she realized she'd left home without her wallet, went back and knocked on the door. He handed her money for taxi fare like a grumpy husband to a profligate wife.

Sala's body fought off the infection that developed at the site of her wound. She made a full recovery, minus, of course, her leg. It was a given that she could not continue to be a doctor and equally impossible that she could chain Jacques to a peg-legged wife: she at last granted him a divorce. He settled enough money on her to allow her to open a bookstore, where she perched on a stool behind the counter and deftly made her way down the aisles with a pair of crutches.

Civil

As Jacques and Simone walked down the flight of stairs after their civil union had been registered—Simone carrying a bunch of lilacs, the two friends who had served as their witnesses behind them—Jacques had such a look of hangdog misery that Simone feared those who passed them were giving him looks of bemused sympathy.

No sooner had they shut the door of her flat behind them than Simone turned toward him, wrapped her arms around his shoulders, longing for him to embrace her. He returned her embrace and then gave her one of those husbandly pat-pat-pats which signifies leave taking.

"Aren't you…?"

"I have some correspondence to attend to…you needn't carry on like that!"

"What do you mean 'carry on like that'? I haven't said a word!"

"You don't need words. Your face says it all!"

(Later on, her face will assume the mask-like expression of those with Parkinson's. Jacques will no longer be tormented by her looks.)

"I can scarcely be expected to govern the expressions which—oh, please, let's not row, not today of all days."

"Oh, today of all days!" he mocked.

She turned away from him, weeping.

"Oh, don't cry. You know I can't bear to see you cry."

He took her in his arms. He did not hold her as firmly as she wished to be held, but nonetheless, he held her in his arms.

"Aren't you happy? At last we've gotten what—for so many years—"

"No, I'm not happy."

"You're not happy?"

He kissed her tears away, repeated, "No, I'm not happy." Then: "It's not uncommon—this sense of melancholia, disappointment, even—when one achieves a long-sought goal."

"You speak—so dispassionately."

"I rowed with Sala the day I married her. I imagine you quarreled with Luc—"

"So you see this as a marriage, like any other—"

She began to weep again.

Jacques grabbed her wrist, pulled her towards him. "All right, I'm happy," he said, a forced smile on his face, his head nodding back and forth idiotically. "I'm happy, I'm happy. Does that make you feel better?"

Flag

When they were hanging out their wash in the courtyard of the block of flats on the rue Campagne-Premiere, the women who were allied with the Spanish anarchists argued with the Communist women. The fights began over the Popular Front and ended up with grousing about clothespins or began over how sheets should be properly hung and ended up with shouting about the Moscow purge trials.

One of the less politically astute and more reckless women shimmied up the minaret, took down the red flag flying there and replaced it with a brassiere.

Later, it would be replaced by black flag, and then by a pair of men's undershorts.

Nuns

Paris had its own orders of nuns. Not quite like those ferule-wielding women of Simone's girlhood, in their habits that made them seem walking triangles, but not entirely unlike them, either.

They dressed in black and strictly adhered to the dictates of their ad hoc orders.

There was Simone Weil, the Red Virgin, a saint in the guise of a schoolgirl, or perhaps a schoolgirl in the guise of a saint. She wore steel-rimmed glasses, the sort that might have been worn by a monk who'd ruined his eyesight reading arcane texts in poor light. Her hair was chopped off, perhaps by her own hand, with a pair of blunt scissors. She'd been baptized in hot oil in an accident at the front in the Spanish Civil War. Later her fasting would lead to her death.

Jacques, needless to say, had seen that other Simone's legendary virginity as a gauntlet thrown down before him and had done his best (and failed) to make off with the prize of her hymen.

"In France," he said, with one of his legendary shrugs, "even our Jews are Catholics."

There was Simone deBeauvoir, with her magnificent carriage and hair styled into a coronet, Mother Superior of an order of one.

Not all the nuns were named Simone. Adrienne Monier, Sapphic prioress, whose postulants pledge themselves to the opposite of chastity, joined them once for dinner. She didn't retire afterwards with the men, as was her usual custom, like that of Miss Stein. Instead, a cigarette hanging from her lip like a tough guy in an American gangster film, she joined Simone in the kitchen, drying dishes while Simone washed.

Ashes floated down from the tip of her cigarette, flakes of grey snow, drifting into the dishwater, onto the just-washed plates.

Stump

In the afternoons, when Simone did not go to the cinema, she walked. Sometimes she had a destination: a café a kilometer or so from their flat where the coffee was served in gold-rimmed cups, Sylvia Beach's Shakespeare and Company, to pick up some books for Jacques. Sometimes she followed a circuitous route, not wanting to walk past Sala's shop.

Sometimes, when she was walking near that bookstore, she'd start to ruminate on Sala's missing leg. Was it made of wood, painted a yellowish-grey color meant to suggest human flesh? Or did she go about in trousers, with one leg pinned up, like the mutilated soldiers one saw hiking along on crutches along the place des Invalides?

Stump.

How could the image of something she had never seen be so vivid?

Years later, lying flat on her back in Dr. Balmant's office, she will confess: "I think about Sala's stump."

He will answer with his silence.

"I think about it a lot."

Again, his silence, his vast and impenetrable silence.

"I'm rather ashamed of how much I think about it. Sometimes—in the afternoons—I go out for walks. And I want to walk past her shop."

She will hear the sound of his pen moving across the page. He should get the pen repaired so the ink flows more easily and doesn't make this scratching sound, which distracts the analysand, or perhaps that's the intention of it, conscious or not, to make her wonder what he has just written down. She will say that to him, and he will respond, "Your concern about my pen is a defense."

"I want to walk past her shop, and I'm hoping that somehow I'll happen to see…but I'm terrified of seeing it…"

You don't marry just a man, Simone realized, you marry also his clan, his ex-wives, his ex-mistresses, his mother, his aunt, his father, his sons from his former marriage, his sisters, even his future mistresses, a point that was brought home to her when, shortly after she offered this confession to Dr. Balmant, Sala died, and Jacques entered into a strange, shapeless mourning.

Curve

It was perhaps a good thing that Simone followed a serpentine route through Paris to avoid Sala's shop. Had she not, she might well have glimpsed Jacques opening the bright red door beneath the sign *Librairie Babylone* and, a few minutes later, Sala sellotaping a handwritten notice to the glass, stating that the shop would be closed for the next hour.

They coupled on a couch in the rear room—Sala often stretched out on it when there were no customers in the shop, since her stump needed to be elevated to keep it from swelling. In the wake of her injury and their divorce, Sala had not only become a Sapphist, but something of a dandy—she who had once been so nonchalant about her appearance. She wore starched white shirts with French cuffs—musketeer cuffs, the French call them—and plucked her eyebrows into the thin arches that had been fashionable a decade earlier. She did indeed, as Simone imagined, go about in trousers, although not with one leg safety-pinned up: her tailor adapted the left leg with a neat seam.

What Simone could not have imagined was how the end of Jacques' and Sala's marriage had freed them both. The divorce had liberated Jacques in the expected way, allowing him to marry Simone, and had permitted Sala to follow an inclination which perhaps had always been a part of her makeup.

In the parlor years before Jacques had examined the photograph of Simone attired for the costume party as a man and stated: "I prefer her as a woman." The fact was he preferred Sala as a man. In addition to her quite masculine attire, Sala had also adopted the gestures belonging to the male realm: she shot her cuffs, sucked contemplatively on her pipe, and even managed to swagger on her crutches.

The decades of recriminations, squabbles and out-and-out fights (their sons had on occasion been forced to physically come between them) had been an acid wash, abrading all that was inessential between them: post-divorce, they faced one another with the rawness they'd had when, as little more than children, they'd met on the back staircase. Their lovemaking—and it was lovemaking, even if neither of them would have used that word to describe it—proceeded in a forthright manner. Sala hung up her sign, and the two of them went into the back room. The rule was that they did not kiss, although that stricture had never been explicitly stated. The frank conjunction of their organs was what mattered. They were not embarrassed by their grunts—the odd, unnamed noises that two bodies make when fucking. Sometimes he turned her around, yanked down her trousers, and took her in the ass as if he were a pederast and she a youth. Sometimes she stretched out languidly on the couch smoking a cigarette while he worked in and out of her.

"Ah," she said, "if only women had cocks."

Sala felt that at last she truly had him: that his other dalliances—even that with his new wife—were mere ornaments.

Rue des Arenes

An apartment was bequeathed to Jacques by one of his mother's former lodgers. As if to prove that nothing in their lives would ever go smoothly, the tenants in residence refused to vacate, and a solicitor had to be engaged. At last they moved from the thin-walled, rickety block of flats on the rue Campagne-Premiere.

Jacques was often a bit peevish on first entering the apartment, partly because he saved up his ill-humor during the day, hiding it while at Gallimard, but also because the sight of his building's exterior discomfited him, with its rather garish melange of styles—Gothic and Second Empire, gargoyles and palm fronds. Its facade was a daily reminder to him that he hadn't gotten all that he wanted from life, and at his age—nearly fifty already, how had that happened?—in all likelihood, he never would.

Patience

May, 1940. What the French called *La drôle de guerre,* their British allies "the phony war," had come to an end, the eight months during which, despite the declarations of war, the two blocs had merely glared at one another.

Germany had invaded France.

A half-played game of patience on the kitchen table, abandoned: Simone had been playing it to try to absorb her anxious energy as she listened to the wireless: "The German high command issued a communique today declaring that the Maginot Line has become a mousetrap for a million men…A spokesman for the French Army countered that its troops were continuing to fight bravely…"

She leapt to her feet and began to clean the flat, not just tidying it up—running a feather duster across the books and knick-knacks—but the kind of cleaning her mother and Cecile used to undertake each spring, as soon as it was warm enough to fling open the windows to air the house, the contents of shelves taken down and piled on tables, kettles of water set to boil, the soot of Paris blackening the water as the curtains soaked in the tub.

France had fallen. Simone understood how it was possible for an individual to trip, lose balance, slip, tumble: but how was it possible for a nation to do so?

Like a mother hen who, seeing the shadow of a hawk gliding across the earth, runs around in circles uttering frantic cries of alarm and trying to gather her chicks under her wing, she was unable to be still. She sat down to eat and managed no more than a few mouthfuls before she leapt to her feet and scrubbed the baseboards, rearranged objects in a drawer.

Jacques burst through the door: "Joë is going to take us in. I have tickets for a train—for all of us—that leaves in five hours. Simone, calm down! Why have you suddenly become a *hausfrau*? Pack, and be sensible about it. I'm going to go and round up the children." They were hardly children anymore. He also telephoned his current mistress from a call box to let her know that despite his promises, he would be leaving Paris without her, and she would now be more or less on her own.

They left for the train carrying worn canvas valises, which attracted less attention than ones made of fine leather, packed with practical items—a sweater, two changes of underwear, salamis, dried fruit. They left behind the shelves of books, annotated in the margins by Jacques' hand, warmly inscribed by those seeking to curry his favor; letters from other members of the literati, drafts of articles and books; boxes of jigsaw puzzles with missing pieces, a three-footed teacup Simone had bought at Les Puces. The furniture, draped in sheets, seemed ghostly, and it was quite possible to imagine that in their absence phantoms might take up residence, arranging their weightless bodies on the settees and chairs, helping themselves to a meal of air and dust from the bare larder, finding the Montecristo Jacques had tucked in a desk drawer and forgotten, and smoking it despite its staleness.

At the post office in Carcassonne, they were handed pre-printed postcards:

Date__

_in good health_tired_slightly, seriously ill, wounded_killed_
prisoner_died_without news of_The family_is well_in need of
supplies_of money_news_luggage_has returned to_is working in
_will go back to school at__is being put up at__is going to__

Best wishes. Love___Signature.

Each person was given a single such card, allowed to do no more than enter proper names in the blanks, cross out what did not apply.

All of France was in motion. Anything with wheels—cars, farm carts, prams, wheelbarrows, children's wagons—was pressed into use.

Women who had never before driven— their husbands, now called up, had taken care of that—got behind the wheels of overloaded cars and, mistaking the clutch for the brake and the brake for the accelerator, set off, while a helpful stranger shouted instructions through an open window. These cars, could, of course, move no faster than the mass of people around them, intermixed with farm animals, lost children, inmates of prisons and mental institutions released by the Germans, the latter group with nuns trailing after them, the good sisters sweating in their thick habits, which dragged in the muddy road.

The radio broadcasts of dance music—singers crooning of moonlit chapels and lost springtimes—were occasionally interrupted by communiques from the octogenarian Maréchal Philippe Pétain, also known as Philipe le Gaga. It was impossible to tell if the crackling sound which accompanied his voice was radio static or caused by the trembling of his hands holding the paper from which he read, telling his people that a rough peace would be made with the Nazis.

Photographs appeared in the newspapers of Hitler touring Paris. Posed in front of the Eiffel Tower, he looked like a grumpy *pater familias*—a lower level employee of an insurance firm, a man who, loathe to admit how small he is, buys clothing a size too large. His brow disappeared beneath his cap, his hands were half-hidden by the sleeves of his great coat.

A friend of Jacques summed it up well: "The man's a nebbish."

Grime

Their refuge at Joë's was short-lived. As Paris settled into a grumpy détente with the Germans, Jacques brought them home where at least they could resist rather than accommodate themselves to the Occupation. He fought to keep *La nouvelle revue française* from becoming a collaborationist journal. When he was unsuccessful, he resigned his editorship, undertaking the publishing of a clandestine paper.

He was arrested in the early months of '41, held for a week during which he endured both the worst boredom and the worst fear of his life, before being released through the intervention of a colleague whose personality was even more *alambiqué* than Jacques'.

Fearing the flat would be searched, Simone got rid of the mimeograph used to run off the paper. Too heavy to lift, she'd had to break it down into pieces. Not having a screwdriver in the house, she'd attempted to make do with Jacques' letter opener, ruining it in the process, finally procuring a set of tools from a friend (*Don't ask, don't ask,* their wartime chant), working on an oil cloth she'd laid on the table, disassembling the machine, carrying it out, piece by piece in her shopping bag, tossing it into the river, feeling like a moll from an American gangster movie disposing of a hacked-up body.

Home, she saw that her fingers were rimmed with grime. She used the vegetable brush to scour her hands. The blackened brush itself might be evidence—it followed the machine parts into the Seine.

Soup

During the war years Simone often ate soup. One could make it from almost anything: water, of course; salt, almost as necessary; a carrot or two, a turnip or parsnip, or a potato with the moldy bits scraped off. If one was flush, one might even have a bit of meat—a wing or even a thigh from a hen too old to lay. A bit of oil always helped, it certainly didn't have to be olive oil from the first pressing, or even the second or the third, a bit of grease left in the pan would do. The butcher had a soft spot for her. He'd shrug and say, "Alas," in front of the other customers, but give her a wink so she was to know to come back when the shop was empty, when he'd pull a few bones from beneath the counter. She'd walk home with her bounty in her string bag, through the quiet streets—the lack of petrol allowed one to hear the plink of the cobbler's hammer, a child's sobs from a distant open window.

Home, she cracked the bones to free the marrow.

Boil, boil, boil, boil.

She set the table and served the soup out of a tureen so it seemed like a proper meal and almost filled them up. Only later, when they were trying to sleep, their hunger would keep them awake.

One's body, after all, has a mind of its own.

Jacques came home one night with his briefcase bulging, opened it to reveal a cache of eighteen beets, four turnips and a carrot, dirt still clinging to them. "Don't ask." For months afterward, every sheaf of papers he pulled from the satchel was redolent of earth.

Letter

Jacques managed to keep his sons from being sent as laborers to Germany by getting them certified as tubercular. For Marcel there had been no shadow on his lung, no wheeze that could serve as a precious bane. After a number of unsuccessful feints and sallies, he had been enlisted in the *Service du travail obligatoire*. Thereafter, she received a monthly postcard from him—the postcard eagerly awaited, which left her depressed for days after its arrival: *I am well…I am well, all things considered… As Chekov said, "Life isn't easy for any of us." I am managing to stay fairly healthy…*

Maybe there was a woman who loved him—sometimes Simone pictured a fellow worker from France, gave her the name of Adele.Years later, at parties, he'd be able to say, "Ah, how my wife and I met? That's quite a story. It might be said that Adolf Hitler was our matchmaker…"

Other times, when Simone couldn't bear the thought of him living on iron rations, she turned his lover into a German woman, the widow of a soldier who'd frozen to death on the Russian front, she sneaked soup to him, real soup, barley and carrot, golden, with a mound of clotted cream floating on top. Simone could picture the globules of white fat spreading through the soup in almost molecular detail. But she had trouble envisioning the *hausfrau*: her mind kept casting up children's book illustrations of plump, rosy-cheeked German *madchen*, complete with red scarves with white polka dots, dimpled cheeks and dimpled knees, or athletic blonde women with their hair in a single braid down their backs from German films—not that she'd gone to see any of these, but she couldn't help seeing the posters for them, even when they were half torn down, lettered over with *FILM BOCHE-N'ALLEZ PAS*. Simone decided to make her young, practically a child-bride, now a child-widow: it still surprised her when shopkeepers noticed the ring on her finger and addressed her as *frau*. Gretchen had it bad for him and he had it bad for her soup, he gave her what she wanted in an alley behind the men's dormitory, but he didn't give it to her the way she wanted it, not only no kisses but he made her face the wall and took her from behind, not so much as a twiddle of his thumb against her clito, he just rammed himself in and out. *Whatever you do, Marcel, don't come inside her, don't give me a half-German bastard for a grandson.*

Other times, she thought it was impossible for anything to happen just as she imagined it. The trick to keeping him safe was to picture exactly what she could not bear to have happen. Lice crawled through his hair, gnawed at his scalp, the itching was fierce, he clawed at his head until it bled, the other guys kept telling him to stop, he'd get typhus, but he woke up in the night and his pillow was streaked with blood. All right, he was safe from that. To keep him free of dysentery, she imagined him racing for the latrines behind the barracks, the cramps were like labor pains, he was doubled over, and what poured out of him was brownish liquid, a stinking potion witches would use to toast the devil, the acid of it searing the flesh between his buttocks. A Nazi guard had it in for him, or perhaps he'd fallen in love with him, it was impossible to tell the two states apart. Fat Bruno was fucking her Marcel in the ass, driving his stumpy dick in raw, her poor Marcel was crying out, the Nazi was laughing at his cries of pain. Every day, she had to feed him moldy bread, soup with maggots swimming in it, she herself started gagging just thinking about it.

Also arriving—every fortnight rather than every month—were courteous and inane letters from Odette, who had had a whirlwind romance when the family was in Carcassonne, and had stayed behind with her fiancé, now her husband.

Rue des Arenes

Jacques said to her, "We may need someone to carry messages. Stop plucking your eyebrows. Go to the flea market and get something really plain, and worn. A coat. Run-down shoes. Dress like a woman who no longer enjoys catching a glimpse of herself in a mirror."

Two weeks later, he handed her a cyanide capsule. Yet another of those clichés of the war years, jackboots on the stairs, the knock on the door, the clandestine radio. And like all those other things, the reality so much messier than the image. By the end of a long day those jackboots weighed a ton, those wearing them think: *Not another flight of stairs, just my luck, not a single building with a lift today. Can't wait to get home and soak these dogs.* The potassium cyanide wasn't easy to get hold of, the correct dosage was uncertain, the stuff lost effectiveness, you might swallow a capsule and find yourself, after hours of writhing in physical torment, dry heaves, repatriated to the land of the living.

"There's an old man, he'll be walking a Pomeranian—one of those silly little dogs, fluffy, yap-yap—every morning along the rue Monge. At eight a.m. You must time it quite precisely, so that you encounter him every morning. If any one should ask why you've suddenly started taking a morning constitutional—advice of your doctor.

"The old man will greet you, exchange pleasantries. Sometimes he'll have a message for you to deliver—and you'll be given some messages to deliver to him. That's all I'm going to tell you—the less you know, the better. We won't ever speak of this again."

She who was never ready on time was dressed—coat, gloves, hat, mended silk stockings— purse in the crook of her elbow, perched on the arm of the chair, glancing at her watch: 7:27, 7:32, 7:34. Usually she arose before six, made Jacques' coffee, threw something on to run to the corner and get the morning's bread, set it out on the table for him with some preserves, and then crawled back into bed, skimming just below the surface of wakefulness in case Jacques should call to her: *Simone, where are the postage stamps? I need a clean handkerchief.* But this morning she had tidied up the flat, was ready to leave the house at ten minutes to eight.

"Ah, for Christ's sake, Simone, you're making me nervous! At least go in the kitchen and—make yourself useful, instead of lurking about like that!"

She set her watch next to the sink, washed a glass, glanced at her watch, washed another glass. At last, it seemed enough time had passed so she could go downstairs—how long, she wondered, would it take her to go down five flights of stairs? One minute, two? Ninety seconds?

Then she was walking, at the appointed time, along the rue Monge, and coming towards her was an elderly man with a thin mustache and the erect bearing of one who had served as an officer in the Great War, a man who wouldn't think of leaving the house, even to walk his dog, without being well-attired. The Pomeranian, with its magnificent brushed coat and thin legs, looked like an elderly woman, beautiful in her youth, who still carried herself as if before an admiring public.

"Madame," he said, and tipped his fedora.

"A lovely day," she said.

The dog, taking advantage of her master's pause, lowered her rear and peed, staring abstractedly into the middle distance as she did so.

"Yes, the autumn air is quite bracing, especially after the heat of summer, which I find more enervating as the years go by. Ah, I wish I could offer something more than such a trite statement to a charming woman…Good day." He gave the dog's lead a jiggle and set off.

The next four mornings she again left her flat at the appointed hour, encountered the elderly gentleman, exchanged pleasantries with him, petted the Pomeranian. It occurred to her that this man might be the anonymous private collector for whom she and Jacques had written erotica. It became rather an *idée fixe* with her.

Dada

On the sixth day, the dog yapped and wagged its tail when she was half a block away.

"Ah, you've made a conquest," the elderly gentleman said. "You are to go to Orleans, there's a train that leaves in two hours. There's a park opposite the train station. (Smile and nod your head, as if I were paying you a compliment.) You'll wait on a bench there—the bench closest to the gate. A man will sit down next to you and remark on your hat. You will tell him:

'Jeanne has baked a cherry tart. Lucien has gone to the country. The apple trees are in blossom.' Now pet the dog, and repeat it to me."

"A train to Orleans, a park opposite the train station. A man will compliment me on my hat. Aren't you just the sweetest little dog. Yes, you are, you are. Jeanne has baked an apple tart."

"No!" the man snapped, *sotto voce*, jerking slightly on the dog's leash. "A cherry tart. And don't forget: the bench closest to the gate." When Simone glanced up, she saw a false smile plastered on his face.

"I'm sorry."

Her apology only irritated him more.

"The bench closest to the gate. Jeanne has baked a cherry tart. Lucien has gone to the country. The apple trees are in blossom."

Now it was her turn to become a Dadaist, a chanter of absurd poetry, cryptic lines.

Home, she donned the drab brown coat purchased just for this purpose, pulled a hatbox from the shelf and took out a turban fashioned from straw mesh with a pink grosgrain ribbon bow. It wasn't the sort of hat the woman she was pretending to be would wear, but nonetheless, she needed a hat, and was worried enough about making the train that she couldn't allow herself the time to rummage about for something more suitable.

"Ah," Jacques said when he saw her emerge from the bedroom in her second-hand coat. "Ah, so you're..."

"Yes," she said. "Yes."

"Well," he said. He paused before saying again, "Well," and then wrapped his arms around her, squeezing her close to him. She was the one who broke off the embrace, fearing she might start weeping.

Turtle

At the train station, she found she had changed her way of walking, making it a little short of a waddle, becoming a member of the race, of dowdy women past their prime, lurching towards old age.

"And what sends you to Orleans?"

The question was asked by a fellow passenger, not by a member of the Milice, a thin-nosed, thin-lipped man with whom she had just exchanged pleasantries of the sort swapped with the elderly gentleman. Unprepared for this question, she nearly blurted out: "Jeanne has baked a cherry tart." Instead she said, altogether too hastily, "My mother is dying."

He murmured a banal condolence and went back to reading the collaborationist *Aujourd'hui*.

"Yes, my mother."

She found she was trembling

"Cold, Madame? Let me shut the window."

"Oh, no, no." Simone knew that if she continued to shiver with the window closed she would be casting further suspicion on herself. "It will be so close in here." She wrapped her coat around her like a blanket, a turtle with its head jutting out of its shell.

"As you wish, Madame."

Simone was relieved when others entered the compartment. Nevertheless, she feared the reader of *Aujourd'hui* might give a half-bow to those in the compartment, saying, "If you'll excuse me for a moment, please," and whisper to the conductor, "Thought I should let you know. There's a woman in my compartment who's terribly jittery…You never know who's a saboteur, eh?"

Years ago, at a gathering Simone had found herself backed into a corner by a man who'd more or less imprisoned her by bracing his arm against the wall. He was well over six feet, so he bent over her, his body twisting itself into the shape of a question mark. It wasn't so unusual for her to get cornered. Sometimes these men had no ulterior motive—or at least none Simone could discern—but more often they saw her as a key which would unlock the door of the inner circles of the Paris literary world. On other occasions they were Theosophists, Vedantists, sometimes Trotskyist opponents of the Popular Front or supporters of the anarcho-syndicalist tendency in the Spanish Civil War.

This man, dank wine on his breath, spoke to her of mysteries passed down from the builders of the pyramids, the sadhus of India—Simone was fuzzy on what had been said, having herself had quite a few glasses of wine. His forelock kept falling forward into his eyes, and he would jerk his head back, like a horse flicking its mane.

Simone murmured polite assents as he spoke of mental emanations and the material power of thought. Mistaking her courtesy for genuine interest, he drew closer, forcing her to tilt her head back in the attitude of a supplicant. A few days later—she must have given him her address, perhaps as a way of detaching herself from him—a brochure arrived in the mail, printed on cheap newsprint, a line drawing of a turbaned man with winged orbs flying from his head, underneath an explanation of how you could beam your thoughts into the minds of others: "Concentrate intently on another person in a room with you, without his noticing it. Observe him gradually become restless and turn and look in your direction..." She had buried it in the bottom of the wastebasket, afraid of Jacques seeing it, scolding her for foolishness. She had not given those long-gone events a moment's thought until now, when she remembered the feel of that cheap newsprint beneath her fingers, the line drawing. Her mind, quite against her will, might be beaming her fear towards the man with the thin lips.

Simone often longed for time to slow down, and now it had, although this prolongation was more like what one experiences in the antechamber of the dentist's office awaiting one's turn to undergo some bloody procedure, overhearing the high-pitched whir of the drill, the muted clatter of instruments against the metal tray, the dentist's murmurs, while the patient, mouth stuffed with cotton batting, responds with an indecipherable word, "Glaptor-fara" or "Fankuzzi." Simone's dentist not only had fingers that were hirsute but also were sausage-like, so that after his ministrations her jaw ached.

And just as Simone thought "sausage-like fingers," the carriage was filled with the odor of pork fat and garlic. The thin-lipped man had spread a linen napkin in his lap and was slicing up a *saucisson sec* with his penknife. Simone knew it was quite impossible that she had conjured up the sausage by thinking about the dentist's fat fingers. Surely, it was the smell of sausage, at first reaching her subliminally, which must have brought to mind the thought of the dentist's fingers, which had attached itself to the thoughts of time at last slowing down.

At the same time, she believed quite firmly that she had summoned that sausage into existence. And just as her mind had manifested this sausage, it would create two members of the Milice, who would knock firmly on the door of the carriage, bow to the innocent parties, one of them pointing a finger at Simone and saying, "You."

Ever have any bizarre thoughts? Disordered thinking?

With the stink of sausage filling up the carriage, there was an excuse to look at the weasel-faced man. He brought the edge of the knife so close to his fingers that Simone could not help think that at any moment—should the train sway unexpectedly—he would slice into himself, the gap opening up in his flesh before the rush of blood. He seemed to not only enjoy the envy of his fellow passengers—a man who could eat meat, meat in the morning—but also was taking some pleasure in their anxiety as the blade sliced close to his flesh. *What was he like as a lover?* Like Luc he would make love with a precision bordering on cruelty.

She wasn't the only one staring at him. There was a woman seated to his left, with a broad-brimmed straw hat—fraying at the edges and with its garland of fabric tea roses gone dusty, one not really suited to the season, or quite frankly, to the woman's age, a hat which, like the woman who wore it, was past its prime. Perhaps this woman, who gave the impression of being the sort of woman Simone was pretending to be, might be carrying a message as well: she might also have been told that a man would sit next to her on a bench and compliment her hat, might have rifled through her hatboxes to find the proper headgear for the assignation before rushing for the train.

It also occurred to her that just as it was possible that the thick-thighed woman with the girlish hat was a Resistance courier, that could also be true of this man. The newspaper, the air of sour rectitude might all be part of his disguise.

The blade of the knife came so close to his finger, she found she was not so much fearing it slicing into his soft white flesh as yearning for it. She imagined him lifting his thumb to his mouth, sucking his own blood.

She longed for the thing that would end her terror: for the Milice officers to knock on the door.

The next day, doing the things she ordinarily did—going to the post office to buy stamps, picking up Jacques' shirts from the laundry—she yearned once again to be on the train. Three days later, knowing that she should not, but unable to resist the temptation, she would ask the man with the Pomeranian, "Do you know when I will be sent again?"

"No, Madame," he said, conveying his disapproval of her foolish question despite his impeccable manners. "I most certainly cannot answer such a question."

Once she delivered the message: "The water-tower has sprung a leak," and watched a man's face collapse in grief. He repeated her words as a question, his voice shaking, "The water- tower has sprung a leak? Anything else? Quickly, please." He had already risen to his feet, his pupils ricocheting back and forth in his eyes, his breath coming shallow, ready to run.

Sometimes no one showed up.

She would wait on the appointed park bench, reading, or pretending to read. Or at a café table, slowly sipping a cup of dark fluid, a brew of chicory and roasted acorns or a glass of sour wine.

Once, sitting in a café, her right arm began to shake, which she found puzzling because it was just a single limb, and she didn't feel any more on edge than usual. (Later, of course, she would see this as a harbinger of her condition.) She clasped her left hand over her right to stop it from trembling.

"Nervous, madame?" the proprietor asked.

"No, monsieur." Then: "A tremor. Familial. It comes on—when—in the prime of life." She had a friend to whom this had happened, yet was surprised that such an explanation had sprung so readily to mind.

"Sometimes my patrons get nervous," he said, as he wiped the table next to her with a damp bar towel, "from drinking too much coffee. Others from the presence of German officers. There are some who come in here every day about noon for drinks."

"Thank you. What do I owe you?"

Blame

Jacques knew himself well enough to know that he always needed a woman in his orbit for whom he felt contempt. He could have great respect for a mistress, even see her as nearly an equal, as long as there was another woman he regarded with a sense of superiority which bordered on disdain. Once, at La Vigie, very drunk, he had berated Simone so ferociously for her intellectual shortcomings that two of the other men present had forcibly removed him from the parlor, arms clasped around his shoulders, fingers hooked into the belt loops of his trousers, walking him around and around the courtyard in hopes of sobering him up or at least keeping him from doing any more verbal damage, one of them saying over and over again, "Come now, old man. You married beneath you. You mustn't blame the poor girl for that." The next morning Jacques had awakened with a headache so ferocious it felt as if his temples were being squeezed in a vise. He had no memory of the previous night's events. He was only aware of the pall, as vague as it was intense, hanging over the assembly, and knew, through the calculus of gestures and glances, aversions of his companions' eyes, that he was somehow the cause of the discomfort. Occasionally, in the years to come, the words that had been chanted, *Come now, old man. You married beneath you. You mustn't blame the poor girl for that* would billow up into his consciousness, often in echoing fragments: *Come now, old man*. Or: *You mustn't blame the poor girl for that, blame the poor girl* although he had no memory of their origin. Like the Latin dirges he had heard chanted in his boyhood, the lullabies his nanny had sung to him, these fragments were tucked deep in a lumpy sack at the back of his mind.

Then the war and the Occupation had come along and changed everything: the hour of the last Metro, the availability of petrol and turnips, their national pride, the essential nature of his relationship with Simone. They had become compatriots—impossible to believe it could happen between the two of them, but yes, it had—and the rancor and passion, the quarrels and reconciliations that had punctuated their years together dissipated. In August of 1942, she had looked up from her reading one night—they were both on the settee, her bare feet resting in his lap, being idly massaged by him—and said, "How long has it been since we had a row?" They tried to remember their last one. There had been the business about the cabbage gone moldy—but that, they both agreed, had been a mere squabble. "Just before we left for Carcassonne..." she ventured. Yes, yes, a piece of crockery she had hurled at the wall was a decisive marker: that had been a real fight, although neither could remember the source of the discord. Jacques said, "I remember seeing the casserole dish flying through the air, headed for the wall, realizing that was the last moment it would be intact," and they had both laughed, then squeezed their hands together: so they would become the sort of couple who would say, twenty years hence, "In the beginning, there were some rough spots in our marriage, but for many years we haven't exchanged so much as a cross word." The prospect both comforted and terrified them.

Comrades

On the night of October 5th, 1941, Simone wasn't served soup but rather a meal of the sort one had eaten before the war—rabbit stew, good country bread. Some grumbled at opening their home to members of the Resistance. Others treated them like visiting royalty. She had eaten so much, drunk so much wine—the farm woman kept refilling her glass—that the sleep she'd fallen into was more of a stupor.

A few hours later when she was rousted from it, she felt as if she were being dragged up from the grave. The man who prodded her awake was a comrade—even those who weren't members of the Party used that term now—to whom she had delivered a message earlier in the day. He smelt of garlic and machine grease and the acrid sweat of fear.

"Hurry up."

He turned his back while she pulled her clothes on.

The moon, full two days before, was a lopsided circle drawn by the hand of a child. He had a bicycle, but the ground was too muddy to ride, so they walked to the road while he whispered. "Alain. They arrested him yesterday. We found him sneaking up an alley. Saw me, ran." His unfamiliar dialect, the whispering, meant there was a lag of a few seconds while Simone sorted out his words.

"Did he talk?"

Even in the dim light, she could see his look of scorn.

"It could have been any of us," Simone said.

He didn't need to say: *it could have been but it wasn't, it was him.*

Having reached the macadamed road, the man climbed onto the

bicycle, indicating that Simone should seat herself on the handlebars. She tucked her skirts between her legs, a girl of forty, fighting with the teasing air for her modesty.

At the garage where he took her, a hand-painted sign in front had misspelled *pneus* as *pnues*.

"He's downstairs," the owner of the garage said, filing the end of a metal pipe as he spoke, the noise so grating she felt as if he were rasping the ends of her nerves. He had a protuberant lower lip which shimmied as he spoke.

She shook hands with the two men—one scarcely more than a boy, really—lounging amongst the half-disassembled cars, scattered parts, the youth's hip against a fender, the older man slouched behind a steering wheel, fingers idly tapping the dash.

The man who had roused her from bed indicated with a jerk of his head a rough plank door, said the word "Cellar."

How foolish she had been to imagine that the Alain she had known two days before, the Alain into whose bed she had crept in the middle of the night for the laudanum of sex, that Alain would be waiting for her down below. His eyelids and sockets were so blackened they looked like a bandit's mask. Simone thought: *We are creatures of flesh, we lug our souls about in bags of skin, although no one believes in the soul anymore, we're blood and sinews and habit and some animating impulse, and if those sacks of flesh get sundered, and some of that stuff, that stuff that made us alive, trickled out*—as it had leaked out of Alain, poured out more likely, judging by the blood caking his mouth, his wrists—*were we still the same person we had been when we were all of one piece*?

The other inhabitants of the cellar, the mice and spiders, the woodlice and centipedes had withdrawn into their crevices, trembling, waiting for the humans to be done with their business.

He slumped against the beam he was tied to. She went weak-kneed as it dawned on her she hadn't been spirited away from the safe house only because it was no longer safe. She clutched the railing to keep herself upright. Rough wood, not a polished bannister designed for the soft hand of a woman from Paris to glide along: a thick splinter entered the flesh of her palm, causing her to start.

Hearing the sounds of her footsteps on the stairs, Alain looked up. The click of heels, not the tromping of feet clad in boots, work shoes.

He sighed with relief. He sighed and then said her name, which was not Simone but the alias she had whispered in his ear forty-odd hours ago. Odile? Dominique? Germaine? Monique? Matilde? He said it as if he were saying, "Mama."

"So," Simone said. She did not know what else to say, and so she said "So." It occurred to her that the Germans who had arrested him had been as inexperienced at interrogation as she was. War, after all was about making do: you ran out of butter and used rapeseed oil. You ran out of rapeseed oil and used rendered bacon fat. You ran out of rendered bacon fat and did without. You ran out of skilled interrogators and used spotty-faced lads who had watched the odd spy movie or wide-girthed Bavarian men who had worked in a hog slaughterhouse. Perhaps those bodies "battered almost beyond recognition," another cliché of the war years, weren't so much the product of cruelty as bungling. Not knowing what else to do, fearing the wrath of their superiors, the interrogators had used fists and cudgels, well beyond the point where such things might produce information.

She touched his shoulder. "They roughed you up pretty good."

"I didn't talk."

"Everyone talks."

Everyone talks she said, but then there was silence, nothing being said, nothing at all, nothing.

The garage owner lifted his eyes from the monkey wrench, which he had been tapping against the open palm of his hand, with a look that said: *Come on, get on with it.*

Just after the start of the war she had read, more or less on Jacques' orders, in manuscript, Arthur Koestler's *Darkness at Noon*. It had been a chore, her German wasn't fluent, and she'd read with a translating dictionary at her side, one that had come from Jacques' father's library, the letters of the German words in Fraktur. The serifs and ornamentation, the thickness of the lines made the words she was forced to look up ponderous. She had resented reading it, especially as it had to be done quickly, someone else was eager for the manuscript, of which there was only one other copy. She tried now to remember the techniques the interrogator, Rubashov, had used in the novel. No, Rubashov had been the one interrogated. Sleep deprivation had played a central role—but, of course, they hadn't the time for that now. She was as ill-equipped for this task as the Germans pressed into service.

"Can I have some water?" Alain asked.

"No," the garage owner answered.

"Tell us what happened."

"Oh, just let me give him a good one with this," the garage owner said.

So it happened like this: you couldn't help it from happening. You turned into the good cop and the bad cop from a B movie.

"Please, can I have some water?"

Simone called to the boy at the top of the stairs. He brought down a glass of water. She held it to Alain's lips, carefully tipping it into his mouth, watching his Adam's apple as he swallowed. Odette at her breast had been filled with the same mix of greed and submission. She felt the same thrill with her power over him and disgust at his need.

She pulled the glass away from Alain's lips and flung the water in his face. "Who did you give up?"

"No one."

"They let you go."

"So that my blood would be on your hands, not theirs."

"Ah, the well-known conscience of the Gestapo."

"To sow dissension among us."

"And then the moans ceased and the cries began. Alain's bowels unloosened in fear. The stink in the room. Of shit, but also of fear. Not just his fear, but the torturer's fear as well. "You know how this is going to end. So why draw it out?"

As the life went out of him, his feet kicked wildly at the dirt floor, like a child having a temper tantrum. A cloud of dust rose up from the floor.

Earlier, when she had so wanted them, the specifics of *Darkness at Noon* had hovered beyond her consciousness, but now one sentence came to her almost whole—Rubashov, the old Bolshevik imprisoned by his Stalinist warders, musing that he knew from experience that coming close to death alters one's thinking and causes surprising reactions. She could see the last words of that sentence as they had been printed on the page: *wie die Bewegungen eines in der Nähe der magnetischen Pole gebracht Kompass*—like the movements of a compass brought close to the magnetic pole.

The boy at the top of the stairs wept.

"Get a hold of yourself," the garage owner said. "Come on," and gave him a punch on the shoulder that was somewhere between a real swing and a hey-buck-up-pal gesture. Then, jerking his head towards Simone: "Walk her over to your sister's place. Don't go inside—the shed. We'll deal with this."

This.

What was left over when life was gone.

This hunk of meat that would start to stink, to draw flies and maggots. Ashes to ashes, dust to dust the priests intoned, as if death were thin and dry.

The garage owner was saying to the other man, who perhaps was his brother or a cousin,

"We can't bring the car in now. Someone might hear and—"

"Yes, in the morning."

"In the morning," the garage owner said. "But we'd better get him ready to go in the trunk now."

"Now."

Knees bent to chest, arms wrapped around knees, head bowed as if in prayer—the shape an end-of-term fetus assumes, no longer floating willy-nilly in its amniotic sea, but having folded itself into a snug parcel about to be delivered to the world.

Forty-odd hours ago, Alain's breath had been ragged in her ear, he had leaned his head back and cried out, "Ah, Germaine!" or "Ah, Michelle!" a name that had been hers and not hers, with a look on his face that had not been so different from the one when the fan belt started to tighten around his neck. Forty-odd hours ago, he had collapsed on top of her, spent and gasping, a fish on dry land. She had felt the beating of his heart through her own chest.

Now Alain was dead. Someday she would be dead. The garage owner with the shaking lower lip would die. The youth at the top of the stairs who had not yet begun to shave would die. His children and their children and their children's children, and their children's children would die. But this was nothing new, she had known this since she herself was little more than a child. Hitler would die, Stalin would die, Pétain would die, Roosevelt would die, Africans living in villages who had never heard the names Hitler, Stalin, Pétain, Roosevelt would die.

Her hand throbbed with pain. She looked at her palm, the red outline of the sliver. This was the soul: the intersection of the world of mind and the world of flesh, the sliver and the pain caused by the sliver. Her hands were gritty, perhaps from the dust kicked up by Alain's feet, a child's protest, *No, no, I'm not going! I'm not going! I'm staying here, here with you! I'm not going!*

When she opened the cellar door and stepped into the garage itself, she was startled by the sound of rain against the roof, the windows. She had forgotten there was a world beyond that underground room.

The boy took her along alleys, lanes, her feet sinking into the muck, the mud slurping inside her shoes. In the distance the dark outlines of houses, wisps of smoke rising from chimneys; behind those walls people had gone on reading, staring into the fire, listening to the wireless, idly scratching their flesh, sleeping, dreaming.

The pressure from her bladder was urgent and she said "A minute," and squatted beneath a bush, the vinegar smell of her urine mixing with the smell of damp earth. During the course of their walk, the rain stopped falling: there was just the sodden earth, fat drops of rain water plopping from leaves, the gibbous moon appearing and disappearing behind the clouds.

Sleep

The shed was used for storage by those with the peasant habit of never throwing anything away—a broken horse yoke, tins of hardened paint. The boy moved wooden crates to reveal a camp bed, covered by a blanket with a black stencil across the green wool, declaring it the property of the French Army. She dusted off the bed, grit and cobwebs, carcasses of dead insects sailing into the air, drifting down onto the floor.

"Is there water? To wash with?" She yearned for hot water, soap, a washcloth, thought of Shakespeare's Richard, offering his kingdom for a horse. What had she to barter?

"I think the pump would—too much noise."

"Yes, of course."

It would have made more sense, given the chilliness of the night, the stiff wool blanket, to have slept in her clothes, but Simone wanted to get out of them, although she knew her naked body would give off a foul odor. She began to unbutton her blouse, not coyly, but as she undressed in front of Jacques before retiring.

"Stay here with me. Please. I don't want to be alone."

How long those seconds before he spoke. Her fingers paused above the third button from the top of her blouse.

"I—" he finally managed to say. "I—"

She knew the look that must be on her face, having seen it often on the faces of men, the naked look of one rejected before it has a chance to rearrange itself into the guise of anger or apathy. The boy was frightened of her aging flesh, frightened of the rawness of her need.

"I only meant," she said, "only…"

"I'll be back for you in the morning. Or someone, someone will."

❦

When she returned to their flat in Paris the following evening, she at first said nothing more to Jacques than, "A messy business."

She lay next to him in bed, unable to sleep, but not wriggling about, lying flat on her back, arms parallel to one another atop the comforter, staring up at the ceiling with wide open eyes.

Although she was still, her inner agitation seeped out—through her pores, her breath— and kept Jacques awake. Finally, he said, "I have some Nembutal. I took it from Christophe's apartment, after he—"

They had always been sound sleepers. The Nembutal had been brought home because suicide might become a necessity.

She got up and went to the medicine cabinet, took one.

After half an hour he sat up, propping the pillows behind him, said: "Go ahead and tell me."

"We had to kill someone."

"We?"

"I didn't actually—that is—I didn't—it was with a fan belt, because we were in a garage—"

"Simone! Be careful what you say. Don't tell me any more than—"

"Yes, yes. I'm sorry."

She too sat up, drawing her knees around her chest, hugging them to her. She did not touch him. She never wanted to touch another human being again. He patted her hand. How odd, that everyday gesture, now.

"A German?"

"No."

"A collaborator?"

"No. One of us. He'd been arrested and—he loved us. Even while we were—doing what we had to do to him, to find out what he'd told the Milice, torturing him, really, even while—"

"It would be better for me, not to hear this."

"All right."

Jacques went to the medicine cabinet, came back with the bottle of Nembutal, taking one for himself, giving her another; although she had to take a third before she finally fell asleep.

If one could call it falling, if one could call it sleep.

Resistance

Half a decade later, she will be sent to a psychoanalyst, Dr. Balmant, who will tell her, "Your shaking is an attempt to recreate the excitement of the war years. After all, you have told me, many times, that it was then you felt yourself to be most fully alive."

"Ah, no, I don't think that is true…"

"I know very well that 'no,' you utter. It is the door that consciousness slams in the face of the unconscious." He considered saying, "The resistance with which you cling to the Resistance," but, although he had warned her against discussing her treatment with anyone, he feared she might repeat this remark to her eminent husband, and he might find it trite.

Train

Simone's carriage was nearly empty, just herself and another woman, a woman with marcelled hair. Having given Simone the necessary greeting and forced smile, the woman with the blonde hair that reached in undulating waves to her shoulders began to read, a work of light fiction taken from a lending library. Simone stared out the window.

About an hour after they had embarked, the train screeched to a halt. They waited.

They waited.

They waited, waited, waited, waited.

Rumors went around the carriages: some said that the Resistance had blown up the tracks. *You'd better prepare yourself to be here for a good long while, it'll be days before…*Others said, *I have it on good authority*, a nod and a sideways glance to let you know the speaker had a pipeline to some greater source of knowledge, *it's German troop movements, give it an hour and we'll be on our way.*

It was nine o'clock in the evening.

It was ten o'clock.

It was eleven o'clock.

Simone went to the lavatory. All during those years, she had a bad taste in her mouth. She brushed her teeth three, four, five, ten times a day. When toothpowder became impossible to obtain, she sprinkled baking soda on her toothbrush, and when she was no longer able to get baking soda, salt. In the toilet on the train, she scraped the nail of her pinkie finger along her gums, along her teeth, smearing the whitish stuff that caught beneath her nail—she knew of no word for this in French or English or German—onto a square of toilet paper. She used the fingernail of her other hand to tamp down her eyebrows, turned up the rim of the cloche which she had previously worn almost as if it were a balaclava, half-obscuring her face, cinched the belt of her jacket about her waist, unbuttoned the two top buttons of her blouse.

Simone came back into the compartment having shed her guise of the drab *femme de maison* and become, if not exactly the woman she was in her ordinary life, a version of her everyday self: a woman mature in the sense of ripe, a piece of fruit most succulent at the brink of decay, a woman who had spent decades learning the knowledge of a community of lovers, secrets passed tongue to tongue, fingertip to fingertip. She gave the woman with the marcelled hair a cool appraisal, and, although the woman barely looked up, the air was charged.

Simone prepared herself to say, "I heard that the Resistance has blown up the tracks. We may be here for quite some time—days even." She had no idea what the woman might say in response. She might answer with a noncommittal shrug of her shoulders or say, "People say a lot of things." She might give a sly smile, shifting her gaze upwards, the smile growing broader as Simone returned it. Or she might say, "Those bloody terrorists," going on—that mix of boredom and fear so often experienced during the war years making her voluble. "Them, and the goddamn Jews." Seeing the look of shock on Simone's face, the other woman would go on: "I had a friend when I was a child who was a Jew, you can't say that I'm not open-minded, but still they do rather know how to manipulate situations for their own ends…" If the woman said that, Simone wouldn't drop her seduction, but she would be rough with her, she wouldn't slip just two fingers into her, but all four of them, her whole hand, if she could manage it, she'd shove it hard against the woman's womb, Simone would nip at her breasts and then grab her nipple between her teeth until the woman cried out—not, of course, loudly enough to be heard in the other compartments—*no, please, stop, you're being too rough with me, you mustn't leave marks on me, you're hurting me, you're hurting me*. Simone was surprised to find herself excited by the idea of causing this woman pain.

And then she said the words she had been preparing to say: "They say that the Resistance has blown up the tracks. We may be here for quite some time."

The woman said nothing, her expression did not change, there was neither a smile of complicity nor words of scorn about the Resistance, merely that look of infinite blankness which is seen on faces of people waiting, in rooms designated with that name, waiting for a train, waiting to see a dentist, who stare at the horizon where the plane of time meets the plane of eternity.

Simone sighed and sat down, not in the seat she had occupied before but next to the woman, seating herself at an angle so that her knees brushed against the woman's knees.

They were playing a game like any other one might play to pass the time when stuck waiting with a stranger, when one tired of solitaire: blackjack, hangman. And just as in those other games, you ruined it if you showed your cards.

"Oh," the other woman moaned, "oh, oh, oh, oh, oh." Those syllables that mean everything and nothing.

Parachute

Sent to wait for an English parachutist, she scanned the sky methodically for hours until her neck grew aching and stiff. She stamped her feet, trying to keep them warm. At last, she heard the rumble of a plane's engine, then saw a patch of lighter grey against the grey sky. The shape became more distinct until it resolved itself into the dark form of a man swaying almost comically, suspended in a leather harness from the parachute above.

She fell in love with the man who was a slave to the wind.

Simone had a knack for falling in love: if she had been an actress, she would have been said to be a quick study. (Fortunately, she also had a knack for falling out of love.)

She walked across the half-frozen marsh towards him as he reeled in the billowing silk. She had loved the man helpless before the wind, and now she loved this man who gathered the wind in his arms, like Aeolus stuffing a leather sack with ill wind for Ulysses, so he would only have the fair. She did not stop loving him when she drew close enough to see that his skin was splotchy, hands too big for his body, like a puppy. Younger, even, than Marcel.

She tucked the crumpled parachute under her arm, then helped him with the buckles and clasps that bound the leather straps to his body. As she did so, her hand brushed against his penis. It stiffened. She let her hand rest there for a few deliberate seconds. A grin spread across his face.

They walked towards the grove of trees from which she had just come. He pulled a shovel with a folded handle from his rucksack—which also held a condom, a change of underwear, a few tins of vile meat, and of course a cyanide capsule—fiddled a bit with it, and buried his parachute and the leather harnesses, the shovel itself, patted the loam of decaying leaves back over it, dusted off the palms of his hands. How sad to bury the beautiful silk. It briefly crossed Simone's mind that she ought to mark this grave somehow so she could return after the war. But by then the silk would have rotted, been devoured by slugs and larvae. Like nearly all other French women, Simone wore schoolgirl ankle socks now. She missed silk stockings, the act of pulling them on, unfurling them up her legs, the sensation spreading from her toes up to her ankles, calves, knees, thighs, stopping just below the cleft of her sex.

As they walked along the verge of the road, the English parachutist told her his name, which was doubtless not the name with which he had been baptized, the name on his official papers.

She gave him a name, which was not Simone. She no longer remembered what she said: Germaine? Dominique? Françoise?

In place of a greeting, the farm woman said, "They told me you would have your own food." They were quartered in the barn's hayloft.

"I know nothing," the farm woman said, rehearsing an excuse. "I heard the dog bark in the night, but just a bit. I made nothing of it—"

Simone had a bit of cheese, a baguette too stale to slice. She managed to get their reluctant hostess to put some hot water in her companion's tin cup and soaked the bread in that. They scooped it out with their fingers—they'd forgotten to ask for spoons. She offered him some of her cheese. He used a penknife to cut it exactly in half, then used the penknife to open the tin of meat. The counterfeited French label declared it contained horse meat, but she suspected it was whale. If this was what they were feeding their soldiers, Simone could only imagine what they were eating at home.

It was February. The sky had been gloomy all day. Dusk had fallen by four, full night by six. Their meager rations left them hungry. The straw upon which they were to lie was scratchy, the barn cold.

Silence, instead of those words which we usually use to fill up the air between strangers: *I was born in…I have three sisters and a…a dog, she's getting old, her muzzle's gone grey…once, on a Greek island in the Aegean…Do you…Yes, me, too…*If this were Jacques, he might enjoy the chance to lie, to make up a life he'd never lived: *Born in China, the only son of missionaries…*And, if the woman he happened to be sharing a makeshift bed with stroked her index finger along his naked chest and said, *Say something in Chinese*, he'd comply, like Adam on naming day in Eden, pulling language out of the void, making her laugh.

But she did not have Jacques' relationship with the truth.

The man lying next to her might be anyone: bookish son of an Oxford don who'd read not just Marx but Hegel, believed he was an infinitesimal part of humanity achieving its destiny. Or a maladjusted lad, who, out to impress the neighborhood toughs, had robbed the local sweet-and-ciggie shop and got himself sent to borstal, from there paroled to the armed forces where his eagerness to please and recklessness had led him here, despite trepidation on the part of his superiors: *—I worry about that boy. —I'm afraid he's the best we've got. —Not saying much at this point. —True enough.* Arm clapped on the other's shoulder: *—But no great loss to the nation's germ plasm if he doesn't come back.*

They made love to drive away the boredom.

They made love to drive away the fear.

They made love because he asked and it was her habit to say yes.

His body was so boyish that it was a surprise to see a man's sex between his legs, the dark shock of his pubic hair. His tongue in her mouth tasted of rancid fat and peppermint tooth powder. His fingers fumbled with the condom packet, and he brought it close to his eyes so he could make it out in the dark. He just managed to get the condom on and get inside her, giving a few thrusts before he cried out, "No, no, no, no, no," and collapsed on top of her.

The rubber had rasped against dry flesh. Poor Simone: she was dry as a piece of newsprint cracked and yellowed by the sun. A few months later, at another farmhouse serving as a safe house—this one more hospitable—she will sneak to the kitchen in the night and scoop her hand into the jar of carefully hoarded grease next to the stove, rubbing the mix of chicken schmaltz and pork dripping, duck fat into her skin. The farm dog, a big-eyed hound, will moon after her—or perhaps, more accurately, after her rancid perfume, pushing his snout against her while the farm woman will sniff her suspiciously.

He pulled quickly out of her.

Had she herself become wartime rations: like that meat from the tin, had she become unappetizing, even repulsive, but necessary?

"Post coitum omne animal triste est, sive gallus et mulier," she said.

"What?"

"It's Latin: After sex, all animals are sad, except roosters and women."

It was wrong about women. And who knew what lay beneath the rooster's postcoital crow and round-the-barnyard-strut?

Poor child.

She laid her palm flat against his chest, a gesture of comfort.

After the war, in a café with some comrades, they'd boasted about how many times they'd had lice. In fact, someone will say, the medals the state presented them should have had a louse holding sheaves of moldy barley instead of rosettes and crosses.

The war dragged on, like a bad cold one couldn't shake. You grew sick of it, you grew sick of the bombast, the exhortations to valor. You grew sick of the thrill. You grew sick of your own nobility.

Long

During their long engagement, Simone had yearned for the banalities of life with Jacques: muddy galoshes, fetid breath in the morning. She'd also longed for the knowledge that arises from two bodies sleeping next to one another, night after night after night, their speaking to one another in a language deeper than words, through the muffled smells given off during dreams, the sighs, the punctuation of a hand finding its way onto a thigh, a weary, aging body furling or unfurling limbs.

Now her body telegraphed to his the truth of that night, that night in the cellar of the garage where the hand-lettered sign misspelled *pneus* as *pnues*, the events which, even if speaking of them had not been forbidden (*Don't ask, don't ask, don't tell me anything I don't need to know*), she would have found impossible to put into speech: her thrill at Alain's degradation, her love of her power over him. It seeped out of her pores, it inflected her moans, it even caused her to thrash about to such a degree that Jacques said to her, his voice filled with forced jocularity: "My, that must have been some dream you were having last night."

Simone shrugged. "I don't remember a thing."

Their lovemaking, which had during the first years of the war been companionable, now became fraught. She ceased to be the one who initiated, and in general, approached sex with the air of one carrying out her wifely duty. Jacques assumed this was caused by her discomfort with her aging body, by the sag of her belly and breasts that were becoming quite unmistakable—and certainly were being exaggerated by war-time hunger.

He was not much put out by this. He had once said to Simone that Sala was aware that his attentions were no longer flitting about, but had fixed themselves quite firmly on an object. This time around, Simone did not seem aware that another woman had come to occupy a rather secure position as his mistress. Dominique was a colleague, indeed, the only female to sit on the editorial committee. He had been impressed by the rigor of her intelligence and the breadth of her knowledge, which she did not flaunt like a bluestocking, but rather was quite modest about. For instance, once when the committee had been discussing the publication of a translation of Osip Mandelshtam's works, it became clear that she was fluent in Russian—although when this was commented on by the others present, she dropped her gaze and seemed genuinely flustered, like a shy schoolgirl who has just been complimented by the teacher and fears that she will later be taunted in the schoolyard for being the teacher's pet. Her appearance was rather mousy. Her black, gray, and dun outfits seemed a habit, and Jacques saw her as another one of Paris's secular nuns. He was vaguely aware that she had children—two sons, if he recalled correctly—she had once had to miss a meeting because one of them had been ill—and lived with her parents.

One day, she had come to his office to discuss a manuscript. As she was always quite correct, the annotations were made in her neat and legible hand. At first he had thought that her skirt had ridden up quite by accident, but then, as it rose higher and higher, it became clear that its lift was not haphazard. She was wearing frilly black garters of the sort worn by streetwalkers. He lowered the blinds, locked the door, and had her on the desk—she had taken care to move the manuscripts out of the way before they coupled.

Turtle

Simone walked along a country road with a lad of seventeen who'd perhaps shaved three times in his life, who'd carried out an act of great—and foolhardy—courage, and then fled to the arms of the Resistance.

"I am your mother. Here is your identity card. Our names are different because I remarried. Our address is…"

He repeated her name, his name, their address.

"Say it again."

"I know it," he protested, for all his bravery a truculent adolescent. (That night, he would climb onto the pallet where Simone was sleeping and curl himself against her as if he were an infant.)

She answered him only with her silence, and he groaned underneath his breath and repeated details, names, dates of birth, "You have a different name from me because you remarried, I was brought up by an aunt…"

A turtle ambled across their path. Simone knelt and grabbed it as it pulled its head and limbs into the safety of its shell. She handed it to the boy, who tucked it inside his jacket, cradling it with his left hand. After a while, the animal's terror eased, and it began to tentatively poke out its head and appendages, and then pull them back inside his shell, which made the boy giggle.

At the house where they were to spend the night, Simone set the turtle on the kitchen counter. As she was about to plunge a knife into its belly, the turtle craned its neck and gazed up with melancholy eyes. It seemed to be saying, with an air of Buddhist resignation, *My whole life has been nothing but weariness and slow toil. I have always known it was going to end like this, and now it is ending like this, just as I have always known it would.*

Rue des Arenes

She took a right on rue Rollin, another right on rue Monge, empty string bag slung over her right shoulder, pocketbook hanging from her left arm. If anyone—an inquisitive neighbor or a member of the occupying army—were to say to her, "Didn't I just see you walking along here?" she would say, "I need some garlic. Excuse me if I rush off, it goes quickly these days."

She had set out at the appointed time, but had not encountered the elderly gentleman with the Pomeranian.

He must have been arrested.

No, perhaps—after all, he was quite old, white hair, liver spots on his hands and face—some medical calamity, a stroke or a heart attack. Ordinarily, of course, one kept one's feelings in check, not so much one's hatred of the Germans, that was given free rein, but one's love for one's comrades—love, an odd word to use for a man whose name she didn't know, a man with whom she had exchanged nothing more than mundane remarks and odd fragments. He might be lying sprawled on the floor of his apartment, moaning in pain, alone. How old would her father be now if he had not died on the cusp of middle-age? Roughly the same age as the elderly gentleman. Perhaps he didn't live alone. He might have a wife, or be cared for by a daughter who saw it not as her duty but as her privilege to aid him. Lying on a white-sheeted bed in a clinic, a stroke having made him aphasic, he might now be attempting to tell that wife or daughter that she needed to reconnoiter with a certain neighbor, the words profuse, random, incomprehensible.

Or the Germans might have got him. Would it be easier or harder for an old man to resist? After all, he must have grown used to physical pain—ah, but an arthritic knee, sciatica—were nothing like a cudgel to the gut. A shove might terrify him, fragile as a porcelain doll.

And then she saw him.

"I was a bit worried when I didn't see you earlier." She hoped her voice did not betray the happiness she felt. "I hoped you weren't ill or —"

The Pomeranian was excited, leaping about and waggling its behind, issuing a series of sharp little barks, almost commands.

"The poor girl. Her routine's been thrown off."

Simone knelt down next to her, ruffled her fur. "Yes, yes, yes, I'm petting you, I'm petting you," but this did not seem to soothe the dog, who continued her series of sharp barks. Simone stared into the dog's eyes, which might have been the beads sewn on a child's stuffed animal.

"Unfortunately, I was a bit under the weather—"

"Nothing serious I hope."

"No, nothing serious. Of course, when one gets to be my age, one can't help but think that every cough is an omen."

Was he trying to warn her of something? Had the Germans arrested him, forced him to take this belated walk with the dog?

The Pomeranian stared up at her. Perhaps it was not really a dog but an automaton, or perhaps the Germans had killed the dog, skinned it, and wrapped its hide around a mechanized device, maybe a tape recorder inside was taking down what she said. Or perhaps the dog itself was a German spy, perhaps its true master let himself into the old man's apartment with a pass key late at night, when he was sure the old man would be asleep and the dog, through a system of wags of its tail, movements of its paws, conveyed their secrets.

Of course, these were crazy ideas. Ideas that would, in the ordinary world, have flitted through her head, scarcely noticed, whispered by the madwoman who lived in the back of her mind—who lives in all our minds, whose mutterings are ordinarily drowned out by the din of the everyday.

"So, you are quite sure it was nothing serious?"

"Ah, madame, I see that I have alarmed you. I assure you quite wholeheartedly, that it was nothing but a digestive disturbance that kept me from my usual rounds. And now, pardon me, but my faithful companion is agitated because her morning routine has been thrown askew. The body is the master, and we its obedient servants. Good day."

Soup

During the war years, Simone often ate soup.

On the days when she was lucky, when the butcher had been generous, she walked home with the hoof of a cow or the neck bone of a pig in her string bag. A calf's foot and a veal shank would have been the choice before the war, but who, in these times, could afford to slaughter a calf? She doubted even those in Hitler's inner circle dined on veal these days. Of course, Der Führer himself didn't, being a vegetarian, his tastes extending only to the flesh of his fellow man. The hog jowl or marrow bone in her bag made her feel like a figure out of a fairy tale, a stout peasant with the golden goose tucked under her arm.

Back in the flat, she'd crack the bones with a mallet, then roast them. Our tongues prefer what's been roasted to what's been boiled, it's a throwback to the days when we hunkered around the fire clad in skins, feasting on the ribs of a mastodon. The smell would start to fill the flat, she'd worry it was seeping out underneath the doorway and those Parisiennes who spent the war years sniffing the air—for the scent of fear coming off German soldiers, for the smell of frying sausage—might start to chew over her business: *I can't say if what they say about her and the butcher is true…all I know is I smelled meat roasting, there's a smell you can't mistake…*

Simone was a slattern, but like many slovenly women she had real gifts in the kitchen—not as a baker, nothing that required exact measurement, careful timing—but as a maker of roasts and stews, where her haphazard ways and willingness to let things rest (be it the film on the mirror in the bathroom or the slow simmer of a pot on the stove) worked in her favor.

The smell of roasting bones filled her with—there was no other word for it—lust. Anyone who has ever been truly hungry can tell you you can feel it not just for a man or a woman but for the knucklebone of an ox. Once or twice, she'd taken the bones from the oven and gnawed at them, working her incisors at the bits of flesh still clinging, licking up the oozing marrow. It was one of the few times she really betrayed Jacques.

When the bones were roasted, she'd stew them with water and perhaps a bit of sour wine, celery leaves, onion, skins and all, vegetable parings, salt—the long, slow boil releasing the essence of the tendons, the cartilage, the bones going backwards in time, becoming soft and fetal, the soup amniotic. At last, setting it on the counter to let it cool, covering the pan with a towel to keep the flies off, the flavors marrying.

But the memories of the war years never became a soup, never melded one into the next so that they became indistinguishable: *I used to go… every day I walked…I often rode the train…* Instead they stayed whole: each day, each train ride, each coded message, as sharp and distinct as those rough pebbles she had put in her shoes as a girl.

June

On June 10, 1944, Simone slept with a thousand strangers, give or take a few hundred, on a Metro platform in Montmartre.

The air raid siren had wailed when she was far from home, having been told by a friend that tobacco was available at a certain apartment *take a left when you come out of Lamarck-Caulaincourt…say that I sent you…* The tobacco was to be a special gift for Jacques.

Simone had gone less than a hundred meters from the Metro station when the siren howled. Within seconds, a herd of humans were stampeding for shelter, Simone stock still as they rushed past her, parting around her as waters around a rock in the river: women whose house scuffs slip-slapped against the pavement; clean-shaven men with one hand planted on their fedoras to stop them from flying off; grizzled men wearing berets, one with an unlit cigarette dangling from his lip; women who'd grabbed pillows and blankets before tearing out of their flats; women clutching children, shepherding children, one with a line of children trailing after her like goslings after a goose; men with winter coats and bathrobes tossed over their shoulders; women carrying the satchels they kept by the door for just such an emergency, containing the two bars of chocolate they'd been hoarding throughout the war, framed photographs of their late mothers, their children's christening gowns, a ball of wool and a pair of knitting needles, and, if they were particularly flush, a few francs tied up in a handkerchief.

Really, it wasn't much further to the apartment. If she hurried, she'd be able to get there before the bombs started falling. And in all likelihood, this threatened air raid was the Germans' attempt to keep the population panicked. That, or a plane spotter whose nerves were on edge. And the tobacco would make Jacques so happy.

The shriek of a gendarme's whistle. "Madame! Are you mad?"

She was still and alone, a pillar of salt in the desert of a Paris street.

The cop grabbed her elbow, propelling her into the crowd shoving its way into the Lamarck-Caulaincourt.

The crowd of intimate strangers clumped to a halt.

—Quit shoving.

—I'm not shoving. The people behind are pushing against me.

—I can't move forward.

—I know you can't! But I can't help it if—

Down below, the station master, the St. Peter of this subterranean heaven, was rattling his ring of skeleton keys at the crowd that had surrounded his booth. *—Move back! Move back! I can't open the door!*

Those spry enough to vault over the turnstiles were doing so.

—Just let me get over, Granny, and then I'll help you over, too.

—Granny! What do you mean by calling me 'Granny?'

—I'm terribly sorry. I meant it quite affectionately…

—Move back! Move back so I can open the gate!

Up above, one of the fedoraed men was ordering —*Quiet*! *Listen*! *Isn't that a Messerschmitt*?

The word Messerschmitt took on a life of its own as it passed from mouth to ear, ear to mouth, wriggling its way down the stairs, moving in a worm-like fashion, contracting and expanding and then contracting again:

—*There's a squadron of Messerschmitts. Maybe they're on their way to bomb London.*

—*London's about to be bombed.*

—*Are you sure it was a Messerschmitt? A Lancaster engine sounds very much like that of a Messerschmitt.*

—*Listen, they're headed east, not west.*

—*I don't hear anything.*

Simone, forced to halt roughly a third of the way down the station steps, clung to the railing, holding her own against those pushing her downwards. She, of course, wanted to live, but if she had to die, she'd like it to be a heroic death—saving one of her Resistance comrades, perhaps—not as the result of being crushed to death in a panic. (Although these last few years, she'd come close enough to violent deaths to know that they were only noble in retrospect. Up close, it was only different from the slaughtering of a pig or a lamb in that it was carried out less efficiently.)

Simone, an old hand at being occupied, dreaded the remote prospect of death, and the far more likely possibility of being stuck for hours in a throng of strangers who would grumble endlessly about their wartime hardships—the stomach cramps from too many turnips, the terrible attack of diarrhea caused by soup made with rancid meat served at the canteen, to which a listener might well respond, *Ah, I'm in such a state with my blocked-up bowels dysentery sounds good to me*. Another member of the haphazard clique might carry on about her neighbor's dalliance with the butcher —*A snout like a pig, but it's not her face he cares about. Gristle and bone for us, his fat thumb on the scale…and then to top it all off, the smell of frying sausages—real sausages, mind you!—coming through the wall…* Then, leaning forward, an exaggerated whisper: *She'll get hers, soon enough…*

Simone yearned for Peace with a capital P, but also for lower-case peace—an end to that endless hymn of grievance and plaint the whole of France had been chanting for the past four years.

Bodies pressed against Simone, their smells filled her nostrils. Hot water was beyond a luxury. A human ripeness hung in the air of Paris. It was the Germans who were clean-scrubbed, reeking of carbolic soap and laundry starch.

This

A week before, the BBC had broadcast lines from Verlaine: *Les sanglots longs des violons de l'automne blessent mon coeur d'une langueur monotone.*

A smile had broken across Jacques' face. He tried unsuccessfully to squelch it, a man who prided himself on his haughty equanimity.

"Yes?" Simone asked.

Jacques would do no more than shrug his shoulders, wink, raise his finger to his lips, which he was attempting to purse, although they were turning up at their corners. He knew, although she did not, that these lines signaled the invasion was imminent, that the Resistance was to begin a general uprising, that this might soon be over.

"This," by the way, was the war. Along with everything else, the Occupation had upset the rules of grammar. When there was no other immediate referent, "this" meant the war; "they," the Germans.

Simone and Jacques had been hunched over the radio, the volume turned as low as possible, Jacques sucking on his empty pipe, Simone with a dowdy crocheted shawl around her shoulders. Although it was spring, the hardships of the last half-decade had burned away every extra ounce of fat from their bodies: the things one never missed until they were gone, the layer of fat enveloping you just inside your skin, more protective than a lover's embrace. Without it, one was almost always cold, even on a balmy spring evening in Paris. One's heels ached from the raw pressure of bone against the soles of shoes. Like most of the women of Paris, Simone bundled herself in worn and patched layers of clothing, swaddled like a caterpillar in its cocoon.

Resistance

After the war, across Europe, museums will be dedicated to the Resistance, the capital letter befitting the proper noun, as if the Resistance had been contained, structured, organized, rather than something amorphous, everywhere and nowhere, the edges of it bleeding into collaboration. Black and white photographs will be displayed showing people leaning towards radios as if they were domestic altars, the captions underneath reading: *Listening to the wireless/to the BBC/to Stalin/to Roosevelt/to DeGaulle.*

The photographs, like the ones that will show the Maquisards being trained in the use of Sten guns or a makeshift printing press on a kitchen table being operated by a *femme maison* who wouldn't look out of place shopping at the Galeries Lafayette, were fakes, obvious to anyone who lived through that time. For a start, no one would have been so foolish as to take a photograph which would have got its subjects sent to a camp—at the very least—should it fall into the wrong hands. In the photographs, the Maquisards have clean-scrubbed faces and clothes without a tear or a patch, but during the war, they were always filthy, their clothes grimy, torn. Above all, in those pictures, they had the untroubled looks of victors on their faces. During the war, everyone in the Resistance went about with the sour expressions of men with peptic ulcers. And when one listened to the forbidden broadcasts of the BBC, it was often necessary to assume rather ridiculous postures in order to get one's ear as close as possible to the radio speakers, lest a neighbor hear the rumble through the walls and sell you out for a kilo of butter or for the defense of civilization against Bolshevism. Listeners hunkered on the floor, knees drawn up to their chests, ears pressed against the radio itself, or crooked their heads at odd angles.

So even at that moment when the smile was bursting over Jacques' face, they both looked more pathetic than heroic: a middle-aged couple, she in a suit fashionable a decade before the war, topped by the ratty shawl inherited from her mother, he in a suit that had, through long wear, developed such a pronounced greenish sheen that it could no longer accurately be described as black.

"I repeat: *Les sanglots longs des violons…*" The rest of the words disappeared in a fog of German-made static. Jacques rose to his feet, held out his arms in waltz position, hummed a few bars of Mendelssohn—a waltz was permissible if it was danced to the tune of a Jew—took Simone in his arms and spun her a few times around their front room before he knocked his shin on the edge of the sofa—even when he was a young man, he had been anything but a graceful dancer.

He whispered in her ear, "*Les sanglots longs des violons de l'automne blessent mon coeur d'une langueur monotone…*I can forgive the British many things, but this choice of poetry is simply unpardonable."

Götterdämerung

It was impossible to feel hope without also feeling dread. After all, the French nation had been hopeful before. In September of 1938, after refugees had streamed through Paris pushing ox-carts, wheelbarrows, driving ancient black cars stuffed with packing crates, piles of clothing—mattresses, bicycles, prams tied to their roofs with rope, stone-faced grandmothers sitting by the front passenger window—Daladier had come back from Munich to cheering crowds, children lifted up by their mothers above the barricades holding out bouquets of flowers to him, the newspaper headlines one enormous word: PEACE!

When the German Army collapsed at Stalingrad in '43—How many Boche losing toes, fingers to frostbite? How many frozen to death? How many prisoners of war dying on their forced march to Siberia?—no one is sure, not Field Marshall Friedrich Paulus, not General Vasily Ivanovich Chuikov, certainly not Jacques and Simone, who were only sure that however many it had been, it had not been enough. They had waited all the rest of that winter—ears pressed against their radios, searching the faces of German soldiers for signs of fear—waited hourly for an invasion which did not come and did not come and did not come.

At last it had. Four days before, a window had been flung open and a voice had called into the courtyard: "They've landed!"

But perhaps this was like the respite granted to a dying man who, after days of delirium, has an hour of lucidity before the end. Will the Germans scorch the earth as they retreat, a version of the Romans plowing the fields of Carthage with salt, Vercingetorix torching his own people's granaries and villages as the Roman legions advanced? Perhaps those rumors about the German's doomsday device were true, that when all hope was lost, they'd switch it on, modern-day Samsons bringing down the pillars of the world around them. Of late, the entire population of France had become expert on Norse mythology, especially the war between the gods that brings about the end of the world: Brünnhilde spurring her steed into the funeral pyre, Valhalla consumed in flames. The end of the Ring Cycle didn't seem at all overblown, tragedy so overblown it became farce. The word *Götterdämerung* had become commonplace: *La porte, la table, oui, non, Götterdämerung.*

Mob

The gates below were at last opened, and the mob shambled forward. They were no longer individuals, stuffed into sacks of skin, possessors of identity cards which listed their names, their dates and places of birth—rather multiple souls fused into a colossal millipede.

A few years later, a doctor at the Salpêtrière will ask her, "Any bizarre thoughts? Disordered thinking?" While she will be hastening to assure him, "Oh, no, nothing of that sort, no," she will remember this journey into the underground, the sense of humanity having evolved into some great beast. Where does the line lie between a bizarre thought and the everyday meander and poke-about of the mind?

Simone stumbled.

Perhaps she stumbled due to muscular weakness caused by wartime nutritional deprivation, so that when her brain sent the command to her tibialis anterior to flex her ankle, the muscle was unable to respond with the requisite force. Perhaps the steps of the Metro station were in poor repair, strips of anti-slip stair tread meant to provide an extra margin of safety had come loose, performing the opposite function, and the heel of Simone's shoe caught on the end of one of these, causing her to pitch forward. Or perhaps this was an early symptom of her Parkinson's disease, the brain's order rappelling down her body via the ropes of her nerves swung too far in one direction, ricocheted, and by the time it reached her foot had reversed itself, causing her to lurch.

Fortunately, due to the pressure of the crowd, she was borne up by the mass of bodies around her and did not tumble headlong down.

She gave a little cry.

A young man squeezed his way through the crowd towards her, no mean feat this, and took her arm. He was roughly her son Marcel's age, in a rumpled, misbuttoned shirt with frayed cuffs. A strand of rope held up his sagging trousers.

"Really, I'm quite all right. I just…I just…" she murmured. Then looked him full in the face: "You are very kind."

He stared back at her. "Yes." His unflinching gaze was the only thing about him that was steady. He trembled, and worked for air, like a swimmer surfacing after too long underwater.

"You yourself are having difficulty."

"Heart condition." He held up his hands, fingers splayed. Beneath his nails, his skin showed pale blue. How many times a day, Simone wondered, must he answer the question, rarely asked verbally, just in a challenging look: *You aren't in the Maquis, in a German labor camp, in prison—are you a collaborator*? and then offer in addition to his words, the evidence of his flesh, assuring the asker that "heart condition" was not a euphemism for tuberculosis, pederasty. You need fear no contagion, bacterial or moral.

Lucky you, Simone thought, lucky your mother: I wish my Marcel had a bad heart. I almost wish he had been born an idiot, that the midwife had raised her head from between my legs with a doleful gaze. But she only said aloud: "I have a son, roughly your age."

"What a coincidence," he gasped, and winked. "I have a mother." The Germans may take our potatoes, our grain, our meat, our sons, our pride, our daughters, our wine, our coal, our petrol but they cannot deprive us of our banter. "Although, you do not seem old enough to have a son my age."

"You would say that to me no matter what, wouldn't you?"

"I would say that to you even if you were an old crone, with a face thick with wrinkles. But in your case I am quite sincere."

"Simone," she said.

"Henri." Then mouthed, "Away? Your son?"

She nodded. It was not that her son being in a German labor camp was shameful, only that if it was spoken of in whispers, it seemed less real than if it was bruited about.

A hunchback a few steps below Simone eyed the crowd, wary of his hump being rubbed for luck, insinuating his back against the wall. It was almost as if he could read the minds of those who were casting furtive glances at him…*Silly peasant superstition. Still, what could it hurt? …And at a time like this, a little extra luck could…*

Ah, Simone thought, this is what has become of the children of Voltaire—we have become believers in omens, amulets, divination. Perhaps the war won't end in either victory or defeat; we'll simply devolve back into pagan tribes. The Eiffel Tower will become like the Sphinx, its origin shrouded in mystery.

Henri glared at the poor man, his contempt undisguised.

The wa-wa wa-wa, wa-wa wa-wa of the sirens persisted, the wailing of a monstrous regiment of mechanical babies.

Fat

At long last, they reached the platform. Henri spread his coat down, indicating that Simone should be seated upon it. She placed herself to his right so that the gap left when one of her teeth fell out a few months ago—the result of vitamin deprivation—was not immediately visible. (Add that lost bicuspid to the mountains of bones at the feet of Der Führer.) She was glad she'd taken the time to make herself up before she left her flat. She'd discovered a stub of lipstick in the back of a drawer—her slapdash housekeeping meant that occasionally she unearthed such bounty: a half bar of soap—a half bar of soap!—beneath the sink, last year two francs in the pocket of an old pair of slacks. Of course, she was wearing a turban, the fashion in Paris for the last few years, owing to the fact that the hair of nearly all Parisiennes had become dry and wiry, like the coat of an Airedale, their bodies having declared, "I need what little fat I have for essential functions," and requisitioned it for use elsewhere. She'd even taken the trouble to get a little soot from the fireplace, mixing it with spittle, and applying it to her eyebrows with the edge of her fingernail. For a while, she'd had a supply of homemade rouge, made from dried-out beet juice mixed with lard, but it had gone moldy. Her cheeks though, had been rosy on their own of late, due to a persistent low-grade viral infection.

When you were in a state of semi-starvation, other organisms started to devour you. It should be pointed out to these microbes and parasites that it wasn't sporting to go after those who were in a debilitated condition—the equivalent of kicking a fellow when he was down. Not only that, but right over there was a German, next to him a member of the Milice, they were plump and well-fed. *Listen, you louse, crawl off of me and over to Heinz, go guzzle his blood, he's got plenty to spare and his is rich and thick.*

Fat chance.

These were the things there were shortages of in Paris: Meat, of course, flesh of any sort, including cat meat, dog meat, fats, bread, sugar, noodles, fresh fish, vegetables, offal, charcuterie—*Would you stop it please*! *You are making me hungry*! —potatoes, wine, milk, coal, gas, petrol, rubber, tobacco, coffee, salt, eggs—although a twelve-year-old boy in the 14th arrondissement had just killed a pigeon with his slingshot and shimmied up a drain pipe to her nest, was carrying his bounty home, one hand holding the dead pigeon by her legs, the other cradling the eggs in the marsupial pouch of his upturned shirt tail— lucky kid! There was above all a shortage of young men: men smelling of Gitanes and *vin rouge ordinaire*, men with stubbly faces, men with hands that slip between a girl's legs, make their way through the slippery folds, thrust fingers inside, move the heels of their hands against the women just so, *yes, right there, oh, yes, yes, don't stop. There. Yes.*

—*Would you stop it, please*! *You are making me lonely*!

But there was no shortage of hunger pangs, lice, or rumors. Ah, there were rumors galore, heaps of rumors, mountains of rumors. Hitler was dead. Stalin was dead. Tons of butter were stored in a cave in the Alps and when the war was over, every Parisian who hadn't collaborated would receive a chit good for five kilos of it. No, I heard quite authoritatively: ten kilos. The Americans were about to sign a separate peace. The British were about to sign a separate peace. The Americans were building a bomb so powerful it turned flesh to shadow.

The rumors coupled with other rumors and gave birth to litters of fresh rumors: Mussolini was marching an army out of Salò, he'd raised legions from Greece, Albania, Croatia. They were at that very moment poised to take Rome back from the Americans. The Pope had given sanctuary to Hitler in the Vatican.

Rumors floated down from the sky like snowflakes. Rommel was dead. Hitler had fled to Argentina. Hitler had fled to Tokyo. The Germans had kidnapped the Pope. The Communists had assassinated DeGaulle. Eva Braun was pregnant. Eva Braun had given birth to twins.

If rumors were wine we would all be staggering home, drunk and happy. The Jews were being gassed in the concentration camps. Mussolini had been killed and his body thrown into a ravine and eaten by a she-wolf, a descendant of the one who'd suckled Romulus and Remus. The English Channel was so thick with the bodies of dead Allied soldiers one could walk across it. The Resistance had drawn up a list of collaborators who would be executed after the Liberation: there were over a million names on it. That army marching out of Salò under the command of Mussolini? Subhas Chandra Bose was joining them with a legion from India, riding elephants, crossing the Alps like Hannibal.

Here

Henri leaned back against the wall, gasping for breath. His right hand, slightly cupped, rested above his heart as if it were a puppy taken too soon from its mother.

Simone uttered a single word, "Là," tapping her ribcage just above her breast as she spoke. They arranged their bodies, her arm cradling his shoulder, his head resting upon her breast, and he was soon asleep, having been exhausted by the effort of making his way onto the platform. It might seem an unusual degree of intimacy between two people of such slight acquaintance, but the war had not only played havoc with the rules of grammar but with other norms as well.

Simone closed her eyes. Was she sleeping? Awake? Flickering on the border between the two states? Lines of poetry ran through her head:

> Here you are in Marseilles, surrounded by watermelons,
> Here you are in Coblenz at the Hotel du Géant.
> Here you are in Rome sitting under a Japanese medlar tree.
> Here you are on a Metro platform in Montmartre…

Perhaps fifteen minutes had passed. Perhaps twenty, perhaps less than three. Simone no longer possessed a watch, having long since sold the one Luc had given her and used the profits to buy four liters of oil, a pack of Gitanes, and a ham on the black market. This despite the fact that she had risked imprisonment to chalk on walls: NON AU

MARCHÉ NOIR. The Resistance believed it showed a lack of solidarity with one's fellow man to purchase that which was being held back from official channels and sold to the highest bidder. On the other hand, she'd seen the sallow faces, the boils on the skin of those who, out of steadfast principle (rarely) or poverty (far more likely) neither patronized the black market nor were able to call upon relatives in the countryside—yokels once looked down upon by their urbane cousins, now courted by them for their bounty. Among the things they had lost in the war was the belief that one could go through life without hypocrisy.

A woman down the platform yanked the needles free from her knitting and pulled the strand of wool, unraveling it and winding it into a ball, the Penelope of the Metro. "The knitting helps me keep my calm," she explained; "but I've no more yarn."

"May keep you sane, but that incessant clack-clack-clack drives me mad," someone muttered.

Henri was daydreaming, imagining the Americans marching into Paris, men named Rocky and Jake and Chuck, cowboys and gumshoes and stevedores who'd signed on for the duration and would become his pals, chocolate bars and packs of cigarettes showering down from the sky. (No one expected much from *les rosbifs*, everyone knew the Brits hadn't had a slice of roast beef in years: whale meat, horse meat, soused herring). If Simone were to daydream about the Fifth Army, she'd imagine them pushing wheelbarrows filled with corn and rye and barley from the vast fields of Iowa and Nebraska, zucchinis and pumpkins and rutabagas from their grandmothers' backyard victory gardens.

On August 29, 1944, the 28th U.S. Army Infantry Division will march along the Champs Élysée, legions of corn-fed boy giants with goofy grins. Simone and Jacques will cheer them, caught up in the orgy of joy, shouting out *Vive la France*! *Vive l'Amerique*! shedding, even if only for a few hours, their stance of detached irony.

Simone will fix her eyes on a gawky lad with a cigarette dangling from his lips. "Where are you from?" she will call to him in English. "Brooklyn? California? Kalamazoo?"

"Carbondale, Kentucky," he'll call back.

"Ken-tuck-ee! Ken-tuck-ee! Give me a cigarette, Ken-tuck-ee." Simone will lift her skirt, show her thigh.

The GI will blush: back in Carbondale women her age had settled into doughy middle-age. He'll toss a pack of Luckies to her, even as Jacques will be reproaching her: "Simone! You're hardly a girl any more."

Simone swam up from the borderlands between sleep and wakefulness, and daydreamed about her son Marcel, the fantasies that had preoccupied her for the last two years: sometimes Marcel had escaped, he was on his way home, traveling on foot. She saw him hunkering by a mountain stream, drinking cold water he'd scooped up with both his hands. Other times he was back in France with the *Maquis*, the rural guerillas. He and his comrades had just found a farmhouse abandoned by its owners. In the cellar were shelves of preserves, apricot, strawberry, raspberry, peach, plum, the jars glinting in the shaft of light from the open hatchway like precious gems. He'd just broken the paraffin seal on a jar of raspberry jam, he was scooping it into his mouth with two crooked fingers, laughing with joy.

Waiting

The steady bleat of the all-clear did not sound. *I'm bored, I'm hungry. When are we going to get out of here*? The Occupation had turned them all into squalling children. *I'm bored, I'm hungry. When is the war going to be over*? They were sick of that plaintive voice in their heads. If it were possible to give one's brain a good cuffing, they would have done so.

They were waiting.

Waiting for the all-clear to sound.

Waiting for the train, held up by troop movements or because the Resistance had blown up the lines, to roll on.

Waiting for the Allies to reach Cherbourg.

Waiting for the Allies to reach Paris.

Waiting for the Allies to reach Berlin.

Waiting to taste butter again.

Waiting for their sons to come home.

Waiting for their sons not to come home.

Waiting for a stone-carrying mob to come shuffling through the eons, out of Leviticus, rocks ready to lob, this time not at fornicators, defilers of the Sabbath, but at killers of Jews and Communists, those who had collaborated with the killers of Jews and Communists.

Waiting to be done with waiting.

Henri's head lolled forward, then jerked up, which woke him.

"I wasn't asleep," he declared, as if sleeping were a crime.

At the moment when Henri was speaking the word "asleep," in the waters off Omaha Beach a piece of shrapnel was piercing the lung of Pfc. Wilbur Desmond of the 320th Antiaircraft Balloon Battalion (Very Low Altitude) (Colored), who was only able to say one syllable of the word "Mama," before his throat filled up with blood. The enormous barrage balloons, tethered above the landing craft, meant to keep the Luftwaffe at bay, strained as if yearning to rise into the air, Gullivers held fast by the ropes of the Lilliputians. Their shape suggested both a stubby penis and the tumescence of a pregnant belly.

A second piece of shrapnel pierced the skull of Pfc. Desmond, the grey-yellow pudding of his cerebral cortex jetted out, some of it splattering into the water. A school of whiting flicked its tails, rising through the turbulent ocean towards the surface to feast on this bounty.

In response to Henri's, "I wasn't asleep," Simone murmured, "Sleep. Sleep," in the voice with which a mother soothes an infant. As she spoke, she remembered Marcel's babyhood, her own mother grabbing her by the shoulders as she headed down the path away from their home, on her way to the train which she would take to her lover—

my lover, she had said to herself. *I have taken Jacques as my lover*—her mother's fingers digging into her shoulders like talons, forcing her around, then hissing in her face: "You unnatural creature! You call yourself a mother! Abandoning your own children!" Throughout the train ride from Aix to Carcassonne, the words had waved through her mind, defiant banners fluttering before her as she went off to do battle against bourgeois convention: *I am an unnatural creature…No kind of a mother, I…I have taken Jacques as my lover.*

Marcel had paid back her poor mothering with the coin of resentment. It was this that had kept him from using his father's connections to keep himself out of the STO. Simone's maternal feelings had at last been aroused—partly by guilt, partly by, after nearly two decades, the inevitable diminishment of her passion for Jacques.

She did not believe in the God of the Hebrews who kept a ledger which he balanced at the end of each year. Or maybe she did, momentarily, believe in such a God, believe that if she were good to Henri, God would take note of it, transfer the assets she'd racked up, pay her back with a bowl of barley soup sneaked to Marcel by a woman named Gretchen or Solvig.

She stroked her hand across the sleeping Henri's cheek, tucked his hair behind his ears. He nestled against her like a cat. Not only, she noticed, was his shirt misbuttoned, but one of the buttons was of black jet. It might have come from a pair of evening gloves. Did he live alone in some lumber room that had been repurposed into lodgings? Was there a landlady who had scavenged this button from the bottom of her sewing basket? A kindly woman in fingerless black gloves who worked at the greengrocers and slipped him an extra onion, a few Brussels sprouts, darned his socks, did her best to keep his clothes mended?

Tobacco

An image of the tobacco she had been on her way to buy arose in her mind, piled on a piece of butcher paper, a confetti not in garish colors, but in browns and golds, smelling of whiskey and earth. It did not seem to Simone that she was thinking this thought: rather, that this idea had lodged itself in her brain and was refusing to budge. This fixed image stood stock still amidst the flow of thought, as she had stood, rooted to the spot, when the air raid sirens yowled.

There it was, spread on the piece of butcher paper, a piece of butcher paper that had been reused and reused so often that it resembled fine crepe. She could see, quite distinctly, each wrinkle and fold of the paper, each strand of the tobacco.

Galoshes

Simone pulled a book from her purse. One thing she had learned about being Occupied is that one must never leave one's house without something to occupy one's time. At the beginning, it had seemed the Occupation was geographic: it was a matter of the number and locations of German garrisons in France, of the demarcation lines that ran between the Occupied Zone and the Free Zone, the Forbidden Zone and the Enlarged Forbidden Zone. But it had soon become clear that Occupation was not so much spatial as temporal. The Germans were notorious for their punctiliousness. If the curfew had been administered by the French, there would have been a grace period of ten minutes to a quarter of an hour between the stated beginning and when the last stragglers might be told to hotfoot it on home before they'd be subject to arrest, while for the Germans the hour was the hour and it was exactly the hour, and moreover it was the hour from the clock's first chime and not the last. Every morning at precisely ten o'clock the first roll of the drum would be heard as the Germans prepared to march along the Champs Élysée, beneath the Arc de Triomphe and at the same exact moment each morning, the drums having rolled, rat-a-tat, rat-a-tat, rat-a-tat-tat, the first line of goose-stepping legs would rise in unison.

But for those being occupied, an hour was infinitely mutable. Simone felt as if she had been handed an enormous and ungainly box filled with dead time—time spent waiting in queues, time spent waiting for a contact to show up, time spent lazing around the flat in hunger-induced doldrums—which she was forced to lug about with her. Her arms and her back ached from hauling around this leaden weight. Despite the fact time was passing, that it flowed around her—hours disappearing into fresh hours, mornings turning into afternoons, days being swallowed up by weeks, weeks by months, months turning into years—*yes, this had been going on for years, years and years*—her burden never grew any less.

"A love story?" Henri asked.

Simone raised a quizzical eyebrow.

"Your book."

"Ah," she said, realizing that Henri assumed that as a woman she'd be reading a romance novel. "After a fashion. Also, a mystery." She moved her hand so he could see the front cover.

"Ah, Simenon. He's not so bad." He jutted out his lower lip. "I don't go for those writers who tie themselves all up in knots."

"I could read it aloud to you, if you'd like..." As she launched into the book's first sentence—"'So intimately blended was the sense of danger with the consciousness of everyday reality and all that was conventional and commonplace...'"—she could sense Henri's disappointment, his desire for something more straightforward. He seemed relieved when she began the second paragraph, with its mention of January, a winter coat with a sealskin collar, galoshes.

She read aloud, as she had once read aloud to her children on summer afternoons, *Arabian Nights*, tales from the Brothers Grimm, and when Marcel objected that they were too girlish— fairy tales!— *Around the World in Eighty Days, The Three Musketeers, The Last of the Mohicans.*

Simone would have preferred to have a full skirt spreading around her, like a pool of butter melting in the summer, the sort of full skirt she had worn when Marcel and Odette were young, but her skirt was straight and short. War-time clothing rationing had forced her to make and remake the garments hanging in her closet, which got narrower and narrower each time they were resewn. Given that, it was fortunate she too grew narrower and narrower.

The Murderer was set in the Netherlands. Whenever Simone uttered certain Frisian names—*Herr de Schutter, Workum, Sneek*—Henri would repeat them under his breath and snicker. When she said the name of a certain town the murderer passes through—*Hindeloopen*—he not only repeated it several times but said, "*Hindeloopen*! That's a good one."

After a while, Simone's throat grew dry. Some wine was offered by a neighbor eavesdropping on her reading—or attempting to do so, for Simone was speaking very low, partly to conserve her voice, partly because she and Henri were quite close to one another, almost literally *tête-à-tête*. The wine soothed her throat, enabled her to continue for a while, but then her voice decisively gave out.

Henri took the book from her hands and began to read aloud, although he read rather ploddingly, word by word, and stumbled over several words—and not only the Dutch names. After little more than two pages, he complained of a headache and pinched the bridge of his nose between his thumb and forefinger. It was a gesture Simone's Jacques also made, but he made it at the end of one of his long days, after many hours of reading and writing.

Knit

A dry cough of the sort that seems a tic. Again. The hunchback she'd glimpsed on the stairs was standing before her, offering a half-bow which he followed with a forced smile.

"I wonder if you and your—friend would be so kind as to permit me, permit me to join you?"

She was surprised the man's voice was so sonorous.

"Of course." Simone had not known what else to say. Shifting her bent legs slightly, she made room for him on the nest of coats. Henri opened a single eye, surveyed the situation, and closed it again.

"I hope I am not intruding."

"No, no." Simone said. "We are actually, ourselves, just—strangers ourselves, who happen to be thrown together by circumstance."

The hunchback steepled his fingers. As he did so, Simone noticed that his hands were quite normal. Indeed, he had the long, tapered fingers of an ectomorph. His nails were well-manicured to the point of fastidiousness, each perfectly shaped, cuticles pushed back to reveal a half-moon rising from the horizon of his flesh.

"Ah, circumstance! As Cicero said, 'By some fortuitous concourse of atoms…' But where are my manners—allow me to introduce myself: Francois Quatrevaux." He followed the announcement of his name with another of his dry coughs and half-bows.

When Simone offered her own name, he immediately asked, "Any relation to Jacques Melville?"

"Yes, he's my husband."

"Ah!" The man clapped his hands together with delight. "How very, well—surprising! Ah, ah! Well, well!"

Simone was a bit put off by this man's enthusiasm, fearing he might attempt to maneuver this chance encounter into a literary association, would shortly mention, making an effort to sound off-hand, "By the way, I have a manuscript—I don't know if, by any chance, your husband would be willing to take a look at it?"

Despite Simone's trepidation about unwonted intimacy from this man, when he filled up the rather awkward silence with "I'm quite honored, Mme. Melville," Simone heard herself saying, "Please, let's not be formal. You may call me Simone."

"I myself was a teacher of Greek and Latin languages at a lycée which the exigencies of war forced to close." He paused, swallowed, his eyes shifted, and then he spoke quickly, as if diving into cold water: "Circumstances—ah, we come back once again to circumstances—have forced me to offer my skills as a tutor, ahem, and of necessity to take on as pupils anyone who can pay my fee—that, alas, includes those who, ahem, feel themselves to be the inheritors of the torch of civilization."

Ah, Simone thought, so it's not a manuscript I'm to be offered—rather, he's attempting to make a timely alliance, foreseeing the day when he might be hauled before some tribunal, whether duly and legally constituted or an ad hoc assemblage and he'll attempt to call upon his connection with me, my husband's well-known antipathy to the Nazis. She judged the man to be something of a weasel. If things had gone the other way, he might well be dropping the names of certain Germans he'd coached in the fine points of Attic grammar, speaking of the detrimental effects of Christian pity, the resurrection of the cold rigor of the Greeks.

"Are you worried?" Henri asked.

"Worried?" François feigned puzzlement.

"I'd be worried, if I were a collaborator."

"I would hardly call what I have been forced to do collaboration."

"What would you call it?"

"Henri." Simone tapped her fingers against his forearm, a gesture both soothing and reprimanding. After years spent acting as her husband's aide-de-camp in the Paris literary world, she'd become adept at the role of peacemaker. Although she found this M. Quatrevaux distasteful, she scarcely wanted open conflict.

There was more than a touch of the maternal in Simone's relation to Henri, and now, like an adolescent, her chiding had the opposite of the effect she had intended, making him bolder:

"Do you go to them or do they come to you?" Henri spoke in the tone of voice an interrogating officer might use to a petty criminal.

François flushed: "Both, that is to say, that for some pupils I—travel to their place of residence and for others—"

"Ah, it doesn't really matter, does it? Their eyes are everywhere."

Perhaps the knitting woman seated a meter or so away was the great-granddaughter of one of *les pétroleuses* who, in the waning days of the Commune, had set fire to the Tuileries Palace and the Hôtel de Ville. She might, while pretending to stare into the middle distance, be taking mental notes on their conversation. In a day or two she could be reporting to some new Tribunal. Later, she'd creep through the Paris alleys after midnight with a flask of kerosene in her hand, purging the city of its bourgeois monuments and edifices, creating a clean slate for the proletarian future which was to come.

"Really, I don't much care for the turn this conversation has taken."

"Ah, but you were the one who brought it up. Told us of your little sessions with the Germans. Tell me, did they serve you little cakes? Coffee—the real thing?"

"Henri, please," Simone murmured.

"Food from the Vaterland? Peppermint schnapps? Ah, I can't drink that stuff myself, it tastes like cough syrup. But I've noticed that cruel people have terrible sweet tooths, it's a mystery, I can't explain it. Sausages," and here Henri's hand briefly, almost imperceptibly, grazed his own genitals. "Ah, yes, the sausages. What were your favorite kinds: *weisswurst, leberkäse, blutwurst*?"

François shifted a quarter turn away from Henri, and said, "Madame—I—Madame—"

"She's told you that she doesn't want to be called 'Madame.'"

"Please," Simone said, laying one hand on François' forearm, the other on Henri's. "Please. None of us are perfect. As Chekhov says, 'Life isn't easy for any of us.' We have all had to make compromises—"

The party lapsed into nettled silence.

Was Jacques wondering when she would return? Was he walking to the window, peering down into the street, searching the crowds spilling out of the Metro station for the shape of her shoulders, her distinctive gait? Was he glimpsing a woman he thought was her, and, not wanting to be seen looking for her—he likes to keep his women a bit off-balance—resuming his seat at his desk? Or was he holding court in a bar—an aging silverback, thumping his chest, letting the upstart males know he wasn't done for yet. Would he shortly head home, guilty at arriving so late, thinking that Simone must have been waiting for him, keeping the soup warm and worrying, only to enter a dark and empty flat?

Grub

A Milice officer appeared, flanked on either side by two underlings. He stood in the curved passage leading onto the platform, legs spread in an upside down 'V', hands clasped behind him. His minions' backs were ramrods. They had all sworn a vow to fight against democracy, Gaullist insurrection, Jewish leprosy. Beneath the militia officer's cap, one could see waves of brilliantined hair.

The officer cleared his throat, shouted: "Food is being brought to you. An orderly queue will be formed. There is to be no panic!" His throat tightened and became more high-pitched as he continued: "No one is to leave until the all-clear sounds! Order is to be maintained!"

We are not panicking and we certainly aren't going to be foolish enough to rush out before the all-clear—but it doesn't have anything to do with your commanding us to do so.

Simone, Henri, and François dutifully lined up for their dose of grub, Simone half-hoping that when they reseated themselves this interloper might attach himself to someone else. But neither man was going to cede the field to the other: the three picnickers resumed their places on the nest of jackets.

Hunger is the best sauce, but the best sauce in the world couldn't make the dish of beans and lard and salt they were served appetizing. Still, they ate: the hinges of their jaws swung open, metal spoons were inserted into their mouths, their teeth chomped away, their tongues thrust the food down their gullets, they swallowed, and from there the dark mills of their innards took over, grinding up, breaking down, stewing in acid baths, turning those piles of beans into piles of shit, just as they would have turned a perfectly ripened peach, a plate of oysters into a stinking mound of excrement.

The sound of a fart, not a single loud honk, but a blubbery trumpet blowing its own version of reveille.

—Oh, for the love of Jesus!

—Oh come now, it's not deliberate…

—Jesus, the stink!

It wasn't just this one poor man who had been unable to control his innards as they worked at the beans. The station filled up with a sewer-like smell that suggested the stench of the ocean, reminding them that we humans are, despite being builders of the Sphinx and the Eiffel Tower, despite sending armies back and forth across Europe, despite having produced Voltaire, bags of stinking wind.

A woman, returning her empty metal bowl, attempted to pass her hand across François' hump, but he ducked out of her way, glared at her.

"It wouldn't have been any skin off your arse," Henri said.

François said nothing.

"Did you hear what I said? I said, 'It wouldn't have been any skin off your arse.'"

"Henri," Simone murmured, as she had so often uttered her husband's name, her son's name, as if she were a sheepdog nudging its flock into line.

"A harmless old woman. It might have given her some comfort."

François addressed Simone: "It is an interesting superstition that I find myself—on the receiving end of, on account of my kyphosis—the correct medical term." He cleared his throat. "The ancient Egyptians had amongst their gods one with the same condition, called Bes. A minor deity, but quite ubiquitous. He was commonly rendered full-faced, rather than in profile, as was the Egyptian custom, and his genitals were revealed, which indicated his status as marginal to the normal world. When an infant in its cradle smiled for no reason, it was said that Bes was pulling faces at it. Professor Jung would no doubt say the behavior we just witnessed was the result of a welling up from the collective unconscious, while those with a more materialist bent would assert that certain folkloric superstitions have been handed down through generations.

"It might be of interest to you—you are, after all, a sophisticated woman"—and here François darted his tongue out and licked his lower lip—"hardly naive, I'm sure, to know that at the Ephesus Museum in Selçuk, Turkey, there is a statue of Bes with an enormous phallus—"

"Hey," said Henri.

Both François and Simone ignored him.

"I lived in Istanbul—for a few years—my first husband," Simone said. "Selçuk was…far away." She met François' gaze.

In her early days in Paris, Simone had often found herself at loose ends in the afternoon—a headache looming after three or four hours of reading the text she had set for herself in an attempt to make up for the slapdash education she had received from the nuns. Of course, there were always dishes in the sink, glasses with a few dregs of wine, the morning's coffee cups bobbing in a pond of dishwater and fermenting vegetable peelings, dust bunnies peering out from beneath the settee—but she would ignore them. She'd leave the flat and wander into the city's museums. She'd never cared for the grand palaces of culture, the Louvre and the Jeu des Palmes, preferring the quirky, the ateliers of dead painters. Sometimes she would fix her eyes on a portrait hanging on the wall, and stare and stare and stare at it, not taking in the brushstrokes, the composition, the use of pigments, staring at something beyond all those things.

Now she stared at François in just this way, and he, back at her, with the intimacy of strangers who knew that whatever occurred between them would be in brackets.

"There is speculation," François said, "that this figurine may have been used as a sort of sacred dildo."

"Ah. I won't have you talking to her like that."

François shot the lady's protector a glare that was both fierce and fleeting, while for Simone, Henri might have ceased to exist.

"Of course, the word 'sacred' is a mistranslation. Whatever that word's origins—in Sanskrit, if I'm not mistaken, and having a connection to the notion of religious purification by fire—we can't now hear it without its Christian overtones. Impossible for us now as modern men—and women"—and gave her another of his little half-bows—"to strip that word of the connotations that have accreted to it over the centuries. The ancient Egyptians had none of our notions of sin and virtue, so the word 'sacred' as it applies to this venereal object..."

He isn't flirting with me, Simone thought, he's propositioning me. If we weren't in this place, he would jerk his head—*Follow me*—and lead me up some alley, unbutton his flies, show me his erect member, take me standing up against the wall.

She found the man repulsive, but after all, she had made love with men who repelled her before. The English parachutist. A squat Belgian painter who had smelled of mutton and garlic and beer: she had been settling a score with Jacques. (Those moves and countermoves in their marriage, the feints and sallies, those reckonings as complicated as the ledger kept by the God of the Jews, those alliances and betrayals that put the machinations of the Allies against one another to shame.) What would it be like to stroke this man's crooked back? Kierkegaard had been a hunchback. It was one of those scraps of knowledge, like those fragments of poems, she'd picked up along the way.

And then the lights went out. Flickered on again momentarily, then went out. In this cave underground, blackness, a blackness beyond what Milton imagined.

Henri found her hand, a frightened child in the dark.

Maybe the Resistance had cut the lines.

Maybe Paris was being bombed above their heads.

Maybe that weapon that turned flesh to shadow which the Americans had been building had been detonated, setting off a chain reaction that was racing around the world, gobbling it up.

Maybe the war at the end of the world had happened, those barrage balloons hanging over the English Channel were the wombs of ancient deities who'd waited patient eons for their hour to come round again, they'd split open like spider's sacs and gushed forth the embryonic new race that was repopulating the earth.

A woman's voice called into the darkness: "Did we all enjoy

tonight's dinner of *cassoulet à la Petain*? *Sans canard, sans porc*…without lamb, goose fat, olive oil, onions, spices, garlic, wine…"

"Silence!" A flashlight beam raked the crowd.

"But, sir, I am only doing what we have been urged to do by the Occupation authorities— sharing economical recipes making use of ingredients at hand—"

"Silence!"

Dark

The lights stayed out. There was nothing for it but to give up and sleep, the grudging sleep of a bear that had no choice but to lumber into its cave and curl up for the winter.

A few bodies away from Simone a woman in a polka-dot dress was dreaming of a heaven in which a mountain of figs rose above a lake of drawn butter. The woman dove into the lake, breaststroked through the yellow liquid. Now, she was on the shore, it was snowing enormous flakes of crystallized sugar: archangels, seraphim, dour medieval saints were rushing around with their tongues stuck out to catch the lozenges drifting down from the sky. Wan St. Veronica who ate but five orange seeds a day on earth had here in heaven grown plump, she was holding out not just her tongue but her hands.

A hand at Simone's breast. It could be her husband's hand, a lover's hand, Marcel's hand when he was an infant.

The hand rolled her nipple between her fingers.

"Henri?" she whispered.

"Yes," the voice attached to the hand responded, but it could be any man's sleep-thickened voice, speaking a single syllable. His mouth so close to her ear that his "hush, hush" was more physical than verbal, grazing the whorls of her ears.

He unbuttoned the top button of her blouse, freeing her neck and throat. The next two buttons released her breasts, but then he kept on going, began to tug her blouse free from the waist of her skirt.

"Oh, no," she whispered, "suppose the lights come on."

He did not answer her, but hiked her skirt up, began working his fingers between her legs. He met her kiss like a child forced to swallow cod liver oil. She tilted her head back, allowing his lips to graze along her neck. His mouth on one side of her neck, bestowing a series of tiny nips, not so tiny nips.

She began to unbutton his shirt, and without his mouth pausing, he pushed her hand away, roughly enough that fear flickered through her.

She ran her hand down the front of his shirt, and did not come to the spherical jet button, the one that would have felt different from all the other buttons, and she knew this was not Henri. The hunchback? Perhaps that was why he'd kept pushing her away, spurning her embraces. A member of the militia? One of her fellow refugees who'd seen the lascivious glances she'd exchanged with François? Was that the smell of brilliantine? Could it be that officer who had stood with his legs forming an inverted 'V,' his arms linked behind his back?

"Get on all fours," he whispered.

If the lights surged on, she'd be caught, presenting her tail like a sow. But her sex had become the mouth of a greedy ogre, one so ravenous the world could be stuffed into its maw and it would still not be satisfied.

"All fours," he hissed in her ear.

She did as she was commanded. He tugged her panties down, entered her from the rear. A sear of pain.

Knees to the platform, made from rock that had been pulverized and remade, her own fist in her mouth to keep her from crying out, dull ache from her knees. *Rock me. Rock me. Rock me. Hold me.*

It no longer mattered who he was.

Fill me up. Rock me, rock me, rock me. Never stop. Back and forth, in and out, back and forth, in and out.

She had become like one of those saints she had revered as a girl, who, loving carnally and impersonally, had strode into leprosariums, bedlams to wash the running sores of syphilitics, lance the buboes of plague victims, loving the vomit, the black shit that poured forth.

He slid his hand from her flank up to her shoulder, stroked her neck: beneath the flesh the jut of collarbone, the tendons, the jugular vein, the Adam's apple, the larynx, the windpipe. He gripped her throat with his strong fingers. She gave a mewl.

"I won't hurt you," he whispered, his breath hot in her ear.

His words might be a taunt. His fingers tightened around her neck.

It struck her that she might be found dead on the platform when the lights went up. The Germans would blame the Resistance, the Resistance would blame the Germans.

But he only had one hand on her throat. Surely it would take two.

"I don't want to die." She had said many true things in her life, but she had never before said anything quite as true as this.

Then his gush of come.

The human animals around them twitched their noses, their sleeping senses drew closer or recoiled. The lake of drawn butter in the dream of the woman in the polka dot dress became a field of new-mown hay. The tongue of a woman near them thrust against the roof of her mouth, as if she could spit out disgust, the stink of sin.

Simone had not been satisfied. If she hadn't been afraid, she might have slipped her hand between her legs, brought herself to orgasm. But she was afraid. And, anyhow, that moment of sweet spasm, when that series of little cries escapes from one's lips, *Oh, oh, oh, oh, oh,* that simple moment of pleasure felt quite irrelevant.

This

In a few months, Simone and Jacques will go to the cinema. The American First Army will have just broken through the Siegfried Line, the Red Army will be on the east bank of the Vistula River outside of Warsaw, and Marcel will be somewhere in between, or nowhere. Before the feature, the newsreel, the announcer's bombastic voice: "From Dachau come pictures that shock even those who thought they had been hardened to the horrors of Nazi depravity…"

The piles of corpses.

Simone's nausea will not be just from her stomach but from every organ within her, gall bladder, pancreas, spleen, kidneys, liver, the vermiform appendix, all those organs threatening to turn themselves inside out, to disgorge their biles and fluids. The taste of sick in the back of her throat. Bending double, as if she were in labor.

Jacques will seize hold of her hand as if she were the one in hysterics, as if she were the woman in the next seat over, groaning and calling out "Oh, God, no, no," without the slightest effort to control herself. Simone will want to hit the woman, not a quick come-now-get-hold-of-yourself slap but really haul off and give the cunt a good belt. *Listen, we've all suffered, quit carrying on like you're the only one. Shut up, would you just shut up*!

Jacques will be saying to her urgently, "Those are the concentration camps—in the labor camps they needed the workers—"

As she shoves her fist in her mouth, she'll realize the seat next to her is empty, she is the bitch moaning and carrying on.

"Come," Jacques will say, fumbling for their wraps in the dark. "I won't let you sit here and torture yourself." Tugging on her arm: "Simone, come!"

But she won't be able to take her eyes off the screen. A naked survivor, he might be a rag doll with black buttons for eyes, will be held up by a GI, a boy from Brooklyn or Kalamazoo.

Ribs.

Pelvis.

Knee cap.

Tibia.

Femur.

Skull.

Wrist.

She won't be able to stop staring at his penis and testicles, enormous against his skeletal flesh.

His body will have said: *take my muscles, devour them, eat the light from my eyes, gnaw my bones down past the gristle, suck the marrow out of them, but leave me this. Leave me this.*

This.

Blare

At 6:27 on the morning of June 11, 1944, came the full-throated, unceasing blare of the all-clear. The collective body on the Metro platform became a behemoth, giving off a groan as it lumbered to its feet, its thousands of joints protesting the previous night's ill-treatment. Simone, who had not slept the entire night, got up with eyes cast down, not wanting to meet a leer, a look of disgust.

Dust and detritus were flicked off blouses and trousers. Mothers licked index fingers and rubbed smudges from their offsprings' faces. Those with enough foresight to have brought combs were tugging them through dishelved hair, the rest making do with fingers. The inside of Simone's mouth tasted as if she had been eating library paste and yeast, and when she moved she caught a whiff of a rank odor emanating from between her legs.

Simone made her way to the address she'd been given, taking a left when she came out of Lamarck-Caulaincourt, right at the first corner, rang the bell of Apt. 5A, answered the sleep-thickened voice's "Good Lord, it's not yet 7," with, "I'm a friend of Martine's." The door opened, the hinges giving voice to their weariness: *day after day, these strange gods, the ones who brought us into being, swing us open, swing us shut, we do as we're commanded,* while the sigh of the woman who opened the door was anything but resigned. She, a self-respecting Parisienne, would be a traitor to her kind if she failed to moan about the ungodliness of the hour.

The woman's bleached blonde hair was rumpled. She wore a red velvet robe that must have been quite the thing in its day, but its day was long past. The nap of the fabric had worn away, leaving bare patches like mange on the hide of an ill-cared-for dog.

"Martine said you had some tobacco..."

"Oh, for the love of God," the woman grabbed Simone's wrist, pulled her into the apartment. "Don't yammer about it in the hallway."

Simone tumbled over her explanations, aware she was talking too much, the air raid, sleeping in the Metro, "I'd come all this way, and gone through so much—"

"Well, that's hardly my fault, is it?" The woman stalked out of the room, did not close the lavatory door behind her. Simone heard the sound of piss hitting the side of the bowl.

In exchange for her francs, the tobacco was passed to her—in a rolled-up paper pouch, not at all the way she'd envisioned it. She was right, nothing ever happened just as one imagined it: Marcel was being electrocuted against a wire fence. A bullet was entering his skull. He was being force-marched East.

On her way home, she passed a graffito—*Cherbourg is liberated*—still wet. It left a smear of red on her index finger.

(In fact, the U.S. Army won't take Cherbourg for another 16 days, by which time this slogan will long since have been painted over by one of those members of the Milice who were everywhere, carrying paint brushes and cans, their collars turned up and their caps pulled down, hedging their bets.)

Sleep

Jacques made his way from his bed to the toilet, not-quite-yet-here. He'd come fully awake five or six times the past night. He tried to put his insomnia down to difficulties digesting his evening meal, a stew of beans and vegetables, although he knew it had more to do with Simone's absence than his dyspepsia. Surely her absence was a simple matter of her having missed the last Metro, forcing her to bunk with a friend. Suppose she simply didn't come back? To whom would he make inquiries? No one official, that would only bring suspicion down on his head.

He sat down on the toilet, which gave him a view of himself in the full-length mirror opposite, hunched over, pajama bottoms pooled at his feet, face scrunched up. He pushed, was rewarded with the sound of a fart escaping, and had a brief wash of pleasure at being alone in the flat, shitting—or attempting to—with the door open. The unwritten rules of his ménage decreed that Simone always shut the lavatory door, while he did so when he was defecating. He overheard something—footsteps on the stairs, a rustle at the front door—and, thinking it might be Simone returning, leaned over and shoved the door closed. But he did not hear her moving about the apartment.

It took a while for him to accomplish what he had come there to do—age slowed everything down, one's step, one's wit, one's response to the opposite sex, even one's bowels. He regarded his production—not without a sense of childish pride (*Look at the fine egg I have laid*!)—before pulling the chain. A rust-orange ring leached up the porcelain bowl, which gave off a stink of stale urine. Since resigning his editorship, he'd had no regular source of income, and got along by cadging off his friends, taking loans against a promised inheritance from a great-aunt—a far from princely sum to begin with—as well as writing the occasional piece of pornography under a pen name. (Sometimes he described himself, with a wink and a half smile, as "a social parasite.") In order to cut back on their expenses, he and Simone had long since let their charlady go. He felt it was a small enough sacrifice for Simone to take over her duties, but she seemed not to notice, or at least not to be troubled by, the smells and stains in the bathroom, the clogged drain in the kitchen sink, the line of ants marching along the window sill. Jacques, like Henri and Simone, was filled with fantasies about what would transpire at the war's end, his having not to do with American GIs named Buddy and Hank nor cornucopias overflowing with rutabagas and aubergines, but with a lavatory that didn't reek.

He went to the kitchen to make himself a cup of the roasted chicory and barley decoction that substituted for coffee. Although it had no caffeine in it, he never came fully awake until he had had a cup of it.

The apartment had been chock-a-block with things even before the war: when his father had died in the mid-1930's, Jacques had inherited a number of family heirlooms, which only a man of the most avaricious sort would have thought of selling, furnishings meant for the rooms of country estates and not for the cramped quarters of a Parisian apartment. They were also hanging onto items which they hoped someday to sell—an art deco lamp, a half-naked nymph holding aloft a globe of light; a baroque gilded mantel clock with matching candelabras in which not just the hour, not just the half hour, but the quarter hour was sounded by a cherub carrying a mallet, a clock which they had long since ceased to wind on account of its infernal chiming, and which showed the hour as perpetually twelve minutes past three. The market for such items having been dampened first by the Depression and then by the war, they were holding onto these as investments—ones which, unlike stock certificates, could not be tucked neatly into a drawer.

Wall

Books were stacked on every flat surface. It sometimes seemed as if the volumes were breeding, coupling with one another in the dark, finding hidden corners in which to drop their litters, like the rabbits in the hutch behind Simone's girlhood home. On the bottom shelf of a bookcase in the corner, an odd sight: books with their spines inward, so that their titles could not be seen. Heidegger's *Sein und Zeit* had been the first volume Jacques had turned to the wall. He wasn't a Nazi, he didn't burn books, he simply didn't care to display the work of this man who had allied himself with the burners of books. Later, it was the turn of Nietzsche and Schopenhauer. Once the Germans invaded Poland, he could no longer stomach the sight of any of them and stacked all his German authors on this bottom shelf, backs to the wall—even Brecht, Mann, Döblin—although he recognized the irrationality of treating those who had resisted Nazism in this manner. His revulsion towards the German language was like that for a food which had sickened one: instinctive, visceral, utterly immune to rational persuasion. He hated the Nazis more for this than for anything else, for teaching him that he, too, could hate a race.

The front room also contained canvases, old silver, coin collections left with Jacques by friends who had been forced to flee on account of their ethnic background or political beliefs. For all the intrigues he carried on in the Paris literary world, they judged—quite correctly—that in the matter of valuable objects entrusted to him, he would behave with utmost rectitude. When they returned after the war, they would find their old family silver, tarnished but otherwise untouched, their Braques and Picassos and Manets wrapped up in the sheets in which they had been delivered, with Jacques refusing most adamantly—he even seemed to take umbrage at the offers—to accept even a bottle of wine for his troubles. His friends would not fail to note that they were now in his debt. Perhaps "friends" is not the word which should be used here—"associates" would be better. In truth, Jacques had very few friends.

Clichés

After his first cup of ersatz coffee—as a rule, German words were disdained, but for this product they were allowed, even demanded—he returned to the lavatory to clean his teeth. The routines one got into over the years. He carried his second cup of Pero to his desk, taking his seat, as he did every morning, before six. He picked up his tobacco-less pipe and clenched it between his teeth, then hooked the stems of his reading glasses behind his ears. He set a blank sheet of paper at the precise angle at which he always set his writing paper, stared at it. It was his habit—and he was a man of habits, even, perhaps especially, at a time like this when—it was impossible to express save with a cliché—*the fate of civilization lay trembling in the balance*—to begin his morning by replying to his correspondence. But yesterday—in fact for the past three days—there had been no letters received, no doubt due to the chaos caused by the invasion and the fact that his regular correspondents' minds were hardly on literary matters.

He began to write, with the same unquestioning determination with which a bee makes honey: *My wife, Germaine*... This was not exactly a work of fiction. He sometimes assumed another persona in his writing, calling himself "Jean" and Simone "Germaine." These alternative names were not disguises, for he did nothing else to otherwise obscure either his or his wife's identity, nor were they meant to suggest alter-egos, for the characters "Germaine" and "Jean" were little more than a hair's breadth removed from their everyday selves.

He wasn't usually a restless man, quite the opposite, an innate quality that was being reinforced in late middle age by his sciatica, the consequent difficulties presented by the acts of rising from a seated position and lowering himself into one, but now he removed his reading glasses and trundled to his feet, went to the front window, which looked out over the Metro station. Passengers were trickling out, but he did not recognize the shape and gait of his wife among them. Past the Metro station was the ancient arena, now a park, where old men were playing boules. Later, boys would come from school, shrugging their rucksacks off their backs and tossing them, along with their school jackets, in a pile on the bottom seat of the old stone bleachers. One could still make out the caves where the lions had been kept before being released to savage the Christians, the crowds laughing as the dying cried out: "I recant! I recant!" or prayed to their useless Lord. The gladiators had called out *Ave legatus Augusti*! *Morituri te salutamus*. Hail Provincial Governor! We who are about to die salute you. Not quite the same ring as: Hail Caesar! Two millennia hence, his descendants might picnic, play games on the grounds of the concentration camps. He hadn't any pride in being a member of his species when this war began and felt even less now. It might be a good thing if it brought about the end of human civilization. Let some other species evolve to have dominion over this planet. They couldn't make a worse muck-up of it than *homo sapiens*.

He continued to put his restlessness down to the break in his routine caused by the lack of correspondence, to the heaviness of his liver, to his anxiety about the lack of progress of the Allied landing on the Normandy beaches, to any number of other factors besides concern over Simone's absence.

He had long believed that both of his wives had maneuvered him into marriages he did not want—Sala by taking advantage of his psychic and physical disintegration when he returned from Madagascar; Simone by loving him so steadfastly, so wildly, turning what he had intended to be only a somewhat brutal reply to her flirtations into a true affair of the heart. Of course, he was a mature man, he knew that all marriages of long duration had their share of disgust, boredom, resentment—there was always one partner who went about thinking, *How am I going to extricate myself from this*? while the other thought, *I can hold on to him. It is worth holding on, isn't it*? He had assumed that if the marriage were to end it would be because he would leave Simone. Indeed, he had often thought of divorcing her, had been on the brink of speaking of it, but had stopped himself, thinking of all the poor girl had given up for him.

Sleep

He sometimes worried she might leave him for another man.

Ever since that night when she'd come home and filled the air with her restless despair, come out with her confession, had needed three Nembutal to sleep—he kept good count of them, knew she'd sneaked a third after he'd fallen asleep—he'd had the discomfiting knowledge that this woman—his wife—this woman he thought he knew better than she knew herself, had things within her he could not have imagined.

He did not admit this worry to himself: it flitted, in a series of disconnected thoughts and images, at the edges of his consciousness. He was as little aware of them as any of us are of the myriad processes of digestion, circulation, the movements of bile, gall within us. She might find a simpler man, one who offered her the ferocious purity of a

Robespierre: a man who, when DeGaulle's name was mentioned, didn't steeple his fingers and having said, "Well…," begin a long disquisition in which the range of forces within the Resistance and the Free French were duly noted, astute observations about the man's character were made, with an aside (referencing a witticism of Molière) about the general's bulbous nose and jug ears, but merely curled his lip and spat.

Perhaps Simone had been with him the night before, sleeping curled against him in a narrow bed in a dirt-floored cellar, tattered sheets nailed to the rafters to make a room of it, the smell of damp earth and cat urine. A rough table next to the bed, a kerosene lamp or just a candle for light. The man a decade younger than Simone, two decades younger than him. (Jacques saw again the image of the man on the brink of old age sitting on the toilet, pajama bottoms drooping onto the floor, his face reddening.) Of course, a fellow member of the Resistance. Jacques' fantasies of the two of them having sex were not so troubling as the thought of them sleeping together, the intimacy of a long night, wrapping their arms around one another, shifting together and then apart, murmuring to each other in sleep, taking in the smells of their night bodies. Her lover might have extracted a promise from her that she would, at last, break the news to the old man.

And then he heard the sound of Simone's off-kilter steps on the stairs. Later, when she will be diagnosed with Parkinson's, this will become a symptom, but for now it is just a charming quirk. Not wanting to be seen looking out the window, he returned to his desk.

He swiveled around in his chair as her key turned in the lock.

"Simone!"

"I hope you weren't worried," she said, although the opposite was true. She was trembling slightly and averted her gaze rather too quickly, but before she did he was struck by the glassiness of her eyes.

"I'm glad you're home." With a jerk of his chin and a raised eyebrow, he indicated the piece of paper she had in her hand.

"An air raid. I spent the night in the Metro. This, this was shoved under the front door."

"Ah, I heard something—"

A red fingerprint on the corner. She held up her index finger, to show the smudge from touching the graffito, quoted: "Cherbourg is liberated." She delivered this with a certain ironic intonation: she, like he, would be embarrassed to utter the millennial language—*liberation, the struggle against the Fascist invader*—abroad in the land without it.

Without his eyeglasses, Jacques could not make out a blurry photograph in the corner of the paper Simone was holding.

"I have a present for you," Simone said. "That was why I had gone to Montmartre…oh." She had just seen the headline of the flyer. "No, no." Weak-kneed, she reached behind her, groping for a piece of furniture against which to lean. "I have a tulle scarf."

"Simone, what is the matter?"

"I had always wanted one, and I said something to Luc about it…"

"Are you having some kind of a—a fit? You are making no sense."

"It was when we were on our honeymoon…the flyer: a reprisal. At Tulle. *Ninety-nine dead.* They hanged ninety-nine of the townspeople."

He was hooking the stems of his wire-rimmed spectacles behind his ears as he moved towards her, taking the paper from her shaking hand.

"They ran out of rope," she said. "The Resistance had held the town for two days." The Resistance fighters had heard the call *Les sanglots longs des violons de l'automne blessent mon coeur d'une langueur* monotone and begun the general uprising.

He imagined, briefly, the last moments of those men's lives: those who had cursed the Resistance, those who had collapsed in fear, had to be dragged to their deaths. He felt cold, more cold than he had ever been before, and wished it were possible to have a hot bath, of the sort one had before the war, steam rising from the tub, fogging the bathroom mirrors and windows. When this was all over—if he survived, if Europe survived—he and Simone would go to a spa. They would lower themselves slowly into the steaming tubs of water. Their pasty flesh would turn boiled-lobster red. Later, they would be massaged: he imagined a slight yet surprisingly strong Indochinese girl who would, at the end of his session, walk along his back. For Simone he imagined a homosexual, the sort of man who had tended to an invalid mother throughout his boyhood, to whom offering physical comfort to women (of a certain limited sort) had become second nature. Perhaps, afterwards, their aging flesh aroused by the ministrations of these youths, the two of them would make love.

Jacques thought: we race of mortals, we are a shameless lot. We read that 99 men were hanged, a number which seems too perfect, made up, as does the detail that the Germans had at that point run out of rope; as does the fact that this town had given its name to the fine cloth woven there. We are horrified, we are sickened, and then we think: I'm cold. I want a hot bath. I hope that if it happens to me, if I'm herded into a square somewhere that I'm not one of the men who pisses his pants in fear. Jacques planned to write an editorial about this in which he would attempt to skirt the usual clichés, to speak of horror and outrage and depravity and courage without actually using those words. If he were to write: "I wanted nothing more than to take a hot bath," his readers would be shocked—although they themselves might have felt such a thing.

(Actually, he will not write about the massacre at Tulle. A few hours hence, shortly after he starts to draft his piece, he will receive news of another reprisal, the massacre at Oradour-sur-Glane, 642 dead, women and children herded into a barn, burned alive, making the events at Tulle pale in comparison.)

The body in the fuzzy photograph could have been a side of beef hanging from a butcher's hook.

Jacques pulled his lips into a thin line, his back grew straight: "We must prepare ourselves for a number of eventualities. Having been arrested before—they're great keepers of lists. I'm no doubt on one. We have to prepare for the fact that I may be arrested again. He gestured towards the flyer with its headline GERMAN REPRISAL: NINETY-NINE INNOCENTS HANGED. "This may be an aberration—the actions of a rogue unit. Or it may mark a decisive change. We've been protected until now by Hitler's—love, it seems an abomination to use that word about the man—for Paris, the fact that we French aren't, like the Poles and Slavs, subhumans. But that may be changing. We may become the lover who has spurned him."

We could become refugees, Simone thought. Those things that bound you to a place on the earth—your identity card, your ration book with its yet-to-be-used coupons, your friendship with the local butcher: none of those would matter anymore. She and Jacques—yes, Jacques would be with her, he had to be with her—would be moving along some road, moving because they were moving, one foot in front of the other and then the other foot in front of that. They would join a herd who walked en masse, not knowing what lay before them, only what lay behind. They might descend on a field like a swarm of locusts, stripping it; grubbing bare-handed in the dirt for potatoes. Later on, in a displaced person's camp, an official would ask her name and she'd furrow her brow, unable to remember it.

(But these things don't happen. The Allies advance, the Resistance continues its uprising. In a little more than two months, barricades will be built in the street below them. Simone will make a cup of Pero and carry it down the six flights of stairs. She will pause in the doorway, and then scuttle over to the sandbags. "Sorry it's not the real thing." Posters had called upon all patriots between the ages of eighteen and fifty capable of carrying a weapon to take to the streets. The man who turns, winks, takes the cup from her hand, takes a sip, then downs it in a gulp, will be at least a decade past fifty. He will give her a kiss on the right cheek, then the left, and then grabbing her, thrust his tongue into her mouth.)

"We must eat," Jacques said.

"Eat?"

"It will calm our nerves."

"I couldn't possibly."

"We must."

She did not rise. He did. It was unimaginable, his going into the kitchen and filling the kettle with water, turning on the gas, taking down a plate, while she sat. Sometimes, when she was late coming home, and he was forced to make his way around the kitchen, she'd return to find every cupboard door open, a puddle of water on the floor. His actions struck her as tender, but at the same time she felt that she was being shepherded along. He came back with a tray, and buttered an end of bread for her—they still used that verb, although it was a mix of bacon dripping and gelatin he had spread thinly on the crust.

The bread was tough, she washed it down with the ersatz coffee, chewed and chewed. Mastication was a better word for the process. Yes, a word from the Roman conquerors of the Gauls. Her jaw, tongue, teeth were like a marching regiment, *do what has to be done, don't ask why, just get it down that gullet of yours.* She drank another slug of the Pero, set the heel of bread down on the plate, hoping Jacques wouldn't notice.

She could see the strain of Egyptian blood that ran through his veins, the cold calculation of those ancients who had faced down eternity with mathematical precision. He spoke as if he had been ferried, eons before, across the waters that separate the dead from the living, was able to watch with infinite detachment the hurly-burly of the mortals on the river's far shore.

"The British and the Americans may have a tough go of it."

"But they've reached Cherbourg already." Simone held up her thumb, smudged with red.

"Yes. But this lull on the Eastern Front worries me. It may mean that the Red Army is gathering strength, waiting for the rest of the Allies to be tied down, and then they'll sweep across Europe. The end of this war may resemble the end of the previous one, we may see revolutions in its wake, but this time with the might of the Red Army behind them: we could find ourselves living in a second Paris Commune." He briefly considered offering Marx's opening salvo from the "Eighteenth Brumaire of Louis Bonaparte," about history repeating itself, the first time as tragedy, then as farce, but there was no chance the threatened Paris Soviet could be laughable. Stalin's armies might keep right on marching, sweeping across the Vistula, the Oder, the Elbe, the Rhine, the Seine, spreading red across the map of Europe as Hitler's armies had spread black, his Resistance comrades becoming apparatchiks. It was quite possible to imagine that he might find himself arrested, even put on trial: *—Ah, so he used that very phrase to describe himself: 'social parasite.'*

"The safe deposit box key is in the upper drawer of my desk. There's an emerald necklace in there—it belonged to one of my great-aunts…"

"An emerald necklace? You never—"

"Now isn't the time. I'll speak to Frédéric about looking after you, should the necessity arise."

"He's always resented me so."

"Yes, but at times such as this, people overcome—they set aside—"

He came and sat down on the couch, kitty-corner to her, their knees touching, holding both of her hands in his.

"I sometimes feel—your life would have been so much easier if I hadn't knocked on your door that night." He had never told her—it would be cruel for him to do so, that he had stood in the corridor that night so long ago and thought, *knock on her door, don't knock on her door, knock on her door, don't knock on her door*, like an adolescent girl pulling petals off a daisy. *Knock on her door*.

If he hadn't followed that whim of his, she would have stayed married to Luc. She'd have been one of those millions whose crimes were nothing more than having a plaster of Paris bust of Pétain on their mantelpieces, than returning the smiles of German soldiers—they were just boys far from home. She might have found a way to wangle Marcel out of the STO. She would have had nothing to fear now but a certain chilliness, perhaps even outright rudeness, from neighbors who thought she had been a bit too friendly towards the occupiers.

"Your gift. I'd almost forgotten." She pulled the packet of tobacco from her pocket.

"Ah, Simone." He lifted it to his nose.

He moved to embrace her, but she pulled herself into the corner of the settee, afraid she would give off the stink of sex. "What's the matter?"

"I feel ill—I—" She put her hand over her mouth as if she were about to vomit and rushed to the bathroom. Kneeling before the bowl, she stuck her fingers down her throat so she would retch. She welcomed the wave of nausea that billowed up from within her, the bitter vomit. After that, she cleaned her teeth, removed her clothes, scrubbed herself—thank God for that half-bar of soap she'd discovered a few days before—took her night robe down from the hook.

"I hardly slept last night, I'm going to lie down."

Jacques surprised her by undressing and climbing in bed with her.

But sleep did not come immediately. She told him about the Metro journey to Montmartre to buy the tobacco, the air raid siren, the young man with the heart condition, the hunchback, the attempts to rub his hump. She repeated her observation, about the children of Voltaire, the Eiffel Tower becoming like the Sphinx. She was hoping he'd offer some sign of appreciation for her wit, but he just said, "Go on."

She described the three of them seated together, a bit like *Dejeuner sur l'herbe*, the wartime version, so they'd had the vault of the Metro and not the vault of the sky, not the baskets of fruit, the loaves of bread. (Simone misremembers the painting—there is a single loaf of bread, four peaches, four plums, and a handful of cherries. These half-starved Parisians imagined food everywhere: the clouds in the Venice sky of a Canaletto seemed to be in the shape of a brioche. Surely the Mona Lisa's sly smile was directed at an off-canvas platter of fried smelt.)

They drifted off to sleep, together.

Hate

There is an emotion which is not hatred, not despair, not love, not sorrow, not hope but all those things mixed together. Of course, they hated the Germans, that went without saying, it was hardly worth putting on the list, it was a given, one couldn't imagine the world without it, as one couldn't imagine a world without gravity or water. They hated the British with their stodgy food and pasty skin and bad teeth and *we shall fight on the beaches / we shall fight on the landing grounds / we shall fight in the fields and in the streets / we shall fight in the hills*—not like those cowardly French who just fell into a swoon before the German Army. They hated the Americans, cock-eyed optimists, Yankee-Doodle-Dandy, bluster, clean-scrubbed, well-fed. They hated the Russians, the Russians who had suffered as no one else had suffered, 15 million dead, 18 million dead, 20 million dead, was there some special department within the vast Russian bureaucracy which numbered the dead, working round the clock, tallying up the corpses, punching numbers on an adding machine, a strip of paper hundreds of kilometers long?

They hate their aging bodies. Every day, gravity tugged at his balls, tugged at her labia, tugged at the skin under their arms, a fraction of a fraction of a fraction of a fraction of a millimeter, every day, day after day, down, down, down, down. They hated those dark blotches that appeared on their skin. They hated themselves for being so petty as to think about dark blotches and sagging genitalia and dimpled skin.

They hated the dead. They certainly didn't believe in the spirit world, the dead turned into bits of foggy ectoplasm that jostled about amongst the living, making the drapery flap when there is no wind, the lights flicker, sending chills down our spines. No, the dead were dead, solidly, firmly dead, gone forever, and that was why they hated them.

Tobacco

They slept, thick sleep, dark sleep, sleep without dreams. They slept without touching, two bodies lying like those Greek koroi, holding themselves tight against the chill of eternity.

Jacques woke first, trundled into the front room, making himself another cup of Pero, then sitting down at his desk, filling his pipe with tobacco. The strike of the match against the flint of the matchbox. He sucked against the mouthpiece, the flame dipping down into the bowl each time he drew in breath. Smoke curled into his lungs.

Simone, in the next room, smelled the odor of tobacco and a half-smile passed over her sleeping face.

Lifts

The U.S. Army crossed the Siegfried Line.

Rommel committed suicide.

The year 1944 became the year 1945.

Dresden was firebombed.

The Soviets took Danzig.

A new fear: that the guards will abandon their prisoners, leave them to starve, the final twist of the knife, making them long for the German order, for the bread made of chaff and the soup of filthy water and rotting cabbage and a bit of salt.

Three months without a letter from Marcel. Four months.

Five.

Hitler committed suicide.

The red flag was hoisted over the Reichstag. Peace.

Jacques treated Simone as a bit of an invalid, bringing her tea and toast in bed, massaging her feet at night. She trembled at times and her sleep was often interrupted by nightmares so vivid she flailed about and cried out, but they both understood that these were symptoms of her worry over Marcel. They entered into an unspoken pact to be faithful to one another "for the duration," as it were—that is, until the situation with Marcel was resolved. (Jacques assured Dominique, who had come to be his steady mistress, that this was a mere sabbatical: he would return.) Their marriage was carried on by two somnambulists, shuffling alongside of one another.

It did not seem surprising that Simone frequently dropped things. She began to use both hands when picking up a glass. ("Two hands, two hands," she had chanted to her children when they were young.)

Every morning Simone left the flat and made the rounds of the various agencies: the Red Cross, the French Ministry of Prisoners, Deportees and Refugees, squinting at the lists posted in the windows, jostling with other mothers to get to the front, never going so far as to give the jab of an elbow, although she took a few sharp thrusts herself. She heard that names could be garbled and after that she didn't just glance down the list until she came to the place where Marcel's name would be, but studied every name carefully, looking for the date of birth as well, 11-04-1919, possible misspellings.

The women who studied the lists posted in windows formed an amoeba-shaped community. On occasion a part of it would split off because a representative from one of the ad hoc agencies or a fellow deportee, fulfilling a promise, had knocked on her door with news, good or bad—generally, the latter. That, or the letter "D"—for *décédé*, deceased, would appear next to a name.

Train

The sound of the club-footed concierge on the stairs, step-clump, step-clump, step-clump, calling out, "Madame Melville! Madame Melville!" A train carrying deportees had just arrived at the Gare du Nord.

The clatter of Simone's wooden-soled clogs on the stairs. She flagged down a passing car, the window rolled slowly down, a man leaned out to ask, "Are you ill, Madame?"

"No." Her hand on the door handle already. "No, a trainload of deportees. My son, he— the Gare du Nord."

She produced a handful of notes, "For the petrol," which were, of course, refused. She leaned forward, as if that could speed the car through the streets.

"I wish you all the best, Madame," the driver said as he pulled the car to a halt, but Simone was already racing towards the station.

"Lilacs!" a street seller cried. "Lilacs for our returning sons!" The flowers made it seem as if this were a ritual. Red roses for lovers, lilies for the dead, lilacs for deportees returning from Germany.

A metal barricade had been set up. Women and a few men pushed against it, until an officer appeared and threatened to clear the station unless they comported themselves properly.

—Has the train arrived? —How many are on it? —What camp has it come from? —Do you have a list of passengers? —Where are they?

And then there was a shout. The returnees were there, you could make them out through the grimy windows. The crowd surged over the barricade. That old sour song: *—Stop pushing! —I'm not pushing! The people behind me are pushing!*

The piercing sound of a gendarme's whistle.

—Please! Stop pushing or someone will get trampled! —What can you see? Can you see anything?

The whistle shrieked again.

—No, no, no. You are going to break my eardrum. Stop! —I am here looking for my daughter! My daughter! My daughter! She was nineteen years old. Nineteen! —Can you see anything? —Stop pushing. —Only nineteen!

Wafting above it all, the odor of lilacs as the flowers were crushed.

Simone, caught up in the crowd like flotsam in an eddy of water, found herself propelled to the front, able to peer for a moment into the holding area. The line of naked men wobbled, and the men themselves swayed back and forth, someone occasionally grabbing a nearby shoulder to steady himself.

The men were dusted with white powder. They looked as if they might have been members of an avant-garde theatrical troupe.

Later she would learn it was delousing powder, later this would make sense.

The policemen, their batons in front of them, shoved the crowd back. *—This is how you treat the mothers of France? —Nineteen, she was nineteen!*

The first of the men emerged, clad in a British military uniform, the baggy pants held up with a belt, the pants so short they revealed his shins and ankles, military boots which it took an effort for him to lift. When a woman in a uniform with a clipboard laid a hand, meant to be reassuring, on his shoulder, he started and then cringed.

A woman in the throng started to sing *The Marseilles*, belting it out, off-key. Every crowd had one of them, a take-charge gal. This one was stout, built like a fireplug—Mussolini or Picasso—childbearing hips, she might have given birth to six or seven or eight sons, she had a barrel organ in place of lungs and heart. The rest joined in because they were embarrassed for her, because they couldn't bear the sight of this man, because they wanted to drown out the voices inside their heads: *Why did you come back in this state? It would have been easier if you had just died there, been our valiant, fallen son.*

The man—thank God, thank God, they could not have borne one more minute of his cowering—lifted his head and smiled, revealing a row of black stumps for teeth. Soon some good dentist would offer his services for free, digging into his own thin purse to pay for the set of artificial choppers. When a young woman darts her tongue into his mouth, she'll stroke vulcanized rubber and porcelain.

Marcel had not been in that group of returnees, nor had he been in the next, nor the one after that nor the one after that, nor the one after that, nor the one after that, nor the one after that, nor the one after that. The tremors in Simone's arms increased in frequency, and she showed odd lapses in conversation at times, but it would have been surprising, given the strain she was under, if she had exhibited no nervous manifestations.

Knock

And then one day there was the knock on the door.

On the other side of it was neither an official from the displaced person's office nor a fellow deportee with news, but Marcel himself.

Simone and Marcel stared at each other, neither moving. She saw there had never been a Gretchen, no carrot and barley soup.

He slumped his body against hers, muttering the single syllable

"Ma," over and over into her hair, the nape of her neck, "Ma, ma, ma, ma, ma." In response, she uttered the syllable *oh*, over and over again. The stench of the grave came from him. She walked backwards across the floor, as if she were in a dance marathon with a sleepwalking partner in her arms. The two of them collapsed together on the couch, she wormed her way out from under him, onto the floor.

Ring Jacques. Yes, ring Jacques. She crawled across the floor, not trusting her legs to hold her up. She lowered the phone from its table, set it in her lap, a comforting heaviness, the black umbilical cord leading into the wall. A few moments before it hadn't seemed possible that she could speak, that if she had attempted to do so strange syllables would have issued from her mouth, not even rising to the level of Marcel's stuttered *ma-ma-ma-ma* and now she was saying, "Jacques Melville, please. This is his wife. It's quite urgent. My son has come home." How strange that this could all be expressed in such simple language.

A voice reached her, not Jacques' voice, that of one of his colleagues. Jacques was not in at the moment, someone had gone out to search for him; in the meantime, would a doctor be required?

She heard herself say, "Yes."

Doctor

After an hour, a doctor and Roger Morel arrived. She was disappointed to see that it was Morel who had been dispatched. He had the reputation about the publishing house as being willing to take on tasks which others disdained, quite unambitious and rather dry. No one had any notion of whether his romantic inclinations were towards his own sex or the opposite, or even if he had any such inclinations. It was quite impossible to imagine him lost in passion, even more difficult than it was to suppose he could have reached late middle age a celibate. On the rare occasions when he joined his colleagues in a café, he sipped his glass of wine, remaining sober while others became less and less so, seeming to take notes. The camelhair coat he wore, a touch old-fashioned but with excellent tailoring, suggested reserves of family wealth—although it had in fact come from a secondhand shop that catered to those with discriminating tastes. As Simone was dutifully embraced by Morel, she leaned into his solid weight, smelt the wool of his coat, the leather of his gloves, his aftershave, was sustained by the upright masculine world.

The doctor approached Marcel gingerly. Simone thought of boys prodding the carcass of a dead animal with a stick. The doctor was afraid of lice, scabies, infection. Nonetheless, he took Marcel's temperature, his pulse, listened with his stethoscope to his chest, said words meant to be reassuring. "He has a fever, but not an alarmingly high one. His pulse is weak and rapid, but there's nothing that suggests an immediate crisis…He should be cleaned up." This last statement was uttered with an air of bewildered disapproval—why hadn't she started on this already?

The poor doctor had spent his life treating pneumonia, asthma, tonsillitis, ushering those afflicted with cancer, TB, incurable ailments out of the world. He had never before encountered a creature like Marcel, who had stumbled into Paris from the pages of a cheap horror book: a zombie, belonging to both the world of the living and the dead. His role was to act as if he were certain, to murmur, with an air of authority, "The next few days will be crucial," or "Rest is of the utmost importance," to give hope while at the same time preparing for the worst. Although, really, he was flummoxed.

Morel stepped into the foyer with the doctor. Simone overheard a murmured conversation—perhaps concerning payment for the doctor's services.

When Morel returned, he opened the window. The wind gusted in, sending the curtains billowing, raising gooseflesh on Simone's arms. "I'm sorry," he said, "the smell…it's really quite…"

"Yes," Simone said. "Yes, of course, I quite understand."

"Well," Morel said, and cleared his throat, stared at Simone, finally giving a sigh and saying, "Clean him up. I suppose we should start with his"—he stared at Marcel's feet—"footwear."

The precision of the man! He was quite right, one couldn't say either "boots" or "shoes," for Marcel had one of each, a wooden clog on his left foot, a boot on his right, the boot with a lace many times broken and many times knotted.

"Scissors will be required."

Yes, scissors, of course, scissors. Why, during all the months she had been waiting for Marcel to come home, hadn't she prepared herself for this eventuality, stocked a kit with iodine, salt tablets, aspirin, rolled bandages, scissors? A sewing kit, she had one in a shoe box, she was sure of that, but it was neither in the closet nor under the bed nor in any of the bureau drawers.

"A knife," Morel called into the bedroom. "If you can't locate your scissors, a knife will do." In his own home, he could no doubt lay his hand on any needed domestic implement—tweezers, razor, corkscrew, garlic press, lemon reamer—within seconds. At least his fussy sadism offered the illusion of a universe in which some moral order remained.

A sharp knife from the kitchen, then, a bit more work than scissors would have been, sawing away at the laces, sinewy from rain and mud and sun. The kettle coming to a boil and screeching—she didn't remember setting it on the stove. Perhaps Morel had.

The lace at last cut free. She tried to pull off the boot, but her actions made Marcel, who had been more or less in a stupor despite all the activity around him, cry out and jerk his leg back.

"Oh," she murmured. "I'm sorry, I'm sorry."

"For God's sake, just yank the thing off." Morel was standing, his posture erect, arms folded across his chest.

"He's my son…I hate to cause him pain…"

Morel removed his jacket, his cufflinks, rolled up his sleeves, grabbed hold of first the clog, then the boot, ripped them from Marcel's feet. He held the boot in his hand, at a distance from his body, and said, "Where shall I dispose of this?" He followed that with orders for rags, a basin of hot water, newspapers, towels. Simone scurried about, bringing him first the wastebasket kept next to Jacques' desk; the other items he was demanding; last of all, she pulled the sheet off of her and Jacques' bed, then stood, mute, skittish, waiting to be ordered about.

Scissors were needed to cut off his clothing, and also some kerosene, for the lice: Morel would go downstairs to the concierge.

"His feet," Morel commanded from the doorway.

The socks, like a winding sheet around a long buried corpse, had become almost one with his skin. His flesh came off in scales, yellow and thin as commune wafers. Take, eat, this is my body. She lay the coins of flesh on a rag, folded it up, shoved it under the couch. *Mary kept these things and pondered them in her heart.* If he died, she would at least have these—no, she mustn't think that.

Morel returned, knelt next to Marcel's head, dabbing at lice with a kerosene-soaked rag, while the insects, some almost translucent, others swollen with dark blood, scuttled away.

Simone, meanwhile, was cutting off his clothes—he was shivering, but Morel, worried about the fumes from the kerosene, said that the window should on no account be shut. In fact, until the fumes had completely dissipated, she and M. Melville should step out to the corridor to smoke, and Marcel should on no account be permitted a cigarette in the aftermath of this procedure. He might, Simone thought, turn into a Biblical pillar of flame.

She gave him a sponge bath. Reaching his genitals, she washed them tenderly, as she had hundreds of times when he was an infant. That rosebud had turned into a man's penis, a tangle of dark above it. With her fingernails, she removed the lice nits clinging to the shafts of his pubic hair. His penis stiffened. Simone had thought he was asleep, but when she looked up, she saw that his eyes were open, staring down at the procedures his body was undergoing as if they were happening to a stranger. She saw that Morel was also staring at her, at her son's genitals.

"I think this is a losing battle," Morel said. "The infestation is simply too severe. We shall have to shave his head."

Marcel allowed himself to be propped up, Simone sat next to him, lathered up his head, but when she started to work Jacques' razor across his skull, he winced and cried out in pain, and then put his arms over his head, curling himself up as if he were a fetus.

"It hurts, it hurts, it hurts," he wailed.

"It will hurt, but just for a few minutes."

He shook his head wildly back and forth, "No, no, no, no, no."

She stroked his head and felt beneath her hand hundreds of tiny nubs of scars. How had humanity kept itself clean in the days before wells and fire to heat water? Had we licked ourselves clean like cats? Plucked insects from one another's hair, popped them in our mouths?

She sheared his hair so close to his skull that he resembled the *totenkopf* of the SS, then dressed him in Jacques' pajamas.

Egg

At last, the sound of Jacques' footsteps trudging up the stairs; the slight hesitation in his left step, caused by his sciatica. He embraced his wife, shook Morel's hand. Morel accepted his thanks with the air of someone who was making notations in a ledger, retrieved his hat and gloves, his overcoat, gave a rather stiff half-bow, and departed.

"What a horrid little man." Simone leaned her weight into Jacques.

"He's quite capable in a crisis—Morel. And I understand he volunteered with alacrity. But let's not—There, there." He stroked her hair, rocked her back and forth in his arms.

"A doctor came. Morel brought him. He was filthy—Marcel. You can't imagine."

"How did he get here? What did the doctor say?"

"He was just there. At the door. He couldn't have come through a processing center—" Jacques lowered himself onto the floor next to her, no easy task between his rheumatism and his sciatica. He put his arm around Simone's shoulder, held her close, a strange Holy Family they, two aged parents with this lummox of an infant. The possibilities that had been dislodged from her womb had been reborn here, in this Marcel, being guided by the two of them through this perilous infancy.

"Have you sent a telegram to Luc?"

"Ah, no, I didn't even—"

Jacques glanced at his watch. "Let me do it now, before the office closes," and scrawled the address from the book bound in red Moroccan leather kept next to the telephone.

"And Odette, too," Simone called down the stairs after him.

At eight that evening, the doctor reappeared, once again took Marcel's pulse, his temperature, pressed a stethoscope against his chest. Before he departed, having uttered his guarded reassurances, he wrote down a diet for Marcel: "A boiled egg; one-quarter liter of milk." He might as well have written, "Eight rubies, nine pearls."

"I'll see what I can do." All the shops were closed. She could not imagine where Jacques would go, to whom he would turn, but in less than an hour he was back, with three eggs and a bottle of wine.

For the first few days, she had listened to Marcel's ragged breaths, praying in the terrible eternity between them for the next, praying to a God she did not believe in, just one more, one more as the midwife had urged her to push Marcel into the world. Unlike the midwife, her pleas were silent, for she did not dare to let Marcel know how close he was to death. She fed him by dipping her finger in the pap of boiled egg and putting it into his mouth, dropped wine between his lips with an eyedropper. She cradled his head in her lap, holding his hands so that he could not scratch the insect bites which covered him. The first night, Jacques had brought the eiderdown from the bedroom and slept next to her, but when she saw the terrible pain his rheumatism gave him as he rose in the morning, she forbade him to do so again.

It seemed to her that she did not sleep at all, although Jacques said that when he rose to check on the two of them during the night, she had been asleep, her head leaning against the wing of the armchair, her eyes closed, unaware of his entrance into the room. How could she explain to him that while perhaps it was true that her physical body slept, inside she did not sleep, or at most slept for a few seconds at a time.

It occurred to her that this might not be her son, perhaps it was some other piece of human detritus who had knocked on her door, uttered that monosyllabic bleat into the hair of the middle-aged woman who answered, like one of those aliens who emerge from women's wombs, claiming love as their due.

After four days, Marcel could manage to eat a few bites of food at a time. She would say "Open up," and swoop a spoonful of food into his beak, wide open like a just-hatched bird.

That night, Jacques ordered, "Come to bed."

"Oh, no, I—I—"

"You must," he said, with more anger than tenderness in his voice.

She could not bear the thought of being separated from Marcel by even a few meters, yet she obeyed her husband: she needed the comfort of having someone else in charge. She did leave the door open.

Jacques turned the serrated knob. The electric light, seeming to protest being extinguished, flared momentarily brighter before it plunged the room into darkness. Since Marcel was wearing his only pair of pajamas, Jacques lay naked. Simone had pulled on the nightgown she had dropped onto the floor that morning, one inherited from her own mother, the tattered silk now thinned by age and with spiderwebs of mending spreading out from the armpits, the buttonholes: Simone was as poor a seamstress as she was a housekeeper. How strange it was to be covered while he was naked. Usually, they occupied their own side of the bed, a region roughly halfway down the middle of the mattress a no-man's land, but tonight she pressed herself against her husband and after a moment's hesitation, he reached out and wrapped his arm around her shoulder, pulled her head onto his bare chest, kissing the top of her head, saying, "After all, he's come home, he's come home."

"Yes, he's come home."

"You must keep your equanimity."

Throughout the night, they rearranged their bodies as they clung to each other, now her head making a pillow of his chest, then his head making one of her bosom. Several times, she slipped out of Jacques' grasp and rose, disturbing the equilibrium of the bed as little as possible to tiptoe into the front room and check on Marcel. The radium hands of the clock next to the bed glowed: twenty minutes past twelve, twelve minutes to one, nine minutes past three. Returning to bed, she curled against Jacques, caressed the loose flesh of his arms, his buttocks.

Rabbit

Those first weeks after Marcel's return, Jacques was a conjurer. He managed to obtain not only two duck eggs, but a piece of salami, and a four-week old Belgian hare, its fur still pale and fluffy, which they kept in a cage in the kitchen, fed grasses culled from the park, and which figured prominently in their daydreams, sometimes fried, sometimes stewed.

He did not, however, spend much time at the flat. On the fifth day after Marcel's return—they measured out time as Christians did from the birth of Christ—Jacques attempted to resume his old habit of taking his place at his desk in the corner of the front room at six in the morning, lighting his pipe, and answering his correspondence. The smoke from his pipe made Marcel cough, so he took to leaving the flat as soon as he had dressed and often not returning until ten or eleven in the evening. She could not fault Jacques for absenting himself. After all, there was nothing much for him to do here, and he was busy with *La nouvelle revue française* which was about to be resurrected under the strange name *La nouvelle nouvelle revue française,* to differentiate it from the collaborationist journal. The atmosphere permeating the flat was depressing, she saw it in the faces of friends who stopped by to offer encouragement in the form of a bunch of wildflowers, kind words, an enameled bedpan.

"Come to bed, then," he would say when he came home, and she would rise, like an automaton that had been rigged to follow whatever order it was given.

Jacques returned one evening with a cream-colored box tucked under his arm. She smiled, thinking he had somehow managed to get enough money together to buy her a gift. Wanting to stop her before she embarrassed herself by fluttering her eyelids and saying, "Ah, for me?" he said, rather roughly: "It's for me. A gift from a colleague."

"A colleague?"

"Someone noticed how tired I looked, and I explained that I hadn't been sleeping well, I'd been deprived of my pajamas. And—a few days later, I found this on my desk. Don't, Simone. Don't give me one of your suspicious looks—"

In their previous life, before Marcel had come home, Simone would have said, "And don't I have reason to be suspicious?" to which Jacques would have responded, "Ah, you needn't act like a wronged innocent—" but now Simone said nothing, merely looked placidly into his eyes, did not even say, "But I'm not giving you a suspicious look."

"After all," Jacques went on, defending himself against accusations which had not been made, "people want to help those who are suffering—a poor old man, for instance," and he winked, "forced to sleep bald as a coot. And furthermore, some have guilty consciences which they want to assuage."

She did not fail to notice that his sentences skirted the necessity of using a personal pronoun, which would have been either masculine or feminine. He needn't have bothered: it did not matter to her that a woman had given him a pair of pajamas. She didn't mind if he was getting his physical needs met elsewhere. He was not made of stone. The plain and simple fact was that she had fallen out of love with him and in love with her son.

For the next few weeks, Simone and Jacques had the same conversation over and over again:

—How did things go today?

—All right. He seems a bit stronger.

That would be followed by a brief description of the food that one or the other of them had managed to scavenge: the kindness of Richard, a friend with a cousin who had a farm near Evreux, who had passed along a wedge of Camembert from said cousin. The check that Luc had sent. Simone's useless journey that same day to several grocers. At the fourth visit, she'd paused outside, putting on the air of a faded beauty of the bruised magnolia sort. Perhaps it was that which did the trick. "My son, you see, my son..." she sighed. This man's daughter had made the acquaintance of several GIs—"What can I say? They may drive us mad, but nonetheless—" a shrug. "She brings them round to the flat, they appreciate the opportunity to sit on a couch…some of them have been kind enough to…powdered eggs, just like real eggs, only they don't taste quite the same…This, another product of American know-how—" He produced a packet of KLIM, powdered milk, with dire warnings printed on the label about the penalties the occupation authorities would visit on any unauthorized parties found to be in possession of said packet. When she had attempted to bargain him down from the inflated price he quoted her, he responded with outrage: "Madame, I am doing you a favor!" This was not the feigned umbrage sometimes exhibited in such negotiations, but the real thing—this from a man who pimped out his daughter for pilfered U.S. Army rations.

Hunger

Simone herself had almost ceased to eat—sometimes, at the end of the day, she would realize that she had had nothing but a cup of Pero, the crust of bread too tough for Marcel to chew, a bit of Marcel's boiled egg licked from her finger. The hunger she felt at this period in her life was different from the hunger she had experienced during the war proper, which had been a hunger filled with lust, a hunger that wanted the answer of food, a hunger filled with rage at the Germans. Now she treasured her hunger.

"This fasting is for medieval saints. You must eat. If something were to happen to you—and something will happen to you, it is inevitable if you keep on depriving yourself—then where will we be?"

Flush

Jacques opened a letter from Luc. "Someone's feeling flush. Or guilty." He waved the enclosed bank draft in the air, then jutted out his lip. "He suggests that Marcel might come and stay with him—"

"What a foolish notion!"

Jacques jutted his lip further out. "Country air," he averred. "And surely the whole matter of food would be a good deal simpler there." Luc had, upon his retirement, become a gentleman farmer. What had seemed a self-indulgent hobby had proved quite fortuitous.

Simone mouthed at Jacques: "The trip would kill him."

"Woonsocket, Rhode Island," Marcel said one day, and Simone was not sure whether he was talking in his sleep or merely speaking with his eyes closed. "What did you say?"

His eyes fluttered open. "Woonsocket," he repeated, seeming to be puzzled by the words coming out of his mouth.

"'You a kraut?'" the GI leaning out of the Jeep had asked him.

Even in his filthy state, his hair unwashed for weeks, his eyebrows and eyelashes revealed him to be a blond, therefore suspect, as a few months before a circumcised penis had been a death warrant.

"*Français*."

The sergeant's hand was on his pistol. "*C'est vrai*?"

When Marcel answered him in French, the American winked and said in English, "Hop in," then switched to French. "Have some cheese, my friend. Not the good French stuff, I'm afraid. Limburger or something. Found it in the cellar of this German bitch last night. Man, you should have heard her holler when we were giving it to her. Woonsocket, Rhode Island, that's where I'm from. My people are Canucks, came down from Quebec to work the mills there. When I started kindergarten, I only knew two words of English, 'Hello' and 'pee-pee.'"

Wink

For the next month, the rhythm of her days varied little. In the morning, she went out and foraged. She walked to save a Metro fare—although she was exhausted, promising herself a ride home if there was anything left over after buying a cabbage or an aubergine, dangling the possibility in front of herself like a talisman. She batted her eyes at the butcher in the rue Tournefort—the one she refused to venture into before the war on account of its filth and flies—but that did her no good: his face slammed shut like a gate: *I'm sorry, Madame, I play by the rules*. When a coy smile failed to elicit the desired response, she appealed to him on the grounds of her son's suffering—another fruitless tack: "Life's hard, Madame." Finally, at the third butcher, she set a few extra coins on the counter. He gave her a wink and a nod, and when the shop was empty, handed her a packet of bones and trimmings she could use to brew beef bouillon for Marcel.

It was on one of these outings that she felt dampness between her legs. She ducked into a stall at a public lavatory. She laughed, laughed as Sarah laughed, when, a crone, she was told she would be got with child. No winged messenger in Simone's case, instead a shock of red on the strips of newspaper used for toilet paper. Ah, it hadn't been menopause but deprivation that had brought about the end of her periods. Her youth—well, perhaps not quite her youth—was returning to her.

Knit

To do nothing—although most of the time there was nothing to be done—seemed heartless, to merely stare at that form lying on the couch, and so Simone boiled water and poured it over dishes and glasses, got down on her knees and scrubbed the corners of the front room. She even sewed, by hand, a second pair of pajamas out of a worn bed sheet so that she could launder one pair each day.

On one of her forays into the wilds of the city, she passed a second-hand shop which displayed in its window once-fashionable hats, a hodgepodge of household items, a ball of yarn with two needles stuck in it—the things people parted with, in order to get a few sous that would enable them to keep body and soul together for one more day. She was surprised to find herself entering the shop, inquiring the price, and purchasing the wool and needles. In the afternoons when nothing more could be done around the house she would sit in the armchair which had, up until this time served as Jacques' throne, now faced kitty-corner to Marcel's berth, and knit. "I learned to knit during the war, when I was a schoolgirl. The other war. For the soldiers at the front. We were allowed to knit in class, with wooden needles, steel ones would have clacked and drowned out the teacher. I made a pair of socks and the teacher—Mme. LeDuc, I adored her—held them up before the whole class and said, 'These are socks for mutilated feet.'"

Had she told him this before? No, she remembered, she'd told Jacques on their first train ride together.

She finished the ball of yarn, unraveled her work, began again.

She bathed him every morning. The sores on his body began to heal, the callouses which had covered his feet sloughed off, revealing underneath the feet he'd had as an infant.

Luc sent not just another check, but a hamper of food delivered by one of his men—one couldn't possibly trust such a tempting parcel to the post: a ham, two dozen eggs, two jars of pickled vegetables, a honeycake, fruit—both fresh and dried, a wheel of Bray Picard, two kilos— two!—of butter, a bottle of Calvados and a bottle of *eau de vie*.

"Ah, Madame, you are fortunate indeed," the doctor said when Simone informed him of this bounty, hoping she might take the hint and offer him, in lieu of his overdue payment, a slice of the ham or wedge of the cheese, but the thought did not even cross her mind.

Indeed, when she saw Jacques coming out of the kitchen that evening munching on a slice of the ham, she cried aloud, "Ah, no!" Then: "After all, it's for Marcel."

"Allow an old man a little pleasure. Ah, it's not my fault. The ham more or less seduced me." It was their old row, with a slab of *jambon sec* taking the place of Jacques' latest dalliance.

Sometimes she read aloud to Marcel, picking up whatever happened to be at hand: the first story her eyes lighted on in the previous day's *Le Monde* or a copy of *Vogue*—a gift from one of those friends who still dropped by on occasion. "I don't suppose you care about the shape of this year's bodice, do you?" He said nothing in response, and she longed for the irritable boy he had been but a few years before, the one who shot scowls at her and occasionally muttered under his breath, "Of all the stupid things you have ever said, that was the stupidest!"

She flipped through *Vogue*.

The women of France had hatched from the grimy cocoons of the war years, reborn as butterflies with cerise, plum, cobalt, sapphire, amethyst wings, courtesy of M. Christian Dior. Dior—Cri-Cri to his friends—painted in this vivid palette, although he himself had flesh of such unnatural whiteness it made him seem pupa-like, aside from his blue-blue eyes which seemed filched from a doll's face. He'd gotten some grief for having dressed the wives of the Untersturmfuehrers and Fregattenkapitains, Obergruppenfuehrers and Obersturmbannfuehrers, those German words piling up on themselves like box cars ploughing into one another in a derailed train. Now he claimed, "You must understand—I practiced my own form of resistance! When I dressed those great German trout, I put ruffles on the bodice that made their bosoms look like battleships. And I chose the least flattering color and then gushed at how becoming it was in a way that any Frenchwoman would have recognized as mockery, but they—not an ounce of subtlety in them—I had them strutting around, thinking they looked like queens, while in fact everyone was laughing at them behind their backs!"

Shutter

Most days, Jacques brought home a new set of galleys, an outpouring from all of those who had decided not to publish under the Occupation. Occasionally, Simone would pick up one of these, but it was hard to concentrate on the opening pages of a novel when she knew that Jacques would take it back to the office before she'd had a chance to finish reading it.

She read aloud to Marcel from a manuscript: "'The open shutters. The breeze coming through the unshuttered window. I do not yet know the words 'window' or 'shutter,' only the sensation of wind on my face.'...Did I ever tell you, it was terribly windy, the day I met your father?" As soon as the words were out of her mouth, she realized it had been windy the day she met Jacques, not the day she met Luc.

She went back to her reading: "'At dusk, I heard the whir of bicycles, punctuated by the bellow of a water buffalo, the cry of a klaxon, as a motorcar sought to part the human waters. Darkness, the rise of the moon, the streets growing quiet, the nightingale, kept by the family across the way, singing: all these things seemed, to my child's mind, to bear a relationship with one another. I believed it was the trill of the songbird that caused the clatter and thrum of the bicycle tires to cease as surely as the white-gloved hand of a traffic policeman indicating halt.' What a curious book. Don't you think?"

Marcel merely grunted.

"Ah," his mother said, having turned back to the title page. "Pierre Laurent. I know this man." Before the war, she had had a flirtation with him, culminating in nothing more than a prolonged kiss in which he substituted ardency for skill. He was a queer man, chronically disheveled—shirts always misbuttoned, stained, given to wild gesticulations which occasionally knocked over glasses of wine: bug-eyed, finger-tapping, manic. Forgetting he had a cigarette already lit, he would light another, and sometimes a third. His manner of speech was the polar opposite of that of her husband: while Jacques set forth each word carefully, a chiseled stone being laid precisely atop the chiseled stone that preceded it, Laurent—no one ever used his Christian name—allowed words to pour from his mouth. They tumbled over one another, one idea would spark a further idea, and he would interrupt himself—he also had the habit of repeating some of his own words in a softer voice than his usual one, echoing himself. This outpouring was accompanied by clearings of his throat, curlicuings of a strand of his forelock around the index finger of his left hand: all in all, giving the impression of being kin to those one-man bands sometimes seen busking on the streets of Paris in the thirties, cymbals, guitar, Jew's harp all at once, accordion at the ready.

Sometimes, Jacques would lean over and lay a hand on Laurent's shoulder, say, "Have a rest. Let someone else speak." Laurent, red-faced, sweating, looking like a long-distance runner giving one last push as the finish line came in sight, would respond, "Yes (yes-yes), but just let me finish my point (my point)," and he would be off again.

It seemed impossible that this text, with its air of elegant inevitability, could have been produced by him. But perhaps, like stones tumbled in a wild river until they were smooth and perfect ovals, his words underwent a similar burnishing in the tumult of his mind.

"Shall I keep reading?" she asked Marcel.

He made a sound which she took to be no.

She slept fitfully in her chair, woke, saw that Marcel was sleeping, read another page of Laurent's manuscript, fell back asleep. As she did so, the manuscript tumbled down between her thigh and the edge of the armchair, rumpling a few of its pages.

The symptoms of nervous instability that had been put down to Marcel's absence continued unabated.

Jacques, sensing that her turning of attention away from him was not just a temporary phase, would now sometimes stand in the doorway between the bedroom and the parlor, saying, "Come to bed," plaintiveness bleeding through his imperious attitude. "In a few minutes," she would answer. Sometimes she'd join him, sometimes she'd fall asleep on the floor next to Marcel. If she did join Jacques in bed, he would immediately turn towards her, even in his sleep, and wrap his arms around her, press his body, damp with night-warmth against her. If she did not come to bed, at three or four in the morning she would wake to him, barefoot, unrobed, bending over her, shaking her gently awake: "Come to bed. Come to bed."

At last, Marcel began to grow stronger, although his progress was by no means an even upward line. His face grew—one could not possibly use the adjective plumper—less lean, although his mouth still had the sunken-in quality of an old man's. One day Simone ordered him to open his mouth—he still spoke rarely, and almost never spontaneously, but now, when told to do something, he would generally obey the command. She counted: he had only eleven teeth left.

Gas

One day she made him cabbage soup, and when she presented the bowl to him, he said, "You know cabbage gives me gas." It was the longest sentence he had spoken since returning.

"Cabbage gives everyone gas," she answered. She was delighted at the return of his old sourness.

"Mine is worse," he stated, with the air of someone giving a fact which cannot be contravened: two plus two is four, hot air rises. As if to prove the truth of this, within a quarter hour after finishing his dinner of cabbage and carrots and bread, he began to pass wind.

"Ah, Marcel!" she rebuked him.

"I told you so!"

Doctor

The next day the doctor arrived with a cumbersome device beneath his arm: a portable scale, with a dial in its base which gave one's weight. Marcel stepped on it, as ordered, and the verdict was given: he was a mere 5 kilos beneath the ideal weight for his height.

A week later, Jacques returned home at the unheard of hour of three in the afternoon.

"Are you ill?"

"No, the doctor wanted to speak with both of us."

"But—how—why wasn't I—?"

"He telephoned me at my office."

Once again, the doctor set his device on the floor, and Marcel stepped on it. In the past week, he had gained half a kilo.

"If we could speak in private…"

Jacques, Simone, and the doctor retreated to the bedroom, shutting the door behind them. The doctor seated himself, while the two of them stood—it would indeed have been awkward for the three of them to have clambered onto the bed together. The doctor lit a cigarette, without offering the pack to them—American cigarettes, Lucky Strikes. He knew he was being discourteous but was miffed by the fact that he hadn't been given even the smallest portion of the ham.

"I asked that both of you join me this afternoon because I need to speak with you quite frankly—"

"Oh, no!" Simone cried.

"Ah, Madame, I apologize for alarming you. What I have to say is the opposite of bad news. Your son's physical recovery is now nearly complete. The fact is that we, my colleagues and I, are beginning to see that in these situations—what's needed is a reconnection of his"—the doctor briefly considered using the word *soul*— "his spirit to life, to the world. It is of utmost importance that he get outside. The fact is, one's connection to life can atrophy, just as a unused muscle can waste away—"

"If only the building had a lift," Simone said.

"Exercise is essential—he may as well get it going up and down the stairs. There's the park across the street—"

"Oh, but the six flights!"

"Simone, we can hardly move house. He will have to walk down the stairs."

The following day, Jacques asked how the stair climbing had gone.

"He's had a hard day."

"Marcel, how was your day?"

Marcel shrugged.

"We're going to get you dressed."

"But he has no clothes," Simone protested.

"He can wear mine."

"They won't fit."

"They won't fit well, but they'll do. Perhaps tomorrow we'll get him to a haberdasher—"

"Oh, how on earth—" Simone motioned with her head towards the kitchen, an imperious gesture more befitting Jacques than her.

Behind the closed door she said to him, "I will not allow you to be cruel to my son. A haberdasher—he could not possibly—"

"We won't know until we try. After all, he was able to make his way here from Germany—"

"Yes, and you saw the state he was in!"

"But that was three months ago. You heard what the doctor said yesterday." He steepled his fingers. "We must force him out of this infantile state."

"Oh, there you go, with your goddamn fingers—" She imitated him. They had had many, many rows in the course of their long connection. Many cruel words had been uttered—Jacques had even sometimes found it necessary to apologize—but this comment moved them to a decidedly different plane. Simone had never before expressed scorn for one of Jacques' essential traits.

"I have nothing more to say to you, Simone." Jacques let the door swing shut as he exited, calling out: "Marcel, you are going to get dressed and we are going outside."

"No," Simone said, "no, it will be too much."

"Ignore her."

Jacques returned from the bedroom with a pair of his trousers, a shirt, a pair of shoes, even some of his underwear.

"Leave the room while he changes."

"But I have been caring for him in the most intimate way—"

"Yes, and it is time for that to end." He fixed his eyes on her quite firmly, said in the voice of a stern *paterfamilias*. "Leave the room."

She did as she was ordered, but stood by the door, listening to the orders Jacques gave her son: "Button the shirt. Tuck it in. Now button the flies. Stand up. All right. Quit scratching yourself. You will soon get used to the feel of a waistband. Let's go."

When she heard the front door of the flat close behind them, she scuttled to the stairway, and stood peering down over the railing.

"Dizzy."

Jacques took Marcel's arm so he wouldn't fall, although Simone feared that if Marcel began to reel he would send them both tumbling down. They reached the landing of the fourth floor, turned around and came back up. Marcel tromped around the flat with the flat-footed gait of a madman.

Simone had picked up his pajamas from where he had dropped them on the floor, smoothed and folded them, and now presented the packet to him.

"No," Jacques said, single finger of his left hand in the air. "He should do as ordinary men do. Get up in the morning, get dressed, sit in a chair. Read the newspaper. Go for a walk in the park."

"For a walk in the park!"

"Yes, a walk in the park."

"But he almost fainted on the stairs."

"Let me tell you, Simone. I am familiar with what it is like to walk up and down stairs when one has become unfamiliar with the practice—because of my war wound, and then because of the illnesses I suffered in Madagascar. One experiences vertigo after a period of prolonged bed rest. In fact, in the military hospital, when I was recovering from my wound, the nurses had an odd contraption, like the reins for a horse, which they would fasten around the newly-arisen patient as he made his way along the corridor for the first time. One lurched and stumbled, like a newborn foal—"

"Oh, please!"

"And quite rapidly, one becomes accustomed—again the analogy with a just-born foal is germane here—to the upright world, which only a quarter of an hour ago seemed so foreign as to be positively bizarre."

Jacques returned from his office the next day in the early afternoon, and was well pleased to see Marcel not only dressed but seated in the club chair that had, until the start of this crisis, been used exclusively by Jacques, although he was less well-pleased to see the youth's feet swaddled in bandages.

"What is this?"

Although his question had been directed to Simone, it was Marcel who responded: "Your shoes gave me blisters."

Jacques went to his desk, fetched two sheets of paper and a pencil, knelt on the floor and outlined his stepson's feet. Having stowed the papers in his pocket, he headed out the door, returning within the hour with a new pair of wingtips. He fetched a box of sticky plasters from the medicine cabinet and handed them to Marcel, who did not even need to be told what to do.

"Ah, no," Simone said, "his blisters."

"One puts up with aches and pangs. My sciatica shoots pains down my leg when I climb the stairs, but I am hardly going to allow that fact to make me a shut-in."

Jacques took his wife's son all the way down the stairs and across the way to the park. When they returned, Marcel looked faintly bilious.

He slumped in the chair and would have vomited on the floor had not Simone rushed over with a basin to catch his sick.

"You see—"

"Ah, please Simone. This reaction to the sun isn't at all uncommon in one who has been shut away from it. The doctor was saying to me just the day before yesterday—"

"Why are you having conversations behind my back?"

"It's not behind your back, I am telling you now what he said, if you will only be quiet and listen."

"Be quiet and listen," Marcel put in. Simone was cowed into silence.

"The doctor said, he specifically asked that I repeat it to you, that when Marcel was a boy, you no doubt threw him into the lake, or his father did so, in order that he might learn to swim."

Neither Simone—nor to her knowledge, Luc—had ever done such a thing. In fact, Marcel was unable to swim.

When Jacques came home during the day—which he had taken to doing so at unexpected hours, like a husband seeking to catch an unfaithful wife—he often found Marcel back in his pajamas, staring at the wall. Once he came home when Simone was going round to the shops and discovered that Marcel had pissed in the bowl in which his morning porridge had been served and had left it on the end table for his mother to remove.

Rattle

She and Jacques were sitting opposite one another in a restaurant. He'd made the suggestion about dining out before he left in the morning, and she'd sensed there was an ulterior motive. The salad having been served, a sign that they had gotten to the point in the meal where he'd better have out with it or it would be too late, he poured her another glass of wine—he had been filling up her glass quite liberally—and gave off one of his interjections, a "*Bien*," somewhere between a word and a sigh, followed by a pregnant pause, and said: "I've arranged for you to see a doctor."

She almost laughed at the puniness of what he'd just said after all she'd been imagining. "A doctor?"

"A psychiatrist."

"A psychiatrist? For me?"

"The fact," he was saying, "that you are so surprised at the suggestion reveals a—"

Oh, there he goes, plodding along through his well-rehearsed words, here they come, it's all laid out very logically, very neatly—she said as much.

"I would ask you to exercise some self-control, especially given that we are in a public place," he said.

"And why is it that you think I need—"

"The fact is that you have developed what is, to speak perfectly frankly, a shared madness with your son."

"My son most certainly isn't mad. And neither am I."

"You are quite right. 'Madness' perhaps is rather too strong a term: an unhealthy dependency. However, the fact that you don't see how close to madness this situation has come, speaks volumes in and of itself. And surely you see that this—arrangement—cannot continue indefinitely. I'm not going to say anything more—only ask that you consult with this specialist— who comes most highly recommended."

"Perhaps you should be the one to visit this highly recommended specialist."

"Simone, you are being childish. I should tell you that I've had a preliminary conversation with Marcel."

"A preliminary conversation? Whatever does that mean?"

"I've spoken to him frankly. I've told him that your health is suffering."

"Ask for the bill, please. I want to go home."

"The fact is, that your misplaced guilt is actually causing harm, not just to you—and you, after all, are the one I am most concerned about in this situation—but to your son, as well."

"I want to go home. I am worried about Marcel."

"You are exhibiting the very behavior I have been speaking about. Marcel is fine."

"Marcel is not fine."

"Marcel will be in the state he is in, whether you are there or not. When he was a child—"

"When he was a child, I was not a good mother to him, because I was so in love with you."

"This is precisely what I am talking about. You act as if this whole tragic circumstance is an opportunity for you to expiate your guilt. But he is a grown man and your infantilizing of him—"

"Stop pontificating. He is my son. He has suffered things we cannot imagine. Do you want me to turn him out on the street? Expose him on some hillside? You will not deprive me of my son a second time."

Jacques slammed his hands down on the table, rattling the dishes, making her jump, give off a little cry.

"People are looking at us."

"Listen," he said, leaning over, taking both of her hands in his.

"I want to leave. I want to go back to the flat—"

He grabbed her wrists. "You are going to hear me out. Do you know what you are like? You are like an addict. And just as we've sometimes had to deprive Joë of his morphine for his own good—"

"You are shouting."

"I am not shouting."

"People are looking at us."

"I will lower my voice if you promise you will sit here and listen to what I have to say."

"Don't bully me."

"Will you agree to see this doctor? He comes very highly recommended."

"Will you ask the waiter for the bill?"

"If you will agree to see this doctor."

"Once." Simone held the index finger of her right hand up in the air. "Once. I will see this doctor once, just to appease you."

"We will start there." Jacques signaled to the waiter, reached into his pocket, removed his pen and diary, and wrote "Dr. E. Balmant," his address, the date and time of the appointment which had been set up, and handed the torn sheet to Simone. He leaned back in his chair, lit his pipe, called the waiter over again, this time asking for two glasses of cognac—and the bill—with the air of a general who is satisfied with himself for having won, not the war, not the battle, but an important skirmish.

Confession

Dr. Eric Balmant, not yet thirty-five, a mere stripling in the venerable world of psychoanalysis, had in an attempt to appear older grown a goatee—although much to his distress it grew in ginger-colored, despite his dark hair and eyebrows, looking as if it had come from the costume room of a provincial theater company, pasted on for a play in which a youthful actor assumed the role of an elder. The redness of his beard made him wonder if he might have some Viking blood running through his veins—perhaps it was this that had made him choose the name Eric to replace the Esau he had been given eight days after birth. He no sooner thought this than he banished it from his mind: he did not believe in the racial unconscious or any other such mumbo-jumbo.

In addition to his youth, there was the matter of his voice—rather high-pitched for a man, so much so that he was occasionally mistaken for a woman over the telephone—and his tendency to articulate phrases in rapid bursts, followed by long pauses between them. His nickname as a schoolboy had been parakeet. (Small wonder he became a psychoanalyst). He labored at making his voice deeper, and hoped, by a slowness of enunciation, to suggest sagacity not pomposity.

He cleared his throat, cleared it again, and opened the door between his office and the anteroom. He was surprised at the ordinariness of the woman waiting for him: her New Look skirt had obviously been purchased recently, but her coat and her gloves had seen a good deal of wear, and her jewelry—a pearl necklace (perhaps a good fake), simple gold hoop earrings—was unexceptional. Given who her husband was, he had expected someone rather more flamboyant in appearance, perhaps a former artist's model with blood-red lips and sculpted brows. He might have passed this woman on the street without a second glance. He made note of his own feeling of disappointment—his mentor had been lecturing Dr. Balmant on his insufficient attention to issues of counter-transference—and inclined his head, shook her hand, and ushered her into his office, not neglecting to switch off the reading lamp in the outer room. The office, although high-ceilinged, was not much larger than the anteroom, forcing his patient to turn sideways to get past the couch. Despite the snugness of the office, the electric fire, in a corner of the room, failed to generate sufficient warmth.

"Before we begin," he said, touching the fingers and thumbs of his hands together, making them into a 'V' pointed at Simone—it was one of a series of gestures he'd cribbed from his own analyst—"I would like to warn you against two things: one, discussing your treatment with others, and secondly, reading the analytic literature."

"Oh, but," Simone said, "I do not think we are actually going to embark on a course of treatment. That is," she added quickly, seeing the look of hurt that crossed his face despite his attempts to suppress it, "I only agreed with my husband that I would come here once."

He said nothing in response, merely stared at her, and she became quite discomfited by his gaze.

"Should I lie down?" she at last asked.

"If you like."

Ah, she's quick to get on her back, he noted, and, quite unconsciously, moved his hand in front of his face to hide his smirk.

The leather in which the fainting couch was upholstered had absorbed the odors of thousands of cigars and cigarettes, the cheese and fungal smell that wafted from the feet of Dr. Balmant's patients, the cheap perfume and aftershave of those who coupled on it in the days before Dr. Balmant bought it secondhand.

She waited for the doctor to speak.

He did not.

She had thought there might be some rituals, like that of the confessional. *Forgive me father, for I have sinned*. Perhaps, here: *I have had three dreams since our last session*.

"Well," she said after a while.

"You seem ill at ease."

"Well, yes, rather," she said, reaching for her handbag, drawing out a cigarette. He handed her an ashtray which she balanced on her sternum. "Should I just start talking?"

"You must allow yourself to simply speak, without censoring. This isn't a drawing room or a dinner party—"

"I'm well aware of that," Simone said. Dr. Balmant, annoyed by what he took to be a reference to the meagerness of his office, frowned.

"My husband," she began, "he thought I should come here. He made the arrangements." She cantilevered her wedding ring up her index finger, shoved it firmly back down, repeated the action. "He, we—the war was difficult for us, of course, it was difficult, I know, for everyone—for some more than others—and we imagined that when it was over that life would just be—all we had longed for. And my son, my son was in a labor camp, in Germany, and—now he has come home, but he is in very poor health...Is Balmant a Jewish name?"

After a minute or so he asked, "What do you suppose?"

"I think that it is. Balmant, yes. You must be thinking: her suffering is nothing in comparison to mine."

"Do you often feel that your suffering is made light of?"

"No, of course not. I'm not the sort of woman who feels self-pity. I've led a charmed life, in many ways. The daughter of—ordinary people—and now I find myself married to—and Paris, I always dreamed of living in Paris as a girl. And my son did, after all, come home. And he is—slowly—he is slowly recovering."

"And yet you find yourself here."

"Yes, because my husband—there's a very harsh side to his nature. He's rather proud of it. He brags of it sometimes. I've deferred to him throughout our marriage, but about this particular thing, I won't."

"'This particular thing'?"

"My son. I wasn't a very good mother. Neither to him, nor to Odette, my daughter. And now, now I've been given the chance to more or less redo things, a second chance. The first night when Marcel came home—he was in terrible shape, more dead than alive—Jacques and I slept on the floor together, next to the couch where Marcel was lying. And it seemed as if—I know it sounds silly to say this—as if our souls merged. Not just mine and Jacques, but Marcel's as well. I think that frightened him. Jacques. That he is afraid of the depth of his love for me."

She craned her neck.

"You just turned to look at me."

"Yes."

"And—your reason for doing that?"

"I suppose—I was wondering what expression was on your face."

At last he said, "What expression did you imagine would be on my face?"

"I didn't imagine anything."

He said nothing, and his silence seemed to cast doubt on the last sentence she had spoken, doubt which grew with each passing second.

She thought of Alain, the game of cat and mouse she had played with him.

"What are you thinking?"

"Nothing," she said. "Nothing." She took a long drag on her cigarette. "What was it we were speaking of? Ah, yes, my husband. The night Marcel returned. How united the three of us were—or maybe that is only wishful thinking on my part. I was, I was pregnant with Jacques. With, that is, Jacques' child. Twice. I had two abortions. He, he was married to someone else. And the process of extricating himself from that marriage—well, it wasn't an easy one. Do you think I am a murderess?"

"A murderess?"

"The children—the children I didn't have."

Dr. Balmant said nothing. At last, he observed: "Your hand is trembling."

"It does that sometimes. Essential tremor, that's how it has been diagnosed." The lie she had told in the provincial café seemed to have come true. *Nervous, madame*?

"By whom, may I ask?"

"Marcel's doctor. He was visiting once when my arm—went off, like that. He gave me some neurological tests—'track my finger with your eye, count backwards from 100 by sevens,' that sort of thing. And then he said it was essential tremor. He said it sometimes developed in"—she hesitated, and then put on a flirtatious voice—"in the prime of life. He asked if there was a family history. On my mother's side, no; but on my father's—well, I'm not sure, because, because, he died so young."

She began to weep, wiping her cheeks with the backs of her hands. "Ah, I'm sorry." She reached for her handbag, took out a lace-edged handkerchief, blotted her eyes, her nose. Since she was lying on her back, her tears coursed along the tops of her cheekbones and drizzled into her ears, where they pooled in the bottom whorl. The sensation of warm, wet ears was a strange, yet not entirely unpleasant, one.

She wept and wept and wept.

Her tears filled up Dr. Balmant's office, his desk and chair floating on the salty water—although the flood hardly disturbed his equilibrium, only occasionally did he reach out his hand to the wall to brace himself against it as one steadies a dinghy against the pilings of a pier. Her tears flowed down the stairs, ran through the streets, the barges on the Seine rocked and lifted, and still, she went on weeping.

As a French Jew, Dr. Balmant had always been fascinated by the Catholic rituals of his fellow citizens—the clouds of incense pouring out of the cave-like churches, the miracle of transubstantiation, and above all, the confessional. Having made himself a secular father-confessor, he'd learned that the revelations entrusted to the listener were hardly those he'd imagined being whispered in that mysterious box—incest, murder, betrayal. Instead, they were as common as grass, as air: *Those who should love me do not. I do not love those I should. I lust. I am filled with petty cruelties. There is something nameless and corrupt at the core of me.*

Dr. Balmant waited for her to compose herself. He didn't adhere to the hydraulic view of the psyche, the emotions dammed-up fluid that needed an outlet. He thought of himself as akin to a surgeon, peeling back the layers of skin, fat, muscle, to reveal the diseased organs. His scalpel was the harsh light of reason. Her carrying on in this fashion confirmed his initial impression of her as a woman who, despite being middle-aged, was given to overwrought flights of emotion. He took note of the movement from the tremor—he had little doubt that it was hysterical in nature—to her playing the coquette— quite unbecoming in a woman of her age—to the histrionic weeping.

"How old were you, when he died?"

"Eleven, I was eleven," she managed to say at last.

"Tomorrow, then?" Dr. Balmant said. "At the same time?"

He removed the linen cloth on which Simone's head had rested and replaced it with a fresh one, although he did not have another patient for several hours. He made note of this action which exhibited not just an anal desire for order but also a wish to be rid of the residue of this rather unpleasant woman.

The next day, Simone said: "It's very seductive, this process, being attended to so closely. Listened to, with such care."

"Seductive," Dr. Balmant repeated.

Gone

On their fifth session, she entered Dr. Balmant's office in a rage: Marcel was gone. It had been done behind her back. His father had taken him away to Picardy. Picardy! Frédéric's wife had invited her for lunch—yes, she had plotted along with the rest of them. Simone should have known something was up—her daughter-in-law never invited her anywhere. When Simone had returned to the empty flat she had been told: It's all for the best, not just best for Marcel, but best for you, as well. And when she had asked, Why wasn't I consulted, why wasn't I even told?

"He said, 'We feared such a scene from you.'"

"By 'he' you mean your husband?"

"Yes, of course, I mean my husband." Then: "I'm sorry. I didn't mean to lash out at you."

"Can you tell me their reasoning? What you understand of it?"

"Ah, the fresh air. Food will be easier to obtain there, in the country. And of course, there is my unnatural attachment to him."

"And what were Marcel's thoughts on this matter? Was he aware that he was going to be—?" He stopped himself. He could not think of a word to use, "removed," "transported" were now so freighted.

"Yes. They got him in league with all the rest of them."

After a long silence, Dr. Balmant spoke. (He rarely spoke except after a long silence, and over the course of her treatment she at times found herself deliberately silent, hoping this would provoke him to speech.) "Marcel will be better off with his father."

"Ah, not you, too! Can't you see how I am suffering? Can't you offer me the slightest bit of kindness?"

"The cruelest thing I could do would be to offer you my kindness."

He said nothing, and she was drawn into the void he thus created, might even be said to be falling into it, a sensation not easily distinguishable from falling in love.

Towards the end of the session, Simone said: "I said to Jacques, 'Well, the problem for which you sent me to Dr. Balmant has been solved, so we can rid ourselves of that expense.' And Jacques said, 'Yes, that will be a relief.'"

"It would be a grave error if you were to end your treatment prematurely. The outer manifestation has been removed, but the psychic conflicts may well now loom even larger. I will see you tomorrow."

Simone lay on her back and stared up at the plaster ceiling with its rococo image of a faun holding aloft a bunch of grapes, although the faun's rear leg was sundered by a wall, the once ornate ballroom having been divided into a warren of offices and anterooms. Swags of dust, seeming to defy the laws of gravity, hung from the ceiling.

She reached into her purse and pulled out Marcel's most recent letters, which she read aloud. *Dear Mother, With my father now. I am doing well. Love, Marcel.* Two weeks later: *Dear Mother, I have gained 3 kilos. Good to eat apples again. Love, Marcel.* Gradually, his letters became longer, more detailed, but no more intimate: reports on the weather, on his weight gain, the need to buy a new belt for his expanding girth. They sometimes seemed love letters to the foods he had eaten: figs, a roast chicken, berries, asparagus, country bread. The cook at first tried to make him soup, which he refused to eat, he never wanted to see another bowl of it as long as he lived, it reminded him of the factory canteen.

Dr. Balmant said, "You carry your son about in your black bag. You wish to have him inside you again."

"No," Simone said. "I merely—after all, I wanted to read you these letters, I find them disturbing. Where else would I carry them, save in my purse? They are so impersonal. And seem, quite frankly, ungrateful. When he was"—she did not want to use the phrase "at death's door," it seemed trite, the sort of set phrase her own mother would say, but no other term sprang to mind, so she said, "When he was at death's door, I, I, I went to such lengths to procure food for him—"

"The word 'no' is the door you slam against the unconscious. And do you note your use of the word 'procure'?"

Cure

To summarize Dr. Balmant's view of the treatment—Simone was a woman not untypical for her age and circumstances. However, in her case, the death of her father at a critical juncture had made it especially difficult for her to navigate the rocky Oedipal shoals. Therefore her relations with men—her husband, her son, Dr. Balmant himself—were filled with a thinly disguised adolescent yearning, with resentment, with a healthy dose (perhaps an inept term) of masochism. All her life, she had chased after thrills— the older man with the extravagant mustache and the open motorcar who had whisked her off to Istanbul, the affair with Jacques, his betrayals, which caused her enormous pain, pain without which she was adrift. The war—her involvement in the Resistance—had satisfied these needs for excitement, as had the drama of Marcel's return. Now, no longer young, the war over, she had resorted to these strange flailings and tremors.

That was Dr. Balmant's view. And what was Simone's?

For the first few weeks after Marcel's departure, she found herself staring out the window when the post was expected. When one of the figures beneath her resolved itself into the postman, she rushed pell-mell down the staircase. She did this even if there had been a letter from Marcel in the previous post—and although his telegraphic letters left her in a cold fury.

As has been said before, Simone had a knack for falling both in and out of love. The plain fact of it was that Marcel's betrayal of her had caused her—after this period of sulky hysteria—to fall out of love with him.

Out with Marcel, in with Dr. Balmant. She knew full well that this love was an expected consequence of the analytic process, and therefore illusory in nature, just as the patient, given an injection of morphine, can be fully cognizant that the rapture he feels is a mere effect of the medication: but nonetheless, there is that incontrovertible feeling of bliss. When she rode the tram home from her meetings with him—she did not like to use the word "appointment," it sounded so cold-blooded and medical—she watched a private theater in which she and Dr. Balmant played the lead roles, the sorts of fantasies she had indulged in as a schoolgirl; so much so that she felt a sense of disappointment when her stop came close. The fantasies were cobbled together out of the romantic novels she had read long ago, the cheap melodramas she had watched at the cinema on lonely afternoons, and involved tears, letters gone astray, operatic episodes of sexual intercourse. She did not confess these fantasies to Dr. Balmant. One wants, after all, to be loved back by one's beloved, and she knew whatever he might say, her revealing of them would deepen his contempt for her. (Yes, she had once again found herself engaged in a love affair shadowed by disdain.)

The two of them were kept busy by dissections of her ragbag collection of intermittent symptoms: her legs had on occasion begun to flail about as well as her arms—"It's a good thing we live in this modern age," she observed to him. "In former times I might have been burned as a witch." Her voice sometimes cut out, like a distant radio signal. When this happened, Dr. Balmant would ask, "What is it you are stopping yourself from saying?"

Although she had not been thinking of this prior to Dr. Balmant's question, the image would immediately rise before her of Alain, purple-faced, his tongue lolling out of his mouth, the fan belt around his neck, but she could not bring herself to say this.

"I don't know."

Sometimes he would say nothing in response, allowing the foggy collection of syllables to hang in the air between them. Sometimes he would say, "You don't know," in a way which made her feel taunted.

She had switched roles with Alain—she was the one with a secret she would not give up and Dr. Balmant was now playing her part. Although Dr. Balmant had warned her against reading the analytic literature, it would have been impossible in her milieu not to have absorbed a rough knowledge of it: she believed that uttering the truth about what happened that night, that night in the garage where the hand-lettered sign in front misspelled *pneus* as *pnues*, that night, would be like uttering an incantation in a fairy tale, "Abracadabra," for she had no doubt that her strange spasms were caused by this secret. She wanted to please Dr. Balmant by confessing her secret, and at the same time, she was certain that doing so would cure her and would end their affair.

Although occasionally she still went out with Jacques, her tremors had increased to such a point that she thought it best to largely absent herself from public gatherings. She did not want to be a source of embarrassment to Jacques, and so her connection to Dr. Balmant took up a greater portion of her life. No longer did she act as Jacques' deputy at gatherings, drawing out the shy and awkward, soothing egos bruised by her husband, seducing some bright young man from the provinces into her husband's faction. No longer did they have confabs prior to an evening out, in which they went over the forces on their side and those arrayed against them, the objective they hoped to achieve—for instance, a writer whose work had just been published in a contending journal, for whom her husband was about to make a play. No longer, during the course of an evening, did Simone hurry to her husband's side to report some unexpected foray, like the subaltern who rushes into the commanding officer's tent to deliver the news that a platoon has been spotted moving stealthily behind a ridge.

She had hardly stopped loving Jacques. Although in her fantasies she pictured confrontations between her new lover and her old, in which the latter ceded possession to the former, she knew full well these were mere daydreams. Jacques was, after all, the one who had put her in Dr. Balmant's hands, and her love for her doctor was part of her love for her husband.

Sometimes at Dr. Balmant's Simone spoke of the things she thought she ought to. "In the assembly hall at school there was a frieze with a procession of stylized Greek women, holding lyres, torches, tablets, their tunics frozen in identical folds. In an illustrated magazine from Paris, I'd seen a picture of the scandalous Isadora Duncan in a similar dress. The priest spoke of the sacred state of matrimony and I thought that—the marital act—must be carried out in special clothes, like priests' vestments, and I imagined the husband and wife striking such poses, perhaps chanting religious vows. I grew up in the country, I knew how animals—but hadn't God, after all, made us in his image?"

To which Dr. Balmant replied, "You cannot have been as innocent as you pretend to have been."

Simone told Dr. Balmant that on a shelf near her parents' bed, a pale green bottle had stood: *L'Eau du Pluton, Purgatif* written on it. Had she asked her mother what it was for, been reprimanded, or had she known better than to ask? She knew that Pluto was the god of the underworld, of sin: had she imagined that his water bubbled up from hell and was bottled by resourceful locals? Was sin a shit-like physical substance? Did the suffering in Purgatory involve passing of this stuff from the body, a process like birth, but far more painful? Did the cries of those in torment make the bellowing of cows calving pale in comparison? Had her dead father bent double, holding his stomach, crying out as he tried to pass his iniquities from him?

Dr. Balmant said, "You are regressing to the anal stage because you are seeking refuge from your Oedipal conflicts." After a few moments, he noted: "Your arm is trembling."

Simone grabbed it with her hand, attempting to still it.

"Your body is speaking, and you are trying to silence it."

Having said this, Dr. Balmant yawned. It was Friday, and in honor of the end of the work week he'd allowed himself a second glass of wine at lunch. Its soporific effects were beginning to tell on him. He was aware of not being in top form at the moment, a knowledge he tamped down by turning it into annoyance at Simone: if she were more original, he wouldn't be so sluggish.

He shifted in his seat. As he moved the scent from his body—of tobacco and old wool and sweat—reached Simone. While Dr. Balmant washed himself at the kitchen sink in the flat every night and every morning with water heated on the stove, it was only at the weekend, when he and his wife Lisette journeyed to her parents' country house, that he was able to take a full immersion bath. It was an unspoken understanding between the two of them that his daily sponge bath be carried out unobserved by her. She did not want to see his body when it was pale and naked, his member shrunk—as it was these December days—with cold, nor did he want to be seen by her when he was in such a state. He never got completely clean with his cursory washings, and by Friday, he gave off a smell thick with richness and must, a smell that, like everything enticing, verged on the border of disgust.

Roundabout

Beyond the mahogany door with the brass plate bearing the name Dr. E. Balmant, down the granite steps, a few hundred meters along the rue de l'Université, the rue de Bac Metro station was disgorging passengers, who rushed up the steps as a trickle of others descended. Jacques walking along the street watched a yellow Citroën 2CV, called a *deux cheveux*, although it in fact had a horsepower of nine, as it puttered past the Metro station and entered the roundabout ahead, the tiny car seeming almost comical, as if it might disgorge a passel of clowns, who would emerge honking their noses and tripping over their gargantuan shoes, although the owners of these cars didn't find their vehicles at all risible: having an automobile marked them as having status, not just financial, but also a connection to the powers that be, one that allowed them access to petrol, still an iffy proposition. This wasn't, after all, America—which had been able to get into the fight without taking any body blows—awash in postwar prosperity, refrigerators, televisions, proving once again that it's always better to be the one who comes to the rescue of the damsel in distress rather than the damsel herself, especially if she's gotten a bit of hard use from her captors.

Jacques had picked up his paycheck a few minutes before from the office of the financier. The clerk had rolled her blotter back and forth across the wet ink while the waiting Jacques tried not to betray his anxiety. Then she'd blown on the check and fluttered it in the air before she finally handed it to him. A few weeks ago the bank manager had taken him discretely aside and murmured to him, "I understand, *monsieur*…and certainly we don't want to embarrass you…but nonetheless we must insist that a positive balance be kept in your account…" Afraid that the checks he had written would arrive at the bank before he did, he was in a bit of a hurry, although he didn't want to race through the streets. It was the Germans who barreled along the avenues and boulevards, disdaining the Parisian meander—and later their American liberators. When he was sitting in a cafe with Dominique in 1945, watching a gaggle of American soldiers hotfooting it down the street, the honeymoon of the first months of freedom long since over, Jacques had amended Phyrrus: Another such liberation and we are done for!

He was a bit nervous as he entered the bank, like a guilty schoolboy who catches sight of the headmaster out of the corner of his eye, but the manager merely nodded in his direction and returned to the papers in front of him on his desk, didn't call M. Melville over to speak in that tone, simultaneously unctuous and threatening.

Run

In Dr. Balmant's office, Simone crossed her legs, felt the prickling sensation on her inner thigh of a run in her stockings beginning. Today was the day Jacques got paid—she could ask him for a little extra in the housekeeping so she could buy a new pair of hose. These had been mended so many times she was starting to feel embarrassed wearing them. A few years ago, she had been a woman who could be either flamboyant or devil-may-care in her dress, but now she had reached an age where flamboyance shaded into peculiarity, threatening to tip into the bizarre, and where casualness suggested despair, so she had taken to wearing well-tailored outfits, a black wool skirt and starched linen blouse, the polished pumps that sat next to the couch on which she lay.

Since Simone was lying flat on her back, gravity smoothed away the incipient wrinkles and creases of her face. A few weeks ago, she had been shocked to see, looking in a mirror at the end of the day, that her lipstick had seeped up into the fine lines above her lips. The woman who ran the local beauty salon instructed her in a technique to keep this from happening, involving the application of a thin rim of vaseline around the edges of the lips: more or less building a dam. This was the future of her face, Simone thought, a feat of engineering: I shall fight back age as Mussolini drained the malarial Pontine marshes, as the Dutch built their dikes to hold back the sea. A smile flickered across her face, she was quite taken with her own wit on the subject, and half-inclined to share it with Dr. Balmant. Being a Jew, he'd appreciate self-deprecating humor. But then again, she didn't want to make herself a woman who felt she had no choice save to make herself a buffoon.

Jacques reached the hotel where Dominique was waiting for him, sitting on a park bench across the way. The kiss they exchanged was not perfunctory, but it certainly couldn't be said either to be passionate: the kiss of two long-time lovers. Jacques put his hand in the small of Dominique's back as they crossed the street. The business of the room was conducted almost silently—bills pushed across the counter, an iron key taken down from its hook on the wall. This was their usual place of assignation.

She sat on the end of the bed, smoking a cigarette, legs crossed, smiling at her lover. Sometimes—far too often for her taste— they didn't make love at these meetings, just lay next to each other in the crepuscular light, talking idly, smoking cigarettes. Jacques was getting on in years. She didn't want to imply, either by action or word, or even the slightest of gestures, that she was disappointed in his decline.

Their last meeting but one, Jacques had actually addressed his organ, referring to it as "my little companion," trying to cajole it into action, as footballers, past their prime, are said to address their legs before a match, urging them onto the pitch. Dominique had considered kneeling before him, taking his limp cock in her mouth, but feared that even this might fail to do the trick, and then he would be truly humiliated. "The spirit is willing, but the flesh, alas…" he'd said. They'd lain naked next to each other, talking in a desultory fashion, whatever came into their heads. "This is its own kind of intimacy," Dominique had said.

Dr. Balmant coughed. "Our time is up."

As Simone descended the steps from his office, she clung to the railing. Her gloves were stained with a diagonal smear of black along the palm, having lifted grease and dirt from the bannisters against which she steadied herself.

In Paris in December twilight began well before mid-afternoon. The motorcars and taxis passing Simone, shivering at the bus stop, had long since put on their headlamps. The chill of a winter's night descended across the city. Simone would be warmer if she took the Metro, but she could not face the descent down those long steps. Fatigue was another in the ragbag of symptoms of her curious condition.

Cave

Jacques was bestowing a kiss on Dominique's forehead. They had finished making love a quarter of an hour ago. She had imagined they were going to spend the rest of the evening together, in a drowsy state of semi-hibernation, their bodies drawing warmth from one another, snug in this cave of blankets. She'd aroused him with words. More and more, she realized, the sight of her body no longer excited him. Like Scheherazade she bound him to her with the power of her stories. The comparison with the writer of *A Thousand and One Nights* did not feel at all inapt to her: if she were to lose Jacques she might as well have her head lopped off.

Once he said to her, as he had once said to Simone, "Pretend you're in the confessional, I'm the priest," and Dominique dropped to her knees, bent her head, played the role of penitent confessing to impure thoughts, impure acts. Once he said to her, "Pretend you're in a cellar, you're bound to a post, you've been beaten, you're moaning, crying out to me—" The next time they met, she presented him with a pair of leather cuffs with which he could bind her to the bedstead.

She heard him sigh. It dawned on her that his kiss had perhaps been a full stop at the end of a sentence. As he sat up, the covers shifted, allowing a blast of cold air against her skin, which made her cry out.

"Sorry," he said. He picked up his trousers from the floor. "Well, my love…" She recognized a certain false heartiness in his voice, designed to deflect any claims she might make on him.

"Oh, you're not—that is, are you?"

"I'm dining at home this evening."

"Oh, yes, well…"

He'd buttoned up his flies already, was smoothing the wrinkles from his shirt, quite businesslike about this leave taking. While the look of quickly-suppressed pain that passed over Dominique's face caused him some guilt, he also derived pleasure at his power over her.

Jacques stepped out of the hotel, drew in a deep breath. The air seemed to him not so much cold as bracing, and, giving his scarf an extra loop around his neck, he decided to walk home. There was a bit of cocksure strut to his perambulation. The mingled smell of him and Dominique wafted up from him—as soon as he got home he'd duck into the bathroom for a wash. He and Simone had their rough understandings, but it would be cruel to fill her nostrils with that scent.

It wasn't yet seven, but there was a quality of benediction to the evening air and light. The cafés he passed were only half-full, the boulevards, while hardly abandoned, easy to make his way along. For the first year after the war ended, it took a lot more than a chilly night in December to send Parisians indoors, but now they had got fed up with peace, sick of it, as they had once got sick of war. No one could wish the war years back, and yet—Parisians looked at one another now with the doleful eyes of the turtle before Simone had plunged the knife into its belly.

Jacques wondered if Dominique was napping in the hotel or had returned to the flat she shared with her parents and sons. He tried to imagine her in that space he had never seen, standing like a flamingo inside the front door, taking off her heels and pulling on a pair of slippers, tasting the *potage de choufleur* simmering on the stove. Did she sleep on a narrow daybed in the front room, making it up each evening and unmaking it each morning? He was glad there were still things about her that remained quite unknown.

Roundabout

Simone was certainly not ignorant about Dominique. A year or so before, there had been a luncheon they both attended, and Simone had understood, through telegraphed glances, a whispered conversation, and the hostess' quick rearrangement of place cards that Dominique was her husband's mistress.

Simone had switched the place cards back, so they were, after all, seated at the same table.

A mousy creature, still wearing wartime kit. She couldn't be so badly off, could she, that she couldn't afford New Look knock-offs? The padded hips that had replaced the wartime padded shoulders?

She understood that she was described to Dominique as Sala had been described to her: a troubled unfortunate, one who must be handled gingerly. She could imagine Dominique saying of her, as she had once said of Sala, "I can't say anything against the poor woman. I know she suffers and that I bear some responsibility for that suffering."

Sphinix

Simone woke up each morning she was scheduled to see Dr. Balmant with a resolution: today I will tell him about Alain. I will tell him this even though my speaking will be the equivalent of prying open the clam shell, which kills the poor mollusk.

Every afternoon, when she left his office, she said to herself, "Ah, today, although I meant to, the right moment didn't present itself, and one doesn't simply blurt out such a thing..." And then, after several weeks of such prevarication, she at last said: "I have something to tell you."

He said nothing, as was his wont.

"I, during the war, I killed a man."

Silence.

She craned her neck to look at him, but he had his usual blank expression on his face. "You have no reaction to this?"

After a while he said: "I am waiting for you to go on."

"That is, I was complicit in his death."

Another long silence ensued.

"Ah, the Sphinx."

"My silence angers you. You want to castrate me."

"To castrate you?"

"You know very well the Sphinx is female."

"I don't think I knew that. The Sphinx, a woman?"

"You wanted your words to shock me. As soon as you had come out with your 'secret,' you turned to look at me, and said, 'You have no reaction to this?' You see, it is precisely the tactic you always engage in. You try to arouse my interest, my pity, by your bodily jerks and tremors. When that tactic fails, you try this one, attempting to shock me with this revelation. The 'secret' itself is of little importance. It is rather the way that you expected it to function between the two of us."

Had she said what she had to say, or had she not said it?

As she journeyed home, the words he had spoken to her at their very first session came back to her, "Do you often feel that your suffering is made light of?"—a question that had not seemed to be a question at all, but rather a taunt. She recalled the sight of Alain's feet, stirring up clouds of dust from the earthen floor, like a child having a temper tantrum, *Don't make me go*! *I won't go*! *I won't! I want to stay here*!

The sound of footsteps coming towards her roused her from her preoccupation. As she returned to the ordinary world, the everyday world, she was shocked to realize that she had been moving her lips.

But during her weekend absence from Dr. Balmant, her shakings slacked off to almost nothing, and when she woke up Monday morning, the first thought in her mind was: Ah, yes, Dr. Balmant is right. These shakings of mine are an attempt to keep him near me.

Stone

In fact, that Saturday she had felt well enough to accompany Jacques to a party. There, another of those *litterateur*-doctors had ushered Jacques into a corner. Laying a soothing hand on his shoulder—Jacques was discomfited by this quasi-paternal gesture, especially coming from a man who was quite junior to him, both in age and status—he asked, "Is Simone under a doctor's care?"

"I don't see what concern that is—"

"Believe me, I wouldn't interfere in this way if my concerns didn't outweigh my respect for your privacy." He spoke in a tone of voice not unlike Jacques' bank manager when his account was overdrawn.

"She is seeing a psychiatrist. Balmant, do you know—"

"Get her out of the hands of those witch doctors. Take her to a neurologist. Let me give you the name of a colleague—an excellent man." The doctor searched his pockets. Finding a matchbook, he tore the cover off it, then patted his pockets searching for a pen. With great reluctance, Jacques handed him his fountain pen, took the scrawled name and telephone number, gave a bow of his head, and withdrew. The nib had caught in the rough cardboard, it would have to be cleaned.

The words "Please don't hesitate to use my name" were tossed at his back.

It would not be accurate to say that Jacques had stalked off in a state of high dudgeon. Low dudgeon might rather describe it. He had no idea what the man—who had interrupted him in mid-sentence not once, but twice!—was going on about. Certainly, he didn't care to have his wife's body dissected in an anteroom at a party, even if that dissection were merely verbal. Still, what was it that the man had noticed? Jacques kept worrying at the encounter, as a tongue does at a bad tooth. But his concerns were soon washed away by the host's excellent wine, so much so that when he woke up in the morning—with something of a headache—he had no recollection of the conversation.

It was only when he thrust his hand into his pocket and pulled out the torn matchbook cover that it came back to him.

Queſt

A fortnight later, Simone and Jacques were sitting in the office of the eminent neurologist, a man with a lachrymose air and bags under his eyes which extended below the tops of his cheekbones.

"So, she has been under the care of psychiatrist?"

"Yes, Dr. Balmant."

"And?" the physician asked Jacques.

Jacques jutted out his lower lip, shrugged. "I'm kept in the dark." He gave the man a conspiratorial wink, the sort that put psychiatrists and silly women in their place.

"I will speak with him," the doctor said with a wave of his hand.

Jacques asked whether an X-ray of the brain would be of any use. It was the neurologist's turn to jut out his lower lip, shrug, and say: "An X-ray tends only to show gross abnormalities, and in this case"—he turned to Simone, smiled—"in your case, Madame, I don't think we are…" and his voice faded into silence.

So began the quest for a diagnosis, which, like any good quest, could not be accomplished in a straight-forward fashion. One must wander in the forest, stand before a fork in the path and go left or right, find oneself held captive, navigate past treacherous rocks.

A second eminent neurologist, called in for a consultation, offered yet a different theory than the first. And a third, called in to resolve the disagreement, offered not concurrence with either one but yet another dire possibility. Like a troupe of circus performers, the physicians tossed about possible diagnoses: brain tumor, hysterical paralysis, multiple sclerosis, rheumatoid arthritis, Parkinson's.

She reported these visits to Dr. Balmant, the tests she had undergone, the latest theories about the causes of her condition. Dr. Balmant said nothing in response to this. "I wish you would say something. I wonder, for instance, if you feel that you were wrong all along, that your interpretations were—actually dangerous, in that they kept me from pursuing the true cause of my, my malady?"

He said nothing.

She said, "I wonder if you feel guilty—"

He said: "You are being hostile. You are rejecting the work we have done together."

"No, I don't think that's true. I see the end of our, of our—association coming into view, and you cannot imagine—Jacques speaks of it quite openly, he says there will be expenses—and we will have to end. I try—because you have warned me how my hysterical outbursts damage my marriage. I cannot bear the thought of losing you."

"Do you see how you take the role of supplicant with me? The spoiled child, down on her knees, begging—begging God, begging her lover, begging her husband, begging her psychoanalyst? Crying out that she cannot bear to be abandoned."

"Yes, doctor," Simone said. Sometimes she said 'yes,' to him just so that she wouldn't be accused of resistance, but this time when she said 'yes,' it was a 'yes,' came from the core of her being.

In the waiting room of one specialist, a man moved ceaselessly about, his arms making winglike motions. When he had been taken into the inner sanctum, the nurse who presided over the outer sanctum said, "*La maladie de Huntington*. In English, they call it Huntington's chorea." Added: "You could have it worse."

Simone had learned this much during her journey into the land of the ill: there was always someone, more fortunate than you, to call you lucky. Chorea: the Greek word for dance. Had she seen the man with the waving arms and thrusting tongue on a stage, she would have judged that like much modern dance, it substituted the shock of the new for artistic quality.

She exchanged pleasantries with a woman she found herself sitting next to in one of those waiting rooms and then—it was the custom of the country in which she now dwelt—exchanged diagnoses, definite or possible. *Charcot-Marie-Tooth,* the other woman said. How elegant that sounded, especially compared to the crass sound of Parkinson's or corticobasal degeneration.

Track my finger with your eyes without moving your head. Without moving your head, Madame.

Touch your right thumb to the tip of each of your fingers on your right hand. Now, the same with the left. Straighten your arm as I press against it.

Each eminent specialist had his own gesture he made when he wanted to say, "I have no idea what is going on here."

One stroked his beard.

One steepled his fingers.

One folded his arms across his chest like a Red Indian chief.

Track my finger with your eyes, without moving your head.

"Any disordered thinking?"

"Oh, no."

"For instance, do you ever take ordinary events as omens? Or think that people are whispering behind your back?"

"Oh, no, nothing like that," although mothers certainly did whisper to their children, "Don't stare at the lady!"

"Difficulty sleeping?"

"Yes."

"Has your handwriting become smaller?"

"Yes."

"Are you often fatigued?"

"Yes."

Yes, yes, yes. She had never known the word could sound so grim.

Blue

Simone often thought that had she not worn the billowing dress of blue linen that long-ago day, she would have she stayed with Luc. Her symptoms would have impelled her into the arms of the Church. Her illness would have had meaning—punishment for the peccadilloes of her youth, a path bringing her closer to God. That other Simone would have set out on rounds to holy sites—Lourdes, of course—and other, lesser-known places of pilgrimage. She would have lit candles before St. Bartholomew the Martyr, who'd been flayed alive and who was sometimes shown in paintings with his own hide draped over his arm, and whose bailiwick was twitching and tics. She would have collected vials of holy water, medals imprinted with the images of saints, rosaries. An old priest, holding his finger to his lips, would have allowed her to kiss the finger bone of St. Someone or Other not just the glass box in which it was encased.

But she had worn that dress of blue linen, Jacques had fallen in love with her, and she had not become a woman who, in middle age, returned to the Church. Instead, she had embarked on a medical pilgrimage, where the rituals involved being stuck with needles, peeing into cups—a messy task at the best of times, made more so when she got the shakes. She didn't kneel on a *prie-dieu* before flickering candles. In the place of prayer cards, she clutched her X-rays, medical records. Once, she had suggested to Jacques that if modern medicine failed, she might make a visit to the *quartier chinois*—it was called that despite most of its residents being Vietnamese. But that was a joke: she and Jacques were not believers in miracles, hokum.

Instead of saints, there were the various men who'd bestowed their names on diseases and signs. Huntington, Parkinson, Tourette; Friedreich with his ataxia, Babinski with his sign. Uhthoff, possessor of a phenomenon. She imagined Babinski as a Russian with the magnificent and unruly beard of an Eastern Orthodox priest; Parkinson as an American, from Sioux City, Iowa, or Cincinnati, Ohio, a man so gaunt that his flesh dangled from the tendons of his neck like a rooster's wattle.

Dada

On the day when the verdict was rendered in final form, when it was no longer possible to entertain the slightest possibility that these symptoms were the result of neurosis, when the words *maladie de Parkinson* were hung around her neck like the titulus of a Roman slave, there followed a stunned silence. Both she and Jacques had the blank looks on their faces a man has after he's taken a blow to the head, his brain jarred against the side of his skull. This was all about her brain, the metaphoric and the literal were also banging against one another.

The doctor who had just delivered the diagnosis—more of a professor than a clinician—had a model of the human brain which he pulled out of the top drawer of his desk. He quite warmed to the lecture he was giving. He became a Dadaist poet, flinging a salad of words at them—*substantia nigra, superior temporal gyrus, calcarine sulcus, postcentral gyrus, medulla oblongata*. Simone was feeling quite dizzy, he was speaking faster, yes, getting more and more excited, he used his index finger as a pointer and tracked the neural pathways that ran from the brain stem down through the conduit of the spinal column. "Although this is hardly your field of expertise, you're an intelligent man," he said to Jacques. "The brain on examination…" he was saying.

"The brain on examination…?" Simone repeated. An image rose from black-and-white horror movies, the sawn tonsure of her skull being lifted off, the doctor peering in, poking around at that mass of coiled white spaghetti, a cousin to the *tête de veau* displayed at the butcher's.

The doctor answered her question by saying to Jacques, "the examination of the brain on autopsy."

Jacques shepherded her out of the office, arm on her shoulder. An old ewe, she'd become mutton, tough and gamey. Jacques hailed a taxi, an extravagance. He ushered her into the cab with the deference he might have shown a maiden aunt. His face was a stone.

"Poor Jacques. You don't seem to have much luck with your wives."

He stared at her as if she were speaking a foreign language.

"First Sala with her leg, and now me with this—ailment."

"You needn't treat me as if I'm going to—behave in a monstrous fashion. Throw you over."

"Are you going to throw me over?" She tried to make her voice sound light, almost devil-may-care. She remembered tales from Russia, sledges chased by packs of wolves, someone thrown off to keep them at bay.

"Simone, Simone."

"What does that mean? 'Simone, Simone'?"

"It means that this isn't easy for—for either of us. There's a period of—adjustment, a time during which one—makes sense of, this news, this, this that certainly neither of us wanted to hear." He half-turned his back to her, retreating into his corner.

This. This. The word became spongy, immense. It swelled up and enveloped them. This, this, there was nothing but this. Of course, he would want to run away. She, too, would have liked to run away, to dash back through the years, to become a hoyden again, to elude illness's tag, "You're it!" zigging and zagging away from the skeletal finger.

Egg

For the next several days, Jacques remained withdrawn from her. He performed the expected little duties of a husband—the bestowing of morning and evening kisses, compliments on the soup. He did, however, avoid that all-purpose marital question, customarily asked after his disquisition on the events of his day, "And how was your day?" (He feared her answer.) At last he said, "An animal, when wounded, doesn't seek out the company of the herd, he retreats, hides himself away, licks his wounds, hides his—his shame."

"Are you ashamed of me?" Simone asked, although she knew the answer to that question perfectly well.

"I am ashamed of myself. In some areas of my life I am quite heroic. But not in this one. I could pretend to be a different sort of man, but the fact is that pretense wouldn't get us very far."

Her heart cracked open like an egg, lay on the floor between them.

Jacques continued: "During the war—sometimes there were comrades who deluded themselves about their characters. I remember one young man who was assigned to set charges on a bridge. It was a possibility that when the charges were detonated the lives of innocent civilians would be lost. It was said to him that this wasn't a job that all men could undertake—"

"I am not a bridge."

"—that if qualms of conscience were going to strike him, it would be best if we knew it ahead of time. He pretended—to himself, to others—that he could carry out such an action. But in the end, he was unable to do so. As a result of his pretending to himself to be the person he wanted to be rather than the person he was, a great many more people perished… He took his own life. I do not want to be like that young man—"

"Jacques!"

"One does not always approach a subject directly."

"One?"

"Men in general. This man in particular."

"Are you saying you are going to leave me?"

"No. That is not what I am saying. I am not saying that I am going to leave you. Only that—only that—well, let's leave it at that."

Despite the discomfort Jacques felt at being home, it was preferable to being out in the world during those first few weeks, although he did not break his routines. He still kissed the hand of the bookkeeper when he picked up his check, gave her a wink as he departed her office ("People say he's quite conniving, but towards me he's never been anything but charming"), drank coffee and *vin rouge ordinaire* in smoky cafés, sucked on his pipe meditatively, undertook his correspondence between the hours of six and eight in the morning, read manuscripts. And when no one was looking, scratched himself (his armpits, the chafed flesh at his waist where his belt rubbed, the crack of his ass).

He did let the facts of the matter be known to a few of his colleagues, who saw to it word got around so on only a few occasions did Jacques have to answer an innocent question with: "Ah, Simone. Well, there we've had some rather bad news. What we thought was rheumatism has turned out to be Parkinson's disease." Further questions were met by vague phrases, "…a neurological ailment…really, I prefer not to dwell on it."

Still, some felt compelled to offer him clucks of sympathy, old antagonists took it upon themselves to clasp his hand as if, through the medium of Simone's suffering he was going to be redeemed. He was grateful for his innate aversion to sentimentality. "Thank you." His tone of voice made it clear that he felt no gratitude.

Previously, he had made a point of not being seen too frequently with Dominique. Not that he hid their affair—in fact, he was rather proud of having won this woman nearly twenty years his junior—but only that he did not want it to seem, either to her or to the world, that she had come to occupy a secure position in his life, like a Chinese second wife. When a few weeks had elapsed after Simone's diagnosis, however, he made sure that others observed her in his company, at lunch and even strolling arm in arm: he would rather be thought a cad than be pitied. He told himself—and he was not being completely dishonest—that Simone, too, had her pride: she would not have wanted her husband to be a man about whom people said, "Poor Jacques!"

Plague

The word of her diagnosis went out. A chorus went up: *Hélas*! *Hélas*! A plague of visitors descended on the flat, bearing bunches of flowers, books, pastries: rivals who were secretly happy, those who assumed there was a fixed store of afflication in the world and Simone having been dealt the ace of spades meant their luck had just improved, the curious, the kind. Having heard her disease was neurological in origin, some no doubt expected an in-home version of the *fin-de-siecle* Tuesday demonstrations put on at the Salpêtrière by Dr. Charcot—like his patients she would swoon, convulse, grunt obscenities, bray or cluck. Often, she did not even shake or twitch, merely looked a bit drawn, as one might after recovering from a bout of the flu. No doubt, her appearance caused a few of them to say:

—She looks just fine! *—Do you think it's just a ruse*? *A way to try to get Jacques attention*? *—Perhaps not consciously, but…*

Simone soon ceased to be a curiosity. The flood of visitors became a trickle; the black telephone rang less and less often.

(When, decades later, she does at last die, more than a few old friends and acquaintances will react to the news with shock, having assumed she had been dead for quite some time.)

Cure

Jacques had more or less instructed Simone to ask Dr. Balmant when her treatment would be brought to end. She had relayed Dr. Balmant's response, that a precipitous termination could be hazardous.

"This can't go on forever," Jacques said, and "This man is like those astronomers attempting to keep the Ptolemaic system in place with ever more complicated theories," and "Simone, there is the matter of money. Money, the hard fact of it."

Twice, Jacques telephoned the man, left messages with his service, and received no response.

One day, when Simone arrived at Dr. Balmant's office, she opened the waiting room door to see Jacques sitting there. "I felt I had no choice but to take matters into my own hands. Ah, don't start crying."

Simone pressed the space where her cheekbones met her eye sockets, tamping her tears back inside of her.

Dr. Balmant, no doubt overhearing the rumble of voices from outside his office, opened the door—it was five minutes before the hour.

"M. Melville." Dr. Balmant shook the man's hand, it would have been quite rude not to do so. "I must say I am quite surprised—well, really, these things shouldn't be discussed in the anteroom. If you'll excuse us, I would like to speak with Mme. Melville alone first."

The words "Mme. Melville"—so cold, so formal—plummeted through her like a rock. She tried to reassure herself that in front of her husband, it was only natural that he would be as correct as possible.

She sat down upon the couch, but did not stretch out upon it. "I didn't know that he was going to be here. I'm as surprised as you are."

Dr. Balmant lit a cigarette, although she couldn't recall him ever smoking before. "It's most, most-uh-uh, most. Unusual." The orotund voice he had cultivated abandoned him, and he spoke in quick bursts with long pauses in between. "Well. I suppose. If it's all right. With you. We should invite him in. Have him say why it is. That he has come."

"I know why it is that he has come. He wants, he wants, he wants," and here she began to weep, "us to part, you and me."

"You must compose yourself."

He offered her a glass of water from the carafe on the table and she downed it, then downed another.

"We had rather a row about it last night, I suppose I should tell you. He asked me when the two of us were going to come to a resolution, an ending. He became, he became quite angry and left the house. He was with his mistress. Dominique. Her name is Dominique."

"Now, now. Surely you can't be certain about that."

"I am. I am. Because he came home smelling of her perfume. Usually he has the decency to have a wash, sometimes he enters the apartment and heads straight for the lavatory, and I hear the water running and a great deal of splashing—I'm hardly a fool. But last night, he came straight to bed."

"Do you see how you are once again approaching your marriage with an air of self-pity, a quite unattractive display of the wrongs that have been done to you."

"Can't you just have a bit of—not pity, a little bit of fellow-feeling for me? A little sympathy for the trials I am undergoing? Would you be as sanguine as you expect me to be if it were your wife who had taken a lover? If you were being cuckolded by her?"

"Mme. Melville…Mme. Melville, do you see how you lash out when you don't get what you want? In this instance, my pity, my sympathy, although I have told you from the start that is not what you are going to get from me. My love is my refusal to yield to your entreaties, to force you again and again to confront what you must confront."

Love. He had said the word "love." He had called her Mme. Melville—three times, the number of times Peter had denied Christ—but he had said the word "love." She clutched hold of that word, she pressed it against herself, she would never, ever let go of it.

"What time is it?" she asked.

"We have about twenty minutes left."

Twenty minutes, only twenty minutes.

Once again, as when she had been in the cellar with Alain, a line from *Darkness at Noon* came to her. "Above, it is possible to kid oneself, but below, from the stomach downwards, one knows." Yes, it was true: things between her and Dr. Balmant were over.

Just then Jacques rapped on the door, and Dr. Balmant said, "I must," as he rose to his feet, and Simone wanted to cry out, "No, it's too soon. I'm not ready to go. I'm not going!" although she was silent. She almost wished that her body would start to flail about on its own as it sometimes did, but it was rigid, locked in place.

Dr. Balmant opened the door to Jacques' fist—he'd been about to knock on the door again, he wasn't used to being kept waiting in antechambers. Dr. Balmant stepped back from the doorway, gave a slight bow and sweep of his hand, the sort given by factotums at hotels to show deference towards guests without being servile.

Jacques seated himself on the chaise, as there was no place else. Simone sat with her head cast down, she did not want to display her face, reddened and swollen in the aftermath of her weeping.

"Let me state matters to you quite forthrightly," Jacques began.

"Actually—" Dr. Balmant interjected.

"I request that you not interrupt me." Jacques drew in a deep breath, and said again, "As I was saying, let me state matters to you quite forthrightly. The fact is, my wife came here initially because of her relationship with her son, which had devolved into what I believe you psychiatrists refer to as a *folie à deux*. That problem was resolved—not, I should like to point out, as the result of any efforts on your part, but because we—my stepson, the family as a whole— took decisive action. And then, you put forward the theory—or so I gather, I must interject here that your patient has been dutiful, she has, per your instructions, been quite secretive about what goes on here—but you and I did, you recall, speak directly about this—over the telephone—"

They had spoken about her? Simone darted her eyes up briefly, looking first at Dr. Balmant and then at her husband.

"...and you then put forth the theory that the outer conflicts having been removed, the inner ones would now loom larger. I agreed with this theory, in part because I am an agreeable man—"

Simone glanced at her husband, wondering if a half-smile was at play on the corners of his lips, but there was not. *Jacques, an agreeable man*?

"Agreeable might not be quite the right word," perhaps he was speaking in response to the Simone's quick look, "rather, dispassionate. And the other reason for my concurrence was that my wife was exhibiting a series of rather bizarre symptoms, quixotic ones, so the theory you put forth seemed quite plausible, that the root cause of them was psychological. I accepted this, because you are the educated man and I am the ignorant one—at least in this field of endeavor."

"If I might—" Dr. Balmant said.

"Please," Jacques said, "I ask that you grant me just a few more minutes to finish what I have to say."

Just a few more minutes: but there were only a few minutes left.

"And so, things went on for quite some time. My wife's condition did not improve, and when I spoke to you about this—"

How often, Simone wondered, had the two of them spoken?

"—you assured me that this was a not unexpected turn of events. I believe you made an analogy to a patient who undergoes surgery, a procedure which may, indeed often does, result in a temporary diminution of the patient's health and well-being. However, in this case, the diminution was not brief—

"Oh, please, must you—" Simone said.

"Must I—what?"

"Must you go on and on?" Simone muttered.

"I am going on and on? It seems, rather,"—Jacques had the air about him of a man who had prepared well for this conversation, composing his set pieces ahead of time—"rather, that the two of you have been 'going on and on.' The fact is—and, please, Simone, I must ask that you not shoot me those aggrieved looks of yours—the fact is that it has been well over a month since we received the news—received it most definitively—that the cause of my wife's condition was not psychological but physical. This has been a difficult blow to bear—the most difficult blow in my life, I can say quite honestly—"

For the first time since Jacques had entered, Simone looked her husband full in the face. *The most difficult blow in my life.*

"But don't you see—" Dr. Balmant interjected.

"Please," Jacques said, holding up his hand, his flat palm facing outwards, "please. I really must insist that you not interrupt me. Yes, certainly, I am not such an egoist that I fail to understand that this most unwelcome news is an even more terrible blow to my wife than it is to me, and that it makes sense that she have some time to take in this news, and that the two of you, who have formed, as is necessary in these cases, a close attachment, have some time to wind down your" —he paused for a moment, and seemed to be searching for the correct word, but Simone had no doubt that this pause had been rehearsed in advance by him—

"your alliance. Fine, that is all well and good. But surely enough time has elapsed, more than enough time, for those matters to be concluded. If I may quote the founder of your field, it seems that what we are dealing with now is not 'hysterical misery' but 'common unhappiness,' and such all-too-common unhappiness your field cannot cure."

A pause of a few seconds followed. It seemed that Jacques had at last finished his disquisition. Dr. Balmant began to speak, but got no further than a half-syllable out of his mouth when Jacques held up a professorial index finger and continued:

"I do not wish to state things in crass economic terms, but nonetheless, financial considerations do come into play here. My wife is facing a future as an invalid. Quite frankly, Doctor, we can no longer afford you." He leaned forward, bringing his hands together, a gesture that an attorney might make after having delivered a summation to the jury.

The only sound that was heard in the room was the ticking of the clock on the wall. Simone lifted her eyes to it with the gaze of a petitioner, as if she could move the inanimate object to sympathy and it would tick-tock its hands backwards.

At last Dr. Balmant spoke. "Mme. Melville. Do you have anything you wish to say?"

"I suppose that my husband is right. He explains it all quite logically. What he says makes a good deal of sense. I haven't—I haven't—his decisiveness, his will to act."

"Very well, then." Dr. Balmant had risen to his feet. He gestured towards the clock. "I am sorry to say it, but our time is up." He extended his hand first to Jacques, then to Simone, saying to her, "Mme. Melville, I trust that our work together will continue within you even if we no longer see each other."

Just before he shut the door behind them, he laid a hand on her shoulder, allowed it to rest there.

Spring

Jacques' associates took up a collection so that she might be sent to the hot springs in Czechoslovakia's Sudetenland which had once been known by the German name of Marienbad, and was now Marianske Lazne.

His female colleagues sighed and said, not without a sense of their own good fortune, "It's the least I can do for the poor thing." The men said, "A nasty stroke of luck"—as they reached for their billfolds, the sentence sometimes completing itself in their heads "—although it does rather make one believe in cosmic justice, Melville getting his due."

At the Gare de l'Est, the porter pushed her in the station's wicker invalid chair—she'd have missed her train had they not resorted to this. Jacques lagged a few steps behind, like an adolescent in public with his parents. She did not blame him: if there were any way she could have avoided this gauntlet of stares, she would have done so.

The rocking of the train lulled her to sleep. When she woke up, she raised the shade to see the bombed remains of a German city—she didn't know which one—bricks smashed back to earth. She smiled. If I were a saint, she thought, I could weep for the child who, born after Hitler's death, playing in the rubble—and where else is there to play?—picks up an unexploded shell and is blown to smithereens. But I'm no saint: I cannot feel pity for that child.

On her way to the spa from the train station, she passed a shop sign with the *Fleischerladen* visible beneath a coat of paint, the Czech word for butcher, *reznictví*, lettered on top of it.

The place had once been ostentatious—a hodgepodge of classical styles—Doric columns, fake Byzantine mosaics, gilded ceilings—but now with its cracked tiles, scuffed floors, chipped paint, its overall air of down-at-the-heels seediness, it elicited a mix of sympathy and admiration from her—akin to the response she had to the sight of an old woman, once of the demi-monde, left with nothing but her memories, jewelry and frocks, and who, living on the proceeds of her pawned gems, in ever more straitened circumstances, still made her daily promenade along the avenue de la Bois de Boulogne in her mended, once-fashionable finery.

She told the clerk at the front desk she needed to send a telegram to her husband, letting him know she'd arrived safely. The clerk withdrew to speak with his superior—she could overhear them through a door left ajar, although she could not understand what they were saying. Finally, an obsequious manager appeared, gave a half-bow and asked, "Do I understand that madame wishes to send a telegram?" as if she had demanded a golden coach with eight white horses be delivered post haste. A worn blank was finally produced and a retainer summoned with two snaps of the superior's fingers: an old man—almost toothless, legs bent from childhood rickets, knuckles swollen with arthritis, trousers held up with rope. He took the blank on which she had written "ARRIVED SAFELY. LOVE, SIMONE," and shambled off. Simone imagined he might flag down a passing horse-drawn cart and entrust the missive to its driver or even shuffle off to Paris himself, her message arriving at the rue des Arènes months or even years later.

Her coat and purse were taken from her by a nurse—the term was quite elastic here—and when she objected, was told in a voice both authoritative and derisive not to worry, that her things would be safe, and after all, she'd have no need of them during her stay.

A nurse, who wore galoshes which squeaked against the floor and the sort of rubber apron worn by a worker in an abattoir, ushered her into the mud bath. On the opposite side of the bath, a trio of Willendorf Venuses lounged, the clay hardening on their abundant flesh. A retainer with a mop and bucket—one of a race of Morlocks who existed on the fringes of this world—swabbed up the muddy footprints left by the departing women, dipping her mop in the bucket of filthy water, slapping it across the floor, dipping it again, doing Sisyphean battle with filth.

Simone found herself as happy as a sow in muck, although her baptism in the hot mud did cause her heart to beat rapidly. For the rest of that day, she had shed flakes of dried mud, finding them stuck in the whorls of her ear, the crook of her elbow, behind her knees.

In the dining hall, her elbow was grabbed and she was steered to a table. "You'll want to sit with us," it was declared. She understood that here she was a prize: her face was not speckled with age spots, no disfiguring tumor grew from her neck. She was seated next to a Spanish woman with ancient gnarled hands bedecked with so much jewelry Simone couldn't help but wonder if it contributed to her arthritis. After she left the table, the others referred to her as "the Duchess," the word spoken in English, with an air of scorn. Simone was not sure if the disdain was for the woman putting on airs or if "the Duchess" was in fact of aristocratic birth and the contempt was for nobility itself. Also at the table was a woman named Monique, who seemed to have some connection with a young man, Jan, who bore a striking resemblance to Franz Kafka, and like Kafka had a respiratory ailment—although he hastened to assure her that it was most definitively not tuberculosis. The conversation was conducted in a language said to be Italian, although it seemed to evolve into its own makeshift Esperanto, words substituted in French or Spanish or even, from time to time, Latin—although never, of course, German. (At one point, the factotum at the front desk, unable to make himself understood, wrote down the word he was attempting to communicate in German. Simone nodded her head, and he then tore the piece of paper into almost infinitesimal squares.)

Jan was a treasure in this place that had become the Land of Dead Sons, or perhaps, more accurately, the Land of Mothers of Dead Sons. The kitchen women and nurses stroked his shoulder as he passed them in the hallway, they whispered to him, "Janek, come to the kitchen, I have something special for you."

The next day, her doctor ordered her to undergo a treatment called "the Scottish spray." When she asked the nurse leading her down the hallway why it was called that, she was told: "It has always been called that," as if this treatment had existed from time immemorial—and who did Simone think she was, to question the order of the universe? She was lead into a tiled room and was pummeled with a jet of hot water, followed by a jet of cold water, followed by hot, back and forth. The force of the water was so tremendous that she fell to her knees. One of the nurses indicated to her that she was to hold the bars which lined the chamber. At the Nuremberg trials hadn't there been testimony about medical experiments involving drenching naked people with water? Maybe this whole spa business was a ruse, the place was in fact run by some Nazi cabal that had survived the war. Monique, Jan and the Duchess were Judas sheep. The thought flashed across her mind in a fraction of a second, was tamped down by her reason.

After this treatment, she was ushered to bed, and it seemed that she slept the soundest sleep of her life, sleeping through dinner, not waking until the next morning, to a rapping on her door: it was Jan, who seemed to have taken a shine to her. He ushered her down hallways and reminded her of the treatments scheduled for her that day—although she was somewhat puzzled by how he knew so much detail about her. It began to seem that she had surrendered her will along with her overcoat and handbag.

It was her first, but not her last, trip to the parallel universe of the ill. At some spas, she was served food so light it would not have sustained an angel. At others, she was stuffed with stewed beef heart, potato dumplings. At a bath in the foothills of the Swiss Alps, she found herself wide awake in the night, wandering the corridors. The thought occurred to her: perhaps I am dead. This is the afterlife: walking along deserted halls, past signs that read, "*Entrée Interdit,*" and "*Réservé au personnel,*" entering empty rooms, hearing the murmur of indistinct, distant voices.

Wheel

A woman, Marie-Claire, descended from Huguenot stock, a believer in good deeds, was hired as a maid of all work, living at first in her own apartment (actually, as Jacques vaguely understood, in a room in her niece's flat), then taking up residence in a room of the Melvilles' apartment which had previously served as a lumber room, repurposed into a snug *chambre de bonne.* Jacques had been generous enough to pay for the fabric with which Marie-Claire had run up the matching curtains and dust frill for the bed, and even for a television.

On one of Simone's visits to the Salpêtrière, she was accompanied by Marie-Claire who asked one of the orderlies standing about the doorway to bring a wheelchair for madame. "Ah, no!" Simone had cried, but the man, a cigarette dangling from his lips, had plodded off to fetch it. Being one herself, Marie-Claire was suspicious of servants: she believed them to be, as a class, both insolent and lazy. There was no need for him to walk so slowly. Clearly, he only did it for the principle: *I'll be damned if I'm going to rush around fetching things for some rich cripple. And that bitch with her—putting on airs.*

"No!" Simone repeated, as the man advanced, pushing the wheelchair in front of him.

"But this place is so vast!" Marie-Claire sighed with exasperation, turned to the orderly: "Madame doesn't want one, after all—"

Marie-Claire had been right about the length of the corridors. Simone dragged herself along, stopping every now and again to rest, sometimes leaning a hand against the walls for support. But it was no small thing to leave behind the world of the bipedal.

Knit

She had been warned against giving in to her disease: she must be stalwart, brave, a fighter. One doctor asked her if she had any hobbies. She felt momentarily offended: Do I look like the sort of woman who passes her afternoons in crewel work, stamp collecting, bird watching?

"I used to knit."

"Ah, knitting, that would be excellent. Fine motor and all."

In the afternoon, she sat in the chair which had been Jacques', with the radio playing in the background (Satie's *Danses Gothiques*, an interview with Jules Dassin about his film, *Rififi*, the man's American accent so thick she could barely comprehend a word), knitting.

She daydreamed that her will would save her, that her illness would burnish her—she would be cleansed of her pettiness and made wise. Her left wrist moved, darting the needle into the loop on the opposing needle. Funny how when she'd first started knitting, she'd had to watch so carefully, had pulled the yarn too tight, twisted it. Now her mind could wander off anywhere while her body went on with its business without her. She knit a muffler for Jacques, then one for Marcel. She attempted a pair of gloves, but those proved too difficult—she'd count and recount the number of stitches that were supposed to be put on a holder, only to find that, like the socks she'd knitted decades before for the soldiers at the front that would have suited a man with deformed feet, her gloves turned themselves into crooked paws. Like that descendant of Penelope she'd encountered on the Metro platform years before, she unraveled her work, began again, this time making mittens, which she presented to Jacques.

"Lovely, dear," he said.

"They're a gift."

"For whom?"

"For you."

"I have a perfectly good pair of gloves," he said.

"Mittens keep your hands warmer."

He thrust them into his overcoat pocket. She never saw them again.

She knitted a blanket for Algerian refugees, then another: the long-suffering Algerians had no choice but to accept her offerings.

Sometimes her hands rebelled at the task set before them: they would begin to tremble, the needles would make a frightful racket against one another, it was anything but soothing.

When Jacques came home in the evening—often after having telephoned to say that he would be dining out with this or that associate, which was sometimes the truth, sometimes a cover story hiding the fact that he had been with Dominique or some other woman who had taken his fancy—he discovered Simone sitting on the couch, invariably with her hair carefully coifed and lipstick freshly applied, a book open on her lap, her whole mien making an effort to say: *You see, I am not feeling sorry for myself. I am taking care of myself, keeping up my interests.* The false smile which she offered him enraged him. (He was honest enough with himself to know that had Simone responded to her illness in the alternative fashion, with a show of despair and frank self-pity, he would have been even more enraged.)

Almost always he kept his anger in check, but on a few occasions he was unable to do so. Her innocent response to one of his questions ("How was your day?" "The same as usual.") would cause him to slam his fist against the flat's front door—they were fortunate that the apartment building was old and sturdy, this action doing far more damage to his hand than to the door itself.

"You mustn't rail at me. Your—condition—is hardly my fault."

"If that is railing at you—"

"I asked you a polite question—"

"Ah, are we to be polite with one another now?"

Paralysis

Paralysis was not a neat deadness. Her hands seemed to have a mind of their own. Sometimes when her brain issued the order, *Pick up the glass*, her hand might form itself into the shape of a letter C, her fingers homing in, exerting the correct amount of pressure. On other days, her hand refused to move or, like a child having a tantrum, went into histrionic spasms. Gone was the half-conscious stupor with which she had gone about her daily life, the smooth communion between will and flesh. She became imperious towards her own flesh: *Just pick up the glass*! *Do it*! *Or else*! If her hand had the power of speech, it would have taunted her: *Or else, what*? *If thine eye offend thee, pluck it out, and cast it from thee*? *Just imagine, Jacques coming home and finding your severed arm lying on the kitchen counter*!

It was said that in the colonies the first sign of a rebellion having spread from a vanguard to the populace at large was a momentary delay when a master made a request of one of his servants—for a glass water with a little lemon squeezed into it, say, or to have the blinds drawn. Soon that hesitation would grow into a dull stare, outright sullenness. So, too, with Simone: her body hung fire, her feet shuffled or minced rather than walked. Soon, her feet would be asking, *Now, tell me, why is it that I should get up and walk? I prefer to stay where I am, quite comfortable, here in the bed.* And then, *If it's all the same to you. Madame.*

She became aware of the minute number of actions involved in simply rising to her feet from a sitting position, the plethora of muscles which came into play—her massage therapist had instructed her on their names: the *rectus abdominus*, the *glutei—maximus, medius*, and *minimus*, the *abductor ossis metatarsi quinti*, the *popliteus*, the *sartorius*, following orders conveyed through the *substantia nigra*, the *striatum*, the *globus pallidus*. It was like a Roman legion massing before battle. No, more like a far-flung army at the end of the Empire, waiting for reinforcements which never arrived, wondering what had gone wrong in far-off Rome.

Rut

Jacques still fulfilled his husbandly duty. Once, the two of them about to leave a neurologist's office, the doctor, having walked them to the door, laid a hand on Jacques' shoulder and, trying to sound offhand, had said, "Ah, M. Melville, perhaps I could speak with you alone for a moment." She sensed Jacques' dread, his fear that he was going to be given some news that must be held back from the patient herself or perhaps presented with a manuscript.

He had emerged a few minutes later, a smile plastered on his face. In the taxi, she had cocked an eyebrow.

"When we get home…" With a jerk of his chin, he indicated the taxi driver.

She found his reticence strange, given that, during the course of their long engagement, he had more than once had sex with her in the back of a cab.

After the ascent to the apartment—"Mt. Everest," she said and laughed at one point as Jacques was forced to pick up one of her legs and lift it onto the step above—Simone asked "Well?"

"Well?" Jacques repeated.

"The doctor. What did he say?"

"He informed me of the dangers of erotomania. It happens sometimes, in cases like yours."

"Cases like mine?"

"Those with your affliction. It has nothing to do with your prior—moral attitudes."

"Erotomania?"

"He didn't go into great detail. He is, after all, a proper bourgeois, and I am your legally wedded husband."

Simone could only think of whispered stories she'd heard as a girl, a substance called Spanish fly made from the ground-up bodies of insects, which louts might slip into a girl's glass, inducing such lust that women were said to have impaled themselves on bedposts, mated with bulls.

"He said—the whole topic embarrassed him—that an assumption was often made that an invalid needed to be protected from—the carnal aspect of marriage, but that, in fact, if one wasn't—"

"Serviced regularly?"

"Don't make a difficult matter even more difficult."

"Ah, so this is a difficult matter."

"A man enjoys his brandy and his after-dinner cigar, is even gratified by the fact that he contravenes his physician's orders in partaking of these pleasures. Then his physician tells him that the latest medical thinking is that a glass of brandy and a cigar—or even two—are beneficial, and prescribes them. Suddenly, the indulgence becomes a duty—"

"Ah, yes, a duty."

"Simone, you must have patience with me. You are not the only one who suffers from your illness!"

Their lovemaking was no longer preceded by flirtation, a leisurely dinner, glasses of wine, a rousing argument, a fantasy spun out loud between the two of them: *Pretend that we're strangers, we happen to be in the same train compartment… You're a priest, and I'm in the confessional…* Rather, it happened in the dead of night, what the French refer to as *au plus profond de la nuit*, the word *profond* the same one used to refer to the depths of a lake. Indeed, night seemed like a solid substance which pressed down on them, making their movements both turgid and graceful. It happened without verbal preliminary, with only the bare minimum of caresses necessary to enable their organs to function. In that nest of warmth formed by the heat of their two bodies swathed in blankets, in one of those interludes when they swam up from sleep, he would tumble on top of her or she onto him, they would rut, grunting and panting like animals, not caring that poor Marie-Claire, in her room off the kitchen, might be awakened by the sounds of the bedsprings, their moans, their full-throated cries. (In fact, Marie-Claire, a solid sleeper, heard nothing. Still, she was not unaware of what transpired during the night: she did, after all, change the sheets.) For both of them, their orgasms had less quick intensity than they had had in the past, but were deeper and slower, like rolling thunder in the distance.

And then, wordlessly, they would fall back asleep.

Simone knew he shared this kind of intimacy with no other woman, that with all the others the trappings of romance and sweet words and coyness and surrender were required: it was only with her that he could share this primal union.

During daylight hours, their marriage resembled those countries—North and South Korea, East and West Germany—that forces of history had bifurcated, and which existed in a state of mutual resentment and longing, often on the verge of breaking into outright hostilities.

Coda

Simone thought of Joë with his war wound. War wrapped a narrative around chaos and destruction. The story began: A beautiful woman was carried off and sequestered behind the walls of Troy. Sieges, trenches, armies tromping across deserts and steppes followed. Walls were breached, one army decimated another. The End.

But because no story ever truly ends, there was the coda, of the war wounded. They limped along the place des Invalides, the off-beat syncopation of wooden legs and crutches beating against cobblestones. The passing women gave these brave lads a little shimmy of their hips.

On the Metro, a notice declared: even ancient women with arthritic knees must offer their seats to those who sacrificed so that our once-beautiful maidens might grow into crones with aching joints.

What, Simone wondered, was the meaning of her suffering? She and Dr. Balmant had tried to make a story from it, but in the end, that plot had collapsed.

The memory of Dr. Balmant's hand, resting on her shoulder.

Shades

At night, a rag-tag bunch of shades gathered in the front room, shrill laughter and loud guffaws, a woman who sang operatic arias *con brio* and quite off-key. One of them was playing a tinny piano. These must be the ghosts of the people who lived in this apartment before. The law of the day, the law of bright justice, required them to cede this apartment to the Melvilles, but at night, such strictures fell away, and the lot of them came clumping up the stairs—no wonder they had made such a racket, dragging that damn piano up the narrow stairway.

She elbowed Jacques.. "Someone is in the living room."

"Go back to sleep."

"Listen! Can't you hear them?"

"Simone, you know very well it is a delusion."

"I hear them, plain as day."

"Simone, I need my sleep."

"Just go in there, please, and ask them to be quiet."

Time passed. "Jacques," she whispered, "Jacques."

"Oh, for the love of Christ!" He flung the blankets off, exposing her to the cold, stalked into the front room, returned, shouting: "There is no one playing the piano in there! Edith Piaf is not singing in the front room! There are no Russian monks, chanting, as you thought the night before! Now just shut up and let me get some sleep!"

The next night they were back: this time without the piano, and without the guest who screeched arias. Instead, they had invited the deceased Sala, who had in turn invited all her dead friends. Sala was now busy convincing the assemblage of the wrongs that had been done to her. Simone could overhear only occasional scraps:

—and then she…

—'She' being Simone…

—Yes, of course.

—Oh, my goodness! I had no idea!

—Yes, and then…

—Ah, no!

She woke to the clatter of the schoolchildren's wooden clogs against the cobblestones. She woke. Therefore, she must have slept.

Cud

The doctor had warned her that she might start to experience sleepless nights and daytime drowsiness. But that allowed him to preserve a fiction: that the clean bifurcation of sleep and wakefulness continued. Instead, Simone seemed to be traveling back to a land where neither state existed, a fetal condition, with neither day nor night, consciousness nor its opposite. Or back to an even older state, pre-mammalian, becoming like the never-sleeping shark whose first and last taste of nothingness occurs at the same moment, at its death. (O lucky us, humanity, to belong to a species to which nature doles out little morsels of oblivion—our nightly descent out of the world, *la petite morte* of orgasm—a foretaste of the blankness that is to come.)

How did she spend these long hours when she was neither asleep nor awake? She ruminated.

On the life she lived.

On the life she might have lived.

On the life she wished she had lived.

Like those sheep and goats and cattle who graze, filling up a stomach with raw grasses which they will later regurgitate as cud and work over, Simone called back the past. She was once again fourteen, sitting in the high-ceiling classroom, staring at the map of the world unfurled in front of them: the French Empire in cool cerulean blue, the British in red. She understood, although their teachers did not put it quite this bluntly, that the English Empire was gross, slithering across the globe, like the buttocks of a fat woman spreading across a chair, while the French Empire, smaller, more compact, was a thing far finer.

The alkaline smell of chalk dust. Simone believed both what the science master told them, that chalk was formed from the skeletons of sea creatures that had died millions of years before, and what the priest told them, that God had created the world and all that was in it in six days.

One of her teachers had allowed her to borrow a book of lithographed reproductions of paintings in the Louvre. The paintings were rendered with deeply drenched colors, so that the sky behind La Giaconda was not grey and pale blue, but azure and indigo, and the faint blush on her cheek became a siren's red. (When she saw the originals, they seemed dim and disappointing.)

She ceased her methodical turning of the pages when she came upon Ingres' *The Turkish Bath*, transfixed by the panoply of female bodies. (She would have been equally transfixed by a panoply of male bodies, but the male nudes were always heroic and alone.) (Her own back was scrawny, her backbone protruding through the flesh so that one could count each vertebrae, her scapula chicken wings.) It was on account of that painting that when Luc said to her, "I have a house in

Istanbul," she gave him her fetching smile, and sighed, "Istanbul." She wanted to go some place where women wiled away long afternoons, lolling about in tiled rooms, their flesh displayed. She longed for indolence, debauchery.

The shock of Istanbul. The narrowness of the streets, the press of bodies, the market smells—a dizzying mix of figs and grapes, mint, garlic, sumac. The hands of the beggars. Her homesickness. She had wanted nothing but to get away, and now she wanted nothing more than to return.

In Istanbul, she had been taken to the *hamam,* the steam baths, by Yonca, the daughter of Luc's local engineeer. Ingres captured the excess of sensuality, the easy loll of woman against woman, the amplitude of flesh. But in the Ingres painting, all the women's flesh was unmarked by time.

An old woman sang, not as a gift for others but for her own pleasure: her voice had long since grown reedy. Mothers, slack-bellied, slack-breasted, entered with lines of daughters trailing after them, drowsy infants suckling. A baby's body, naked and slick, would turn to reveal its sex, a cleft or a rosebud. An old woman, her sex saggy, pubic hair gone sparse. (Later, in Rome, Simone would see an ancient wall, its bricks pockmarked by time, dangling grasses having taken root there, and it would remind her of these old women's cunts.) In the corner, a cistern filled with cold water. A ladle, resting on the edge of the cistern. The masseuses would pour water over their heads to cool themselves and tip the ladle above their open mouths. Some of the tiles of the ancient mosaics on the wall had chipped away. Time had burnished others to a blue so rich they were iridescent. When she touched the wall, she was aware of centuries of grime and condensation and sweat. The wool of the carpets scratched the skin of Simone's buttocks and hips and thighs, despite the cotton scarf laid on top of it. An air of torpor which would, as the afternoon wore on, fade into something close to depression.

The women of the European quarter tried to mother her or at least to act like her wise elder sisters. (They seemed so remote to Simone then, women of thirty-five or forty, their features made blurry by time, like faces on ancient statues that have stood exposed to the elements.)

Simone was a wide-eyed girl who might be tempted to go native. When they learned that Yonca had taken her to the Turkish bath, they grasped her sleeve, like the beggars in the market, whispering of the foul water there that spread disease, of the contagious lethargy. The specters of cholera and consumption floated in the air. One could be seduced by the sickness of this land.

Pain

Her body was an orchestra under the direction of a mad conductor. The orchestra tried to play Mozart, but instead found itself playing Stravinsky. And Simone was one of the Philistines at the opening of the *Sacre du Printemps*, catcalling, hurling the pages of the score onto the stage. She wanted harmony and order, the cool mathematics of a Bach fugue, not these wild jolts and jarrings that ran through her body.

No man had ever possessed her. Only her pain possessed her.

Morphine did not remove the pain. It created a woman with her name and body who felt the pain, while Simone watched from a remove.

Rut

At times her mind got stuck in a groove, stuck in a groove, stuck in a groove, as the needle of the hand-cranked gramophone in the parlor at Juan-les-Pins used to do. The simplest thought—say, *I need to go to the hairdresser's*—and there it would be, like a sty in one's eye, like a bit of lettuce caught in a gap between one's teeth: *I need to go to the hairdresser's,* unbudging for hours.

Rose

As well as remembering, she imagined: that one of those two bits of protoplasm wasn't scraped from her womb during the course of her long engagement: her imaginary child seemed more real to her than Marcel, Odette.

Stephan.

When Jacques had a few glasses of wine at a party he would lay his hand on the arm of an old friend and say, "Permit me to be a bragging father…" and boast about Stephan's exam results. He came home on Sunday for dinner with a bouquet of red roses. When Simone chided him for wasting money, he winked and confessed: he'd raided the dustbin in the alley behind a flower shop, pulled off the wilted petals.

This

And then there was the everyday world. Now. Here. This.

Marie-Claire smoothed the hair back from Simone's brow and said, "What is going on in that head of yours?" looking at her imploringly.

"Nothing," Simone said: it was the easiest thing to say.

The rituals of the day: Jacques up at six every morning, Marie-Claire now the one to make him his coffee, the smell of tobacco drifting in from the front room, the perfunctory kiss on his departure.

Gone

One morning Simone awoke to something thin and tenuous in the air of the flat, a smell of fear she could not put into words. Marie-Claire refused to meet her eyes.

It was mid-afternoon before Marie-Claire at last said, "He made me promise. Promise not to tell you. Oh, Madame, Madame, I am so sorry, please forgive me. He has gone."

"Gone?"

"Yes, Madame. He thought it would—be easier this way. Oh, I'm sorry, I'm so sorry, please forgive me. Please don't be angry at me."

"Call Stephan."

"Who is Stephan?"

"Our son!"

"Marcel?"

"No, not Marcel! Jacques' and my son. Stephan. *Ste-phan*."

"Madame. You and M. Melville do not have a son."

"Ah, you don't know anything! Of course we do!"

She said it with such vehemence Marie-Claire considered that the possibility that there had been a son, perhaps born before their marriage, fostered out. "Call him! Tell him what has happened!"

"I could call Marcel."

"Ah, not him. Call Stephan!"

"I don't know his telephone number."

"Look in the book." Simone was almost shouting now. "Right there. Next to the telephone. Look it up. Look it up!"

Marie-Claire opened the red leather address book, searched. "Madame, there is nothing."

"Bring it here. Bring it to me!"

Marie-Claire did as she was commanded, sitting herself down on the settee next to her mistress. "Ah, I told him, I told him, I tried to tell him, I—" She wept, twisting her hands.

"Someone has erased his name." She paged through the book, her tremor making the pages rattle, peering at the entries that had been rubbed out, looking for the pentimento of her son's name.

The ringing of the telephone sliced through the air.

"Ah, that may be him—" Marie-Claire said.

"If it's Stephan, I demand to speak with him."

"M. Melville, he promised he would—" Speaking into the telephone: "Yes. Yes. Yes. She's quite distraught—"

"Stephan!"

"She is saying, 'Stephan.' She believes that—it isn't true, is it?—that the two of you had a son…Madame, it is M. Melville."

"Let me speak with him!"

Simone shuffled over to the telephone.

"Jacques. Where are you? Where are you?" She repeated that sentence over and over again.

"I will be back. In two weeks."

"You will be back?"

"Didn't Marie-Claire tell you?"

She began to wail. "She told me you had gone! She told me you had gone! She didn't tell me you would be back."

Interspersed with her cries of pain came Jacques voice, solid, chanting *You must calm yourself* and *Two weeks, it's only two weeks* like the non-existent Russian monks chorusing in the parlor at night.

Marie-Claire fussed with the cross around her neck, murmured "I tried, monsieur, I tried."

"Where are you? When will you be back? You're with her, aren't you?"

"Come now, I'm losing patience with you. You must get hold of yourself or you are going to force me to hang up the telephone."

"No, don't hang up the telephone! Please, please, just tell me."

"It was because I feared such hysterics from you that I—"

"Oh, please, don't hang up on me. Just tell me where you are. Why didn't you tell me you were going? Why did you sneak out of the house?"

Jacques said nothing.

"Two weeks. Do you promise me you will be back in two weeks?"

"Yes, I promise you. Now you must promise me that you won't carry on. And no more nonsense about a son. You know, don't you, that we never had a son?"

"Yes," she admitted. "But—" she said, and then stopped herself, isn't it possible that his soul—after all, in Asia, they believe in the transmigration of souls—and Pythagoras, he believed it, too—that his soul is encased in some other body, that we pass him on the street sometimes, jostle against him on the tram? But she did not say those things, instead she said: "Where are you? Just tell me where you are."

"Simone." A reprimand.

"She's with you, isn't she?"

"Simone." And then he said, "Goodbye," and the line went dead.

Simone plopped down onto the floor.

"Ah, Madame," Marie-Claire, rushing over to her, grabbed her right arm and attempted to hoist her upright.

"Let me be! Let me be! I want to sit. I want to sit."

"But, Madame, if someone were to come and see you, they would think that I, that I was a poor—servant—" The word was not one Marie-Claire liked to use to describe herself.

"Who will come? No one will come! No one will come!"

Marie-Claire, having failed to lift her from the floor, sat down next to her, wrapping her arm around Simone's shoulder, drawing her close.

"Don't you, don't you, don't you, don't you—" Simone could not stop saying the phrase. She shoved Marie-Claire away from her so hard that her face hit against the edge of the settee (later there would be, not a bruise, but a slight discoloration), all the while continuing to say, "Don't you, don't you, don't you, don't you— You," she finally managed to say, "you, you, you, you were in league with him."

"Ah, Madame, he made me promise. He is, after all, he is, whatever my personal attachments are—he is the one who pays my wages. Oh, Madame, Madame, I never—I never— this is not how I was raised. My parents took their marital vows quite seriously—"

Simone wailed. She wailed like a wounded animal. She wailed like an abandoned child. She wailed.

"Where is he?"

"He made me promise not to tell."

"Where is he? Where is he? Where is he? Where is he?"

"North Africa."

"And is she with him?"

"Yes."

Was he in a house overlooking the sea? In a white house with blue shutters thrown open to the ocean air? Did locals in soft-soled slippers pad around the place, preparing cups of strong coffee for him and Dominique to drink in the morning, running a damp mop across the tiles? Did the household servants know no French, so they said to him in the local language, *Careful, sir, the floor is wet*? Did one of them hurry over to him, taking the old man's elbow so he didn't fall? In response to this humiliation, did Jacques leer at the servant, so that later, in the kitchen, she muttered to the other household help, *Those filthy French*! *He's old enough to be my grandfather*!

Simone hoped he was gorging himself on the local dishes so that his indigestion cropped up. She hoped he filled the air with the stink of his farts, that Dominique heard the sound of his bowels in rebellion.

Her

Dominique had waited discreetly in the other room. Since there was no telephone in the flat, she and Jacques had to walk to a local hotel which charged an unconscionable amount for an overseas call (his concern over the cost of the call had been part of Jacques' rush to get off the line). She took Jacques' arm, leaned her head against his shoulder, and the two of them walked along the roughly cobbled streets to a café overlooking the Mediterranean, where they would spend the next several hours reading, smoking the local cigarettes, the tobacco drenched in aromatics to disguise its roughness, staring at the horizon, staring at the sea, drinking thick Turkish coffee, as the afternoon wore on switching to mint tea, and as the afternoon turned to evening, changing to wine, which the proprietor kept beneath the counter and served them in tea cups—this, after all, was neither Tunis nor El Kef and he did not wish to offend his countrymen's sensibilities.

Although they were only gone for two weeks—Dominique longed for a proper month's holiday, but did not dare say so—on the first day they laid down a pattern which would become a routine and then a habit: the long, indolent morning in bed, breakfast served on trays by the servants. The first day it had been the local croissants, dry and almost tasteless. Dominique had managed to convey to the man who seemed to be in charge—there were so many servants, surely far more than were needed for this apartment—that they wished to eat what Tunisians would eat, and thereafter were served dates and yogurt and bread with honey. When the trays had been taken away, Jacques would read for a while and then yawn and say, "Doing nothing wears me out," and fall asleep. He fell into the habit of dozing and Dominique fell into that of watching him sleep, sometimes stretching out next to him, laying her head on his chest, listening to the steady thump of his heart, taking in his smell, which, as the days went on, became less and less the smell he had at home, and more and more infused with the scents of mint and Tunisian cigarettes, yogurt and honey. Sometimes in his sleep he did pass wind—he was, after all, a man in late middle age—neither of them used the word "elderly" to describe Jacques, even in the privacy of their own minds—and, when the prime of life has passed, one's body, inside and out, grows more and more flaccid with each successive year. She took pride in loving even these smells, as later, the heroine of her scandalous novel would take pride in her willingness to be debased by her lover, her suffering of pain for the sake of proving her love for him.

On their third day—only eleven days remained, really, only ten, nearly all of the final day would be spent in travel—she began to narrate the events of the day, speaking of herself in the third person. Because each day's events repeated the previous ones, the sentences were burnished through repetition. At first she used the imperfect, that is to say, a tense which describes an ongoing state, repeated action, which would be translated into English as "He was sleeping on his left side…" Later, when she returned to Paris and recalled these events, she used—not without a certain ironic detachment—the *passé simple*, an odd tense to use in one's head, as it is never used in conversational speech, but only in formal, written narratives—it might be used, for instance, to describe Caesar's conquest of Gaul or the shenanigans of Louis XIV.

After their lazy morning, they wandered to one of the few restaurants in town and then through the marketplace, or visited the local museum, with its rag-tag collection of second-rate Roman mosaics and sarcophagi, its ancient pottery shards, a page from Qur'an, blue vellum with gold lettering, its rattling floorboards. From there they went to the café they had entered on the first day, and began their ritual of coffee, followed by mint tea, followed by tea cups of red wine.

On the fifth day, walking to their café, they passed a dog, lying on its side, panting heavily, flies feasting not just on the open wound on its left flank, but drinking the liquid from its rheumy eyes. Dominique cried aloud—a slight cry, the tiniest of *ahs*—and then averted her eyes. The next day, neither of them bothered to prepare themselves for the sight of it, assuming it would have been dealt with by now—but there it was, flies more abundant, the wound's stink greater. After that—*why didn't someone take a shovel to the poor animal's head*? surely it wasn't their place as foreigners to do so—Jacques not only positioned himself so he would be between Dominique and the dying animal and held up his hand to block her view, neither of them saying aloud what they were both thinking: *Why doesn't that damn mutt hurry up and die*?

It was on the eighth day—only three days left—that Jacques bought Dominique the scarab ring she would wear every day for the rest of her life on the ring finger of her right hand. She asked that the stone be set not in gold or silver, but in iron. Although she would never remove the ring, she would often push it up and look at the rusty trace left on her finger.

Lying alone in their vast bed, the bed in which she took up so little space, Simone sensed the presence of Jacques lying next to her. She was not a madwoman. She knew she was here in Paris and Jacques was somewhere else, in Morocco or Libya or Tunisia, in a house overlooking the sea or a charming apartment in the casbah belonging to a homosexual artiste. She knew he was dreaming of her now, maybe even muttering her name, poor Dominique overhearing it, as Simone had a few times heard Jacques saying "Sala, Sala" in his sleep. She was glad he had traveled vertically, so their nighttimes were in sync. She would have felt much more abandoned if he had traveled across many time zones, were now in America or Madagascar.

The shadow of his shadow lay next to her. She could feel the few extra grams of weight, the darkness displaced by a deeper darkness.

Jangle

The black telephone was ensconced upon a spindly-legged table, more or less on its own—save, of course, for a few books, a manuscript. It rang less and less often, and between calls waited, a plump and patient Buddha. But did not completely cease to ring: mid-morning, early April 1954, it gave off its demanding peal.

Marie-Claire, standing at the kitchen sink drying a glass, was delighted at the prospect of something out of the ordinary happening—a telephone call!—and, at the same time, dismayed at having to admit that life had grown so straitened that the ringing of the telephone was a cause for exultation. In the face of these two clashing responses, she adopted a pose of disgruntlement: she wasn't about to abandon her duties and leap for the telephone. She was not one to have a machine ordering her about.

For the second time, the machine commanded: *Answer me*!

Simone, seated in her chair in front of an open window that looked down on the street six stories below, turned her neck, which moved in a ratcheting fashion, towards the pealing machine. During the war, one of her comrades, checking to see if the phone was bugged, had unscrewed the base of this telephone, lifted off the Bakelite cover, twisted off the caps that covered the mouthpiece and the earpiece. In doctor's offices when she saw charts hanging on the wall showing the internal mechanics and scaffolding of the body, the skeleton, muscles, nerve pathways on a skinless human figure, she thought of the wires and screws and levers and gizmos beneath the smooth shell of the telephone.

It rang for a third time. Where was Marie-Claire? Simone determined to rise and answer it herself. "Come on, legs," she murmured, her tone cajoling with just a hint of threat, as she used to speak to Marcel and Odette when they were young. She had braced her shaking arms against the steady ones of the chair and was leaning forward, shifting her weight onto them, as Marie-Claire entered the parlor, her damp dish towel draped over her shoulder, her version of the sash worn by the members of the Légion d'honneur.

One of the hallmarks of Simone's condition was difficulty in ceasing action once it had started. Having begun to rise, she could not stop. Marie-Claire rushed towards her, crying, "Ah, no, Madame!" Marie-Claire rocked back and forth between Simone and the telephone. Simone plopped down, the jarring action causing a sharp pain to shoot up through her pelvis, so intense that it made her cry aloud just as Marie-Claire said "Allô," before which her country mouth slipped an "H," rendering it simultaneously German and American.

Simone could tell from the tone of Marie-Claire's voice that she was speaking with someone she considered beneath her: the woman had a immutable social hierarchy in which she not only knew her place but everyone else's. She managed to convey an air of slight disdain as she said, "Oh, that's so terribly kind of you."

The call was from the butcher, asking if the family Melville would like the foreleg of a just-slaughtered spring lamb. The butcher played roughly the same role among the housekeepers and wives of this neighborhood as Jacques did in the Paris literary world. That was to say, he was a collector—and when it suited his purposes, a revealer—of secrets, a giver of largesse, a withholder of favors.

Marie-Claire accepted the butcher's offering—to do otherwise would be to get on the man's bad side. As a special favor to the Melvilles, the butcher's boy would drop it by later. The joint of lamb was quite impractical. It would be roasted on Sunday, the leftovers brought out of what Marie-Claire persisted in referring to as an icebox for meal after meal until Wednesday, when Marie-Claire will raise it to her nose and sniff, half hoping it will have gone off, allowing her to chuck it out, but alas. The lamb will grow grayer with each passing day, the layer of fat which at first had glistened atop it like icing on a cake percolating through the meat.

"I thought it might be the dealer," Simone said, gesturing with her chin towards an Alpine landscape in an ornate frame hanging on the wall. It had been bequeathed to Jacques by a distant uncle, who had little imagined that the inheritor would make a show of grimacing in horror when he saw the painting. Jacques had hung it on the wall so that it could be shown to a gallery owner who was known to traffic in such monstrosities, with the hope that it might be unloaded on some good bourgeois who would be impressed with the academic honors the long out-of-favor painter had once received. Perhaps the dealer could also find a customer for that fantastically baroque clock which had at first offended them with its ugliness, but which they had grown so accustomed to they now ceased to see.

Neither Simone nor Jacques would ask the dealer to look at two canvases, wrapped up in sheeting and stashed behind the bedroom armoire, which were among those that had been entrusted to Jacques at the start of the war, and whose value was increasing with each passing month—they did not dare to hazard by how much. The owner of those canvases had not shown up on any of the lists kept by various governmental bureaux dealing with displaced persons and former prisoners, nor on those of the ancillary voluntary agencies, as either definitively dead or alive. There was always the chance that he was living under an assumed name in Lisbon or a Greek fishing village, still afraid to show himself, or that he had been caught up in the great maw of Stalin's prison camps.

Simone turned her head back to gaze out once again at the Roman arena, now a park. Old men played boules, their thin voices drifting up to her, the clack of metal balls against one another. After a while, the old men shuffled off to the café across the street to drink pastis.

Until a year or so ago, Simone used to hobble over to the arena, with Marie-Claire urging her on, as if she were a child taking her first steps. Indoors, she could manage going downstairs fairly well by walking backwards and clinging to the railing. But once they were outside, she refused this monkey-like method and, maintaining a thin sheath of dignity, and holding her head high, she rested her right hand on the railing and, with Marie-Claire clutching her left arm, began her slow descent down the front steps. But now she could no longer abide the stares of passersby. For a while, they had been ones of curiosity, trying to decipher whether she was sick or merely odd, with her flat-footed march and the fixed expression on her face. Now, cast decisively out of the kingdom of the well, she was glared at in anger for disrupting the passage along the sidewalk, so she merely watched from her perch at the window. At precisely 3:11 each afternoon, an elderly lady was wheeled in a bath chair along the street towards the park, pushed by a thin young woman from Martinique or Upper Volta. The elderly lady had magnificent posture, each vertebrae neatly aligned with the one below and above it like a tower of blocks stacked by a compulsive child. In her right hand she held a gold-handled walking stick.

If Simone were to allow herself to be pushed in her wheelchair along the street, she would not look like an empress on a wheeled throne. Despite all the efforts of the massage therapists and their ilk, her shoulders were becoming hunched, her head lolling forward so she resembled a turkey vulture. Her backbone, that tower we erect heavenwards, had begun to tumble, Babel-like, on its way to becoming the jumble of bones that will lie in the ground.

Within the hour, Marie-Claire was calling from the kitchen, "Ah, that telephone!" This time, she rushed to the instrument, not wanting a repeat of Simone's attempt to rise.

"*Ah, oui, monsieur*." Marie-Claire's voice was reverent, as if she were taking a telephone call from a saint. She slid her hand over the receiver, announcing in a stage whisper: "It's Professeur Laurent."

"Tell him to ring Jacques at his office." Simone's voice was like a radio tuned to a distant station, the signal cutting in and out.

"No, Madame, he wishes to speak with you."

A few minutes later, she had hung up the phone: Laurent would be calling on her tomorrow. Pierre Laurent was the genius whose manuscript she'd read aloud to Marcel when he was ensconced on the couch: the antic, frantic, quirky man who nonetheless managed to produce written texts of such smoothness it seemed his sentences might have been golden eggs laid by the mythical goose. It was quite possible to imagine that he had been born wearing eyeglasses and that his own mother had addressed him as *vous*. He seemed destined to go from being an awkward boy to an ancient goblin, with no intervening period of adulthood.

She remembered him kissing her in the alley, thrusting his tongue into her mouth as if it were a toilet plunger. She had fought to breathe, laid a hand on his shoulder, pushed gently against him. "Ah, you don't want me to…?" he had said, and she had murmured, her voice teasing: "Slow down." There was a queer charm in his clumsiness. She had lovers who executed their maneuvers with such cool prowess one could engage in that most intimate of acts with them without the sense that one came any closer than when shaking their hands. There were other men, geniuses (and Laurent certainly was in that class) who seemed to believe they were doing women a great favor by coupling with them. Although their—conjunction, that was the best word Simone could use to describe it—had never proceeded any further than that sucker-mouth kiss, Simone had been drawn to the frankness of his desire.

These days her visitors were so few they could be counted on her fingers: besides Odette and Marcel, Jacques' sons and their wives, who trudged up the stairs with bunches of lilacs or daffodils and the heavy tread of those undertaking an obligation, there was only a minor female poet who had a habit of glomming onto jettisoned wives and the infirm and a massage therapist who lugged his table up the stairs and delved into her stiffening muscles, rubbing in an ointment which smelled of cod liver oil and naphtha.

Was it possible that Laurent was coming to see her in an attempt to revive what had once existed between the two of them? After all, he had perhaps been intimidated by her, and now—the voice in her head was her long-dead mother's, *Now that you've been brought down a peg, missy.*

It was quite possible that he might not show up. Although Laurent's philosophy was grounded in the concrete, his own interactions with the world were slap-dash, his forgetfulness legendary. He had written her address down—no doubt on a laundry slip or a corner of a page torn from a manuscript—but that scrap of paper might disappear into the maelstrom of his life, and he might remember their appointment waking with a start at three the following morning.

Although Laurent had taken his *agrégation* in philosophy, and had been called to the Sorbonne to take up a chair in that discipline, he claimed to practice anti-philosophy. Philosophers would say that it did not matter that the townspeople of Königsberg could set their clocks by the moment that Immanuel Kant walked past their doorway on his daily constitutional, or that historians in ancient Greece said when Socrates drank his cup of hemlock, he was clad not in a robe the color of Carrera marble but in brightly colored garb, an undergarment of blue topped with a cloak of madder pink, garish colors we associate with a strumpet out on a Saturday night. But to Laurent, these things did matter. It was precisely his aim to return philosophy to the chaos and sensuousness of everyday life: not to strip away the skin of the world to find the great truths underneath, but to understand that such a flaying of the world destroyed what it sought to find within.

The body of Laurent was an inextricable part of his genius. He sometimes walked for hours through the streets of Paris, mumbling, his mutterings turning into full-fledged arguments with himself. The story may be apocryphal, but was nonetheless widely believed: once a policeman, seeing this unkempt, wild-eyed man, gesticulating and shouting, quite oblivious to the consternation he was arousing in his fellow passersby, stopped him. Laurent's amusement at being thought a lunatic, coupled with his insistence that he was a professor at the Sorbonne, only increased the officer's belief that he had a maniac on his hands. It was only the policeman's being led to a nearby bookstore, which had Laurent's most recent book displayed in the window, along with a photograph of the author, that kept him from being taken into custody.

Simone was wary enough that she said nothing to Marie-Claire about the expected guest, knowing she would not be able to bear the looks of sympathy Marie-Claire would shoot her should Laurent fail to show up, the silent monologue which would run through Marie-

Claire's head as she stood at the sink washing dishes, which Simone would be able to pick up with her invalid's antennae.

Although she did not tell her why, she insisted that Marie-Claire iron her black trousers and fetch a pair of flats from the back of the armoire. Marie-Claire, down on her hands and knees, rummaged in the cupboard, muttering: "A perfectly good book, but the cover's bent... How on earth did that end up in here?" as she pulled out a copy of Sartre's *La Nausée*. Simone wouldn't have dared to tell her it was a first edition "warmly inscribed by the author" as the booksellers touted such things, its value greatly diminished by the crease in the cover. No doubt Simone had flung it in there one night when guests were expected and she had spent too long primping and, realizing that the guests would be arriving any minute, had simply gathered up the piles that had accumulated on the dining room table and raced with them to the wardrobe. A day or two later, a sour smell would remind her of the dirty dishes that had ended up in there. Simone believed a home where everything was neat was like a city without a park. A touch of nature's promiscuity was necessary. If Marie-Claire were to hear, she'd say: *Ah, it's more than a touch*!

Pierre Laurent stood outside the Melville flat, his hand raised to rap. He was mentally preparing himself for the sight of Simone, who would no longer be the woman he had walked along the river with, but now a woman in solid middle age, with crow's feet; either greying at the temples or with hair dyed coal black. He prepared himself for the face gone doughy, for jowls, for wattles, for a broadened backside, for her breasts having become a single great bosom held in check by a brassiere that was a feat of engineering, for a face hidden behind a Kabuki mask of foundation and mascara and red-red lipstick.

"You must be careful," he muttered to himself, "careful, careful." When Sally had returned to Paris from America in '48, he had embraced her and then said, "The years have not been kind to you."

"Ah, Laurent, that was cruel!"

He hadn't helped matters by saying, "I wasn't trying to be cruel, it was merely a statement of fact."

Now he murmured to himself, "Don't say 'old,' don't say 'ugly,' don't say 'crippled.' If you can't resist, if the words are going to come out despite your best efforts, go in the bathroom and turn on the taps and say them while the water is running."

Paralysis

He was seated opposite Simone on the settee. Having tossed his coat on the arm of the sofa, he was saying, "Simone (Simone, Simone)." He then threw his head back like a horse about to neigh, reached up with his left hand—his right was busy tapping a cigarette against the ashtray set on the coffee table—and shoved back his forelock. He drew the cigarette to his mouth, where he allowed it to dangle, a wreath of smoke spreading about his head, as he took her hands in his, fixing his gaze on her, his eyeballs so protuberant it seemed they might at any moment pop out of his head. He would have been happier if he had been an octopus or the multi-armed Hindu goddess Kali and could have smoked, held her hand, smoothed his hair, and scratched himself all at the same time.

"The word 'paralysis' was used and I—"

"How did you think you would find me? Like the heroine from a novel, staring in the distance at the approach of the angel of death?"

"Ah, ah, ah, ah," he said.

Her shakings provided a good bit of exercise, so her body looked like that of a former dancer who had kept up the disciplines of her youth. "It is an odd sort of paralysis," she said. "More of—the will than of the body."

"Paralysis." Laurent uttered this word *sotto voce*.

"It is all rather more quixotic than expected."

Quixotic. He did not speak this word, only mouthed it. Although Simone was familiar with his myriad queer habits, she found this one disconcerting.

"You are still beautiful. Beautiful!" His coat slithered down and lay in a heap on the floor. She knew his words were flattery. Charm had always been her strong suit. She did have the kind of looks which aged well: her prominent cheekbones provided a good scaffolding for her face. She had never been so beautiful that others looked at her and mourned what the ravages of age had destroyed.

Marie-Claire on her way out to fetch something to serve this unexpected guest, said, "I'll just put this on a hanger," executing her version of a *demi-plié* as she retrieved Laurent's coat, to which he responded, his mouth like a machine gun, blurting out the word "no" instead of bullets. "That is, that is, to say, I wanted Simone—Madame—Mme. Melville, to—the coat! It's made from vicuña, a relative of the llama (llama)—the Andean highlands. Perhaps the llamas wild progenitor. Feel it! Rosamund gave it to me, I would never have, have—oh, it's absolutely obscene, obscene, what it cost."

Simone touched it and made the appropriate sounds of appreciation, at the same time noticing several dark splotches. "I know! A lovely garment and those—I must remember (remember) to take it to the cleaners. I'm forever leaving things behind. Once I lost a manuscript. Left behind. Café? Metro car?" It wasn't just his repetitions that were at odds with ordinary conversation, but his whole syncopation, as if his body were engaged in a separate conversation: some rough boogie-woogie. "Jacqueline arrived at my room to find me in tears and walked me around to all the places I had been. We managed to locate it, thank God! Its possessor—its temporary possessor had, had unfortunately used a few of its pages to light the fire. But only a few, thank God."

"Or perhaps, thank Jacqueline."

"Yes, thank Jacqueline." As he spoke, he scratched his head, his nose, his crotch, adjusted and readjusted his clothing, occasionally gave an amiable slap to the twitching muscle of his cheek as one would give a friendly smack to a faithful but too eager dog.

The aforementioned Jacqueline and Rosamund were parts of a

bevy of older women who circled about Laurent, whom he sometimes described as "the aunts" and at other times designated by saying, "the—you know—" and waving his hand in a circular fashion to the right of his head, like a gaucho twirling his bolos. The word "older" in this context did not mean older than Laurent. In fact, some of the aunts were younger than him by a good decade. Rather, these were women who were too old to be considered as his romantic partners.

These women—all of whom had a strong maternal streak and substantial wealth, came by his hotel room—the hotels in which he lived were invariably just a few steps above flophouses—first checking at the front desk to make sure his rent was up to date. (Not a few of the proprietors, eyeing these women in their coats of Russian sable, saw little harm in exaggerating the amount owed on M. Laurent's account.) Laurent was always broke, despite making a substantial income. He had a reputation among the denizens of the hotels and working class cafés he frequented as being both an easy touch and quite forgetful about debts. The chambermaids in his hotels soon discovered they could slip a note from the stack left higgledy-piggledy on his desk, and when that went unnoticed, they pilfered a bit more, and then a bit more.

Opening the door of Laurent's room, one of the aunts might discover that not only had the electric fire been left on, but that the philosopher's socks and underwear, draped over the back of a wooden chair to be dried by said fire had been singed. Indeed, had she arrived a quarter of an hour later, the room might well have been engulfed in flames. Furthermore, the table appeared to be undulating: a pullulation of ants were crawling over a piece of cheese and hunk of bread, barely visible beneath their black collective mass. This woman, who within her own Parisian apartment was attended by *two femmes de chambre,* plus a cook and a butler, set about cleaning up the filthy room.

"Once a man chased me down the street, yelling, because I had taken his jacket from a café, it was the same color as mine, he thought I had stolen it, and it was only an intervention by the landlord that—so, I decided not to ever take my coat off, at least not in a public place, but you see, the result is—" and here he displayed the stains on his coat, as bridegrooms used to exhibit the bloodstained nuptial sheet.

In addition to acting as his patronesses and scullions, the women of whom Laurent had been speaking also served—if the matter were to be put quite crudely—as his bawds. The members of Laurent's sorority did not profit from their efforts, save in the coin of Laurent's gratitude. The women kept an eye out for a certain type of girl—fresh from convent schools or daughters of émigré families—with long fair hair which seemed to determine to escape from its hairpins and barrettes and tumble, in lank tendrils, down around their thin faces, with boyish hips and breasts like champagne coupe glasses. Like wise aunts all over the world, they broadened their charges' horizons by giving them works to read—tomes of high literary merit considered scandalous by the unenlightened—and speaking to them, quite frankly, about the way relations between men and women were carried out in this sophisticated milieu. With certain girls the introduction to *la connaissance charnelle* was also carried out on a practical plane as well as on an intellectual one, with the aunts undertaking this sometimes with a sense of obligation, sometimes with delight.

Tremor

A tremor began in her right arm. He stared at her quite openly. "Your hand—it just—does that?"

"Yes." With anyone else she would have become self-conscious, grabbed her right arm with her left, perhaps wedged it between her hip and the back of the couch in an attempt to hide it.

"It's quite fascinating. Wittgenstein (Wittgenstein!) asked, 'What is left over if I subtract the fact that my arm goes up from the fact that I raise my arm?'"

"This."

"Aristotle wrote about the hand, I believe, the palsied hand, and, and, and Heidegger also. Just, just recently. I have the galleys of his new work, because... Yes, yes, of course, of course, there are myriad bodily processes which are not subject to our conscious control. Yes, but surely one of the ways that we come into our own as human beings, leaving behind the, the, the world of infancy—"

A few minutes before, she had been thinking about how she would fend him off when he made his approach, responding with a gesture, a phrase, that would not be an outright rejection, one that might be seen as a feint. Now, her body had sent him off on a tangent.

"—is to discover," he was saying, "part of forming the habit of living is, is, is understanding which of our bodily processes are subject to our will and which are not—" It seemed that his words were directed to an imaginary interlocutor. "Dr. Nalson—"

"Dr. Nalson? It was Dr. Nalson who—"

"Yes, yes, I know. I know! Because there are certain cases, people, that is, patients, and Dr. Nalson has shared with me some of his observations, because they are pertinent to the problems I am grappling with now. He has even allowed me to sit in on some of his— It even crossed my mind that I might—oh, never mind a thought just went flitting across my mind—when I was a boy in Indochina there were certain birds that flew very fast, tiny birds—sometimes one would flit by, and I wouldn't be certain if I had really seen such a bird or if, if, if I had imagined it. At times I have thoughts that seem to me like those little birds, they carom across my mind, they come from nowhere and disappear into nowhere—"

"Dr. Nalson," Simone said.

"Ah, yes, yes, yes, Dr. Nalson! He was showing me some of his files, and I saw your name. And I said, I said, 'I know this woman, I know her!'" He wiped a fleck of spittle from his right cheek, seemingly unaware that there was another one on the left.

"Did you look at my file?" Simone half-believed that her medical file was like the Book of Fate, prised by Napoleon from an Egyptian sarcophagus, said to divine the future.

Marie-Claire entered, carrying a pink box of pastries tied up with a silver ribbon, accompanied by a gust of cold air from the hallway.

"If I had known you were coming," she said, "I would have prepared something myself, but since…" and she allowed the words, unspoken but nonetheless present—*you dropped in unannounced*—to waft through the air, although they were certainly not picked up by M. Laurent. Simone was attuned to Marie-Claire's meaning, and further imagined what else followed: *If M. Melville reprimands me about the housekeeping accounts, I expect you to come to my defense. After all, we aren't the sort of house that serves our guests a heel of old bread.* Both women anticipated a row that might have been recorded in some diminutive version of the Book of Fate, offering prognostications not about the outcomes of military campaigns, but of household spats.

Simone's face was turned towards Laurent. His face was turned towards the petit fours being set on the plate. Because he had put two of the little cakes in his mouth at once, he was silent. Simone was able to ask again: "Did you see my file?"

"When," Laurent said, propelling a few crumbs into the air as he spoke, "I said to Dr. Nalson, 'Oh, I know this woman, this lovely woman,' that was in fact what I said, 'this lovely woman,' he moved it away, he's quite correct, your Dr. Nalson—"

"Ah," Simone said once again, unsure if she were relieved or disappointed. "Have you come to study me, then?" she asked, expecting him to deny it.

He answered her in the affirmative, the single syllable repeated three times, unqualified by hedge or explanation.

"Ah, Laurent, you are so without guile."

"There is a case, a patient"—and here his whole body began to jounce about. He had the air of a boy who believed that all the marvels of this world, from the great pyramids to the orders of ants, had been created for his delectation—"this man, survived a bout of encephalitis only to be left with a kind of 'psychic blindness.' This man's way of being in the world, is quite curious. If he has his eyes closed, and the doctor orders him to perform a simple action, he is quite! unable to do so. To touch his hand to his nose. Whereas your hand—"

"When my arm does that, when it starts to tremble, it seems as if my arm is no longer a part of my body, but a thing apart, like that ashtray or the table. But no, that isn't quite right, because it has animation, so perhaps it is more like the radio or the telephone. And like the telephone, I can no more will it to cease its actions than I can will the bell in the telephone to be still. An alienated object."

"Alienation!" Laurent cried. He took that word, so freighted with philosophical meaning and grasped hold of it like a child who had received an unexpected gift. "Alienation!" Laurent rolled his eyes upwards, as if he were inscribing words on the slate of his forebrain. He was translating her word into its weighty German translations, *Entfremdung* and *Entäusserung*, trying to find a place for it in a vast and jumbled philosophical system, which sometimes seemed akin to the genealogy of a remote and thus interbred Alpine village, in which everyone is everyone else's second cousin once removed, and one's grandmother is also one's niece by marriage.

Still

Laurent blurted: "Do you find me tiresome?"

"No, not at all. Why do you ask?"

"You look so, so—"

"It is part of my condition. My face is losing its powers of animation. When I told you that the paralysis was—quixotic—this is one of its—strange ways. It upsets Jacques so much that sometimes he closes his eyes so he can't see me. It's as if we were talking in the dark."

Laurent had taken advantage of her speaking to eat two more of the little cakes. His fingers were now engaged in smoothing out the tiny pleats in the fluted paper cups which had held them. Some of his fingernails were bitten down to the quick, while the one on the pinkie finger of his left hand was so long it might have belonged to a Chinese mandarin—although Laurent's nail was streaked with black.

After returning with the cakes, Marie-Claire retreated to the kitchen.

Simone pictured Marie-Claire stopped, eavesdropping so she could report to M. Melville on madame's day.

"Ah, ah, ah—the intimacy of voices in the dark!"

She didn't say that when Jacques closed his eyes, it was not two lovers exchanging scraps of words in the night. Household business: —*Did Marie-Claire pick up my shirts*? Accounts of his day, his moan and complaint, the petty insults he was forced to endure, the fools he did not suffer gladly—Simone was still good for something, an infinitely receptive ear into which he could offload the day's detritus, sparing his mistresses from seeing the bitter man whose powers were waning, allowing them only to see the wise old solon. With her, for instance, he could speak quite frankly of the machinations he was undertaking in an attempt to be elected to the Academy. The outgoing member was not yet dead, although his demise was imminent, and Jacques had been calling in favors, making what—despite the language in which they were couched—were threats in the jostle for the soon-to-be-vacant seat.

Tramp

"This view—this picture! I know this view!" Laurent pointed to the painting they were hoping to sell.

"Ah, yes—" Simone felt the necessity of explanation. "It was left to Jacques by a distant relative. It's quite hideous…"

"Yes, I used to hike that path, that very path—"

"…and a dealer is coming over to—"

"It was when I was a youth, at university—"

Simone gave up explaining away the artwork, and attempted instead to dive into Laurent's conversational stream: "It's hard for me to imagine you as an Alpinist."

"I was more or less, that is, ordered to by my mentor, excess of energy—now the doctors feel that part of it may in fact be—well, I won't go into that, or perhaps just for a moment, I may have an overactive thyroid." The statement, which had begun as a parenthetical one, ceased to be so. "Descartes thought the soul was in the pineal gland, but, but my soul seems to be in my thyroid. You may have noticed that my eyes are quite protuberant—"

An artist had once done a quick sketch of him on a linen napkin at La Coupole, in which the face was dominated by the eyes, rendered as concentric circles, the line growing thicker as it came closer to the center, the thin nose and pursed lips almost an afterthought. The café owner had at first stowed it in a drawer, taking it out occasionally and showing it off—to cries of, "Ah, Pierre Laurent!" Later, when the tourists, American, British and Argentine, having learned that this was a place where the bodies that housed great minds could be glimpsed, descended on the café like flies, driving away those they were seeking, the proprietor raised his prices, told the invaders that Jean-Paul Sartre had either just left or was expected at any moment, and framed this napkin and hung it on the wall. The place ceased to be a dim cave, the air thick with cigarette smoke and talk, where the denizens stumbled on their way to the toilet and cursed the darkness, the landlord no longer calling out, "If you would pay your damn tab, I could afford light bulbs."

"The Alpine hike," Simone murmured. Then added—because she really was intrigued by the notion that Laurent's soul resided in his thyroid and wondered in what organ her soul lived, "We will return later to the seat of your soul. The hike, the hike." She wondered if she were picking up Laurent's verbal tics.

"I had such an excess (excess) of energy that I was ordered, the equivalent of a forced march, to go out on Sundays on real tramps, to burn it off. It was on one of those walks, yes, at that very place—have you read Antonio Gramsci's *Prison Letters*?"

"No," Simone said, and then added, "it's one of those things I haven't yet gotten around to," although the truth was that she was not quite sure who this Gramsci was and why he had been imprisoned.

"There's a section that's quite moving." If Simone was in the habit of pretending to know more than she did, Laurent's habit was the opposite. He could have quoted the passage in question from memory in the original Italian and also could have told her, to the precise day, how long Gramsci had been in prison when he wrote this particular letter. "He had been in prison for quite some time, he wrote of no longer using ordinary reason, but of reasoning as old convicts do, through a series of associations and images, and that this kind of reasoning was as effective as ordinary reasoning—and it seemed that my professor, in sending me on this walk, this hike, up, it was really quite difficult, even for me as a lad—I'm very muscular, I know it seems strange, that I should have the body of a stevedore, if I were to take off my shirt—of course, I wouldn't— take off my shirt, don't worry, I'm not about to—" and he gestured towards Marie-Claire in the kitchen— "it seems to be on account of all my tics and jactitations, my-my-my—they actually are a form of exercise. I'm quite hale, I know it doesn't go with my pallor. If it hadn't been for the complete exhaustion that I felt (exhaustion) and, I suppose also a sort of altitude sickness, I was quite light-headed—" and here he circled his hand, the gesture quite similar to the one he made when he was talking about the aunts. "Quite spent, my brain deprived of oxygen, I came out onto, the promontory, and looked down to the valley below. I was flooded with—oh, it's trite to say—a sense of the sublime, the sort of emotion that becomes in some people a belief in God. I felt as if *I* were God, looking down on the world, the hills beneath me, the Alpine meadow in the foreground. It is a grand thing to stand on top of a mountain and look down upon other mountains, into the valley below. And that at the same time there was something false in it, that it's the world that painters give us, painters who in the end are rather trite—ah, no, now I've insulted—"

"No," Simone put in.

"Ah, please don't repeat that comment to your husband."

"Believe me—"

"I wouldn't want to get on his bad side. Not of course that he, that he has a bad side—"

"Laurent," Simone said, putting her hand on his arm. "Laurent. I need you to listen to me."

"Listen to you," Laurent whispered.

"The painting is an inheritance. From an uncle, a great-uncle of Jacques. We have hung it on the wall—"

"(Hung it on the wall.)"

"Because a dealer is coming over to look at it. We hope to unload it on someone with more money than taste."

Palilalia

"I must just—tell you this. When I am listening to someone very intently, this. I repeat—people sometimes think I am mocking them—(my psychoanalyst thinks it is a disturbance stemming from the mirror stage). Anyhow, the painting—that's a relief that you too find it hideous. And the point I was making—when I recall that walk, reaching the peak and looking down into the valley, and now here it is hanging on your wall—how odd. The very same view. I didn't reach the summit, no, it would have required ropes and ice axes to—and a companion and I knew that no one would ever be my companion on such a climb, I wouldn't be my own companion on such a climb, the knots that must be double-checked, it's quite possible that I would have got distracted—probable— So there was vision, but not our ordinary vision, which is fragmentary, and self-centered, of necessity. I look at this tea cup, this tea cup—"

"Actually, it's a coffee cup."

"A coffee cup, yes, not a tea—I look at this cup and because it is my cup, not mine by the right of possession, but my cup in that it, it, it is the one I am expected to drink from, it occupies my field of vision in a way that looms larger in my consciousness. Because I am in relation to this cup, because I have drunk from it and of necessity the rest of the world becomes less focused, blurrier on the edges, as I turn my attention to it. The world is only glimpsed fleetingly in those grand images. Most of the time we are down here on the ground, we are surrounded by things, objects, places, places which we have invested with meaning. I narrow my focus because of my affective connections. Indeed, doctors feel that in some types of idiocy this is precisely the problem, the patient appears dull but in fact he is unable to shut down the floodgates, to put on the blinders, and taking everything in he seems to take nothing in."

A few months later, she'll be listening to one of the radio lectures which Laurent will have recorded, his disembodied voice eerie in the flat: "Classical painting gives us landscapes which present a homogenized world, governed by the laws of perspective, which fundamentally distort the way that the world engages us. Such works of art ask little from the viewer; instead, they imbue him with a sense of earthly order which is fundamentally false."

It will be his voice and not his voice, because he will have suppressed its most fundamental characteristics, its staccato qualities, its echolalia, the way it pinged about like a pellet in a pinball machine.

One day, several weeks hence, he will come to her from the recording studio, where he will have been taping this lecture. When he takes off his shirt he will release an odor so acrid she will recoil. "Ah, sorry. (Sorry, sorry.)"

"Laurent," she will say, in a voice that is both loving and reproving.

"I put on a clean shirt this morning! And I bathed. This morning. During the interview, I make an enormous effort to talk as other men (men!) do, without all my little flickers of words, and, and. In order to do this, I must also restrain myself physically, and I can do it, but only with enormous effort, ditch-digging!—it's as much effort as digging a ditch, and I work up a sweat like a common laborer." He will go and have a wash, and when he returns, he will smell of Jacques' soap, sandalwood and clay, so that while he will be moving in and out of her, it will seem as if she is making love to a man who is both Laurent and Jacques at the same time. That will be the fifth time, the next to the last time they make love.

Now, a church bell chimed the hour of four, and Laurent cried out: "Ah, no! This is—ah, ah, there's so much more that—half an hour ago, I was supposed to meet Jacqueline, Jacqueline, oh, she'll be ever so angry, my coat. I'll ring. I promise!" He grabbed his coat, grabbed the last two petit fours from the tray, kissed her hand, and raced out the door.

Long

Laurent did not ring.

But four days after his precipitous departure a letter arrived from him. A love letter—after a fashion.

> *Dearest Simone, Twenty-two hours have elapsed since I took my leave of you. I promised to telephone, but I thought I would write instead, since I am so clumsy in direct intercourse. Social situations are never easy for me; and I must confess that last week's was made more difficult by the presence of your maid. I do hope to see you again soon…*

Simone wrote him back, her handwriting so tiny it might have come from the hand of an elf—micrographia, another hallmark of her condition: *Come Thursday. Marie-Claire has the afternoon off.* She slipped the letter into a stack of mail Jacques was posting, sat by the open window, watched Jacques as he crossed the street, paused at the postbox dropped the letters into the slot. She would have liked to have remained there until the postman emptied the box, but it began to rain. "Ah, Madame!" Marie-Claire exclaimed, seeing her sodden face and skirt. "Why didn't you call me," slamming the window shut, hurrying her off for a good hot bath to get the chill out of her bones. "We can't have you coming down with a cold, on top of everything else. And above all now, when the seasons are changing and your blood thinning." (Marie-Claire was certain that just as sap in trees began to run in spring, so too in that season the blood of humans became less dense, preparing itself for the lassitude of summer, just as she believed the time between the full moon and the new was the best time to castrate farm animals and that a black snake coiled on a fence post was a sure sign of foul weather.) So Simone, rushed to the bath to be warmed—she did rather enjoy the sensation of Marie-Claire rubbing the flannel across her flesh, being wrapped in a towel as if she were a child—did not get to see her letter picked up.

And then it was Thursday. Marie-Claire, who made it a habit of going to visit her sister on her afternoons off, puttered about. Several times she was on the verge of leaving, had her hand on the doorknob, then remembered something—her handkerchief, her Metro tokens, madame's glass of warm milk.

"Surely, your sister will grow concerned if you are late."

"Ah, no, she's not the worrying sort."

Knock

At last she departed, and Simone was left alone in the empty flat, to wait, with an infinity of possibilities in front of her. Had Laurent received her letter? Would he come?

But then there was a knock on the door, only five minutes after Marie-Claire's departure— almost too soon. She would have liked that frisson of anxiety to be prolonged a bit.

"I was here, I was waiting in the café opposite, I wanted to make sure, to make sure, she had gone, that Anne-Marie—"

"Marie-Claire."

"Yes, gone, I wanted to make sure that-that—she's rather a horror—"

"She's very good to me."

"Yes—oh, I hope I haven't offended you, I'm sure she is, good—"

More or less to rescue him, Simone asked, "Would you like something to drink?"

"Coffee, no, perhaps not coffee, I'm on edge enough as is, I just get anxious in the presence, well, in the presence of a beautiful woman."

"Would wine be better?" Simone asked, and without waiting for him to answer—who knew what kind of a knot he might twist himself into?— she went into the kitchen, making two trips— one for each glass of wine—from kitchen to parlor.

When she returned the second time, he was scrabbling through his pockets, "Ah, I'm terribly sorry, I am going to have to disappoint you—"

An abyss opened up around her, she plummeted through empty space: "You have to leave?"

"No, no. Not disappoint you in that manner. Remember last week we were discussing Heidegger, the hand, the passage—remember!"

Simone made a vague murmur of assent.

"Here it is—no, that's not it, that's the hotel bill (past due)—ah, no, it must be in the pocket of my other trousers—or perhaps—" and he delved into his worn leather satchel, rifling through papers.

Simone did not get to hear Laurent read aloud the passage from Heidegger: "'The hand is a peculiar thing. Every motion of the hand in every one of its works carries itself through the element of thinking, every bearing of the hand bears itself in that element. All the work of the hand is rooted in thinking.'" Nor to hear his commentary, "Your hand is particularly peculiar. And therefore, is your thinking peculiar? Oh, I hope I haven't offended you by, by, by saying that."

"No, no, no Heidegger, but this, this!" he cried, holding aloft a paperback book with her husband's name on it.

"What is this?" Her voice was monotonous, her face impassive: neither conveyed her pain. She took the book from his hands; Jacques hadn't authored it, but merely written the preface. Still. Why had he hidden its existence from her?

"Ah, you haven't, you haven't… But everyone is talking about it. It's quite scandalous." He began to read aloud, sometimes word for word, sometimes summarizing: the lovers walking in an unfamiliar part of Paris, René ushering the woman who has no name other than 'O' into a taxi, the trip to the chateau where she will be bound and whipped.

"Who is this woman? This Pauline Réage?"

"Ah, no one knows. People say that it is so explicit that no woman could have written it. Some, many, people say that your husband wrote it."

"No," she said, decisively. Of that much she was sure.

He gulped his wine. "So, we are alone."

"I should tell you," Simone launched into a set piece she had rehearsed: "Part of my—condition—is a difficulty in initiating action. It isn't just physical, but psychological as well." Perhaps soon she would get it printed on a card, like those deaf-mutes hand to shopkeepers. Not for the first time, she envied Joë's neat deadness, the line of demarcation that ran across his body. How much easier for others to make sense of than this paradoxical state she found herself in. "Do you understand what I am telling you?"

"You (you, you), need me to take the initiative. Is that it? I need to seize the reins, I need to…"

"I am like a clock that needs to be wound up."

Clock

Laurent leapt to his feet. By the time she realized what he was doing, and got the word "No," out of her mouth, he had already wound up the baroque monstrosity that sat on the mantelpiece.

"Oh, no."

"I'm so terribly sorry. Didn't you say, I quite distinctly heard you say wind up the clock?"

"No. I said, 'I am like a clock that needs to be wound up. It makes such an infernal racket, we never wind it—" As if on cue, the bronze cherub within the clock emerged and began to bash away at the gong.

Laurent winced at the noise.

"It's actually quite valuable—hideous, but valuable—"

"Yes, yes, hideous."

"Our plan is to someday sell it—but it's one of those things we never get around to. And it chimes like that every quarter hour—that's why we never wind it up."

"Ah, I'm so sorry. I…"

Simone saw he took a certain pleasure in humiliation. As it was in her nature to cater to the whims of men, she reprimanded him further: "Yes, not only were you not listening to me, you've created a problem between me and Jacques. Now that the damn thing has got started up, there's no way to stop it. He's going to know someone's been here—"

"Isn't it possible to say that you, that you—"

"We never wind it up. It clangs all through the night, too. Anyhow, I lack—the fine motor control necessary for such an action."

"Well, perhaps you could say that Anne-Marie accidentally—"

"One doesn't accidentally wind a clock."

She saw that he wanted to be comforted, as a child who has been punished by the father is then secretly consoled by his mother.

"Come now," she said, "don't fret, we'll think of something. I could even just tell Jacques the truth—"

"The truth!"

"Yes, that you came to call, that you were interested in my condition, part of your phenomenological investigations, tell him exactly what happened, what I said, what you heard…"

"He won't…"

"After all, nothing untoward has happened, has it?"

"…be angry? No, nothing, no."

Once again the cherub emerged and began to peal another passing quarter of an hour: they both started and cried out.

"I must," Laurent cried, rising to his feet and crossing to the mantel, busying himself with a bit of paper from his pocket (what flotsam must be accumulated in those pockets, half-smoked cigarettes, notes to himself, bits of paper napkins he'd twisted into long curlicues, perhaps even the ends of his own fingernails, chewed off and stowed there to be disposed of later), managing to still the mechanism.

Before the business with the clock it seemed he had been on the verge of declaring himself, but now he lurched off in another direction:

"I am—I have written—I am writing—an essay, in which I speak of how illness breaks the bonds of the everyday, thrusting us into another reality, hurling us—quite (quite) against our wills into another world, that is to say, one which bears a skewed relationship to our own (skewed), and I feel that I have gotten stuck. I have my own experience of illness, but I feel rather cowed about writing about it, it isn't much, indigestion, colds of course, the ordinary, liver, liver attacks—a few fevers that really—a terrible toothache. It was during the occupation, and the pain shot up my—the fact is that I neglect my physical well-being just as I—and Sally who schedules these things for me, dentist appointments, and, and she had gone back to America on account of the war—it shot up through my face as if my brain were going to be pierced by the pain. I took a bicycle taxi—a human being forced to pedal another about—but I was in such pain, and so it seemed—that illness might—well, upend everything, as the brave man under torture finds out, finds out, that he is not so brave after all.

"Dr. Nalson says that when we see the human body broken, it is at those broken moments, those places that we have insight into, into our nature— Ah, how was it, how was it, that I got started on this whole thread of conversation?"

"I must confess, I have difficulty in following—"

"Ah, yes. In my last book, the critics rather took me to task for, for, for concentrating too much on my own experience. I sit down to write, about, about that toothache, and I can imagine certain critics—your husband, for instance, I hope you won't be offended—calling me to task, saying I have built an entire philosophy on a bad tooth."

"Am I to be your lover or your means of philosophical inquiry?" She had meant for these words to be coy, but because of the increasing monotonousness of her voice, she was more forthright than intended.

"Both! If that is, if —"

It was impossible for her not to feel tenderly towards him, like a dance partner who treads on one's feet and then blushes with shame at his ineptness. "Ah, Laurent. You are so without guile."

"Could you call me Pierre? It is, after all, my given name. My mother called me Pierre. Well, of course she did, she would hardly have called me by my surname. The girls with whom I have—relations!—sometimes they call me Professor Laurent… I know people speak of me as if I have the habits of an oriental potentate, having girls delivered up to me, but really (really) it's only that I'm so frightened—that is why I have the"—he made the gesture which indicated the circle of protective aunts. "I understand some men, most, most?—enjoy the chase, it's a bit like hunting—my uncle took me hunting once—stick to the subject!—the flirtatious smiles, the winks and nods—the first caresses—you see, I comprehend it all very well, it's just carrying it out that I find so—

"Anyhow, all along, I have congratulated—that's too strong a word, no—on organizing my affairs in a way that disdained the conventions of bourgeois life, but in some ways I was like the banker who has a wife for whom he feels a sort of fond contempt— The girls often strike me as silly, hysterical, gullible—of course they are!—they are little more than children, and fobbed off on—I like to think that in years to come, the memory of my flesh, my pasty flesh, its boils—I have terrible boils, on my back!—my rank odors—will disappear from their memories, that I'll become—ah, sort of like a marble statue, that they'll be able to say—perhaps to their confidants, perhaps only to themselves—that they were once lovers with a member of the Academy—"

"The Academy?"

"Ah, I shouldn't have, I feel that I'm going to tempt the fates by saying, not official, no, but my friends assure me that it's in the bag. I'm a ghoul!" he almost shouted, but seemed well pleased with himself. "The poor worthy scholar isn't dead yet, although—the others engage in deathbed machinations so if one doesn't—"

Jacques would be in a foul humor for weeks—months!—over Laurent getting the place he craved. She both pitied her husband and felt a pleasure in the revenge she would take upon him, now doubled.

"Ah, but the Academy, that's not, I merely, I—I console myself for the wrongs I have done these young women, for the paucity of my, the poorness of my skills as a lover, the fact that I am no Adonis, with the hope that I will provide them, if with but scant immediate pleasure, then with some retrospective pleasure— And yet, my analyst—well, he believes it all stems from my childhood, of course he does—my father was not married to my mother. He had another family, two children who were not dressed in hand-me-downs, who walked down the street hand-in-hand with their papa. My father gave me gifts on my saint's day, and I treasured— A cardboard theater, hand-painted, I realize now it must have been made by Orientals because the eyes of the princes and queens were quite round and their noses enormous, as we are seen through their eyes. It's a bit like the perspective I'm trying to get—oh, never mind, I'm going too far afield, I have a tendency to do that at the best of times and when I am nervous (nervous!) I do it even more." His jaw moved as if he were indulging in the American habit of chewing gum and he lit a cigarette, despite already having one going, realized his error and stubbed it out.

"Laurent, I do not mean—"

"Pierre!"

"Pierre." She laid her hand on his arm. "I do not mean to be rude. But you—I am wondering if there is some point you are driving at."

"Yes! Yes! There is a point I am driving at, there is. I am trying—I am sorry, I don't do well when I get interrupted, I feel rather as if an electrical connection has been short-circuited."

"Take a deep breath."

"Yes, that's a very good idea. There is a point I am making. About how I both longed for my father and deeply resented—hate, it isn't too strong a word, hate. For the pain he caused my mother. For his duplicity, the promise that he would someday make her—and me—

legitimate. And so—this is what my analyst says, that I identified with my mother and, and—it is surprising that I didn't become a homosexual," and here Laurent shuddered. "Oh, I find the thought rather frightening. The idea of—men. They are so big, and—hairy. I am rather hairy myself, but then I don't have to look at —

"And to sum up…?"

"Ah, Simone, I should like to have you with me always, when I wandered off you could whisper in my ear—" He dropped his voice: "'Laurent!'" then raised it again, "Rather, rather, 'Pierre, Pierre,' and I would return to the subject at hand. Citizens of ancient Rome had a slave—called a nomenclator (nomenclator!)—who whispered in their ear the names of those they encountered. You could be like that, only whispering in my ear to remind me what I am talking about."

"If I knew what you were talking about." Then: "I do not believe that you came here to talk about ancient Rome."

"There was another whispering slave. During victory processions, he would whisper *Sic transit gloria mundi*, 'All worldly glory is fleeting.'"

"The time you and I have together is fleeting—"

"Let me get back to the point I was making—" He held his index finger in the air, "Ancient Rome, whispering slaves, ah, yes, you whispering in my ear to keep me on the subject, and the subject was, it was, my father, and the fear I have of being a man, perhaps a boy having his first love affair—although the first time my uncle took me to a brothel I wept, I was so frightened—which is why I consort with those girls. My analyst asked me the other day if I could imagine myself with a woman roughly my own age, someone with some experience of the world, I right away thought of you—you, you!"

He saw that Simone was attempting to say something, and rushed ahead before she could do so.

"I would have told you all this before, before, but that Anne-Marie was here, and— I went right from my analyst—straightaway!—to meet with Dr. Nalson, and that was when, was when I saw your file—and it seemed—ah, I don't believe in a God who rigs coincidences, I don't believe in God at all, and if I did I wouldn't believe in one who—but nonetheless— Sometimes I glimpse another sort of reason—I was speaking of this last week, last week, when I visited, when I talked about the Alpine hike—I can see it in the distance, as one sees dark shapes in the sky, not sure, not sure if it is a flock of birds or cinders. As some great-grandfather of Socrates, some Athenian who planted the saplings in the marketplace, that later grew into the grove of olive trees Socrates walked beneath—must have had an intimation of the dawn of reason."

"Yes," Simone said, with such sonority that he ceased speaking for nearly thirty seconds.

Twirl

Then he said, "When we walked by the river, you wore—do you remember what you wore?—a dress of deep purple. And you twirled."

"I twirled?"

"You wanted to show me something about the cut—is that what it is called, the cut?—of the skirt, you twirled." And he stood up and demonstrated, arms scissored against his bosom, a backwards glance at the imaginary skirt as he spun. The question crossed Simone's mind: Who would he have been had he been born the other sex?

"You were—you had been drinking champagne and you were a bit—well, certainly not drunk, but lightheaded — I think as much with anger—you had just had a row with Jacques—as with the champagne."

"The row with Jacques—that I don't recall. But there were so many quarrels. I still have that dress." If Marie-Claire had her way, that overstuffed armoire of Simone's would long since have been weeded out, the impractical, no-longer-worn garments given to some charity shop where they might increase the quantity of good in the world rather than just molder. "Shall I put it on for you?"

"Would you? Would you twirl?"

"I doubt if I can twirl," she said as she rose, using her arms to push herself up. She added, "But I will try." She had become an anthropologist of the tribe of the normal, and knew that this word, "try," when used by an invalid, exercised an almost talismanic power over them.

Laurent noticed, as she walked towards the bedroom that her gait was odd, a bit flat-footed, almost like a petulant child making a show of displeasure. He stared quite unselfconsciously at her feet, and then himself began to walk back and forth in front of the settee, becoming aware of how he shifted his weight onto the ball of one foot as he simultaneously brought the heel of his other foot down—what a complicated business was this walking, how little heed he had paid it until this moment. Yes, and the more he thought about it, the more difficult it became. In French, to be stupid is to think *avec ses pieds*, with one's feet, or to be *bête comme ses pieds*, as foolish as one's feet, but it seemed to Laurent that there was a wisdom that lived in one's heels and arches, in the sinews and bones of the foot, perhaps even in its callouses and bunions. He must make a note of this, it was exactly this type of insight he had been hoping to gain by coming here. He stubbed his cigarette out on the heel of his shoe and set the butt on the side table. It tumbled to the floor. He felt about in his pockets, finding a stump of a pencil and a piece of paper which had been carried about for so long that its texture had become velvety. He scrawled, "March, walk, attention, difficult," underlining the word difficult twice with such force that he broke the lead in the pencil, and was unable to add the words he'd intended, *bête comme ses pieds*. He thrust the paper and useless pencil back into his pocket as Simone returned, not wearing the purple dress but carrying it slung over her arm, a hunter returning to camp carrying prey.

(It is this cigarette butt, a Balto, that Jacques will find on the floor and toss into the ashtray, making nothing of it, not seeing it as evidence of his wife's betrayal, the unthinkable being simply that.)

Trying not to be obvious about what she was doing, she leaned against the victrola before shaking the dress out. (She could no longer perform the action of standing at the foot of the bed and rippling the comforter in the air to shake out its wrinkles. Such an action caused her to fall flat on her fanny.) The shaking filled the air with thousands upon thousands of motes of lint, which caught in the light streaming through the high windows and formed a shimmering halo. She sat down on the settee and removed her shoes. "I undress for doctors now." That medical ritual of being given a gown—the word strikes her as mocking, surely she could not show up in one of those shrouds at any fancy dress ball without causing a ripple of horror to course through the gathering. The color of these garments was no doubt officially described as white but was in fact a pale, pale grey. These sacks had covered one diseased body after another, male, female, old, young, the halt, the lame. In between wearings, they were laundered by armies of dour women, inmates who had become trusties, who clumped along the corridors, flat-footed, slack-jawed, gathering up piles of these discarded garments, trundling them down to the cellars where they, along with sour-smelling sheets and rags, were immersed in vats of boiling water.

She said: "It's a strange ritual, almost religious in nature. One goes into a little cell, changes into a shift. The doctor will see your body, but the notion of getting undressed in front of him seems quite scandalous—one wouldn't dare to suggest it. Often, I can't manage the business myself—there are always a plethora of ties that have to be fastened in the back, difficult, I imagine, for even the youngest and most limber. Some handmaiden asks, in a voice either disgruntled or condescending, 'Will Madame be able to manage?'"

"Will Madame be able to manage?" Laurent asked, and without waiting for her to answer, began to unbutton the fine buttons at her throat. Then he laid the palm of his left hand against her throat.

The memory of her hand against Alain's throat, his pulse.

Laurent said: "I touch the flesh on your neck, and if I can forget the things I have been taught to think about the flesh of an aging woman's neck—I'm sorry! I'm sorry! I'm so terribly sorry! I've—"

"It's all right," she said. "It's the truth. I am an aging woman."

"It's just that because of the way I arrange things, the poor young girls, they have to look at me—"

She had gone right on talking while he was speaking: "One reaches a certain—point in one's life and one no longer has assignations in the afternoon, or if so one makes certain that the curtains are drawn—"

"Occasionally I've caught sight of myself in a mirror, when I'm on top of them, I look like a basset hound, a basset hound having an epileptic fit, perhaps—"

"And then even that light seems too harsh, one couples under cover of darkness—"

"No, it isn't all right. I've offended you, I've hurt you—"

"Suppose we didn't love one another—in the way that we've learned that such relations must be conducted. Suppose—"

"Yes, yes! If I could just look at your neck, see it as it is!" he said. "The flesh of your neck. The fine wrinkles and frank lines."

"I sometimes feel," Simone said, "that I've been exiled from the kingdom of the well. I live beyond the city gates."

"Yes, this is what I want. I want to go someplace strange with you. Someplace that isn't—that isn't of the everyday world—"

She would have liked to undress coyly, to undo a button, then give a half-glance upwards, but she needed to focus all her attention on the mechanics. Her fingers objected to the task set before them. At the Salpêtrière, she had been told about a dressmaker who specialized in making garments for invalids—skirts with elastic waistbands, easy-to-grasp buttons: the nurse would have been more than happy to give her the contact information. "Thank you," Simone had said, "but I think not. 'Vanity of vanities, saith the Preacher, vanity of vanities; all is vanity.'"

The nurse had guffawed. That's a hoot! You being vain!

Free of her outer clothes at last, she stood, aware of how dingy her nylon slip had become, of the mended ladders in her stockings.

She pulled the dress on, relieved to discover that it still fit her—if anything, it was a bit looser than it had been the last time she wore it.

"Laurent, I need your help." She turned her back to him, gathering her hair up in her arms.

"Pierre."

"Pierre."

"Ah, just to, just to zipper you up."

She felt the fastening of the metal teeth rippling up her spine, his one hand on the base of the opening, at the place where the small of her back gave way to her rump. As Laurent moved the zipper up her spine, she felt each set of teeth engaging, became aware of every millimeter of flesh as the metal slider moved over it, was aware, too, of Laurent's fingers, how, despite their thinness, they were well-muscled. She won't be surprised, later on, at how deftly he will move them inside of her.

And then the cold metal slider touched her neck, resting against the bare flesh.

The heat of her body reawakened the smells that had lain dormant within this dress for years: old perfume, the acrid scent her body had given off during her menses, the apple blossom scented powder with which she had dusted herself after her bath. For so many years she had spun fantasies about the future, whiling away the time while she stared out the window on train rides, lay in bed waiting for sleep. Now, she called up the past, pretending she could still walk along cobblestone streets in heels, that she could whirl before a man with whom she had snuck away from a gathering, a man whose kiss tasted of red wine and sardines, a man whose tongue thrust into her while she arched her back and moaned, "No, no," a word that meant itself and also its opposite.

And then she let go of her hair: falling, the thick tresses on top, the fine hairs at her neck. She turned, flat-footed, a cumbersome about-face towards him and smiled. She would never twirl again. (In Istanbul she had seen the whirling dervishes, spinning like tops set going by the hand of God. The next morning, back at the villa, after Luc had left for the day, she had locked the bedroom door and turned and turned, but had felt no closer to God, only dizzy and foolish.) She wished she could still spin, she wished she could still wear heels—*talons hauts* the French call them, with the suggestion that they nab prey. She would have liked to feel the heels causing her back to curve, suggesting the arch of sexual pleasure, the organs inside shifting so her body was touching itself from within, but she could no longer manage the complications of walking or even of standing in heels, the stresses that would be put on the bones of her feet, almost as delicate as the bones of a songbird.

"I should be wearing stilettos with this dress, but alas—"

"My ayah walked in bare feet. In Phnom Penh (Penh), when I was a boy, on nights when I could not sleep because of the heat, she would take me into the native districts, down to the riverbanks. I would ride on her shoulders, pretending she was a horse and I a knight, and cry out, 'Faster, faster,' while the natives reached up, wanting to touch my blonde hair, my curls. Not barefoot then, no, she was wearing cloth shoes. 'Faster, faster,' I'd cry, rocking myself against the nape of her neck. Paper boats with candles in them traveled down the river, and when there was no breeze blowing, she would say, 'I will make the wind,' and blow on my face. And then I would fall asleep in her arms, and outside the door of the house she would slip off her shoes, her little cloth shoes and pad to our room in her bare feet."

One

When Simone was alone she'd gaze into the middle distance for hours and think nothing but 1=1, staring at that marvelous equation, the seed of the universe.

Albert

But now Laurent unwound her, set her going like a tightly coiled spring unloosed: "You cannot imagine how, in the absence of external stimuli—all that bustle and hurry with which I once filled up my life—whose party we had been invited to and whose party we had not been invited to, the manuscript that needed to be typed for the printer, the young poet from the provinces who had to be brought into our fold, our love affairs, the ending of our love affairs, chopping onions, stitching up fallen hems, reading the latest novels—how, now, in my isolation, my body has become what the world once was. I listen to it as I used to listen to symphonies: The spasm of pain that shoots through my right calf—for no reason I can fathom—is like the cello player tuning his instrument, hitting the wrong note. Sometimes I think that if these sensations were speeded up, they would become beautiful, they would make sense—not medically, but as a piece of music makes sense.

"I used to have a victrola. We sold it to a second-hand dealer, the flat's so full of stuff." She had stopped herself from saying, *and when we tried to maneuver the wheelchair around, it really became quite impossible.* Stopped herself, because she still had her pride, and would rather not have Laurent know that she had spells where things got so bad she could no longer walk. She also stopped herself from saying, "You remember that old victrola, it was in the sitting room in Juan-les-Pins, we listened to Caruso on it the first night you came with Jacques," because she remembered just in time that while in many ways Laurent is Albert—in fact, Albert's name could be made from Laurent, well, almost—both men having those nimbuses of curly hair surrounding their heads, dandelions gone to seed, and also a similar haphazard relationship to the things of this world—that it had not been Laurent who had been in the parlor that night, listening to Caruso as one of the other guests exclaimed over and over again, "A miracle!" As in a dream, he was both himself and someone else.

"Sometimes, I would be alone in the dismal flat where I lived with my son and daughter before Jacques and I wed, they would be at school, and I would crank the victrola very fast, the voices on the recordings would speed up, they would sound like cartoon characters, very high-pitched, comical. And sometimes I would allow the mechanism to wind down, and then they would be monks singing dirges, growing deeper and slower until they gave out. At the time I had no idea why I was doing such a thing. I suppose we all have queer little activities we undertake when we are alone—but now it seems that perhaps I was preparing myself for this period of my life, for this new relationship with time. Do you think I am mad?"

"No. Not mad!"

And then, like a boy diving into a cold pond, he plunged the shucked mollusk of his tongue into her mouth, his action both annoying—could he possibly think this was pleasurable for her, this thrust, without any sweet layering?—and also, somehow, touching—like a child who presents his mother with a gift he has made certain she will love it since it has come from his hands.

He lunged from her throat to her cunt, happy to discover that she had not bothered with underpants. He lapped greedily at her sex.

"Ah, Pierre," she murmured, and then when he did not respond to that, laid a firm hand on his shoulder.

He poked his head out from the swathing of her skirts.

"You don't want, you don't want…?"

"Yes, I want to make love with you. But please, slow down."

"Slow down. Slow down." He hung his head, a chastised schoolboy.

"Ah, Pierre," she said, "I don't mean to cause you pain—when you write, you tease the reader, don't you? You don't give him everything on the first page, you throw out hints, you introduce a theme, just with a few words, a fleeting image, something you will slowly develop… "

He screwed up his face, a man cogitating. "I am trying to translate the one practice to the other. It seems a frightful amount of work. Not, that you aren't worth—only that one doesn't ordinarily associate labor that is, that is, with, with — or does one?"

"When you draw a circle, with your fingertips or with your tongue, my body yearns for the center of that circle to be touched. Wait," she said, and pulled away from him, rose to her feet, turned her back to him, lifted her hair from the nape of her neck. He unzipped the dress, the dress he had so recently zipped up and she pulled it off, allowed it to crumple onto the floor. Then, embarrassed by the dinginess of her slip and bra, she removed them.

"I'm afraid you will be repulsed by my body," she confessed.

"I may be. I am used to the bodies of young girls. But I think my—" he stopped, looked upwards, as if there were a dictionary engraved on the inside of his skull.

"Is 'curiosity' the word you are looking for?"

"'Curiosity' is not quite right, but I suppose it will do for now. If it's possible to combine curiosity with-with-with-ah-ah—"

"What is the word you are stopping yourself from saying?"

"Love."

"Are you flattering me?" she asked. She expected him to lob a remark back at her as one propelled a tennis ball back across the net at an opponent—an opponent one did not necessarily want to best.

"No! I am not, not, not flattering you. I am no good at such things."

The sofa was awkward, too small, the horsehair padding made her flesh itch, she had to splay her right leg against the back, the bed would have been far less cumbersome, but making love with Laurent there would have been too much of a betrayal of Jacques.

"If you stroke your hand towards my nipple, but don't actually touch my breast yet—"

"Ah, yes, and then I do!"

"No, you must make me wait for it, make me yearn for it, make me feel that I am going to go mad with the desire to be touched."

"It seems, it seems—unkind."

"This is how you arouse desire—by withholding. Up to a point."

He did the best he could to follow her instructions, although like a novice learning to drive, oversteering, braking too quickly, he had not yet had the knowledge of lovemaking sink into his body.

And then he came. Not having entered her, still in his trousers, crying out, "Oh, no, oh no," a naughty boy, messing himself. "I'm sorry. Oh, I'm so sorry."

She held him in her arms, "It's all right. These things happen."

"I'll do better next time. I promise I will. Will there be a next time?"

"Of course," she said. "Of course."

He had said the word "love" to her. Luc had said this word to her too, at first passionately and then as if he were yielding a grappling hook. When Jacques said it to her, he pronounced it with a wry intonation. Simone was certain that Jacques also spoke this word to Dominique, although without those inverted commas around it. Simone imagined that it was only after her death, when Dominique would advance from the position of dowager mistress to wife, that Jacques would say the word "love" to Dominique with an almost amused intonation, with a wink so slight as to be almost imperceptible.

Pierre had simply said it.

They would make love six times altogether, if you count this first encounter, although it included neither penetration nor her orgasm. And it seemed to Simone that the sight of him with his messy trousers, his hang-dog face, brought them closer than a successful encounter would have done. For five more Thursdays he would show up, a few minutes after Marie-Claire left for the afternoon.

One

All during the week she thought of Laurent. She did not think about Laurent, about his strange ways of speaking, about his tales of riding on his nursemaid's shoulders, neither did she yearn for him. The thought was simply "Laurent," as she sometimes thought: 1=1.

Laurent

Did Laurent think of her?

Yes.

Sometimes in the night he would be awoken—a rhythmic pounding coming from up above that might have been lovemaking or a pimp beating up his whore—and her image would be in his mind. At odd moments when he was walking—he often became so restless while writing that there was nothing for it but to set out through the city streets—he would think of her, a smile of pleasure curling at his lip, congratulating himself on becoming (or almost so) a full-fledged man, one who was able to carry out relations in an ordinary manner, might even be experiencing this state he had so often read of, being in love.

On one such trek, he encountered Jacques.

"Where are you off to in such a rush?" The ordinary words were imbued with amused disdain, which seemed to extend beyond Laurent to all of the human race and then to the end of the universe.

"I-I-I-am not going anywhere, nowhere in particular that is," and he flushed, terrified that he might blurt out, *I'm not heading for your flat, if that's what you're thinking.* "I have been writing"—and he pulled out the pages he had stuffed into his pocket and held them before Jacques, evidence. "I hope you'll excuse me if I rush off (rush off), I've rather a difficult passage in mind," he tapped his temple.

Jacques gave one of his half-bows as Laurent trotted off.

I did very well there, I didn't let anything slip. His pride at having kept mum gave way to a deeper satisfaction, the knowledge that he was cuckolding this smug man, a pleasure not completely distinguishable from his love for Simone.

Alarm

How odd for Simone that life went on as before. The rituals of the day. The clatter of Jacques' alarm. Marie-Claire moving about the kitchen. The smells of coffee, tobacco, fresh bread. On fine days, Simone was set before an open window as if she were musty bedding being aired. The weekly visit from the masseur. The end of the day, the lugubrious tread of Jacques' footsteps on the stairs, the patter of Marie-Claire's feet as she rushed to turn off the radio: M. Melville preferred to enter a silent flat. And after all, the news of late always bad—the French army trapped at Dien Bien Phu, America teetering on the brink of fascism, acts of sedition not just in Casablanca, but in Marrakech, Fez, Rabat.

Curve

The next time Simone and Laurent made love, they did so in the bedroom. The sofa was simply too ungainly. She led him in there, willing to have him see the collection of pill bottles and tinctures on her nightstand, intermingled with her skin creams and hair ointments.

On account of Simone's awkward gait, they couldn't manage to walk with their arms around each other. Instead, Simone walked a step or two in front of him, and he set his open palm in the small of her back. In French, the phrase is *la cambrure des reins*, the kidney's curve.

This is how he will return to her in the years to come: the physical memory of the slight pressure of his open palm resting at that place where the hard back curves into the soft rump. The human back—broad, brute, supplied with relatively few nerve endings, the place on which our kind, when we have no beasts of burden to carry our loads, bear what must be borne. Then the armor of our rib cage ends, the hank of nerves cast up through the back is gathered together, and our tender kidneys dangle beneath the other internal organs, vulnerable.

This

Decades later, Simone will have forgotten her smatterings of English and German and nearly all her French as well. The words she learned first—mama, ball, duck, cup—aren't the last to go, the words for things that can be touched. At the very end are the words that seem to be spun into a web like a spider's, thin but sticky words with definitions that take up whole pages in the dictionary—this, here, now, some.

Sometimes Frédéric's wife, having trudged up the stairs—ah! those six flights of stairs!—will enter smelling of resentment and exhaustion and the onions and fish heads in her string bag. She will kneel down before her mother-in-law (she will feel a certain kindred spirit with her, both belonging to the sorority of betrayed wives), and say, "How was your day?" And Simone will incline her head almost imperceptibly towards the sound. Time will move with glacial slowness. She will respond to the question she has been asked with a single word, "*Ce*," this. It will take her more than an hour to purse her lips, another hour or so to move her tongue forward and then draw it back: by the time she has finished uttering the word, her step-daughter-in-law will have made the stock from the fish heads and sour white wine, chopped the cabbage, stewed it all together, run it through a food mill, will be sitting slumped in a kitchen chair, rubbing her aching bare feet, muttering to herself, "Well, I suppose my illustrious father-in-law can't be bothered to telephone when he's going to be late." She will hear the slow expulsion of air from between Simone's lips, but will not realize it is part of a word, it will just seem like one of those sounds that escape from the leaky bag of an old woman's body. Still less will she realize that Simone has said the word "this": that all day she had been remembering the feel of Laurent's hand on the small of her back, as they walked across this room towards the bedroom. This.

There

Other times, when she said "*Là*," there, she was seeing her husband Luc buffing his engineering tools with a chamois cloth before returning them to their leather and mahogany cases. The scene will unfold over the course of hours. ("Slowly, slowly," she had whispered in Laurent's ear.) Luc, in this recollection, was not her first husband, a man who occupied a long-past place in the narrative of her life, but came to her as he had actually been at those moments when, not yet nineteen, she had appeared in the doorway of his study late at night, wearing her cream-colored frock with the blue sash pulled tightly around her tiny waist, and saying, "It's late," by which they both understood her to mean, *Please, come to bed, make love to me, I can't bear waiting for you* and he would look at his wife, giving her a look of tenderness tinged with a desire to see her suffer. He would meet her gaze with a steadiness that made her feel all the wilder, and then he would return to buffing his instruments, while Simone lingered in the doorway.

Back

But it was not yet 1961, 1965, 1972, those years when time slowed to lead.

Simone was entering the bedroom, walking ahead of Laurent, his hand grazing the tender indentation of her back.

Laurent sat bolt upright after they had made love and said:

"Well, I—do you mind if I smoke?" He picked up his clothing from the floor, patted the pockets of his shirt and pants, then patted them again, as if they might suddenly have fruited a pack of cigarettes.

She offered him one from her pack, lying on the nightstand.

"Ah, no, no, I prefer, I prefer—" and he shambled off into the front room. She heard him mousing about for his own pack.

She was alone.

He had left her behind for hours, for weeks. She waited for him to come back for decades, for a century. *He's not coming back, that Jacques of yours*, her long-dead mother said: the voice of an ancient oracle, her words echoing off the craggy rocks of time. *Coming back. Back. Back.*

The walls of the room receded. It was many, many kilometers between the bed and the door, the nightstand and the bed. Kilometers was the wrong unit of measurement: these gaps needed to be measured in leagues, fathoms, cubits, *pieds du roi*: distances based on the length of a man's forearm, on his stride.

He came back. Naked, a cigarette dangling from his lips, his penis and balls dangling from between his legs, his forelock dangling over his brow. He came back as if his leaving had been quite inconsequential, as if he had not been gone forever, as if he had merely gone into the other room for a pack of cigarettes. He came back, his body parting time before him, as Moses had parted the waters of the Red Sea. He came back, bringing with him the gift of ordinary time, time as other mortals lived it, seconds flowing smoothly, one-two-three-four, on up to sixty, the sixty seconds adding up to a minute, the clocks all across Paris agreeing: this is a minute, one-sixtieth of an hour, finite, logical.

Stilettos

She waited, she waited and waited and waited, it seemed that Thursday would never come, that she could not bear the waiting, but she bore the waiting because she had no choice but to bear the waiting.

Thursday did, at last, come.

Marie-Claire, as ordered, fetched Simone's stilettos from the closet, then polished them with her apron, a determined Aladdin rubbing a lamp from which a genie stubbornly refused to appear, muttering aloud about their impracticality, silently about the sin of vanity, making Simone promise not to attempt to walk in them. She knelt before her mistress with the look of pained sanctimoniousness Christ exhibits washing the feet of his disciples in Giotti's painting.

Much to Simone's disappointment, Laurent did not seem to notice her shoes. When it was time for them to make their weekly sortie into the bedroom, she asked him to remove them for her. Once again, someone was kneeling at her feet. He, of course, didn't have the look of pious resentment Marie-Claire had exhibited. Simone had thought he might love her feet, that he might have stroked and caressed them, might even have bestowed a row of kisses along the outer ridge, marveled at the tenderness of her soles, so rarely walked on. Perhaps he would once again speak of his ayah's feet, might even suck her toes one by one, as if they were ten miniature phalluses.

But he did none of those things.

Her shoes off, they merely marched into the bedroom, and he began to remove his clothing in a husband-like manner. When he took off his shirt, he released such an acrid odor that Simone started.

He explained about the radio lectures and the effort required of him to speak like ordinary men. He left and washed with Jacques' soap, returning, smelling of both himself and Jacques. He yanked her blouse and skirt free and, having grappled her onto the bed, dove into her, not bothering to remove her garters and stockings. Later she would recall this as a the day when Laurent, aflame with passion (the language she had to describe this was that of romantic novels), could not wait for her to undress, was so wild that he took her almost like those men who bought a girl on the street and then had her against a brick wall in an alley. But at the moment, she was aware of the garter's cutting into her skin, the twist of the nylon stockings against the top of her thigh.

He dozed afterwards, which he had never before done. Actually, dozed was too mild a word—he fell quite soundly asleep. At first she found it to be a new level of intimacy, the sight of his mouth lolling open, the smell of him growing slightly damper and more fetid as he slept, the unaccustomed stillness of his body, but soon he began to snore, and she felt her precious time with him disappearing into an abyss.

Benzedrine

The clocks chiming two did not wake him, nor did the clocks chiming three, but at the clanging of four he started awake. He was a bit abashed as he rubbed his face and pulled on his trousers, felt about on the nightstand for his glasses. "These lectures for the radio, they are—my philosophy boiled down for the common man—I despise that phrase 'the common man,' I can't quite believe I used it."

She would sound like a shrew were she to say, 'We have so little time together and you slept." So she was silent. Even more of a virago were she to say: 'And now, you can only talk about yourself.'

"So ah, ah, the fact is that I have gotten very little sleep this week. It's quite a bit of work, to write a short talk, it's much easier when one can, when one has, as in a philosophical text, unlimited space to roam, and, and, and—my doctor has prescribed a drug for me, one inhales it, Benzedrine, it is called, have you heard of it?"

"No."

"It's really quite a miracle. A whiff and—I think of Delphi where it was said that vapors came up out of the grounds—one feels rather—not capable of uttering prophecies, no, but quite alive—I suppose one could say it's morphine's opposite, although they say it doesn't have addictive powers, only that one can feel rather superhuman, one can work all through the night and on into the next day and—" He looked at her finally, and taking in the look on her face, said, "I'm sorry."

"We have so little time together." She felt like a scold. And because she already felt like a scold, she went on to say, "So little time together, and you slept." She laid her hand on his chest—he had put his shirt on but not yet buttoned it, she could feel his heart, rat-a-tat-tat: "You can't imagine what they mean to me, your visits, how, how—terribly lonely—I know I sound self-pitying, still, it's a fact, my life is—it's terribly constrained, and your love, your love—"

He sat down on the bed and began to weep, quite without restraint. Luc had never wept in front of her, Jacques only once when his father died. He at least had the decency to go into the toilet, closing the door behind him and opening the taps, the water mostly drowning out the sound of his sobs. A few of her lovers had cried in front of her, and she had always found it not just unmanly, but an unwanted intimacy, physically off-putting, as if they had hawked phlegm from the backs of their throats. At first she simply stared at the weeping figure of Pierre, half-dressed, bent over almost in the pose of Rodin's The Thinker. She was not sure of how long she stared at him, her mouth slightly agape.

"Won't you at least offer me some comfort?"

She continued to stare at him, immobile.

"Some, some comfort."

"I am not your mother. Neither am I your ayah."

At this he wept all the harder, no longer cradling his brow against the heel of his hand, but wrapping his arms about his shoulders and rocking back and forth.

She laid a reluctant hand on his shoulder, said the only words she could think of to say, "There. There, there."

"Why are you being so cold to me?"

"I must speak frankly. I am unaccustomed to such—displays."

"No, I suppose, I suppose, one can't imagine your, your, your Jacques carrying on in such a fashion—"

She stopped herself from saying, as she would have said in the past with other lovers, "If you don't mind, I prefer the spheres of my life to be separate."

"I-I-I-perhaps I am frightening you? I think, think, think I am also frightening myself." A slight shaking had been added to the repertory of his usual tics and spasms. "Perhaps I have never really been in love before. This may be the madness of love of which, of which, of which the classical poets spoke. I am sorry," he wiped the hollows beneath his eyes dry with the heels of his hands. "I am terribly sorry, terribly sorry for carrying on so, I can see that—that it is putting us on rather a bad footing."

It struck her that her aura of chilliness was the attitude that her husband must often have adopted towards flighty women.

He began to pat his pockets, lifting his shirt up from the floor.

"Your cigarettes are there," she indicated the night stand with a jut of her chin. His watch was next to them, it read a quarter past four.

"No, it is that Benzedrine inhaler I was looking for, I thought it might, it might—I feel quite despondent. Just, I'll be right back—"

He came back, sniffling, with an object that looked like a lipstick tube in his hand. "There, that's better. It's quite miraculous, this drug, a sort of penicillin for the soul. My doctor says not to worry, that it has no untoward effects, but those who are more at home in the world of, in the world of drugs, medicinal and otherwise, say this is nonsense, that one always pays the piper. I fear that this untoward display of emotions you just witnessed may have been the result, the aftereffect of my indulgence—

"It seems to me to be the refutation to Cartesian notions of the separation between the mind and the body: we imbibe a substance and it alters us. A glass of wine, a glass of wine tilts our soul, not to mention, the more drastic effects of this little device," he said, holding up the inhaler as if he were an emperor and this his scepter.

"No," Simone said. "You must not use it again. You must not."

"Ah, my dear Dr. Melville. I shall do as you command."

Gods

In her life on the other side of the divide, she would have shown her displeasure to a paramour who behaved as Laurent did, perhaps by failing to meet him for a planned assignation, later whispering to him when they happened to find themselves at the same gathering, "Sorry, I simply couldn't get away," indicating her husband with a nod of her head. Now, in her invalid's life, her vexation was no less, but she didn't hold the belief anymore that she could, through force of character, through will, alter her path—indeed, such a belief seemed a delusion to her. Life was made of happenstance. Jacques had fallen in love with her because she was wearing Elise's dress of sky-blue linen that filled with wind. Marcel had come home because a passing American had given him a lift. Laurent had happened to see her file on Dr. Nalson's desk.

When she first received the unwelcome gift of her diagnosis, she had wished for a way to make sense of it. She would have liked to believe in an Old Testament God who meted this out as retribution for sin, or a Christian God who gave it to lead her to redemption. Or a pagan god—some spirit of a spring or a glade or craggy mountain peak whom she'd inadvertently offended by cutting down a sapling or kicking loose a rock, who had avenged himself with this curse. But her disease had taught her there was no way of making sense of this.

Thursday

Thursday.

After they had made love, he propped the bed pillows behind him, wrapped his arms around her. She leaned her head against his chest and felt his heart rate increase, was aware of him swallowing hard.

At last he blurted out: "I have, I hope you won't think I have betrayed you, I have been talking with Jacqueline—don't worry! don't worry!—I haven't mentioned your name. I have told her about the circumstances, that is, that you are a married woman—Don't worry, I have been most circumspect—but I have begun, I have begun—about, the practicalities—"

"What practicalities? I don't know what you are talking about."

He looked crestfallen "Ah, you don't, you don't? I am sorry. I have presumed too much. Perhaps I was premature (premature). I told you, I don't know how to manage these things."

"Laurent, I don't know what you are talking about."

"Pierre! There would be many practicalities to consider, if—of course, the hotel rooms where I reside would be completely out of the question, a flat—I actually—I saw a sign, 'To Let,' and then the specifics, it was a ground floor flat—a ground floor flat!"

She smiled. Although her face was becoming more and more of a mask, she could, with effort, force her old expressions. "You are asking me to leave my husband, my husband of over two decades?"

"I suppose, well, yes. Am I asking too much? I told Jacqueline—she by the way would be willing to offer assistance, to undertake the obligations that are customarily undertaken by the father, of the—well, the groom— That is to see, to see that we are—to the establishment of a household. Don't worry! I didn't mention your name!"

"So you are proposing to me?"

"Proposing, it has such a formal sound. As if I should get down on one knee…I don't know. Goodness, I never thought of that actual possibility. A wedding? Although I suppose, I suppose, if that was what you wanted, I would of course. You wouldn't want a church wedding, would you? Do you think Jacques will be angry?"

"Let's imagine our life. I need you to help me. It is the hardest thing about my current state: that my thought has become so concrete."

He imagined out loud the rooms they might move into: perhaps a warren-like flat, oddly-shaped rooms opening onto other oddly-shaped rooms. Or an enfilade where doors slid open from one room to reveal another room of the exact same size and shape, with another set of sliding doors revealing yet another identical room.

They would hire someone else to care for her. Not Marie-Claire, who belonged to this old life.

"Could the new girl change the sheets every day?"

"Ah, you see, we are so alike, alike! On the days they change the sheets in the hotels—only every other week—when I sleep on clean sheets, ah! Jacqueline will get us fine sheets, fine, fine linen."

And their flat would be on the ground floor. The masseur will be relieved, no longer having to lug that table up six flights of stairs. Might Laurent be allowed to watch while the masseur works on her? He would, he confesses, find that exciting.

Yes, he could watch, but he would have to be discreet.

"Might I, might I undress you for him? I will undo that row of tiny buttons stretching from your throat to the notch below your collarbone. I will reach the notch just below your neck, where the bone—what do you call that bone?—the bone that the ribs grow out of?— We will learn, we will learn, the names of all the bones, won't we?"

"*Le sternum,*" Simone said.

"Yes, of course! Of course it is the sternum!"

"I don't much like that name."

"No! In English it is the breastbone. Breastbone. That is a much more pleasing name. Because it smacks of impossibility: breast and bone, the two words together. When we do not like the official names of bones, we will find other names," and he reached out and touched her fingers, feeling his way along the fine bones, stroking down, rubbing his thumb and forefinger against her wrist bone. "We will search other languages, we will—I will do it!—I will go to, to, to, libraries and find words from African languages, words from Indochina. I will kneel at your feet and remove your shoes. Your bare feet!

"I told you my ayah, my ayah walked in bare feet. Those complications in relations between master and servant. But I was hardly a master, I was a child, although a white child. I slept in a bed, in a European bed, despite it all, despite having been abandoned by my father, despite living in circumstances that my mother described as 'tenuous'—I often overheard her saying that phrase, 'our circumstances are somewhat tenuous,' sometimes she said, 'our circumstances are becoming even more tenuous,' although I spoke Khmer before I spoke French—I wonder what the word for sternum is in Khmer?—I have forgotten so much. And my ayah—I never knew the poor woman's name!—she slept on a pallet on the floor next to me. And sometimes, at night, I would whimper in fear—she would comfort me, she would not climb into the bed with me, that would have been untoward, she would let me get down on her mat. There was a chamber pot and she would go behind a curtain and squat over it. I remember that sound of her urine hitting the porcelain. And the smell, the smell rising up! I could see her feet beneath the curtain. It will make me happy to remove your shoes, to be there next to your feet, to caress your feet. I would try to peek, and see her pissing—my ayah."

"Would you like to see me piss?"

"Ah, could I?"

"Of course."

"It is the sort of thing I suppose I have always wanted to —but I would never have known how to broach the subject with the *jeunes filles* because—well, I was asking enough of them already."

"Now?" Simone asked.

"Ah, ah, ah, could I?" It was the voice of a child who had been told that as a special favor the calendar had been rejiggered and Christmas was imminent, two weeks earlier than expected. He held out his hand for her to take, he didn't yet understand her body, the fact that she needed to use her arms to push herself into a standing position, that the slight assistance offered by an outstretched palm was quite insufficient.

"Could you — my robe? It is hanging on the hook over there."

She was vain enough that she did not want Laurent to see her from the rear, to see her ass gone squarish and saggy, its dimpled flesh. She had no doubt that it would fill him with disgust, as the sight of his wobbling rear did her.

She plopped herself down on the toilet. "This may be more difficult than I imagined. You want to see it, don't you? But it's hard for me to hover, to hold myself above the seat."

"What if—what if, here, I knelt before you. Here, can you stand up for a moment?"

She leaned her hand against the wall and stood. He placed his arms upon the toilet seat, turning his hands up at the back. She sat down, supported by his hands, her legs spread apart, his face very close to her crotch.

"There, are you all right?"

"Yes, fine, although I'm a bit shy." She was aware, too, that seated like this, she had thin folds of loose flesh at her midsection, and her breasts sagged. She moved her pelvis forward, leaned back, looked away from Laurent's eager face, and staring at the wall, felt the warm piss flowing out of her.

"Ah, yes, yes, yes. Oh, could I ask one more thing?"

She was afraid he was going to ask her to piss in his mouth, and was relieved when what he asked was if he could stand and piss between her legs. "Not on you! No, no, I don't want to do that. Just for you to spread your legs and—"

"Yes," she said, "yes, of course. I will do anything that will give you pleasure."

He pulled his hands out from beneath her rump, she slid down onto the toilet.

"Now, I'm shy."

"Think about something else. It will help—this is something my disease has taught me, sometimes one must play a trick on oneself. Sometimes I have to turn my will elsewhere, and while my will is distracted, my body will do what I need it to do. Although I do ask myself, who is this self who fools the self?

"Let's think about what our lives will be like when we are together, when we live in the flat, when we wake up in the morning together, sunlight flooding into our room—"

"I thought our room was going to be windowless. A grotto—Ah, here it comes. Yes, yes." The stream of urine jetted from him.

She thought: if we hadn't defeated Nazism, it would have collapsed under the weight of its own obsession with health, those rows of blonde *madchen* with their gleaming teeth, doing their jumping jacks (*eins, vei, drei, freir, fumpf*), who must have climbed aboard the their lovers and bounced merrily toward their orgasms. Who could live in a world which made no room for the decadent, the sick?

And then, like Adam and Eve, they were aware of their nakedness, aware of the ridiculousness of it all. Almost at the same moment, they clutched their arms against themselves, rose, Simone straightening her robe around her, and began their journey back to the bedroom.

The bells clanged out the hour. Bong-bong-bong-bong. One church's bell, more mellifluous, was slightly off from another's: din-don, din-don. Despite the cacophony, there was no question: it was then four o'clock, the hour of Laurent's departure.

Bones

Simone and Laurent won't ever move in together, they won't ever hire a maid of all work, they won't ever learn the Finnish word for pubic bone, *häpyluuhun,* nor the Latvian word for backbone, *mugurkaula.*

If they had moved ahead with their alliance, shocked conversations would have been held in bars and at soirées hosted by expatriate American heiresses and the salons of long-deposed Russian nobility where tea was served in chipped cups bearing the imperial crest.

—*Have you heard about Simone Melville and Pierre Laurent*?

—*I simply can't believe it.*

—*Do you know what I heard*? *No, no, it's gossip. I shouldn't repeat it.*

—*Ah, that's cruel. You can't say that and then not…*

—*All right, but you must promise, absolutely promise, that you* won't *repeat it. I heard that—well, you know the sort of machinations that go on with the election to the Academy. I heard that Melville threw his support to Laurent in return for Laurent—*

—Taking Simone off his hands?

Her love for Laurent, his for her, had at its core perversion: something disgusting, unimaginable to the vast majority of their fellow creatures (although each of those fellows felt some equally unspeakable desire). It was radical, subverting not just the established order of society but the personality of the lover.

Thursday

It was three-thirty on the following Thursday when Laurent entered Simone's flat and, in place of a greeting, cried out, "Sally! I have been with Sally, Sally, the American! Do you know she is from Memphis, Tennessee, they do come up with the most marvelous names these Americans, Tennessee, it's an Indian word, Red Indian, that is, of course!—and then they throw in an ancient Egyptian city—"

"Laurent—" She laid a hand on his arm.

"There's a Paris in New York state, and also a Rome"

"Pierre—"

"And Mississippi! Ah, there's a word. Mississippi. Ah, how was it I went off on this tangent—"

"Have you stopped taking the Benzedrine?"

"Ah, not quite."

He looked into her eyes, the look of a wild animal caged. "Soon."

Letter

After he left, she picked up a book from the end table, the most recent Simenon. She tried to read, her eyes moved across the lines of type and then down to the next line, back to the beginning, across, down to the next line, across. She saw each letter, the emptiness within and between and around the letters. After some time had passed—and it seemed she no longer had an internal clock, that she might have been staring at the page for a minute or an hour—recognizing that she had taken in nothing, she shifted her gaze back to the top of the first page, the first letter, the letter 'L,' far larger than the rest of the type that followed it. She stared at it as if she had never before seen the letter 'L,' as one stares at the letters of a foreign alphabet. She knew she should stop thinking about the weight and heft and shape of this letter, that this altogether too concrete thinking was a symptom of her illness, and that it is the duty of every invalid to fight against her illness, not to give in to it, and yet she could not stop thinking about the solid, blank shape of this letter.

The sound of Jacques' footsteps on the stairs. His key entering into the lock. The tumblers turning. The faint moan of the hinges. His cough. His words. "Hello, dear." "Hel.lo." Her voice cut out, like the jammed radio signals during the war. Jacques' kiss on her forehead. Time returning, ordinary time, time as others lived it.

The next of his customary actions, that is, his Thursday customary actions: his left arm slipped around her shoulder, his right hand grasping her right hand, pulling her to her feet, leading her to the toilet. (Marie-Claire, of course, was the one who ordinarily saw to these duties.) When Simone was alone, waiting for him, the stoppage of time was not just a psychological phenomenon but a physical one: she had no sensation of hunger, of thirst, of the need to micturate. Indeed, several times lately Jacques had been horrified to come home and find her lower jaw awash with drool: she had neglected to swallow. But now that Jacques was leading her to the toilet she felt the burning pressure from her full bladder, and tried to hurry, but only succeeded in making her gait stumble-footed.

He was businesslike as he worked at the clasps and zippers of her slacks, tugged them down, along with her underpants.

"Can you…?" he asked.

"Yes, of course," she answered, although it wasn't a foregone conclusion that she would be able to seat herself on the porcelain bowl—it was only on her good days she was able to do so.

Not bothering to hide his distaste for the entire matter, Jacques stepped to the other side of the door and closed it behind him. Ah, if only he had known that night when he stood in the corridor thinking *Knock on her door / don't knock on her door* that it would come to this.

There are no secrets in a marriage of long duration, only things the couple do not speak of, even in the privacy of their own minds.

"I'm done." Then, when he had entered the room again, "My fingers aren't working well today."

They both knew what that meant: that he would have to wrap a ribbon of toilet paper around his hand, like a boxer having his hands taped before a fight, and shove his hand between her legs, dab at her damp folds and creases. She looked away while he did so: he could not have borne to have her look at him while he carried out this act.

Retropulsion

On the following Thursday, Laurent arrived so quickly after Marie-Claire's departure that Simone assumed he hadn't been waiting in the bar across the street but had been lurking about in the hallway.

"Here I am! I am here! Right on time, right on time. I am having a difficult, a most difficult—I think a glass of wine—I'll get it for myself, it will be no problem for me to, for me to, for me to, get it for myself."

"You haven't stopped taking the Benzedrine?"

"No, no, not quite yet." He gulped his wine. "I finished with the radio lectures and I swore to myself—I did try, but I get thrown into the most awful state of despondency, I think my doctor is wrong, and my friends who are addicts are right, one never gets off scot free—it has crossed my mind that perhaps I shall have to go to one of these—facilities—in the countryside, where one more or less becomes a voluntary prisoner, so that one can, kick one's, one's—"

They lay in bed and talked after making love.

During their lovemaking and for half an hour or so afterwards, Laurent's frenetic activity ceased, his finger-tapping, clicks of his tongue against the roof of his mouth, leg-jouncing, and he showed an almost feminine languor.

Simone's head rested on his chest—it still surprised her each time she saw the mat of thick hair there, as if his flesh beneath his clothes was an outfit he had put on for a costume party.

She knew that in a little while, he would pick up his watch from the night table, squint at it, cock his head to the right side and say, "Ah, well. It's getting to be that time…" his gestures as ritualized as those of a priest saying Mass. But that moment had not yet arrived.

They talked without the need for logic, connections, without a fear of repetition. "Why did they have such enormous windows in school rooms if they didn't want us to be staring out of them?" Simone asked.

To which he responded, "It seems almost criminal to say it, but I loved the silence of the city during the occupation. Although it wasn't really silence (silence, silence)—the whirring of bicycle wheels turning, the distant clanging of church bells, the birds in the park."

"Yes," she said.

"When I was a child, riding on my ayah's shoulders, the moon followed me, both my vassal and my protector, pregnant and golden. The moment when—I must have been six years old, seven, I'm not sure, six or—I woke early one morning and stared at my ayah, asleep on her mat next to me. She was dreaming—a smile flickered across her face. The realization that she must sometimes be awake and see me sleeping. The terrible understanding that I was the center only of my own world. That once I had not been, and at some future date I would no longer exist…Ah, ah, ah," he said, and Simone witnessed the return of his ordinary way of being in the world. The light outside had shifted, growing thicker. Soon it would be time for him to leave. "I have not forgotten, not forgotten. Where are my trousers?" He leaned off the bed, his arms bent down, his legs behind him as a rudder, reminding her of a salamander, "Here, here, here," he cried, waving his trousers aloft. "This passage from Heidegger, the one I was referring to earlier, where he speaks of the hand—"

"Ah, you've ripped a page from a book."

"Oh, it's all right. Not to worry! Not to worry! Rosamund comes around and sellotapes them back in for me, I don't know why—why!—when I get excited about a passage I often do that—tear it out and put it in my pocket. Like a child with a toy he can't bear to part with."

She rose naked—she no longer felt the need to disguise her bare flesh from Laurent—and began her flat-footed march towards the chair where she had draped her clothing, but half-way there her body took it upon itself to walk backwards. "Laurent!" she cried, for her body was headed for the wall, but he merely stared at her, mouth agape.

Since her feet were doing the exact opposite of what her mind had ordered them to do, she thought she should try to walk backwards—an exercise they had done in calisthenics at school—but how exactly did one walk backwards? Did one lift one's heel first? Or one's toes? But in the meantime she had reached the wall, and her heels continued on their own, like a child's wind- up toy, banging against the plaster.

"Ah, Simone!" he cried.

"I, I—"

"Hold me!" She called out to Laurent as if she were haling him across a long distance, although he was only a few feet away. "Hold me!"

He did as he was ordered, but her feet still flailed away. "Hit me," she pleaded. "Slap me. Please, please."

He did, but not hard enough.

"Please, harder! Harder."

He slapped her and slapped her and slapped her, and at last her body was shocked enough to stop.

He held her tightly against him, as a frightened child is clutched by its mother, held her so tightly that the next words she spoke were muffled by his shoulder, "I need—I think—I need to sit down."

"Yes, yes, of course," he said, but he did not loosen his grip on her, only moved with her, the two of them making a strange lumbering beast, to the bed. "*Tiens, tiens,*" he whispered into her hair. "There, there." Then, clearing his throat: "Ah, that was, that was—"

"I have frightened you. There is a name for this phenomenon. It is called retropulsion. When I asked the doctor to explain it to me, he said that certain wires got crossed in the brain. And when I protested that there weren't actually any wires in my brain, he said that of course, he was only speaking metaphorically—"

Nonetheless, she had imagined that inside her brain a row of women were sitting before a switchboard, in identical chairs, stretching on past the vanishing point. The operators all had manicured fingernails, ramrod posture, feet crossed at the ankles. Each woman's shoulders were squared and she faced straight ahead, looking neither to her right nor her left as she plugged the jacks into the waiting holes on the board. Although these women kept their heads completely still, they were managing to signal to one another via winks, nudges of their elbows, cockings of their eyebrows. They smirked as they sent her connections skittering off in strange directions. Attempting to telephone God, she was instead connected to a baker in Toulouse. Instead of being put through to the butcher down the street, the call was routed to her long-dead sister or to a puzzled shop assistant who repeated *Madame, I do not understand what it is you want. Madame, you are making no sense.*

Puppet

"I am like a puppet, being moved this way and that by a mad puppeteer. I will my body to go forward and the exact opposite happens."

"Ah, ah, ah! There is a passage in Aristotle. He speaks of paralyzed limbs which when we intend to move them to the right turn instead to the left. Ah, it is nearly an exact illustration of what has just happened with you, with you! And he says that in the souls of incontinent people—but I think we must all be incontinent people— In Greek, the word is *akrasia*. A state of mind in which a man acts on the impulses of pleasure, rather than via rationality—we are all slaves to our bodies, no man could remain continent until he exploded, no matter what his judgment told him. Ah, ah, ah—this is such a fascinating discussion—

but I shall soon have to leave. Will you be all right? Will you start to, to, to retropulse again?"

"My nerves are like the anti-colonial guerrillas in Indochina. They rarely go into battle, staging instead lightning raids."

"Ah, but I have not, have not, have not had the chance to read you the passage from Heidegger."

"Next week," Simone said. "Next week."

No

The next Thursday, he did not come. She waited and waited and waited and went on waiting, but he did not come.

Dam

The following Monday, Jacques entered the apartment in a cloud of ill-will. He kissed Simone on the forehead, and settled into his chair with a sigh. He read for a few minutes, then dozed briefly before dinner. This sleeping before dinner was becoming a habit, although he still said upon awakening: "I seem to have fallen asleep."

He recounted the day's events over supper. A luncheon had been held that day to discuss the wording of a petition to be circulated about the events in Indochina. There had been negotiations—that was a polite word for it, he winked—"a frank and open exchange of views," as diplomats describe a shouting match—about whether the Viet Minh should be described as *the* legitimate voice of the Vietnamese people or *a* legitimate voice. The luncheon at the ostentatious Hotel Meurice. It was something of a joke by the organizers: Ho Chi Minh had once been a pastry chef there. Although, at the rate things are going at Dien Bien Phu—Jacques made a show of giving it the proper Vietnamese pronunciation—this petition by French intellectuals would make little difference.

A brief cesura while he forked food into his mouth, sipped wine.

"Ah, yes, by the way, some very sad news today. Pierre Laurent," and here Jacques paused, brought his napkin to his lip, "has died."

Her fork dropped from her hand, clattered against the plate.

But after all, she frequently dropped things.

A good thing, at the moment, that her face had become a mask.

"What happened?"

"A heart attack—" Jacques jutted out his lower lip, rocked his head slightly from side to side. "Perhaps a stroke. They found him in his room. He'd been dead for a few days. Quite a distasteful—ah, well, this is hardly the time to speak of it."

He returned the conversation to the current situation in Indochina. A few days before, *L'Humanité* had referred to the battle of Dien Bien Phu as one between an elephant and a tiger, the lumbering French the elephant, stuck in their valley, the cries of the wounded rising up to heaven like the mournful bellows of those great animals. And the Viet Minh the tiger, stalking above them, pouncing and retreating.

Laurent was dead.

Jacques found it curious how quickly the image had become a cliché, one heard it everywhere, on trams and in cafés.

Laurent was dead.

One of the participants at the luncheon had been holding forth about the Vietnamese emperor, Bao Dai. There was something almost refreshing about his infantileness. To clasp the man's hand was to know him completely—plump palms and fingertips, limpid grip, the way he would cling to a proffered hand long after the act of handshaking should have come to an end. Some men had double chins, but he had a plethora of them extending the length of his neck so that it resembled the ruched bodice of a woman's evening gown.

Laurent was dead.

If only Jacques would stop talking.

"Apparently Bao Dai has always taken a childlike delight in the attentions of women—many women, the more the better, and all together. It is probably a good thing for his wives and mistresses and the call girls he picks up along the way because he has no concern for their satisfaction. They must please themselves, or one another."

She did not care about some Oriental, plump as a Buddha, having his pleasures attended to by a gaggle of courtesans. She did not care even care about the soldiers, whether French or Viet Minh, dying in the far off valley ringed by mountains, nor about the tigers and elephants that had fled the sound of the howitzers and the rumble of tanks, fleeing along the banks of the Nam Yum River, away.

"Will there be a funeral?"

She saw the look of incomprehension on his face, "For Pierre—?

"I don't imagine so. He certainly wasn't one for the church. It may well have been taken care of already—the disposal of his remains."

He would have wanted the body there, physically present.

Who had found him? Jacqueline or Sally or Rosamund, the hotel clerk or maid? Had he been sitting half upright in his bed, pillows propped behind him, glasses half askew, cigarette in the ashtray, a book resting on his right knee, his notebook on his left? Had whatever force went haywire within him, thump of heart, whoosh of blood, made him arch his spine, throw his head back, mouth open *oh, oh, oh, oh,* as if he were in sexual ecstasy? Had it happened in his sleep, had he died curled against his pillows as he used to curl against hers?

The weight of tears gathered, dammed up within her temples behind her dry eyes. These waters might continue to build up, trapped inside her head by her inability to cry. Her brain might burst from the press of tears within it. The doctors would have some name for it: cerebral-vascular hemorrhage, aneurysm. No one would know the true cause.

There

She did not sleep that night. She lay flat on her back and stared at the ceiling. Laurent was dead.

The bells in Notre Dame chimed out the hours.

The hours paced on, as they would go on, hour after hour after hour, after her death.

Between the hours of three and four, she aroused herself by

rubbing against Jacques' thigh, then reached over and rubbed his cock. He scarcely seemed to awaken, but tumbled on top of her, dead weight, and pushed himself inside of her. She pulled him to her with such force that the imprint of her fingers was visible on his back several days later.

Dominique would see it when he was walking to the sink in the cheap hotel to piss, and assume she had an unknown rival.

The bells chimed four, they chimed five, they chimed six.

The business of the household began, Jacques arising, the smell of coffee, of pipe smoke, the sound of Marie-Claire shutting the door behind her as she went down to fetch the morning bread.

The bells chimed seven, they chimed eight. Marie-Claire got her up, dressed her, made her breakfast, took her to sit by the window.

Rend

The patriarchs of the Old Testament had mourned by beating their breasts, rending their robes, smearing their faces with ashes. She had no ash, but she had her hands, her clumsy hands, lacking in fine motor control, true enough, but capable of being fists, claws. She was glad that Marie-Claire had chosen her black cardigan with its pattern of forget-me-nots in seed pearls. She grabbed the neckband and pulled until the outer edge of her palms grew raw and seeped blood. Still, the fabric failed to give way. She managed to get it between her teeth, to gnaw at it, at last to hook a stitch around her incisors, one thread came loose, unraveling, unraveling, the minuscule white beads showering onto the floor. A few of the seed pearls ended up in her mouth. She swallowed them: perhaps they were poison. Perhaps they would lodge within her, gumming up her works and plumbing, bringing a halt to all the goings-on within. It was the sound of her pummeling her chest with her fists, so loud it could be heard over the sound of the radio, that brought Marie-Claire into the front room.

"Oh, my goodness! Oh, Madame!"

The physician was phoned…*yes, doctor, two vials…No, don't worry, I know how to manage the hypo.*

Simone was led to her bed, undressed, changed, not into widow's weeds but a nightgown of white, as if she were an angel or a virgin.

Marie-Claire wept. Not the great resounding sobs Simone wished she could cry. No, Marie-Claire wept good, steady Protestant tears.

Interlude

Two weeks later, she heard his voice: not the voice he had used when alone with her, but his official voice, the voice of him reading from a typescript, a voice almost droning and without inflection, a voice absent all she held dear about his voice, but nonetheless his voice.

Jacques rose to switch off the radio.

"Please don't," Simone said.

"As you wish, my dear. I always found the man rather tiresome," Jacques said. "The"—he wiggled his fingers—"the antic quality, and I did not find his thought particularly rigorous. For instance—"

"I would like to listen," Simone said.

"…the world is inhabited not just by rational beings but by the sick, the primitive, children, the mad. Classical thought had little concern for the experiences of these people, devoting itself to measuring their deficits in contrast to the normal. Why had classical thought so little concern for these experiences? Because it believed man to be the lord and master of nature, set above it by reason, rather than inextricably bound up with nature…"

And then it was over. And then there was the solemn voice of the announcer saying, "That was a radio lecture recorded by the late Professor Pierre Laurent shortly before his untimely death. After a brief musical interlude, we will return with…"

Coda

Years passed.

A decade.

More years.

Laurent, of course, stayed dead. That is the implacable, stubborn, inescapable nature of the dead. They go on being dead. They go on being dead forever.

Marcel began to grey at the temples, as did his step-brothers. Lines etched the face of Odette.

Jacques' health remained remarkably good until, at the end of 1967, the beginning of 1968—he was, after all, entering his eighth decade—his organs began to peter out: his kidneys, his heart, his spleen, his lungs, all seemed to sigh heavily and pull the blankets up around their shoulders, preparing to meet their fate.

Poor Marie-Claire, good Marie-Claire, our steadfast and faithful Marie-Claire! The windows now flung wide open, more grit from the city streets drifting in, Marie-Claire twirling about with vacuum and feather duster and rag. If the air wasn't let in, there was such a sickroom smell about the place—sickroom smell, that was a gloss, to be quite frank it was mostly urine and that other dark and disgusting substance all human bodies produce—but also the fetid odor which oozes from old people's pores. More than once, Marie-Claire had been heard to say—to no one save herself—"I can't help it. I simply must sit down." Having plopped herself down on the couch, she pushed out her lower lip and blew air out of her mouth and up towards her forehead—the weather unseasonably warm for April.

"How are they today?" Marcel asked each Sunday. And Marie-Claire would answer: "She's doing better, but he's worse. One goes up, the other goes down." Or, tears thickening in her eyes: "It's been a hard week." Or, "Your stepfather walked to the bathroom on his own!"

Throughout April, Jacques was ensconced on the sofa, almost as if he were lying in state, as a steady stream of callers came to pay their respects to the man still referred to as the *eminence grise* of French literature, although the hair on his head had long since turned from grey to white and gone wispy. The feathery hair didn't cover the brown splotches on his scalp. He appeared to be a fledging, his natal down not quite shed. Marie-Claire, realizing it was unseemly for a man of Jacques' stature to be receiving guests in his pyjamas, went first to a *grand magasin*—criminal what they wanted to charge for a smoking jacket, equivalent to nearly a month of her wages!—and from there to second-hand store, the sort that catered to those who had taste but not funds in abundance—as it happened, the one Roger Morel had patronized. Although her own preferences were decidedly conventional—witness the fabric decorated with nosegays of lilacs against cream which she had used for the curtains, dust ruffle and duvet in her room—she had been in service long enough that she understood what those of Jacques' ilk found pleasing. She purchased a smoking jacket for him, deep red brocade with a velvet collar, well-tailored, slightly worn, looking as if it might have been passed down from his father, which he wore when visitors were expected.

Jacques had, after all, ended up in the Academy—in the seat Laurent never got to assume. A good proportion of his callers were jockeying for his position within that body, whether on behalf of themselves or their protégés or allies. They had to be offered coffee, tea, a glass of wine, their coats taken, the flowers they brought arranged in vases.

Simone was in no state to be seen by the distinguished guests. When they were expected, she was whisked off to a purdah within, shut up behind the closed door of the bedroom, wearing one of the white nightgowns that had become her habits, solitary in the marital bed, sometimes shaking so hard the bedstead rattled against the wall, causing those seated in the parlor to furrow their brows, although they were, of course, too polite to ask, "What the hell is that noise?"

Other times, she lay quite still, and more than one caller whispered to another as they descended the stairs together, "Do you know if that wife of his is still alive?"

Her symptoms rolled in and out, following the tidal pull of some quixotic and imperious moon. At times she seemed to be like those stone statues she and Jacques had seen in the ramshackle museum on the Greek island of Naxos.

Little did she know that a magic potion would soon free her. The elixir was being concocted, not from eye of a newt and liver of blaspheming Jew, but from an extract of fava beans—not brewed by hags at a cauldron but distilled in a laboratory.

Gaz

May of 1968. The rector of Nanterre shut the campus in response to student demonstrations. A brick was thrown, and then another. Police occupied the Sorbonne for the first time in its history. On the streets beneath Jacques' and Simone's flat, a clash broke out between the police and students. The police lobbed canisters of tear gas, and the students tossed them back, but the demonstrators had only water-soaked kerchiefs while the cops had gas masks. The students ran through the streets, chanting "Adieu, De Gaulle," and chalking slogans on the wall: *Nous sommes tous indesirables* and *Soyez réalistes, demandez l'impossible*. An American woman, studying at the Sorbonne for her junior year abroad, swung herself along on her crutches, although she could not keep up with the rest of the crowd, which parted around her. Nights, back in her room, she soaked her hands, swollen to nearly twice their usual size, in ice water.

Marie-Claire shoved damp towels and rags into the gaps between the windows and the frame, the door and its jamb, although this was not entirely successful in keeping out the *le gaz lacrymogène*, which found its way through the cracks and crevices. As if the atmosphere in this flat wasn't morose enough already, Jacques and Simone wept, tears not of sorrow but of stinging pain. Jacques cursed: "Jesus! Oh, Jesus! Jesus Christ!" (This will later cause Marie-Claire to say, "He was a good man, for all his difficult traits. And at the end of his life, he turned towards the

Lord, I used to hear him calling aloud to our Savior for succor.") Simone did not cry out. The gas merely made tears stream unchecked down her face, mucous and drool run from her nose and mouth. Poor Marie-Claire was forced to mop up even more bodily orifices.

A few days after this skirmish—a portent of events to come—Jacques went from being a man in a general state of decline to one who was in the throes of a definitive crisis: pneumonia. An ambulance was rung for and the medics strapped him onto the stretcher and bore his cumbersome form down the six flights of stairs.

—Say what you like about working in the banlieue. At least there the buildings have lifts. Last week we had to bring a man down seven flights who must have weighed a hundred and fifty kilos.

—A hundred and fifty kilos? Oh, it's not possible!

Jacques moaned in pain. The ambulance attendants stopped grumbling, focused on the task at hand. Neighbors came to their doorways to see the commotion, staring with the sullen, honest curiosity of Parisians. A few, after the frail package had been carried past them, walked over to the edge of the railing, peering down at him.

—It's the old man from the sixth floor.

—Ah, he's not just any old man, he's a member of the Academy.

At the hospital, his heart refused to give up, it went on beating, beating, beating.

Gone

"Does she even know he's gone, poor thing?" Marie-Claire tucked an errant strand of Simone's hair, behind her ear. Of course, she knew. His smell was gone, the stink of his shit wafting up from the bedpan—due to his invalid's diet smelling more sulfurous and alkaline, lacking its usual odor of tobacco and red wine and coffee, but still, unmistakably his. The absence of his weight on the other side of the bed. If she had been capable of forming a resolution, of the physical acts necessary to carry out a plan, she would have gathered up books, the cast-iron door stop, heaped them onto the other side of the mattress until the weight matched his, as she had once, so long ago, taken the comforter and pillows out of the wardrobe and wrapped her arms and legs around them, pretending they were him.

Does she even know he's gone, poor thing?

Simone had what was left behind when language had been subtracted from thought.

Miracle

A kiss awakened Sleeping Beauty in her gown long gone to tatters, lying on her bed become a bier. Uttering the gnome's name freed golden-haired Rapunzel from her walled-up tower. In Simone's case, it was a syringe which pierced her flesh, coursed L-3,4-dihydroxyphenylalanine into her veins: L-dopa.

He sat next to her bed. Once "this" without referent was the Occupation, "they," the Germans. Once "he" was Jacques, "this" the conundrum of her marriage. Now "he" meant Dr. Phillipe, "this" her illness.

He spoke for centuries. Laurent had told her about monks in a Himalayan kingdom who chant a single word for decades: the doctor must be an acolyte. "*Il y'a,*" he said, a phrase that took years to make its way out of his mouth. Ah, those words, as common as stones and dead leaves; words with the inevitability of stones and the fragility of dried leaves; words that seem simultaneously to mean everything and nothing: *Tiens, là, il, çi, ça, y, a.*

"There is a new medication which has shown a great deal of success in treating Parkinson's disease. Your son has given me permission to try it in your case. The results can be quite dramatic."

The syringe was plunged into her flesh, which clung to the needle as the doctor withdrew it. An old, old woman, and still her body was saying: *Don't leave me*! *Stay inside me*! *Don't leave me*! *Don't leave me*!

The sensation of ice water flowing through her veins and then—

"What has happened?" She grabbed hold of his hand, her anchor in this spinning world.

"Do you remember," he said, "before I gave you the injection, I told you that results could be dramatic."

"Dramatic," she said, showering the good doctor with spittle. "Drama, drama. It's a Greek word, isn't it? When I lived in Istanbul, I would see Greece, across the straits. My husband—my first husband—was an engineer, in Istanbul—"

The doctor was pulling his hand away, or attempting to do so.

"You are—"

"Simone. Simone Melville. I was Simone Vidal and then Simone—oh, I had another name—"

"You are holding my hand too tightly."

"Oh, doctor," she said. "I lived in Istanbul because—well, it isn't so important now, not his surname, which used to be my surname—an engineer, and his fingertips were covered with Prussian blue. I'd find it in the morning, doctor, after we had made love, blue on the edge of my jaw, circling my breasts like a faint tattoo—tattoo, tattoo, it's from some Polynesian tongue, isn't it? The places I thought I would someday see. The South Seas. After all—Gauguin. Oh, yes, the blue. The blue of the Aegean and the blue dress I wore and the blue from the drawings—he sucked this breast—" and here her right hand made itself into a greedy anemone opening and closing its fingers over her left breast.

"Mme. Melville—"

"Oh, there is no need to be so formal."

He held up his hand, inclined his head, beneath his kind but firm mien, sheer terror at what he had unleashed.

"I'm afraid I must insist that we be—that we maintain—"

"While he sucked one breast, he stroked the other, the blue from his drawings tracked onto my breast, as if I were the initiate of some ancient cult of Druids. And then, doctor—" and here, she pulled her legs up, allowed her knees to drop apart, "here," and she touched her sex, "where he thrust his fingers inside me and worked the heel of his palm back and forth against me, it would be a deep blue, almost like a bruise. I was so young, doctor. My bush was thick—"

He wondered how those joints, which should have grown rusty like the hinges of an unopened trunk, could move so dexterously.

"The dose," the doctor was saying, "needs to be titrated."

The words stanched back inside her for so long were pouring out, breaching the dam, the gush of words widening the cleft, and the wider the fissure the greater the flow. The words were solid, her poor lips-jaw-tongue-teeth had to struggle to keep up with them. Expressions danced over her face the way they sweep across the face of a newborn: grimaces, grins, Oh-my-God! gape-mouthed surprise, frowns of ancient widows, upturned glances of girls in love. They arrived in no particular order and departed as rapidly as they had come.

"A sedative will be necessary…Madame, set your arm on the arm of the chair. Mme. Melville, look at me." Dr. Phillipe had fixed his gaze on her, or rather was trying to, but she was like a child playing tag, darting her eyes free of him.

She could even, she discovered, turn her head.

At the wonder of it, she pivoted her head back and forth, almost like the owls in the cypress trees on the bluff above Cap d'Antibes.

"If you could hold her arm—" Dr. Philippe said to Marie-Claire.

Finally, after a good deal of wrestling—good God, if she kept squirming about like that the needle might well break off in her arm—at last, he was done, he pulled out the syringe, he saw her face go slack, and allowed himself to dab the beads of sweat on his brow.

"That was—that was—" he said.

"A miracle," Marie-Claire supplied.

A few days later, when Dr. Philippe again came to call, he gave her a radically smaller dose, a tenth of what he had tried before, and this time Simone did not rocket past the stratosphere, in fact, she barely seemed affected. Returned again, a few days later, to administer a fifth of the initial dose, which once again sent her spinning.

Dr. Philippe consulted with his colleagues. These wonders were unlike those described in the Bible, the paralytics picking up their pallets and skipping away. (Or perhaps they hadn't been so simple after all: think of poor Lazarus, stripping off his winding sheets and washing away the scent of death, yet going through the rest of life knowing full well what awaited him—he would become rotting meat, fodder for maggots.)

Out

Not that it had been easy when Madame had just sat there like a lump of rock, but now: "I want to go outside."

"Ah, no, Madame, it will be so difficult."

"I want to go outside."

Day after day: "I want to go outside. I want to go outside."

"All right! All right!" poor Marie-Claire snapped one day. "All right, we'll go outside!" Anything to stop her wailing. "On Sunday, when Marcel comes. We'll go outside."

"I want to go outside."

"I've told you, I've told you, we're going to go outside. Sunday."

"I want to go outside."

Fall

Simone, perched by her window, strange hag in her aerie, had fallen in love.

Fallen in love with a short-haired youth with a ramrod carriage who stood on the street corner, pressing papers into the reluctant hands of passersby. Although she could not see it, a red enameled circle pin with a gold profile of Chairman Mao was pinned to his jacket. She longed to read one of his flyers. Marie-Claire or her daughter-in-law Hélène would have snorted with laughter had she asked either to fetch one for her: *Are you thinking of joining a revolutionary cell*? Such a request would have tried the patience of those who attended her. Perhaps a fixed amount of that quality was kept in a rubber-stoppered bottle in the bathroom medicine cabinet.

HOLD HIGH WITH GREAT REVOLUTIONARY FERVOR THE BANNER OF MAO TSE TUNG THOUGHT! DENOUNCE THE CAPITALIST ROADERS! the headline on the roneoed pages read, the words typed on an old Olivetti, a few of the letters cracked. The aging and cantankerous duplicator had a mind of its own, ink caught in the wrinkles of the stencils, causing odd blue-black rivers in the leaflets. The group of which this young man was a part had just produced the denunciation of Jacques which Dominique will read aloud to him in his hospital room: "The bloodsucking, bourgeois leeches who, not content with physical rape and pillage, treat the culture of the conquered lands as fodder for their jaded, decadent lusts…"

Of course, Simone was not faithful. She was also in love with a female student with dirty blonde, unbrushed hair who passed beneath the window. Estelle—or so Simone had named her—wore the same outfit every day, a pair of black Capri pants topped by a striped Breton fisherman's sweater, her hair flying behind her, the banner of her nation, the young. There was usually a young man with her, although each of her romances seemed to last for no more than a few days.

At Laſt

At last, it was Sunday. As always, Marie-Claire offered a bow of her head to Marcel and his wife Hélène, which Hélène returned with a slighter nod of her own, Marcel with an embrace. It was a point of contention between the couple: she knew the value of respecting the time-honored order of things—one simply didn't go about hugging the servants! As the events of the next few weeks unfold, she'll occasionally turn her eyes from the television to give an *I told you where such things would lead*! look to her poor deluded husband.

Jacques' sons did not bother to ring and say they wouldn't be coming, not even with their frequent excuses. It was a given that they'd show up at their father's bedside, as they had every day for the past fortnight since he decamped from home to hospital. Frédéric made no secret of the fact that he was in his mother's bloc—even more her partisan now that she was dead and no longer able to fight her own battles. He regarded Simone as a seductress who had given no thought to the suffering she left in her wake. He was only civil to her out of a sense of filial obligation. Alphonse, the younger son, might be said to have a more nuanced view of the situation. He was not disturbed by the fact that his father had abandoned his mother—after all, no one could say their marriage had been an easy one. He was only troubled by the fact that his mother had been replaced by a woman he regarded not only as provincial, but to be quite frank about the matter, a dimwit.

They both were more accepting of Dominique—Alphonse because he respected her intellect, Frédéric because she had given Simone a taste of her own medicine. The three of them—Dominique, Alphonse, Frédéric—sat next to Jacques' bed, the IV steadily dripping antibiotics into Jacques' arm, Alphonse with his arm around Dominique's shoulder, Frédéric holding her hand. Dominique had at last achieved what she thought would be her due: she was more or less Jacques' wife.

Back at the flat, Marcel knelt on the floor next to his mother in her wheelchair, while his wife tromped into the kitchen to give Marie-Claire a hand. Pots and pans clanged against one another, the knife thumped steadily against the cutting board. Simone was both an old woman in Paris and a girl in Provence, overhearing the grumble and murmur of her mother and Cecile. The dramatis personae changed, the rhythms of daily life did not.

Marcel was most determined that his mother not go into a home, as those places were called. Everyone praised him for being a devoted son—"Ah, but you don't know what she did for me, when I came back from Germany—half-dead, one foot in the grave—well, really, that hardly begins to describe my state, it was more like just a tiny filament of my being was left in the world of the living and it was that she grabbed a hold of..." while Hélène rolled her eyes, *yes, yes, we've heard it all before, the filament of your being...*

The concierge's son was enlisted to help with the expedition to the park, he and Marcel crossed their arms together, Simone was seated upon that bridge. Hélène and Marie-Claire managed the wheelchair, while Hélène issued warnings: *Mind, the steps get uneven here*! *Marcel, your back*! The concierge herself brought up the rear of the procession, carrying a blanket folded over her arm.

Simone was wheeled, an empress on a wicker throne, towards the park across the street, where she sat in splendor amidst the ruins of the ancient arena.

"Ah," Marcel said, "see how happy this has made her."

Simone closed her eyes, turned her face towards the sun, worshipping that distant god.

What luck! The girl, Estelle, was there in the park, sitting with one of her beaux, on the next park bench. What Simone had taken to be a striped Breton was not. The girl must have draped the sweater over the heater to dry, creating the scorch marks which from a distance looked like stripes. And then, to keep it from getting burned again, she hung it from a hanger, which caused the stretched out sleeves that drooped over her hands, making her appear simultaneously waif-like and simian.

Simone loved the girl, her hand was between her legs, rubbing, rubbing. Marie-Claire was the one who noticed and grabbed her hand.

"Stop!"

"Let go of me! I'll do what I want!"

"Madame!"

The next day, Marie-Claire phoned Dr. Philippe. "She's becoming rather—well, rude—" and after many feints and sallies finally managed to come out with the rough story of Madame masturbating in the park.

"The medication is rather new and for all its wonders—we are seeing a few of these problems cropping up."

"But what should I do?" begged Marie-Claire.

"I'm sure you'll be able to manage," the doctor said and rang off.

Shuffle

It was a good thing Simone had gone out a few days before. It was no longer safe to venture forth. Marie-Claire even tried to keep her away from her window—who knew when an errant missile or brick could be launched? Yes, yes, Marie-Claire knew it was quite improbable that a brick could reach this high, but then wasn't all of this unthinkable?

But Madame—who could now get up on her own two feet and walk right over—well, true enough, it was more of a shuffle—to the window, without so much as a by-your-leave to Marie-Claire—sat watching the events beneath unfold as if they were a private theater put on for her benefit. Estelle ran along the rue des Arènes, leading a V-shaped formation of her comrades, like geese in chevron flight, holding hands, and then collapsing, laughing, into a pile of joy.

They were building barricades in the streets again. ("They" without any antecedent now meant the young.) This time, of course, Simone won't be carrying a cup of ersatz coffee down the long flights of stairs, there will be no ardent kiss from a grateful comrade.

Simone, perched at her window, watched as the short-haired man (MARX! ENGELS! LENIN! STALIN! MAO!) became the petty general of a rustled-up army, his recruits' faces protected from tear gas by kerchiefs folded in half, so they looked like bad guys in American westerns. He gave an order to one of the young women, who skipped off—generalissimo would no doubt have preferred a dutiful march—and tried the doors of several parked cars. That tack proved fruitless—every lock in Paris that could be bolted had been. The girl picked up a paving stone, raced back with it, and hesitated, rock in hand.

Do it, Simone thought, do it. Hurl the damn thing!

And then the girl did. Roosting pigeons, startled by the sound, rose hurly-burly into the air, then formed themselves into a flock and proceeded to wing back and forth, as if commanded by some avian god to wipe clean the skies of Paris. The glass had collapsed into thousands of random geometric shapes which clung to one another out of force of habit. The girl, still a bit timid, pushed against the glass with a half fist until it crumpled, reached in, opened the door, a minute later was holding metal bar meant for prying off hubcaps aloft, like Delacroix's *Liberty with the Flag of the Republic*. The martinet took the pry bar from her hands, set to work on the tarmac, he and his underlings pulling it up in a great sheet to reveal the cobblestones underneath. Another band had shifted the car with the shattered window into neutral, was pushing it into the middle of the street to serve as a barricade. The pry bar, meant for removing a hubcap, proved no match for the stones, and snapped in half. This sent their leader into a rage: in the workers' paradise on earth they were building, not only would the exploitation of man by his fellow man be brought to an end, but crowbars would be decently made!

An old woman hobbled down the steps from the building opposite, calling out, "Comrades! Comrades!" She had various pieces of paper in her hand—Medical certificates? Her husband's union card? A commendation for her work with the Resistance? "Comrades! Comrades!" she shouted into the air. Then, when no one paid her any mind, she surveyed the scene and tottered over to our boy-general. She pointed to an ancient blue Citroën, thrust the certificates under his nose. Simone had never seen this woman before; the old people in this neighborhood were like the fish that live in the bottom of the ocean, only some catastrophe drove them upwards, into the fishermen's nets. He smiled, laid a hand on her shoulder, promised to protect her car.

The ceaseless wail of sirens, police, ambulance, fire.

The girl in the striped sweater had disappeared. Perhaps her father, a good bourgeois or a faithful member of the Party, had driven up to fetch her home. She was ensconced in her girlhood bedroom for the duration, safe from marauding revolutionaries or infantile provocateurs. Or she could be sitting in a café debating a passage from Engels' *Anti-Dühring* or crouched on the floor of an occupied lecture hall, painting demands on a bed sheet of fine Belgian linen that had been liberated from a shop earlier that morning.

The radio was kept on nearly all the time now, as it had been during the Fall of France, the Liberation. The official French radio stations were off the air, having gone on strike, and news must be heard from stations in Luxembourg and Germany.

"Luxembourg! Germany!" Marie-Claire cried, "How can we possibly trust news from there?"

Every day, Marie-Claire received a phone call which she reported as being as from "the hospital," which was not, strictly speaking, a lie, although it was Dominique calling from the hospital. The poor doctors and nurses hardly had time to palaver with family members, the injured from the street battles were piling up in the corridors, the chapel, the admissions office, not to mention the endless meetings being held, with chants of "Strike! Strike! Strike!" filling the air.

Despite the optimistic wash that Marie-Claire put on Dominique's reports, Simone wailed: "He is dying! I know he is dying! Oh, I will never see him again. Never, never, never."

In the corridor, one doctor laid his hand on Dominique's shoulder (ah, how often this gesture had been repeated in the last few days), those masculine arms reassuring, shepherding, weighting her down to earth: "I know you would want me to be completely frank with you." She wasn't, in fact, at all sure this was what she wanted, but she said nothing. "The antibiotics are working, but this is just a temporary change—the pneumonia clearing up, but the underlying disease process…"

"Yes," Dominique said, "I understand what you are telling me." It was her turn to put her hand on him, a flat palm against his chest. She stopped him before he could come out with the word: "death."

A doctor who was also a literary critic, a confederate of Jacques, a man in his mid-forties who, over the last several weeks, had found himself growing more and more stooped, so that from behind he looked two decades older, dropped by and stood looking out the window, his back to Jacques, watching the marchers below.

"They say their lives have no meaning. They say that boredom is counter-revolutionary." He sighed.

Mule

Confabs were held outside the patient's room, Dominique and his colleagues deciding that he'd be better off at home.

—It will present some difficulties.

—Ah, yes, but with the threat of a doctor's strike…

—Have we considered moving him to a hospital outside of Paris?

—I'm not sure he would survive the journey.

For all Jacques' claims to being disinterested in his own fate, he was adept at getting his own way: he wanted to go home. For a start, there was the matter of the utter chaos of the hospital, which meant that although his medications and food were delivered in a more-or-less timely fashion, he had been left in the pyjamas he'd been wearing when he was brought to the hospital, and his sweat-soaked sheets had not once been changed. It made him feel a persnickety invalid to complain about this—he remembered how he'd railed about Simone's fussiness about her bedding, so he did not. He wished Dominique had been able to grasp the situation and remedy it. She, however, was so absorbed in her impending loss she seemed not to understand: one confronts death as much with one's body as with one's mind.

He wanted to go home not only in order that he might get away from these gritty sheets, have the sweat and stink of death washed from him by Marie-Claire's hands, be given a pair of fresh pyjamas, but he also wanted to get away from Dominique's grief.

He at last understood Pascal's "The heart has its reasons that reason knows nothing of." It wasn't some scrap of romantic folderol. The heart's reason is the reason of a mule. The heart plods on because it plods on. Thump, thump, thump, thump, thump. You may have to take a stick to that mule to get it going, hit it not just once but two times, three times, but once it gets going the stubborn thing doesn't want to stop. Thump, thump, thump, thump, thump, thump.

The nurses and orderlies did not seem to be aware they were tending to a member of the Academy. He saw himself reflected in their eyes: he had become the mangy dog he and Dominique had passed in Tunisia, that dog that refused to die.

Prior to Jacques' return, Marcel came to visit him. When he entered the room, Dominique dropped her gaze to the floor. "Excuse me," she murmured and scuttled out the door.

Marcel gave a sigh of disapproval; Jacques thought: *Once a prig, always a prig,* said: "It seems that the age of miracles hasn't passed. I may, after all, be leaving this place and not feet first."

"It is precisely that possibility—of which we have gotten wind at home—that possibility which has brought me here today." Marcel steepled his fingers, which caused his *beau-père* to add "pompous ass" to his mental list of Marcel's faults, although the gesture was one Marcel had appropriated from his stepfather. "I need to tell you that your wife"—he coughed again—"my mother, has also had a quite remarkable turn for the better." He went on to describe the effects of L-dopa—leaving aside the incident of Simone masturbating in the park.

Home

An ambulance couldn't be organized, so it was arranged for him to be brought home in a private motorcar. It twisted through cramped back streets, stopped by police, students, his body exhibited, stretched out in the back seat, a living *laissez-passer*.

The battles between the police and the students had shifted a few streets away, and tear gas no longer drifted in, the barricades in the street below were manned by a rear guard. Simone was in the bedroom, listening to the transistor radio Frédéric had bought a year or so ago in order that his father might listen to radio programs without having to decamp to the parlor. *It is estimated that somewhere between two and eight million workers are now on strike...Despite having declared that he would not cut short his visit to Romania, President de Gaulle is reported to be on his way back to Paris...*Jacques was borne in, on a canvas stretcher, carried by two of his protégés, men hardly in the first days of youth themselves, their foreheads beaded with sweat and their faces reddened by the effort of lugging this parcel up the stairs. Although Marie-Claire had been told of the plan to bring him home, this news had not been shared with Simone—it was feared that something might go wrong (a turn for the worse caused by the rigors of his leaving the hospital, the car unable to wend its way past the barricades) and Marie-Claire simply could not have stood Simone's dismay.

He had come back to her.

He's not coming back, her mother had said, so long ago.

These poor professors performing the role of orderlies had no idea of how to manage the transfer from stretcher to bed. It was Marie-Claire who flopped her ungainly master onto the mattress. It was also Marie-Claire who said, "I think he should rest," and switched off the radio, ignoring Simone's slight cry of protest. By the time Marie-Claire returned to the bedroom after seeing off the bearers, intending to change Jacques into some clean pyjamas, he'd fallen asleep. It wasn't her habit to lie down in the middle of the day, but one could hardly begrudge her an afternoon nap. Within minutes, she was snoring loudly in her snug room off the kitchen.

Simone alone remained awake. Bored, wishing Marie-Claire had not flicked off the radio, surely Jacques would have fallen asleep with it on, but if Simone were to turn it on now, it would no doubt wake him up. Jacques slept, mouth agape, drool escaping from his flabby lips. His legs were like waterlogged tree trunks, swollen yet filled with emptiness. How, Simone wondered, had his body become both so enormous and so frail? She laid her hand on his chest: the fabric of his pyjamas was greasy, almost rubbery. He smelled of the sea, of salt and decay.

He slept for nearly two hours, while she looked steadily at him.

He awoke suddenly, his eyes flashed around the room, the eyes of a sleep-baffled toddler searching for his mother.

"You're home."

He turned towards her voice, smiled, and then—he might be be an old and frail Jacques, a sickly Jacques, but he was still Jacques: he drove the smile from his face. He didn't want Simone to be able to say, even in the privacy of her own mind: *at the very end, he became quite devoted to me, even childlike.*

"So, it's true—Marcel told me you had been—resurrected."

"I walk. I talk."

"Where were you? All those years?"

"Here. Right here. Simply here."

"Can you ring for Marie-Claire? I want to sit up."

"I can do it," she said, and—not without difficulty—she plumped the pillows behind him and tugged on his arms so that he sat, not fully upright, but no longer prone. He was a bit put out by the whole procedure—the awkwardness of it all, the way the flesh on her upper arms flapped about as she yanked him up.

He had wanted Marie-Claire to come into the room so he wouldn't have to be alone with Simone. A few hours before, at the hospital, there had been a messy business with Dominique, tears on her part, the threat of full-blown sobs—thankfully, she had excused herself and run down the hallway so he didn't have to witness it. He'd had quite enough emotion from the distaff side for one day. Wanting to say something that would amuse Simone, that would keep her too from becoming maudlin, he said, "It might interest you to know—I have been denounced as a neo-imperialist lackey. Apparently my counter-revolutionary crime was my writings about Madagascar."

"And who. Is it who. Denounced you?" Despite the changes wrought in her by the L-dopa, her voice still cut out, like a radio pulling in a distant signal.

"Ah, some student group. In their newspaper. It was read to me in the hospital."

"By Dominique?"

He did not respond to her verbally, but stared at a point on the wall, his lips pursed, waiting for her to say: —*She came to see you in the hospital? How many times? Every day? For how long? Did the nurses address her as Mme. Melville and did you not bother to clear up the misconception?* That he will have to respond: —*Stop, Simone. You are not only torturing me, you are torturing yourself.*

But she said none of those things.

"I read that book she wrote."

He turned his head towards her, his eyes darting back and forth, almost the same look he'd had on his face a few minutes before when he'd woken up bewildered.

"How on earth did you get your hands on a copy?"

"Pierre Laurent read it to me."

"Laurent?"

"We had an affair."

Jacques laughed out loud, though his laughter soon devolved into a hacking cough. This miraculous drug the doctors had been shooting into her had not effected a real cure, only regressed her to an earlier state of her illness, the period during which she had labored under delusions, believing that Russian monks were chanting in the apartment above them, that a piano had been hauled into the sitting room, and a raucous party was being held there. Now she believed that she had had an affair during the years when she had been a shut-in.

"He came on Thursdays, on Marie-Claire's afternoon off."

The cigarette butt, the Balto, that he'd found on the floor so many years before, found and then tossed into the ashtray. Nothing, the stump of a cigarette, what could be more inconsequential, but it had stayed, tucked away in some corner of his mind all these years.

He laughed again, laughed in wonder. She had been cuckolding him. The sense of shock was soon overwhelmed by disgust. The whole business struck him as depraved, far removed from the ordinary perversions he was familiar with—homosexuality, pederasty, sadomasochism. Surely, even those publishers of the most outlandish erotica had no volumes that dealt with sex with invalids. During all those years when he had been shut up here in the flat he had had his own life, of course, this was expected, but it had never occurred to him that she— It wasn't at all like him to think so incoherently. The mix of emotions within him blurred together, like a painter's palette gone muddy at the end of a long day.

She saw that he was in pain, and because she still loved him—yes, of course, she still loved him, and hated to cause him pain: "It didn't last long. He only came five times. Before he, before—"

He remembered, as he remembered the Balto cigarette butt, the evening when he had told her of Laurent's death. How offhand he had been. Yes, it had been during the fall of Dien Bien Phu, he had spoken of his disinclination to sign an open letter being circulated on account of a disagreement he had had over some words used in the second paragraph—he remembered that the words had been in the second paragraph, although he didn't remember what they had been. He had repeated a risqué story about the corpulent and infantile emperor. The atrocities the Americans had visited on Indochina had erased his memory of the previous horrors, and then—the gesture he'd made, dabbing at his lips with the linen napkin, more as a punctuation in the conversation than anything else, *Oh, and by the way, I had some sad news today…*

"He hadn't come. I didn't know," Simone could not stop herself from wailing, "I didn't know, that he was dead, that he was dead. I thought—I thought he had abandoned me."

He reached over and stroked her face. "Poor girl."

"Yes, poor me. And poor Dominique. She thought all along, didn't she, that I would die first and she would get to be your wife. I went on living and living and living. They don't like that, do they?" This time the "they" without referent meant those who dwelt in the world of the well. "Did you ever think of putting a pillow over my head?"

He waggled his head from side to side. "The image would sometimes cross my mind. But I never seriously considered it."

"I read that interview with her—was it in *Le Monde*?—and it spoke of her fingering a ring made of iron, in the shape of a scarab, that she wore where one would wear a wedding ring, and I knew that you must have bought it for her when the two of you were in North Africa—"

"Yes," Jacques said. "You are more perspicacious than I have given you credit for." Once again, he gave a compliment which had an insult tucked inside of it.

She considered saying, "Being suspicious makes one perspicacious—one is always looking for clues," but decided against it: the time for rows, for sniping, had passed.

"But why are we talking of this now?" Jacques said. "I've said my goodbye to her. My life with her is over. I won't see her again."

"He didn't read me the whole thing. Laurent. He brought it with him one day, when he came. He thought—it would arouse me. There was something about him of the naughty schoolboy, giggling and nudging his friends over salacious books he had in his haversack. He told me that everyone was talking about it. That you had written the foreword. That the rumor around Paris was that you had even written the book yourself. But of course, when he started to read it to me, I knew that you hadn't written it. One can recognize the voice on the page as one recognizes the actual voice—but when he was reading about V, in the cellar, her utter submission, I knew that Dominique had written it, that somehow that night, that night when I was forced to—"

"Yes, I know which night you mean. That night when you couldn't sleep and I gave you a Nembutal."

"Actually, you suggested I take it. I got up and got it for myself."

"No," Jacques said. "No. I remember quite distinctly, standing next to you with the glass of water and the pill in my hand. But really, that isn't so important."

If you had done that, I would have remembered, Simone thought. There were so few such acts of kindness on your part that I treasured every one. "I didn't just take one Nembutal that night."

"I know. You took three. I kept count of them. I'd been keeping them as a—well, as a sort of insurance policy. If suicide ever became a necessity. I knew—I'd heard about bad lots of cyanide that brought you to death's door, but didn't carry you across the threshold. So, I'd consulted a physician, his instructions were quite particular."

"I said so little," Simone said. "And yet you knew so much. It must have seeped into the relations between the two of you—"

"I have not always been successful in my attempts to keep the spheres of my life separate." That book, written as a gift to her lover, a version of those stories he and Dominique must have spun to one another, as she and Jacques had once made up stories for one another: *Pretend there's another woman in bed with the two of us…Suppose we had a little flat somewhere, and you got there one day, and you found another man fucking me…*These thoughts raced through her. She missed, briefly, the mind she had had until a few weeks before, the mind that had moved with infinite plodding slowness, lumbering, sure-footed.

"I couldn't bear for Pierre to read it to me, I told him to stop… Now it seems there are no more secrets between the two of us," Simone said.

He had never allowed himself to believe that when he was about to leave the world he would be transformed by the experience, repent of his past errors. And he saw now he had been right all along: imminent death did not burnish one, make one holy: it left one as one had always been, only more so. That strain in his personality—which he did not regard as cruel, although it often seemed that way to others—his acid honesty surfaced now.

"Since you are so enamored of honesty, I should tell you: I stood outside your door that first night and thought *Knock on her door / Don't knock on her door / Knock on her door / Don't knock on her door."*

"But you did knock on my door."

"But I might easily not have."

"But you did. Don't you think that now, at this point—when, quite frankly, we have so little time left, that you can cease to be sanctimonious. That you can drop your claim to having an Egyptian nature. That you can admit that you truly loved me."

He steepled his fingers. He was not strong enough to walk up a single flight of stairs, he was not strong enough to get out of bed to walk to the toilet on his own, but at least he could still do this, match finger to finger, pinkie, ring, middle, index, bring the whole assemblage towards his mouth, pressing his pursed lips against the joined index fingers, a gesture which suggested that his better nature was preventing him from blurting out something quite cruel. The spire shape also suggested that what he was going to say when he collected himself would border on some holy verity.

But he didn't. He said nothing.

"Do you remember—"

He spoke over her, "Please. Don't start. I am leaving this world. Like Hezekiah, I have turned my face to the wall."

"No, you haven't."

"It is metaphoric." A smile played on the corners of Jacques' mouth. "But if you like, I can do so quite literally." He winced in pain, as he attempted to turn on his side: the fits of coughing during his bout with pneumonia had battered his torso, albeit from within.

She grimaced in pain along with him, and cried out, *ah. Ah, ah* the syllable she had cried in sexual ecstasy the first night they made love, *ah, ah,* the word she had said when Marcel showed up at her door, one foot in a wooden clog, the other in a boot that had almost become one with his skin, the word she had shoved her fist into her mouth to stop herself from crying out on the Metro platform in Montmartre. *Ah, ah, ah.*

Seal

Half a century ago, they had made love in the cave hidden from the wind—the limitless sky above, the grains of sand which were remains of rocks from earth's first days.

This time, Simone played the role of the bull seal. She aroused herself with her hand, ground her thighs against Jacques who moaned as she rocked her body against him, her ancient, cumbersome, slow, grunting body, finally letting out a string of *ah, ah, ah ah's,* that syllable that means everything and nothing.

Acknowledgments

Thanks to Richard Nixon and my father. "Goddamn you, tricky Dick," my father used to yell at the TV when Nixon appeared. "Burn in hell."

Thus, I learned to holler back. Many decades later, my father and Nixon both long dead, I happened to hear a radio interview about Dominique Aury, the author of *The Story of O*. (At Northfield School for Girls in 1965, we had passed this forbidden text from hand to hand: thrilled, aroused, disgusted, enticed, reading it with the aid of a flashlight and covers pulled over our heads, perhaps a hand drifting to that place that we had no other word for than "the birth canal.") Aury had written the erotic novel to entice her lover, Jean Paulhan. In the course of the interview, Paulhan's wife was dismissed with the words "Oh, she was an invalid," with the unquestioned certainty that one could not be both disabled and a sexual being. "Oh, an invalid," I shouted at the radio.

Out of that germ of anger grew my desire to imagine the erotic life of "the invalid," the woman who was assumed to be beyond the bounds of desire, of desiring. This book is the result.

While hung on the scaffolding of real events, this novel is just that: a novel, with fictional characters—with a few exceptions: Joë Bousquet, the paralyzed poet, deserves to be better known by English readers. The American woman, swinging herself along on her crutches in Paris in May of 1968, is my late friend, Karen Donovan. Karen, I miss you so much—if only it weren't the implacable, stubborn, inescapable nature of the dead to go on being dead forever.

I have also cribbed from Marcel Merleau-Ponty's radio lectures in creating the lectures that Pierre Laurent gives and from Jean Paulhan's writings in creating Jacques Melville's experiences with Madagascar and malaria.

My deepest gratitude to my early readers, Georgina Kleege, Stephen Pelton, Susan Roth, and Brian Thorstenson, for their encouragement and helpful critiques. Much thanks to Michael

Northen for his assistance in getting this book published. I have been beyond fortunate to have a community of wonderful friends who have surrounded me with love and friendship in ways it would take a whole book to detail: first of all, Rosemarie Garland-Thomson; Deborah Agre, Christopher Beck, Gene Chelberg, Cathy Kudlick, Peter Drucker, Lakshmi Fjord, Kenny Fries, Jenny Kern, Vicki Lewis, Lisa Menda, Kenji Oshima, Alan Pulner, Marsha Saxton, Susan Schweik, Alice Sheppard, and Cecilia Woloch.

Cinco Puntos has been a pleasure to deal with, from start to finish. Thanks especially to Lee Byrd for her excellent editing.

East Bay Meditation Center, especially the Every Body Every Mind Sangha, has been a source of comfort and growth to me. I owe a particular debt of gratitude to Deb Kerr, Mushim Patricia Ikeda, and Larry Yang.

My son, Max Finger, and his girlfriend, Lindsay Stanley, have filled my life with love and happiness beyond measure.